The House On the Moor by Margaret Oliphant

In Three Volumes

Margaret Oliphant Wilson was born on April 4th, 1828 to Francis W. Wilson, a clerk, and Margaret Oliphant, at Wallyford, near Musselburgh, East Lothian.

Her youth was spent in establishing a writing style and by 1849 she had her first novel published: Passages in the Life of Mrs. Margaret Maitland.

Two years later, in 1851 Caleb Field was published and also an invitation to contribute to Blackwood's Magazine; the beginning of a life time business relationship.

In May 1852, Margaret married her cousin, Frank Wilson Oliphant. Their marriage produced six children but, tragically, three died in infancy. When her husband developed signs of the dreaded consumption (tuberculosis) they moved to Florence, and then to Rome where, sadly, he died.

Margaret was naturally devastated but was also now left without support and only her income from writing to support the family. She returned to England and took up the burden of supporting her three remaining children by her literary activity.

Her incredible and prolific work rate increased both her commercial reputation and the size of her reading audience. Tragedy struck again in January 1864 when her only remaining daughter Maggie died.

In 1866 she settled at Windsor to be closer to her sons, who were being educated at near-by Eton School.

For more than thirty years she pursued a varied literary career but family life continued to bring problems. Cyril Francis, her eldest son, died in 1890. The younger son, Francis, who she nicknamed 'Cecco', died in 1894.

With the last of her children now lost to her, she had little further interest in life. Her health steadily and inexorably declined.

Margaret Oliphant Wilson Oliphant died at the age of 69 in Wimbledon on 20th June 1897. She is buried in Eton beside her sons.

Index of Contents

CHAPTER I

In a gloomy room, looking out through one narrow window upon a moor, two young people together, and yet alone, consumed the dreary hours of a February afternoon. The scene within doors exhibited scarcely less monotony and dreariness than did the moor without, which stretched black and heavy to the hills under a leaden sky. The room was well-sized, and lighted only by that one window, which was deeply sunk in the deep wall, and hung with terrible curtains of red moreen, enough to kill what little amount of light there was. A large dining-table, of cold, well-polished mahogany, occupied the centre of the apartment—an old-fashioned sideboard and mysterious bureau of the same character stood out darkly from the walls—and hard, angular chairs furnished forth the dining-room, as it was called—but which was, indeed, drawing-room, study, boudoir, everything to the brother and sister who held occupation of it now.

And here were none of those traces of feminine presence which one reads of in books—no pretty things, no flowers, no embroideries, nothing to cast a grace upon the dullness. Perhaps that might be partly Susan's fault; but when one lives all one's life on the borders of Lanwoth Moor, ten miles off from the humblest attempt at a town, without any money, and seeing nobody to stir one's ambition, even a girl of seventeen may be pardoned if she can make little brightness except that of her presence in her shady place. To tell the truth, nobody made much account of Susan; she was not expected to exert much influence on the changeless atmosphere of Marchmain. No one supposed her to be the flower of that solitude: any little embellishments which she tried were put down ruthlessly; and the little girl had long ago learned, as the first duties of womankind, to do as she was bid, and hold her peace. She was seated now before the fire, making a little centre with her work upon the cold glimmer of the uncovered table. She was very fair in her complexion, with hair almost flaxen, white teeth, blue eyes, and a pretty colour. She did not look intellectual, nor interesting, nor melancholy; but sat leaning very closely over her work, because there was not much light, and Horace stood full between her and what little there was. She had a pair of scissors, a reel of cotton, and a paper of buttons on the table before her; and on the back of her chair hang a huge bag, made of printed cotton, which it was safe to believe was her work-bag. There she sat, with a little firelight playing vainly upon her dark woollen dress—a domestic creature, not very happy, but very contented, dully occupied in the silence and the gray afternoon, living a life against which her youth protested, but somehow managing to get on with tolerable comfort, as women unawakened and undisturbed do.

Of a different character altogether was the other inmate of this room. On the end of the table nearest the light lay a confusion of open books and an old-fashioned inkstand, which two instruments of learning had, it seemed, gone towards the composition of a German exercise, which appeared, half finished, and with a big blot on the last word, between them. Twenty times over, while that blurred page was being compounded, the young student had flown at the fire in silent irritability, and poked it half out; and he now stood in the recess of the window, between the red curtains, blocking up the light, and looking out with angry eyes upon the dim black blast of February rain which came with the darkness from the hills. It was certainly a dismal prospect. The very shower was not the hearty, violent shower which sweeps white over a landscape in vehement sheets of water; it had not a characteristic of storm or vitality about it; but, saturating, penetrating, invisible, went chill to the heart of the sodden land, if heart was in that wild, low stretch of blackened moss and heather, where nothing living moved. The young man stood in the window, looking out with a vexation and dull rage indescribable upon the falling night. He had this only in common with Susan, that his features were cast in an unheroic type, and could only have been handsome under the influence of good humour and good spirits, two beneficent fairies unknown to that lowering face. Good health and much exercise kept the colour on his cheeks and the light in his eye—against his will, one was tempted to suppose. He was short-sighted, and contracted his eyes in his gaze out, till the eyelids hung in heavy folds over the stormy stare which he sent across the moor—and querulous lines of discontent puckered the full youthful lips, which were made for a sweeter expression. Weariness, disgust, the smouldering rage of one oppressed, was in his face. He was not only in unnatural circumstances, but somebody had injured him: he carried his head with all the loftiness and superiority of a conscious victim; but it was evident that the sentiment of wrong—just or unjust—poisoned and embittered all his life.

"Rain!" he exclaimed, jerking the word out as if he threw something at fate. "My luck!—not so much as the chance of a run on the moor!"

"Are you tired of your German already, Horace?" asked Susan, as he came to the fire to make a last attempt upon its life—lifting up her contented woman's face, not without the shadow of a smile upon it, to her restless brother.

"Tired? D'ye think I'm a child or a girl like you? Do you think I can spend my days over German exercises? What's the good of it? Have I a chance of ever using that or any other language, unless, perhaps, as a beggar? Pshaw!—look after your work, and don't aggravate me."

"But it would please papa," said Susan, with some timidity, as if this was rather a doubtful argument; "and then, perhaps he might be persuaded to do what you wish, Horace, if you tried to please him."

"To please papa," said her brother, imitating her words with contemptuous mockery, "is an inducement indeed. To please him! Why should I please him, I should like to know? What has he ever done for me? At least, I shan't cheat him with a false submission. I'd rather chuck the lot of them into the fire, than have him suppose that I read German, or anything else, for his sake!"

"But oh, Horace, you would make me so unhappy!" said Susan, with a little unconscious gesture of entreaty, letting her work fall, and clasping her hands as she looked up in his face.

"I suppose so," said the young man, with perfect indifference.

"And you don't care?" cried his sister, moved to a momentary overflow of those sudden tears of mortification and injured affection which women weep over such cool, conscious, voluntary disregard. "I would do anything in the world for you, but you don't mind how I feel; and yet there are only two of us in the world."

"So much the better," said Horace, throwing himself down in a chair before the fire; "and as for those vain professions, what is the use of them, I should like to know? What could you do for me, if you were ever so anxious? Anything in the world, in our circumstances, means simply nothing, Susan. Oh! for heaven's sake, don't cry!—you're a good girl, and sew on my buttons—but what, in the name of fortune, could you do? You know as well as I that it is only a fashion of words—"

"I did not mean it so," cried Susan, quickly—but stopping as suddenly, cast a hurried, painful look at him, and dried her tears with a hasty hand—the look which natural Truth casts upon that cruel, reasonable fool, Wisdom, whom she cannot contest, yet knows in the wrong. A little indignation burning up upon her ingenuous cheek helped the hurried hand to dry the tears, and she returned to her work with a little tremble of haste, such as a discussion with her brother very frequently threw Susan into. She did not pretend to argue with him: she was not clever, but his philosophy filled her with impatience. She "could not bear it." She felt inclined to get up and seize hold of him, and try physical measures to shake this arrogant pretence of truth out of him; for Susan, though she could not argue, was not without a temper and opinion of her own.

Silence ensued. Susan made nervous haste with her needlework, and stumbled over it in her little flutter of vexation; but Horace was too much absorbed to notice this girlish show of feeling. When he had rocked in his chair a little, placing one foot on the side of the old-fashioned grate, he suddenly sprang up and thrust away his seat. "By George!" cried Horace—but not as that exclamation is usually uttered, "I've not got a friend in the world!—there isn't a man in existence, so far as I know, that will do anything for me!"

"Oh, Horace!" said Susan, "think how much better off you are than some people. Don't always make the worst of everything! Think of poor Roger Musgrave at Tillington, who has neither father nor home—his godfather dead without making any provision for him, and nothing to do and nobody to look to, poor fellow—and breaking his heart for grief besides, and Peggy says will either 'list or die!"

"And a very good alternative too," said Horace; "he's very well off for a poor milk-and-water nobody—free! and able to 'list if he likes, or die if he likes, without any one troubling their head about the matter. As to home and father, I heartily wish he had my share of these precious commodities. Do you think anywhere else a man like me would sell his soul for a bed and a dinner? There! there! hold your tongue, or talk of what you understand."

"What do I understand, I wonder," cried Susan, "sewing on your worship's buttons? A man like you!—you are only nineteen after all, when the truth is told."

"I am man enough to make my own way," said the youth, angrily; "it is not a question of years or days, if indeed you were able to judge of it at all, which you are not."

"If I were so very certain of my own strength," cried Susan, following up her advantage, "I'd run away, if I did not care for home, or father, or—or anybody. If I did not mind about duty or affection, or such trifles, I'd go and make my own way, and not talk of it—I would! I know something, though I'm not so wise as you. I think it's shocking to talk discontent for ever, and gloom at everything. Why don't you go away? Think of the great people in books, that go to London with sixpence in their pockets, and turn out great merchants—or with a tragedy, and turn out Dr. Johnson. Think of Chatterton, whom you were reading of. You are better off a great deal than he!"

"Chatterton was a fool," said Horace. "I promise you I'll wait for the tide, and not shoot myself when it's in the flow. I am much obliged for your advice. I've neither a tragedy nor a sixpence that I can call my own—but some of these days I'll go."

Pronouncing these words with slow and formal emphasis, as if he meant something dreadful, Horace marched solemnly to his German exercise, and sat down to it once more. The evening grew darker round the two; by degrees Susan's head drooped down on her needlework, till you could see that she had been seized by a womanish panic, and was secretly putting up the linen on her knee to wipe her wet eyes. This terror and compunction worked its way silently as the early wintry night came on. By-and-by, through the quietness, which was broken only by Horace's pen, the ashes from the grate, and a slow patter outside of the wet which dropped from the eaves, there broke a little hurried, suppressed sob. Then Susan's white work, more distinct than herself in the twilight, went down suddenly upon the floor, and a darkling figure glided round to Horace's side. "Oh, don't think of it any more!" cried Susan; "it was only my ill-temper. Oh, Horace, never mind me!—don't think of it again."

"Think of what?" said Horace, peevishly; "what on earth do you mean, thrusting your arms about me? I did not ask to be petted, did I?—what do you mean?"

"Oh, Horace—what we were saying," said his sister, with humility.

"What were we saying? Can I remember all the nonsense you talk?" cried the young man, shaking off her arms with impatience—"can't you keep to your own business, and let me alone? Oh, you wanted me to be Whittington and the cat, didn't you?—thank you, that's not my vocation. Isn't it bad enough I must stand your sauciness, without standing your repentance—oh, for mercy's sake, go away!"

Susan went away without another word, gathered her work into her big work-bag, and went out of the room, not without making it sufficiently audible that she had closed the door.

"He's a coward! he does nothing but talk!" she said between her teeth, as she went up the dark stairs; but nobody save herself knew that her momentary passion had brought these words to Susan's lips, and ten minutes after she would not have believed she had said them—nevertheless, sometimes passion, unawares, says the truth.

CHAPTER II

The household of Marchmain consisted of four persons. The brother and sister we have already seen, their father, and one female servant. In this little interval of twilight, while Susan puts on her clean collar for dinner, and which Horace, who would rather disarrange than improve his dress, out of pure ill-humour and disrespect, spends in the dark, staring into the fire with his head between his hands, we will explain to our readers the economy of this singular household. At this hour all is dark in the solitary house. Without, the chill invisible rain, the great unbroken blackness of the moor and the night—within, an unlighted hall and staircase, with a red glow of firelight at the end of a long passage, betraying the kitchen, and a faint thread of light coming out beneath a door opposite the dining-room. Thrift, severe and rigid, reigns in this dwelling. In Mr. Scarsdale's own room a single candle burns, when it is no longer possible to read without one; but there are no lights in the family sitting-room till the dinner is placed on the table, and Peggy has nothing but firelight in the kitchen, and Susan puts on her collar by intuition upstairs. Everything is under inexorable rule and law. The family have breakfast between nine and ten, sometimes even later; for Mr. Scarsdale is not a man to modify his own habits for any consideration of suitability. From that time till six o'clock, when there is dinner, the young people see nothing of their father. He sits with them in the evening, imposing silence by his presence; and that, so far as family intercourse goes, is the chronicle of their life.

Let us enter at this door, which marks itself off from the floor of the hall by that slender line of light. It has the same prospect as the dining-room, when there is any daylight to see it; but it is smaller than that gloomy apartment; two large bookcases, shut in by a brass network, stand out with sharp and angular corners from the walls, no attempt having been made to fill up the vacant space at either side of them, or to harmonize these gaunt pieces of furniture with anything else in the room. There are two or three chairs, which stand fixed and immovable in corners, plainly testifying that nobody ever sits there; and before the fire a library table, and in a round-backed elbow-chair the father of the house. He sits there reading with a forlorn persistence wonderful to see—reading for no purpose, reading with little interest, yet turning page after page with methodical regularity, and bending his lowering forehead on the book as if it were the business of his life. He is dark, not so much in complexion as in sentiment—a close, self-absorbed, impenetrable man. It is not difficult to perceive that he is neither a student by ardent inclination, nor by profession a searcher into books; but what is the secret of these solitary studies is hard to discover. He sits with his head leaning upon one hand, and the other turning the pages—sits often for hours in that one position. He is scarcely ever stimulated into interest, and never owns the enlivening touch of that zeal and curiosity which hunts for proofs or illustrations of a favourite theory through a dozen volumes. There is no heap of books by his side, but only one orderly volume, which is not of the class of those fantastic delightful reverie books in which studious men delight. The blank, straightforward manner in which he reads on comes to be impressive in its singularity after a time. He seems to pursue this occupation as a clerk keeps books, and counts his progress, you could imagine, by the number of the pages he has read, and by no less tangible criterion; and nothing moves the settled darkness of his uncommunicative face.

Behind him, hung by the side of the window, in the worst light of the room, is a portrait, a very common work, done by a mediocre painter, but in all probability very like its original, for the face looks down through the gloom with a real smile, which paint cannot give—a sweet, home-like, domestic woman, such another as Susan will be when the years and the hours have carried her into her own life. There can be no doubt it is Susan's mother and this man's wife. There is no other picture in the house, and he cares so little for anyone seeing this, that he has hung it in the shadows of the red moreen curtains, where nobody can distinguish the features. Most likely he knows the features well enough to penetrate that darkness; for though he sits with his back to it most usually, it is for his pleasure it is here.

Nobody knows anything about this man; he has not any family connection whatever with the house or locality. Nobody can understand why of all places in the world he should come here to the tumble-down old house on the edge of the moor, which nobody else would live in. When he came, ten years ago, the country people paid him visits—half in curiosity, half in kindness—which were never returned, till at last society dropped off entirely, even from the attempt to break upon his seclusion. To account for his ungraciousness, rumours of great crimes and great misfortunes were whispered about him; but as the novelty failed, these sunk into abeyance; and it was tacitly understood or believed now that the loss of a great lawsuit, which materially lessened his means, was the cause of his withdrawal from the world. He was then but a young man, scarcely forty; and if neither sport nor society had attractions for him then, it was not to be supposed that his heart had expanded now. He lived in a severe, rectangular, mathematical poverty, which calculated every item, and left room for no irregularity. He kept his children rigidly within the same bounds which confined himself. If they formed acquaintances, it must needs have been at "kirk or market," in the roads or the fields, for he strictly forbade them from either receiving or accepting invitations; while for his own part he gave a certain cold attention to their education as a duty, but spent as little time as possible in their society. It is not surprising, under these circumstances, that this gloomy and brooding man should have roused the kindred temper of his son to a slight degree of desperation, or succeeded in making the thraldom of his life very irksome to a youth who was neither amiable nor submissive, to begin with. Mr. Scarsdale did not even pretend a fatherly regard for Horace; all his life he had treated the lad with a cutting and desperate civility, which would have pierced a more sensitive child to the heart; and from his boyhood had given him a certain position of equality and rivalship, totally contrary to the relationship they really held, and which at once stimulated the pride and raised the passions of the solitary youth. This unhappy state of things had never come to a climax by any outburst of passion. Horace might be as disrespectful, as sullen, as defiant as he pleased. His father extorted a certain hard lineal obedience, but neither expected nor seemed to wish for, reverence, love, or any filial sentiment; and this aspect of affairs had become so habitual, that even Susan did not observe it. Most likely she thought all fathers were more or less the same; her whole heart of tenderness went back to her little recollection of her mother—and Mr. Scarsdale was still human so far as Susan was concerned. He was not kind certainly, but at least he seemed conscious that he was her father and she his child.

Notwithstanding his seclusion, his limited means, and morose habits, he still bore the appearance, and something of the manners, of a gentleman—something which even those neighbours whose kindnesses he had repulsed acknowledged by an involuntary respect. When the half-hour chimed from his clock on the mantel-piece—almost the only article of luxury visible in the house—he closed his book as a labourer gives up his work, pausing only to place a mark in the page, and, taking up his candle, went solemnly upstairs. He was scarcely of middle size, but so spare and erect that he seemed tall; thin almost to the point of emaciation, with marked and prominent features, unlike either of his children. Yet, strangely enough, though Horace's face resembled that of his mother, the expression—the spiritual resemblance—was like this dark and brooding face: possibly, the very pang and keenness of opposition between the father and the son lay in their likeness. Mr. Scarsdale carried his candle up the gloomy staircase, leaving his study in darkness, to exchange his easy dressing-gown for a coat, and prepare himself for dinner. Dinner for ten years, at least, had been to him a solitary meal: during all that time his doors had never opened to admit a stranger; but he never once failed in the customary punctilio, or neglected to close his book when the timepiece chimed the half-hour.

Meanwhile, the preparations of the kitchen were coming to a climax. This was the only cheerful place in the house. It had a large old-fashioned chimney, with a settle in its warm corner, and the warmth centered in that recess as in a chamber of light. Bundles of herbs were hung up to dry over the mantel-shelf, where was a little oil-lamp attached to the wall, but rarely lighted—so that the apartment itself, with its broad but high window, its great wooden presses and tables, was but half seen in the wavering light. There stood Peggy, putting on her "dinner cap." Peggy was, at least, as tall as her master, and very little younger. She was his foster-sister, attached all her life to his family, and knew the secret of his retirement, if anybody did; but Peggy was of the faithful type of ancient servants, and gave no sign. She had been comely in her youth, and was still fresh-coloured and neat when she pleased—and she did please at dinner-time. She had on a dark stuff gown, with a white soft muslin handkerchief covering her neck under it, as is the fashion with elderly women in the north country; a great white apron, and the before-mentioned cap, which had pink ribbons in it. Peggy had rather a large face, and features big and strong. Had she been born a lady, with nothing to do, she would have been a strong-minded woman; but Providence had been kinder to Peggy. As it was, she had her own opinions about most things, and hesitated not at all to express her approbation and disapprobation. She was, in short, very much what old servants were, as we have said, a generation or two ago. But one thing was the pride of Peggy's life: to have everything in perfect order for her master's dinner, which was the event of the day to her; to feel convinced that her cookery was as careful and delicate as if she had been attended by a score of scullions; to do everything indeed, as far as it lay in one pair of active hands and one vigorous brain to do, as perfectly as if a whole establishment of servants waited on the comforts of "the family"—was the ambition of Mr. Scarsdale's solitary waiting-woman. If no one else felt the compliment, Peggy was continually flattered and inspirited by her master's evening-coat.

And it was she, though nearly fifty, who did everything in the house, it was she alone who knew the former history of "the family" which she tended so carefully. If ever Mr. Scarsdale unbended his reserved soul for a moment, it was Peggy who received the rare confidence. It was she who had helped the inherent woman to come to feminine life in poor little Susan's neglected education; and it was she, the only busy, cheerful living inhabitant of the house, who now carried those slender silver candlesticks into the dark dining-room, and disturbed Master Horace in his reverie with the gleam of the unexpected light.

CHAPTER III

There were strange elements of incongruity in the scene presented by that dinner-table. Mr. Scarsdale sat at the head of the table, with his son and daughter at the sides, and Peggy behind his chair, erect and stately in his evening dress. All the furniture of the table, the linen, the silver, the china, were of the finest description, and in beautiful order; and strangely around this little centre of light gloomed the meagre unadorned walls, the homely furniture, the heavy hangings of the cheerless apartment, which, however, scarcely formed a greater contrast to the dainty arrangements of the table than Horace Scarsdale's gray morning jacket, and disordered hair, did to the formal toilette of his father. Susan sat at Mr. Scarsdale's right hand, in her clean collar. Her dress was very homely; but Susan, at seventeen, was one of those women who have a natural fitness for their place everywhere, and never fall out of harmony. Perhaps she was not over-sensitive by nature; at all events, she was not distressed by the silence of this meal, at which there was no conversation. It was their invariable custom, and Susan had seen no other family-table to make her aware of the misery of this. Horace was of another temper: everything was an offence to the unhappy lad; the silence galled almost beyond endurance; and when his father addressed him as he did always, with formal politeness, upon helping him to anything, the blood rushed to the young man's cheeks with such sudden violence and force, that no one, who watched his countenance, could have been surprised to see him answer with some demonstration of passion. But he never did; he replied, in the stifled voice of rage, with thanks and formal courtesy. Thus they sat like two enemies, forced to civility by the circumstances of sitting at the same table, and together ate, as if it choked them, their unblessed bread. "Shall I help you to some soup?" asked Mr. Scarsdale, and Horace made a stubborn bow and said, "Thank you." Neither spoke the other's name, neither even looked in the other's face—yet, by that strange magic of antagonism, which is as strong as love, were aware, instinctively, of every movement, almost of every sentiment, which influenced each other's conduct for the moment. But they had this little duel all to themselves—Susan, dulled by habit, and knowing that it had always been so, observed it not—Peggy, behind her master's chair, saw everything, and said nothing. Sometimes, indeed, an acute observer might have noticed that the faithful servant set down something on the table with an unnecessary emphasis, which answered, instead of words, to give her impatience vent, and which her master never failed to notice. Peggy, too, did not hesitate to interfere in the business of the table—to remark that Mr. Horace did not eat, and to recommend a particular dish to Miss Susan. Peggy's dialect was rather a remarkable one, and difficult to identify. She was a North-countrywoman by birth, but had lived in many districts of England, and had taken up, with great impartiality and candour of mind, their different manners of speech. But Mr. Scarsdale, who had killed all natural utterance in his children, had no power over Peggy; he never even tried to restrain her. Her discourse ran on a cheerful chorus during the whole solemn period of dinner; and this it was, more perhaps than anything else, which prevented a positive outbreak between the father and the son.

"Young Master Roger, Miss Susan, dear, he's agoin' hoam," said Peggy; "he's got father and mother livin' after all, as I hear say, and none so poorly off neither, for all his goin' off in a despair wi' talk o' 'listin'. Natur's a mystery, that's for certain—to turn off a manchild upon a godfayther, and rather to 'list nor to go hoam! I dunno know which is worst if ye ask me. Stewed chicken, master, and done perfect, though I say it as should not; but I'm none so pleased with the peatoes. I'll not have no more from the mill—they're agoin' in the disease. Wine?—this very minute, if I had the keys."

Mr. Scarsdale brought forth the keys from his pocket; and, totally regardless of Peggy's monologue, which ran on in further gossip, broke the silence of the table in his own person—a most portentous and unusual incident. He spoke without either addressing or looking at anyone, though it was, in fact, a question which he asked.

"There is, I believe," observed Mr. Scarsdale, "a spare bedroom in the house?"

Peggy did not hear for the first moment, being taken aback by the unusual event; and Susan said, timidly, "Yes, papa," taking the remark to herself.

"The door was open this very day, master," said Peggy, when she recovered her surprise; "I judge you wur lookin' with your own eyes what like it was; but the good of a spare bedroom in this house I would wish a wise woman to tell to me."

Mr. Scarsdale made no response, but delivered himself of his further intelligence as though he heard her not. "I wish it to be put in order," he said, briefly; "Colonel Sutherland arrives here on a visit, to-morrow."

Even Horace was moved to a momentary start and look of surprise at his father's immovable countenance, while Susan clasped her hands in spite of herself, and cried—"Oh! papa, is it my uncle?" with the most eager and joyful anxiety suddenly suffusing her face.

But Susan's voice was drowned in Peggy's more decided accents. "Master Edward!" cried Peggy, with a restrained shout of triumph—"blessings on his honest face! he never crossed a door but he brought comfort—and as handsome a man as eye could see, and the pleasantest gentleman to speak to that ever said good-morrow. So he's Cornel now!—and well deserves it, I'll be bold to say. Custard, master?—as light as a May breeze—and the very tarts you had in holiday times, when you were a boy. I had a thought of old times, and knew no reason—to be sure, it was for a forewarning of the news!"

Mr. Scarsdale thrust the china dish containing the tarts out of his way with an unusual expression of impatience. Then, recollecting himself, took it up and turned to Horace—that is to say, turned his head to him, without turning his eyes, as was his custom. "May I have the pleasure of helping you?" said the father, with a tone of suppressed bitterness. Horace put forth his plate immediately; Peggy's harmless confectionery was evidently vexatious and annoying to Mr. Scarsdale, and his son took pains to express his enjoyment of it, and compliment Peggy on her handiwork. It was as rare an event to hear Horace's voice at dinner as his father's. The approaching event seemed to have loosed the tongues of both.

This little incident put an end to Peggy's gossip; she removed the remainder of her tarts with a visible flutter of offence, and set down the wine on the table with double emphasis. When Peggy withdrew, Mr. Scarsdale took a book from his pocket, and set up a small folding reading-desk, which had been placed by his hand when the cloth was withdrawn. There he sat, with his glass of purple claret reflected in the shining mahogany, and the two tall, slender candles illuminating a little circle round him, and his head relieved against the dark curtains, which looked almost black in the feeble light. A line of magic drawn round him could not have screened him more completely from the other inmates of the room. Horace thrust his chair away rudely, and leaving it thus at a little distance from the table, went to the window and disappeared behind the curtains to look out on the night. Susan stole quietly round to the side of the table, and produced out of her big bag her evening work—an occupation dear to her heart, though it was only a patchwork quilt, the only fancy work that Susan knew; but before she sat down, withdrew her brother's chair noiselessly to the side of the fire, where it looked human and companionable. Then silence, entire as if these three human creatures were statues, fell upon the room, where still Mr. Scarsdale sat at the shining table with its two lines of reflection, with the claret jug at his elbow, and his book supported on the reading-desk, and the glass before him half-full of purple wine. He turned the leaves at regular intervals, and went through them with mechanical gravity; but his ears were keen to every rustle of the curtain, and with all the virulence of domestic strife the mind of this singular father watched his son.

As for Susan, her whole mind, as she worked in silence, was full of the wonderful intimation she had just heard. Perhaps by this time you are disposed to think that Susan was very insensible and dull in her feelings not to be miserable about the enmity which existed between her father and brother; but Susan was accustomed to it, and had never seen other fathers and sons, and had seen this go on in the same way so long, that, though she felt it uncomfortable, she entertained no apprehensions about it. As for Horace, if he would remain by himself in the window, looking out upon the black night, Susan could not help it. He was not more miserable there than he would be at the table with his father's austere shadow upon him; and conversation was tacitly prohibited in those dismal evenings. Susan's was still an unawakened mind; her brother did not encourage her to think her own influence over him of any importance, nor permitted her to suppose that she had any power to soothe him; and the trembling, timid, mediatory love, which holds a fearful balance in many a divided household, needs love and softness of some kind, on one side or the other, to keep it alive. Love Susan found none in either of her two nearest relatives. She loved them by nature and custom; sometimes a terrible impatience of their discord seized her, and a momentary impulse of passion, to do something or say something which should stir this stagnant, stormy calm, or perhaps change the manner of their existence, had possessed her once or twice in her life; but the tender, anxious, intense love which cruelty cannot kill when it has once developed itself, never can develop itself without the stimulus and creating power of dear love from some one to begin with. Thus it was that Susan beheld with vexation and distress sometimes, but without agony, the unnatural feud beside her, that she took neither side, because either side was equally cold, repulsive, and unaffectionate. She did not know life; she knew not even the fictitious life of books. She did not fear when her brother rushed out into the night, as he did often, that Horace would fall into the rude snares of village dissipation, or run in the way of vulgar crime. She was not alarmed for a possible outbreak of violence between the father and son; such things had never been suggested to her inexperienced mind.

So she sat in the silence, not resenting it for her own part, content in herself, and making out of that dismal quiet a little circle of domestic tranquillity when she arranged her patches and contrasted her colours, and secretly entertained vague anticipations of unknown pleasure, and a warmth of inextinguishable personal happiness, in the very heart of the misery through which her life had grown.

At eight o'clock to a minute Peggy brought in the tea-tray, and removed the claret-jug, which, though he had only once filled his glass, stood all that time by Mr. Scarsdale's side. Then he took his cup of tea from his daughter's hand without even looking at her, and went on with his reading. Comfort was not to be got out of anything in this house. Horace drank his standing—told his sister it did not rain now, and went off out of the room like a wind. And when Susan looked over her tea-tray to see her father's eyes fixed upon his book, and the door closed upon her brother, and herself compelled to sit formally there till Mr. Scarsdale, sipping it slowly and by intervals, had finished his second cup of tea—a certain forlorn sensation of solitude and discomfort moistened Susan's eyes, and brought an ache to her heart. Then her thoughts went back with a joyful rebound to the promised visitor of to-morrow—her mother's brother, an actual relation, whose love and kindness she had a claim on. She lost herself in wonder what like he would be, and how he would treat his sister's children. To-morrow would solve Susan's long and troubled problem—whether all men were like papa: to-morrow would give her a glimpse into that world of which she knew nothing. Nature was sceptical in Susan's heart: she could not believe that papa was the type and impersonation of man. Kindness, unknown and longed for, seemed coming to her in the person of that uncle. She returned to her patches, longing to run into the cheerful kitchen to Peggy, to ask all about the new-comer; but bound by the customary punctilio of the house to sit there silent and occupied opposite the reading-desk—a bondage which Susan had never felt more oppressive than on this particular night—while Mr. Scarsdale still turned the mechanical pages, and Horace roamed through the black moor and the falling rain, cursing his fate.

CHAPTER IV

This same evening, while Susan sat at her patchwork, comforting herself with fancies concerning the unknown uncle who was to make so strange and unexpected a break upon their solitude, an old gentleman, carrying his own carpet-bag, went into one of the carriages of the night-trains about to start from Edinburgh for the south. He was not a first-class passenger, but the railway people put up instinctive fingers to their caps as he addressed them. He was tall, thin, erect—of a soldierly bearing, with a grey moustache and gray hair, wearing thin upon the crown. That he was a little deaf it was easy to perceive, from the sudden stoop he made when the person sitting next him in the carriage put a question to him unexpectedly; and that his eyes were touched by years and usage was equally apparent when, unable to find his spectacles, he held his time-bill at arm's length to read it the better. But there was something ingratiating and prepossessing even in the bend which brought his ear to the level of the voice which addressed him, with that instinctive and delicate courtesy which will not treat the most trivial application with carelessness. The good woman who spoke felt flattered—she could not tell how; it was only to ask when the train would start—a thing which her next neighbour knew no better than she did—but the ready attention, and sincere endeavour which the old soldier instantly made to satisfy her, gave the questioner all the feeling of a personal compliment. When the long line of carriages got under weigh, our friend wrapped himself up in his warm cloak, and leaned back in his unluxurious corner. It was a gloomy, rainy, miserable night; the little lamp jolting in the roof, and throwing a feeble illumination over four benches full of drowsing night-travellers, was the only light visible in earth and heaven, save when the nocturnal express plunged with ostentatious speed through some little oasis of a station, with faint lamps gleaming through the universal gloom. The old soldier, however, was not easily disturbed by the discomforts of his journey; if there were any special meditations in his mind, he showed no sign of them; but, with his face half buried in his cloak, kept motionless in his corner—where, in the very midst of the black night, or, to speak more properly, about three o'clock in the winter morning, the guard awaked him. He had reached the end of his journey. The rest of the night he passed in the Railway Inn of a country town, from which he set out next morning in a gig, to face the raw February blast for a drive of fourteen miles over an exposed country. Colonel Edward Sutherland, though he had been twenty years in India, had come home still a poor man; and habits of economy were strong upon the old officer, accustomed all his life, even in the luxurious eastern climate, to spare and restrain unnecessary expenses. He was a solitary man, but he was not a free old bachelor, at liberty to expend his own means on his own pleasure; wife and many children had been left behind in Indian graves, but he had a boy at Addiscombe, and one at St. Andrew's, and consequently not a shilling of his income to spare; so he placed his carpet bag carefully below the seat out of the reach of rain, and tied a travelling-cap over his ears, and muffled his cloak half over his face, and so turned his face to the wind for his chilly journey to Lanwoth Moor.

"Ay, sure the wind's in the east—it's ever in the east on this road," said the man who drove him. "When it's could as could all the country over, it's double could Lanwoth way. Beg your pardon, Cornel," said the man, touching his cap, "but it's strange for a gen'l'man to goo this gate in ought but a shay."

"That is my business, my man," said the traveller, quietly; "is it a good road?"

"Bits," said the postboy, shrugging his shoulders; "and bits the very dyeuce for the poor beasts; but we never goo this direction, Cornel, not twicest in a year—not all the way. There's Tillington, five mile this side o' Lanwoth, but the road strikes off to the reet—Lord blees you, gen'l'men know better nor to build on a moorside. The wind comes down off the fells fit to pull your skin off, Cornel; and ne'er a shelter, and ne'er a tree, but bits o' saplings in the moss. Rain and snow and hail, they sweep a' things before them. I'd never set a brute beast, let alone a christian, with its nose to Lanwoth Moor."

"Yet somebody must live there," said the traveller, shivering in spite of himself within his cloak.

"Not a soul, Cornel, but the one house," said the driver, eagerly; "not a thatch roof or a clay wall—nought but Marchmain. They say it was built at the riding of the Marches, that's once in the hunderd year, and a' foor strife, foor to part the lands of the twae Allonbys, brothers and foes as should never be seen in God's world. But sure there it stands, black as hate, and—" —the man made a sudden pause, and looked suddenly up in the old officer's face—"Cornel, you're gooing there?"

"Do you know me, driver?" said Colonel Sutherland, with a little curiosity.

The man held down his head with a sly, half-abashed smile, not quite sure whether to pretend knowledge or to confess that he acquired his information from the card on the carpet bag. The result of his deliberations was an equivocal reply. "I know an army gen'l'man when I see him, sir," he said, raising his slouching rustic shoulders, and quickening his speech out of its Cumbrian drawl. "My father was an ould 53d, and Cornel Toppe Sawyer's own man; and, begging your pardon, Cornel, a blind man could see you had borne command."

Colonel Sutherland was human; he was not only human, but a little amiable vanity was one of his foibles. He inclined his ear blandly to this clever compliment, and perhaps thought his driver rather a sensible fellow; but at that moment the blast came wild in their faces—wet, dismal, cold—a wind that cut to the bone, and the chattering teeth and shivering frame which owned its influence was not lively enough for conversation. The horse winced, and turned his unfortunate head aside, making a momentary pause. The hills—low, gray, and piebald, with their yellow circles of lichen, and brown turrets of rock—were blurred into the dull horizon, which expressed nothing but that dismal, penetrating moisture and murderous cold; and when, by a sudden turn of the road, the hapless traveller found himself suddenly under the shelter of high banks and hedges which intercepted the blast, the sudden contrast was so grateful that Colonel Sutherland withdrew his cloak from his blue face, and looked about him with a sigh of relief. There was nothing very particular to see: a common country road descending a slope—for which some necessity of the soil had made a deep cutting expedient—with a village within sight, and a soft, broad valley; green fields, dotted with farm-houses and haystacks, and leafless trees. The houses were all of the silvery-grey limestone of the district, and walls of the same stone, more frequent than hedge-rows, divided the fields. The old Colonel, drawing breath under the shadow of the bank, thought to himself that under sunshine the prospect would be very pleasant, and was scarcely pleased to find that this, the only comfortable bit of the road, was the one on which their progress was most rapid—and to hear that they were still ten long dreary miles from Marchmain.

"There was talk enow in the country, Cornel," said the driver, resuming his discourse, "when a strange gen'l'man coom'd to take that 'ouse. Ne'er a sowl in twenty mile but had heard of Marchmain. I reckon you've never been there?"

"No," said the traveller, briefly.

"He's a terrible quiet gen'l'man too, as we hear say," continued the man; "a great scholard, I do suppose—and ignorant folks have little understanding on the ways of sich. They say strange foot has never crossed the door this nine year. It's a terrible place to bring up children, Cornel, is Lanwoth Moor, and the young gen'l'man and Miss they're kepp as close at hoam as if they were but six-year-olds; never a gun on young master's shoulder, and the young lady ne'er saw a dance in her born days. Them things come natural to young folks. I'm saying but what I hear: it might be a parcel o' stories for ought I know—but Mr. Scarsdale yonder, he's a very uncommon man."

"Poor children!" said Colonel Sutherland half aloud, with a sigh. The open air, the rustle of the wind, and the noise of the wheels improved the Colonel's hearing, as it so often does a gentle imperfection of the kind. He beard every word of these scattered observations, and began to feel more anxiety touching his visit to his morose brother-in-law than he would have thought possible when he started. He knew, it was true, the secret calamity which had driven his sister's husband to the wilderness; but his own simple, pious, cheery spirit had no understanding of the unwholesome passions of a self-regarding soul. He had blamed himself for years for unconsciously feeling his relative's withdrawal from life to be pusillanimous and unworthy of a man; but nothing had suggested to the practical and innocent-minded soldier a gloomy retreat such as that which began to be revealed to him by hints and suggestions now. He was unable to conceive how a man with children could make an utter hermit of himself, "especially children under their extraordinary circumstances," said the Colonel anxiously, in his own heart. He grew silent, absorbed, troubled, as they proceeded on their way. When, immediately after settling himself on his return from India in a home of his own, that home often longed for, to which his sons could come in their holidays, he had volunteered a visit to his brother-in-law—it was the reciprocity of honest affection and kindred which the veteran wished to re-establish between his own family and their nearest relatives. He set out to visit the Scarsdales in the full idea that they too would visit him, and that the father of that household lived like himself in the tenderest friendship with those inheritors of his blood in whom he renewed his own youth; and with an old man's sentiment of tender gallantry, this old soldier thought of Susan, the only surviving woman of his race, his sister's daughter and representative, his baby-favourite long ago. Perhaps a floating idea of appropriating this only woman of the house had dawned upon his fatherly mind with other matters—for the Addiscombe cadet was a year older than Susan, and boys are so likely to marry when they go to India. At all events, it was a sunny, simple picture of family kindness and comfort which had presented itself to the honest eyes of the old soldier when he set out upon his journey. This prospect began to cloud over sadly now; he could not understand nor explain these singular circumstances, which must be facts, and visible to the common eye. A lonely house which no one else would live in, a seclusion which no stranger ever broke, young people shut out from the society of their fellows, and gloom and mystery upon the whole house! The Colonel wrapt his face once more in his cloak and subsided into deafness and silence, pondering painfully in his own mind what might be required of himself under such unexpected circumstances, and what he could do for the relief of Horace and Susan, whom in his kind heart he fondly called "the children." These deliberations had come to no satisfactory result, when, rounding a corner of the road, the bare extent of Lanwoth Moor became suddenly visible, stretching to the fells, and the sky to the horizon, blurred with rain, where it was scarcely possible to tell which was hill and which was cloud.

They drove along in silence, a long half mile, seeing nothing but that same blank expanse traversed by the long, deep cuttings of an attempted drainage, until at last the driver silently, with a certain sympathy for the silence of his companion, pointed out the solitary walls rising on the edge of the moor. The house was a square, common-place erection of two stories, with no remarkable feature, but that one side was raised a story higher than the other, and stood up square and gray, like the little distinguishing tower of an Italian house. Like—yet how unlike!—the rough, gray limestone, unpolished and savage, the deep walls into which those small windows sank like cavernous eyes, the cold blue slated roof, the cold door coming bare out upon the path, without a morsel of garden or any enclosure, all enclosed and backed by that monotonous mystery of moor, the distant spectral hills, the clouds that carried them out in ghostly ranges, the wind and the rain so blended together that they made but one—and they went to the heart with a chill indescribable, and not to be resisted.

Colonel Sutherland looked upon all this with a sensation of anguish. It was incomprehensible to him. That he should find his relatives here, and not in the cheerful village house he had expected, overpowered him with complete wonder. He ceased even to be indignant at the father who sacrificed wilfully the happiness of his children—he suspended his judgment till he should hear what extraordinary circumstances had fixed them thus. In his unsuspecting heart he felt certain that something which he did not know must have produced this exaggerated and unnatural retirement. The sudden impression produced upon him by the sight of this house made his cheek pale, and added a nervous trembling to the shiver of the cold; he got down, stumbling at the door, which the driver watched with undisguised curiosity, as if something unnatural and portentous was about to make its appearance—and, in his emotion, let the money fall out of the purse which he took out to pay his conductor. While he stooped to pick it up, the door opened hastily, and Peggy rushed forth and seized the carpet-bag. At sight of her the Colonel recovered a little from his confusion and tremor.

"Thank God!" he exclaimed fervently, "there is some sunshine here at last."

The driver opened his eyes somewhat disappointed. Peggy was not known at the country town, though Mr. Scarsdale's extraordinary life had been heard of there; and the vigorous servant-woman, who began to scold forthwith between the exclamations of her joyful recognition, reduced the mysterious house to matter-of-fact. The man drove off, not knowing what to make of it; and fearing to hear of some new misfortune, with his honest heart beating with grief, sympathy, and anxiety to mend the position of his friends, Colonel Sutherland, after twenty years' absence, entered at his brother-in-law's inhospitable door.

CHAPTER V

The kitchen of Marchmain was built out from the house, and was a long and somewhat narrow apartment, quite unlike the rest of the building. People said it had been a cottage standing on the spot before this house was built, and arbitrarily connected with it—and the unceiled roof and large old-fashioned chimney favoured the notion. The mud or brick floor had been, however, replaced by a deal one; and the roof was now covered, instead of thatch, with the less picturesque but safer slates, which gave so cold an aspect to the house. Within, two large articles of furniture filled up half the space, though furniture these fixed encumbrances could scarcely be called. One was a prodigious press, in which Peggy kept her household linen—the other, a great square box with a sloping lid, which contained the immediate supply of coals, brought from the coal cellar outside. Beneath the window—which was large but high, so that Peggy, though she was tall, could do no more than look out, and Susan could only reach up to it on tiptoe—stood a large deal table, clean to the utmost extent of cleanliness, where Peggy did her ironing—(Peggy was punctilious in her concerns, and kept everything in its proper place)—another table in quite another quarter was appropriated to the cooking—and a third, a small round one, stood aside in a corner to be lifted in front of the fireplace at nights when Peggy's work was over, beside the big old heavy elbow-chair, where Peggy took an evening nap and sipped a fourth cup of tea.

In this apartment, in the morning of the same day, while Colonel Sutherland drove through the rain, Susan, excited, happy, and restless, fluttered round Peggy at her work. Susan had in her hand the front of one of Master Horace's new shirts, which she pretended to be stitching—but everybody knows that stitching is a delicate operation, and not to be performed on foot, or in a state of restlessness. This was the time of the day when Susan was most free to follow her own desires. Horace was out, and Mr. Scarsdale in his study. When this fortunate concurrence of circumstances was secured, Susan came lightly out of the dull dining-room to the bright kitchen, the only place in the house which had an appearance or sentiment of home. Peggy was better company for Susan than a thousand philosophers; she laughed, she sang, she danced about, she looked like a young living creature, as she was, in Peggy's womanly presence. Her father and her brother were rather hard examples of the rule of man to Susan. Horace exacted endless sympathy—sympathy more bitter than it was in her to bestow—and scorned it when it was given; but Peggy cherished the girl with an all-indulgent tenderness—a motherly, nursely, homely love, advising, and interfering, and fretting, which kept her heart and her youth alive. But something more than usual occupied their thoughts to-day.

"Ay, honey—as if it was yesterday," said Peggy. "R'c'lect him!—he was not the young man to be forgot, I can tell you! Many a handsome lady would have gone over seas to follow the young soldier. He was just the innocentest, bravest, kindest man I ever looked in the eye."

"Why in the eye?" said Susan, who was a little matter-of-fact, and liked to understand a new phrase.

"Eh, child! his heart was in it!" cried Peggy. "When your mamma was alive, she was a dear, blessed creature, and kept religion and comfort in the house; but when Mr. Edward came, it was pleasure to be about, and the world was changed. He never arguified with a soul, nor set up his opinions, nor took slights nor offences, nor a single mortal thing that a' persons beside did. He was just right himself and happy himself without thinking upon't, and was a happiness to be nigh night and day. The master, so far as I can think, had never a cross word with Mr. Edward. Think you any other man would ever have come, or been let come, to this house?"

"No, indeed," said Susan, gravely; "it is very strange. I wonder how he thought of it at all; one would suppose he must like us, Peggy, to come here—though I don't see how that can be either. Hasn't he been in India all our lives?"

"Little matter for that; but you understand nothing about friends' feelings; and how should you, poor forlorn infant!" said Peggy. "He likes you, I'll warrant; and he's held you on his knee, Miss Susan—and besides, for your mamma's sake."

"To be sure, for mamma's sake," said Susan, satisfied; "but surely, other people, when she knew so many, must have loved mamma. Peggy, what can make papa so stiff and hard to strangers, and putting everybody out of the house, and never letting us make any friends—what do you think it can be?"

Peggy drew a long breath, which seemed to end in some inward words, said for her own private relief and satisfaction.

"Your papa has his own reasons, Miss Susan, and that's neither for you nor me; but you see he lets Mr. Edward come. Who can tell how many more?—for Mr. Edward has the tongue of a nightingale, and steals folks's hearts."

"I wish he would sing into papa's," said Susan, laughing; "there's never any music at Marchmain, Peggy. Oh, I wonder when Uncle Edward will come; look out and see if there's anybody in the road; such a morning! and Horace will come in all muddy and sulky, and not get goodtempered the whole of the day.

Peggy," cried Susan, jumping down from the chair she had mounted to look out, "are boys always so dreadfully cross?"

"Indeed, Miss Susan, they're little to be trusted," said Peggy, with a grave face of wisdom, prudently refraining from blaming Horace, while she inculcated the moral lessons supposed to be most advantageous to feminine youth.

Susan shrugged her shoulders with a private internal reflection, which perhaps meant, "I should like to judge for myself;" but which said, "I am very glad, then, that we see so little of them." For people don't permit themselves to be very ingenuous, even in their thoughts—at least women and young girls do not. "I suppose, then," she said very demurely aloud, "there never was but one Uncle Edward in the whole world, Peggy."

"Eh, honey! if there were a hunderd the world would be saved, like the Lord said to Abraham," cried Peggy. "My heart jumped when the master said it last night. I said to myself, 'a good man's coming, and a blessing will come with him.' If I saw you out of this, you two unfortunate things, I would be content to go foot foremost the same day to Lanwoth Church."

"That would be cheerful and pleasant for us, I am sure," cried Susan; "I wonder how you dare say such a thing, Peggy—all about your own nonsense, and not a word of Uncle Edward! But, I say, Peggy—oh! tell me—Uncle Edward's not a young man?"

Peggy took time to consider, pausing in her work for the purpose, with her hands covered with flour—for it was baking day. "I'm bound to allow he cannot be young—nay, it's fifteen years since he was home," cried Peggy, with a sigh. "Time flies!—it was the very same year, Miss Susan, that your mamma died."

Susan paused with a question on her lips, awed by these last words; for she understood dimly that it was in some season of extreme and mysterious calamity that her mother's life concluded. She could not have told how this impression had settled on her mind, but there it certainly was.

"Peggy," she said suddenly, putting into words the suggestion of the moment, "was it mamma's death that made papa so—so—" —Susan hesitated for a word, and at last, with a natural hypocrisy, substituted one that did not express her meaning for a less dutiful term—"so sad?"

Peggy made no audible answer, but she screwed her lips into a tight round circle, through which came an invisible, inarticulate "No," most emphatic and unmistakable though unpronounced, shaking her head violently as she did so. Susan was first frightened, then amused, at the extraordinary pantomime.

"Don't shake your head off, however," she cried, laughing. "But about Uncle Edward—you never will keep to the point, you troublesome Peggy! If he is an old man, what is he? Has he got any children?—where does he live?—do you know anything about him at all?"

"Not a mortal thing," said Peggy, relieving herself by speaking loud. "Who can hear anything here, I would like to know? Not of my own brother, Miss Susan, let alone your mamma's. But he's coming, bless him! I'm strong in the hope nature will come with him, and something will be done for you two."

"Peggy, you never spoke of us two before like that," said Susan. "Has anything happened to us that we don't know?"

"Oh, bless the innocent!—what do you know?" cried Peggy. "If I never said it before, it was because I saw no hope; but I've told your papa my mind, and that I can tell you, Miss Susan; and I'll tell it to Mr. Edward, if Providence spares me, before he's been twelve hours in this unlucky house!"

"You are very odd to-day, Peggy," said Susan, looking at her with curiosity. "But I am sure if Uncle Edward gets us permission to see people sometimes, I should be very glad—but then, we have affronted everybody," added Susan, with a little shrug of her shoulders. "However, he is coming himself—that is the great matter. Peggy, what will you have ready if he comes early? He cannot wait all the time till dinner! How foolish I was, never to think of it before! What shall we do?"

"We'll have in the lunch, Miss Susan, and as good a lunch as anybody need wish for," said Peggy, in triumph. "Is that all the good Peggy is for, to think upon things at the last moment?—for as sure as I'm living, there's a wheel upon the big stones in the road!"

Susan sprang up upon the chair, leaped down again, her colour rising, her heart beating. Then she ran breathless towards the door—then paused. "Oh, Peggy! who must tell papa?" she cried, in great excitement and trepidation. Peggy, without pausing to answer her question, rushed past her and through the hall, to throw the door open and seize upon the carpet-bag, as before related. Peggy was not afraid of papa, and her shriek of joy and welcome, "Eyeh, Master Edward!" penetrated even through the closed windows and doors of the study, where Mr. Scarsdale sat as usual, while Susan stood in the hall, eagerly bending forward to see the newcomer, and speculating with herself whether it was safe to secure herself the pleasure of her uncle's first greeting, without the dreadful operation of telling papa. The issue was, a sudden spring forward on the part of the excited girl, while her uncle—sad, oppressed, and wondering—stooped his deaf ear to Peggy, and tremulously bent over his carpet-bag. Susan had no sooner seen his face than the long restrained heart yearned within her—her mother's brother—somebody who loved them! She sprang forward and clasped his arm with both her hands, and fell a-crying, poor child, as girls use, and looked up in his face, all-conquering in her wistfulness, and her smiles, and her tears. The old man caught her in his arms, and read her face as if it had been a picture, with eager wet eyes that, after a moment, could scarcely tell what they gazed on. In that moment the poor lonely girl woke up, by dint of finding it, to discover the love that had been wanting, the immeasurable lack of her young life. And the old soldier took his sister's child—the only woman of the family—a new, tender, delicate tie, almost more touching and intimate than any other, into his fatherly old heart; and, on the instant, took courage about all the unknown troubles of the mysterious house, and was at home and himself again. They went in together to the dull dining-room, where Susan had no desire to remember that papa had not been told, and grew friends in half a minute, saying nothing but the common words that every stranger at the end of a journey hears from his entertainers. But the "Oh, Uncle, I am so glad you are come!"—the glistening eyes—the joyful young voice—the little figure fluttering about him, unable to rest for anxiety that he should rest, and have exactly what he wanted—spoke more eloquently than volumes of fine words. And Susan's face had already almost reconciled Uncle Edward to the savage solitude of Marchmain, and the dreary blank of Lanwoth Moor.

CHAPTER VI

When Colonel Sutherland had been established for nearly half-an-hour in the angular arm-chair, which was the most luxurious seat this room afforded, where he sat holding Susan's hand and keeping her by his side, it suddenly occurred to him that he had forgotten the other members of the family in his satisfaction with his new-found niece. "But, my dear child, your father?" he said, hastily; "he expected me, did he not?—he is surely at home."

And instantly Susan's countenance fell.

The old Colonel had begun to recover his spirits about his brother-in-law's house. He saw Susan in blooming health, affectionate, frank, and cheerful, and he began, with natural hopefulness, to impute the dismal house and solitary life to some caprice, and to imagine to himself a loving, united family, who were society enough to themselves. But it was impossible to mistake the cloud which fell instantly upon Susan's face. "Oh!—I ought to have told papa," she said, with a hesitation and reluctance in her voice which went to her uncle's heart. He drew her still closer to him, and looked in her face anxiously. But Susan knew nothing of that domestic martyrdom which conceals and smiles on the family skeleton. She was not aware how great a skeleton it was—it was simply a thing of course, to her inexperienced spirit.

"I should think he must have heard—I should think Peggy must have told him," said Susan. "He is not so angry when Peggy goes into the study as when I go; but if you like, I will go and tell him, uncle, now."

"Never mind, Susan. I daresay your father will come when he chooses. A deaf man would have heard Peggy's shout," said Colonel Sutherland; "and Horace—was there nobody but my little girl who came to see the old uncle—is your brother in the study too?"

"In the study!—he would as soon go down the well or up the chimney," said Susan, with a very short and half-frightened laugh. "No, uncle—Horace is in Faneleigh Woods, or on the Moor. He never minds the weather. I do think at this time of the year he gets wet through three times a-week; but I am sure Horace will be very glad to see you—as glad as I was—oh, I am quite sure!"

This expression of conviction, made with some heat and anxiety, had a very different effect from that which Susan intended—it revealed to the Colonel very plainly that Susan was anything but quite sure of Horace's sentiment; and, perhaps, Colonel Sutherland's first sensation thereupon was offence and indignation; and his personal dignity suffered a momentary mortification, from the idea that he had volunteered a visit which was welcome to nobody but this little girl. This personal feeling, however, was but momentary. A deeper pain returned to his heart; he looked anxiously into Susan's blue eyes to find out, if possible, how and why this unnatural state of things existed; or, failing that, what effect upon her the loneliness and the hardness of her life had made. But there were no mysteries in those eyes of Susan's—her girlish, undisturbed heart, clouded by a little terror of her father, which took no deeper form than that of discomfort and uneasiness, gleamed in them with otherwise unmingled joy and satisfaction. All the natural filial love hitherto denied her had sprung to life in a moment in Susan's heart. She looked at her uncle with an affectionate pride, which made her breast swell and astonished herself. To stand by his side, to feel her hand held in his kind hand, to know by intuition that there was interest for all her little affairs, and sympathy for all her unregarded troubles in this new friend, was a new life to Susan. She felt encouraged and emboldened without knowing how, as she appropriated, involuntarily, his affection, his aid, his succour. She kept naming him over and over within herself, with a secret inexplicable swell of pride and comfort. Susan had never been disposed before to use the possessive pronoun in regard to anything more important than pin-cushions and scissors; and now to say, "My uncle!" was something as new as pleasant. But notwithstanding that reference to her father curbed her tongue and brought a shade of restraint over her thoughts in spite of herself; and Uncle Edward's affectionate questions flagged—he too had something else to think of—the change was apparent to both; and Susan, for the first time in her life, moved to exert herself to seek a less unfortunate subject, immediately remembered that her uncle must want refreshment, and proposed to call Peggy to bring in his luncheon.

"Suppose we ring," said Colonel Sutherland, putting out his hand with a smile to the unused bell-rope.

Susan started with terror to prevent him.

"Oh, uncle, we never ring!" she cried, in an alarmed tone.

The sound of that bell tinkling through the house might produce Susan could not tell what tragedy in the study. She put out her trembling hand and caught at her uncle's to stop his intended action. When she did so, to Susan's great surprise the Colonel, dropping the bell, turned round upon her suddenly, and put his arm round her.

"My poor child!" he exclaimed, with some sudden access of feeling, scarcely intelligible to Susan, and with tears in his eyes.

She did not know what it meant, and yet she was very much inclined to cry too.

At this moment fortunately Peggy came in unsummoned, bringing the tray, but not the dainty dish which her care had prepared for Mr. Edward. When she set it down upon the table, she addressed the visitor with the tone and manner of one who has something disagreeable to say.

"The master's in his study, Mr. Edward: he never comes out on't at this hour of the day. Will you please to step athwart the hall, and see him there?"

"Certainly," said Colonel Sutherland, and rose at once, releasing Susan, who could not help feeling a little tremor for the consequences of his visit to her father. The old Colonel himself stepped solemnly, with a certain melancholy in his whole figure and bearing, as he went out of the room. It went to his heart to see the clouded face with which Susan responded to his mention of her father, and he went to meet him forgetting even the discourtesy which did not come to meet him—oppressed, and grieved, and wondering. When he had closed the door behind him he laid his arm on Peggy's arm, detaining her.

"What does it all mean?" he asked, with a troubled face, and stooped his deaf ear to Peggy's voice.

"What does't mean? Mischief and the devil!—and good reason he has to be proud of his handiwork," cried Peggy, vehemently, though in a whisper; "and oh, Mr. Edward! before the two unfortunate things are killed and murdered, save him from himself!"

Perhaps Colonel Sutherland did not perfectly hear this strange communication; he nodded and went on after her, looking puzzled and distressed—he was not of an intrusive or interfering nature. He had no idea of thrusting into any man's secrets, with the view of doing him good. And then, what influence had he, whom after twenty years absence his host would not come to meet. So he went across the hall, stooping his lofty grizzled head, and with a great confusion of grieved thoughts in his mind—while Susan, left behind, went to the window to look for Horace, and stirred the fire into a flame, and placed the tray and the arm-chair in the most comfortable position possible, and trembled a little, in a vague idea that Uncle Edward might somehow dissolve in that awful study, or come out a different man.

In the study, just risen up from his chair, Mr. Scarsdale received his visitor; he scarcely made a step forward to meet him, but he shook him coldly by the hand. They stood there together, two strangely different men—the recluse standing bolt upright, with his wide dressing gown falling off from his spare figure, and his book open on the table—cold, self-absorbed, in a passion of unnatural stillness; the soldier, with his tall stooping figure, his deaf ear bending with that benign and kind humility which made the infirmity a grace, and his anxious countenance afraid to lose a word of anything that might be said to him. Mr. Scarsdale's greetings were few and hurried; he asked when he returned, and how he had travelled, and then, reaching a chair which happened to be within arm's length, begged that Colonel Sutherland would sit down, in a tone which plainly signified that the request itself was a favour. Colonel Sutherland did so, looking at him with a strange wistfulness—and then, reseating himself, his host spoke.

"Since you have come to Marchmain, I have something to say to you at the commencement of what I suppose you will call our renewed intercourse. I will deal with you frankly. I should not have ventured to invite, if you had left it to me, a man of your tastes and feelings here."

"I can guess as much," said Colonel Sutherland, with a passing, angry blush.

"I should not," said Mr. Scarsdale, coldly; "because my establishment is very limited. I live in great seclusion, and I remember that you are a lover of society, and what is called cheerfulness. But you have come, and yours is the responsibility if our life oppresses you. And one thing I would say; I do not fear your discretion, having warned you. You are aware of the very peculiar circumstances under which I stand—you know, in short, the blight of my life. Pshaw! why speak of it, or give it a name?—you know, of course, thanks to your sister's frankness, exactly what I mean. Now this, I beg you to observe, is totally unknown to my children: my son is not aware of his advantage over his father. I do not mean that he shall be, until," added Mr. Scarsdale, with a ghastly smile, "until the time of his triumph approaches; but, in the meantime, I have to request that you will not think of extending to these young people a confidence which I do not wish them to possess."

A flood of painful feelings rose during this speech over the Colonel's face, of which kindness misconstrued and personal dignity wounded were the least and lightest. He looked with an amazed, grieved, uncomprehending wonder in the face of his brother-in-law, and was silent for a few minutes, while the first pangs of indignant pain were subsiding, though he involuntarily rose to his feet, an action which Mr. Scarsdale followed. Perhaps this last rudeness might have roused the warlike blood of the old soldier, had not his eye at the moment lighted upon that portrait in the shadow of the curtain. That touch of old love and sorrow moved him in the midst of his resentment almost to tears. He had to pause before he could speak as calmly as he wished to speak. "I have never thought it my duty," said Colonel Sutherland, "to interfere in any man's house: I will not begin in yours—nor would I remain in it even for a night, but for recollections which neither you nor I can efface by any measure of hard words. But, for heaven's sake, Robert Scarsdale, why is all this?—why do you meet me after this extraordinary fashion?—why do you shut yourself out from human sympathy?—why refuse yourself the comfort of your own children? As for myself, I am neither an enemy nor a stranger. Old ties and kindness have never died out of my recollection through all the sorrows and labours of my life, which have not been few. Why have they passed out of yours? We are relations—not antagonists."

"We were relatives," said Mr. Scarsdale, stiffly.

"Were! And my dear sister—your good wife—do you count her, then, only among the things that were?"

"I beg your pardon: a man is generally the best judge of the goodness of his wife; but there is no question at present of the virtues of the late Mrs. Scarsdale," said the recluse. "I can see no benefit to result from discussing past circumstances. You are welcome to my house, such as it is; but, knowing my position as you do, I think myself quite justified in requesting your silence on this matter. It was not my will, certainly, which made you aware of it at first."

Colonel Sutherland stood before his brother-in-law in a flush of unusual and inexpressible passion. He could not give utterance to the indignant, mortified, impatient surprise with which he heard these words. But what can any one say? It is hard for the voice of kindred to praise a poor woman—even when she is dead—while her husband looks on blankly, and is the best judge whether his wife has been a good wife or not. So he is, of course: therefore, be silent, brother of the dead—say nothing about her—she is judged elsewhere, and beyond human criticism now. But the old soldier stood listening, with the pang of wonder, almost stronger than that of anger and indignation, at his heart. He was so much surprised, that he was speechless. This unexpected sentiment shook him suddenly in his supposed position, and turned all his previous ideas into folly. He was not the brother of a wife beloved, the uncle of children who cherished their mother's memory, but an intruder, presuming upon a past relationship. A flush of deep mortification came upon his face: he made a stately, ceremonious bow to his ungracious host—

"In that case—as things are," stammered the Colonel, "I will make no encroachments upon your hospitality. Pray, don't say anything—it is unnecessary. I—I shall take care to pay due respect to your desires so far as your children are concerned. In short, I beg you to understand that your secret is, and has always been, with me as though I knew it not; but," said Colonel Sutherland, pausing in his haste, and steadying his voice, "it was, as you are well enough aware, known to half, at least, of your former friends, and that by no—no indiscretion on the part of—my sister—and it is open at this day, or any day, to the most indifferent stranger who chooses to pay a fee at Doctors' Commons. What you can mean, in these circumstances, by a precaution so—by such precautions, I cannot tell. Is it not better your son should learn this from his father, than from any ill-disposed companion whom the young man may pick up? But that is certainly not my business. I presume that I may, without objection on your part, see my niece and nephew sometimes during the few days I remain in the nearest village? The children must acknowledge a certain relationship with their mother's brother."

"Oh!" said Mr. Scarsdale, with a slight blush of shame on his cheek, "I shall be glad to have you remain here."

Glad! the word was out of keeping entirely with his aspect and that of the scene; it looked like a piece of mockery. Colonel Sutherland bowed again with still more ceremony.

"It is too late," he said, quietly.

"Your room is prepared—you have been expected," said Scarsdale, awaking, not only to the reproach of sending a stranger away, which, distant as he was from the opinions of the world, touched him still, but to the vexation of being resisted. "My daughter, so far as looks can express it, has been expecting you eagerly. I beg you to reconsider your decision—nay, I entreat, I insist that you should remain."

"Too late for that," said the Colonel, with a smile and a bow; "but I will not detain you from your studies. Susan, I believe, has some refreshment ready for her old uncle. I will not carry a punctilio of welcome so far as not to break bread in your house; but I will bid you now, and finally, good-bye."

So saying, the old soldier made a superb bow, and, without lifting his eyes again to his churlish host to see how he took it, turned round on his heel and left the room.

In the hall he encountered Peggy waiting for him, who, familiar in her anxiety, laid her hand upon his sleeve, and stretched up on tiptoe to whisper her anxious interrogation into the Colonel's deaf ear. He waved his hand to her with an assumed carelessness, which he was far from feeling.

"We should not 'gree, Peggy, if I stayed a day," he said, familiarly, and with a smile. "You must direct me to the next village, where I can get a bed and a dinner—for I will not leave the quarter till I know my sister's bairns."

"But ye'll not forsake them; say you'll never go away till he promises their rights," cried Peggy, in a whispered shriek.

The Colonel shook his head, and put her aside with his hand.

"If I can do anything for them, I will," he said briefly; and so went into the dining-room, where Susan waited, trembling for the issue of this scene: while Peggy, retiring to her kitchen in fierce disappointment and mortification, threw her apron over her head and wept a sudden torrent of hot tears; then comforting herself, repeated over his words, wiped her tears, and carried in the luncheon. She would not lose faith in her favourite with so short a trial. Daylight, good sense, common affection did but need to breathe into this morbid house, and all might yet be right.

CHAPTER VII

When Peggy re-entered the dining-room, she found poor Susan struggling to restrain the sudden sobs of her distress and disappointment in finding that her uncle was not to remain at Marchmain. He had not meant to tell her at once, and even now he told her cheerfully, and without offence, as if he had changed his intention for his own convenience solely. He had just opened the carpet-bag, of which he had been so careful on the journey, and was taking out a parcel very carefully and elaborately packed up, which he proceeded at once to uncover. Susan looked on, a little curious, but not much interested; she had no conception what it was, or that she had any connection with it; and when at last it was all unfolded, and spread out before her, she looked on rather more interested, but no less wondering. What might Uncle Edward be going to do with those snowy lengths of India muslin, the fragile foundation of which was scarcely sufficient to bear the wreaths of embroidery, which Susan had never seen anything like in her life, and instantly longed, with a girlish instinct, to copy and emulate—pretty collars, too, and cuffs, feminine articles which the Colonel could have no possible use for; and wrapped up with these one or two unknown articles, rich with that wonderful tiny mosaic work which embellishes the card-cases and blotting-books of people who are fortunate enough to have friends in

India. Susan had a vague idea that one of these was a card-case; it certainly was like something of her mother's which Peggy preserved as a relic, and had promised to make over to her young mistress when she was old enough to pay visits—an impossible age, which Susan laughed to think of ever attaining at Marchmain. When he had opened them all out upon the shining uncovered table, which reflected the spotless whiteness of the muslin, the Colonel looked down at Susan with a smile, bending his ear towards her, and looking for gratification and pleasure in a face which was only admiring and puzzled. "Are you pleased with them?" said Uncle Edward. "I puzzled my old brains to think what you would like, and there you have the results of my cogitations—not anything very extraordinary, but bought a good many thousand miles off for you, when the only recollection I had of you was that of a baby. I had to count the years very carefully, I assure you, and was near committing myself, and losing credit for ever by bringing you a little frock."

"But, uncle, do you mean they are for me?" cried Susan, in amazement.

"Eh? Precisely—for you," said the Colonel, who had not quite heard her question, but understood her look. "There is but one woman in the family, my dear child: you don't suppose that my boy Ned could wear muslin, or that Tom knows how to use a fan? But eh?—what's happened? Have I vexed you without knowing it, for a blundering old blockhead? What's the matter, Susan? I'll toss them all into the fire rather than make you cry."

"Oh, uncle, I can't help crying—then, I like to cry!" exclaimed Susan, finding the old Colonel really concerned, and disposed to carry out his threat. "To think they should be for me—to think you should have thought of me in India! Do you suppose I could just say, 'Thank you?' Nobody ever gave me anything all my life before—and oh, uncle, to take the trouble of thinking of me!"

"If that is a troublesome operation, I have taken a great deal of trouble about you, one time and another, Susan," said Colonel Sutherland. "Now, dry your eyes, my love, and tell me if you approve of my taste. They are nothing extraordinary, you little goose—you will make me ashamed of my bundle. Why, everybody brings such things from India, and bring them very often to people they care much less about than I do about my little niece. If I had been richer, you should have seen what we can do in the East; but I just managed, you perceive, to get you one shawl."

Which shawl the Colonel extricated accordingly, as he spoke. Poor Susan, afraid he might think her foolish, managed to stop her crying, and gazed—half with dismay, half with admiration—at all the pretty things before her. What could she do with them? Colonel Sutherland, it was true, knew that she never was allowed to see anybody, or to make any friends, but a fact which is alien to nature makes no impression upon a natural mind. He could not remember or suppose that a young girl had no possible use for the pretty, simple dress he had brought, and looked on with a pleased face to see the effect of his gifts, as Susan began to examine them. Peggy, going backward and forward, saw it was now time enough for her to interpose, and, with a genuine woman's interest, plunged into the delightful investigation, which Susan—flushed and agitated quite out of her wont, and tremulous with many new sensations—had just concluded, when Horace entered the room.

That room, all its life, had never looked so homelike, and the reason was not explainable; for, except in the heap of litter at one end of the table, and the old man eating his luncheon hard by, there was absolutely no change upon the apartment. That soldier's face, weatherworn and brown, full of command yet full of tenderness, with grizzled hair and moustache, and erect soldierly pose, was not by any means a common-place countenance, or one which could have passed unnoted anywhere; but it was not even that which made the charm. It was the bright, pleased look which the Colonel, as he sat, lifted upon the girl before him—the amused, kind, tender smile which went over all his face like sunshine—the kindly, homely inclination towards her of that deaf ear—the care he took to hear all she said—the interest and indulgent regard with which he followed her movements and listened to her words. There was no criticism in those kind eyes—they were eyes accustomed to give a genial interpretation of everything—and the light of them changed the aspect of this dismal room. It did not even look so dark or so stifling—the very mahogany brightened, and hearty blazes awoke in the once-smouldering fire. Everything seemed to have become aware, somehow, that living human love and kindness, indulgence, tenderness were there.

Yes, indulgence—though, to be sure, it is very bad to spoil our children; but what would not one give, when one grows old, for that dear, lost indulgence of our youth, which will never come back to us—that consciousness that there is one at least who will see everything we do in the best light, and put the kindest construction upon our failings, and think us cleverer and better, and fairer and pleasanter, than we are and can be! Youth cannot thrive at all without this sunshine; but heaven help us, how it dies and disappears out of the noon of life! Susan had never once felt it before—the feeling came upon her, as she met her uncle's eyes, that she had never really lived before—that she was only awaking to find out what she herself was, and what were the people around her. Somehow the dawning of a happiness unthought of brought with it the sudden revelation of miseries which had not struck her in all her past experience. Fathers, it became visible to her in a moment, were not all like her father—homes were different from this home—even Uncle Edward's presents helped that enlightenment. These pretty things were common to girls of her own age, and in ordinary use among them. Her uncle was even puzzled that she should look at them as she did, and think them so beautiful, so wonderful, so much "too fine for me!" And as Susan came to comprehend this, between the pleasure and the pain, her cheeks flushed, her young limbs trembled, her heart beat loud with strange emotion. Even that excitement helped the effect of Uncle Edward's kind face in the room. This very confusion and commotion was life.

When Horace appeared, wet as Susan had predicted he would be, and sulky as he always was, the sudden gleam of warmth in the familiar apartment penetrated even into his sullen heart. Its first result was the natural one of making him feel more unhappy; but in another moment, and with reflection, a change came upon Horace. He did not desire or care for the kindness of his uncle. He was not a domestic creature!—he longed to escape from home, and was exceedingly indifferent as to what he should have there, if he could but attain that desirable end. And Colonel Sutherland appeared a very likely assistant to Horace—as, his deaf uncle not having heard him enter, he stood for a moment looking at him before he advanced. The young man, in his hard wisdom, perceived the simplicity of the old man who sat unconscious before him. As far as he could comprehend a spirit so different from his own, he read his nature in the Colonel's face, and took up his part accordingly with cleverness and dexterity. He advanced quickly to his uncle and held out his hand, Susan watching him with an unusual anxiety which she could not explain to herself.

"Uncle!—I need not ask who it is—uncle, welcome!" cried Horace, with a heartiness unknown to him heretofore, and perhaps more reality in the expression than he himself could have thought possible.

The Colonel rose with a little stumble of haste, putting his hand to his ear. For the moment he was perplexed, and thought it a stranger; but catching the sound of uncle, hailed his nephew with all the affectionate sincerity of his unsuspicious heart. He shook both his hands as Horace's hands had never been touched before; he looked in his face, too, as in Susan's, to trace the lineaments of their mother, and called him "my dear boy;" and shook his hands again with an effusion of satisfaction and kindness. For Horace, so far as features went, was somewhat like his mother, and, with his smile and his smoothed-out brow, looked a very different person from the Horace of every-day use and wont. "But will he persevere?" said Susan to herself, with an ache of delight in her heart; and "How to keep it up?" said Horace within his own saturnine spirit. The uncle knew nothing of these secret questions—did not suspect for a moment that the young man who met him so joyfully had changed his manners for the occasion, and congratulated himself in his simple heart that both the children had kept their hearts and feelings warm in their solitude. The old man grew quite radiant and talkative. He who had intended to leave Marchmain directly, sat still, opening out his honest heart to the young people like a long absent father. He told them first and principally about his boys, their cousins, whom they must know—about the house he had got, which was exactly what he wanted, and where he only wished he could have Susan to be "mistress and mair!" as he broke out joyfully in his Scotch—about India, where almost all his life had been spent, and which, with Edinburgh, and a peep of London, made up the world to the veteran. And the light had actually begun to wane in the short afternoon, when it suddenly occurred to Uncle Edward that he was forgetting himself, and that he must face the blast again to find his inn. A momentary austerity came into his face as he recollected this, and, rising hastily, begged of Horace to show him or to tell him the way to the nearest village. The nearest village worthy the name was five miles off; there was a miserable little hamlet nearer, with a miserable little public house, but that Uncle Edward shrugged his shoulders at.

"Can Susan walk five miles in a good day?" said the Colonel, smiling. "Then come along, my boy—we'll go there."

CHAPTER VIII

A walk of five miles on that dismal February afternoon was not a pleasure excursion; nor was it pleasant to look back upon poor Susan's face at the window—flushed, tearful, ashamed, mortified, Susan had not experienced an equal vexation in the whole course of her life. To think of Uncle Edward having to go away through the damp and twilight five miles off to find a lodging! Uncle Edward, who had come closer to Susan's heart in half-an-hour than all the rest of the world in all her life! When they were out of sight she subsided into the arm-chair and had a good cry over it, and then went to talk to Peggy, who was actively furious, relieving herself by incomprehensible ejaculations. Still somehow, mortified and vexed as she was, there was all the promise of a new life remaining for Susan. Uncle Edward would return to-morrow; so long as he stayed he would see them every day—and the idea disturbed the stagnant atmosphere, and diffused an indescribable cheerfulness through the house. Even Peggy, though she fumed, was exhilarated by the thought—perhaps on the whole, it was even better that the Colonel's tender, honest heart should not be grieved by the sight of the ghost of family life existing here. So long as he did not see it to make himself wretched with the view, Uncle Edward's sweet and healthful imagination could conceive of no such scene as Mr. Scarsdale's dinner, or the evening hours which followed it. And then he was coming back to-morrow!

So Susan took her presents upstairs, and fell wondering and dreaming over them, making impossible fancy scenes of cheerful rooms and pleasant people, and smiles, and flowers, and kindness unknown. Somehow whispers of all these delightful things seemed to breathe out of that pretty muslin, with its graceful wreaths of embroidery. The horizon opened to her awakened girlish fancy, far off, and almost inconceivable, yet with a vague brightness of possibility—and Susan spent an hour arranging her new riches in the drawer, which was the only scene they were likely to enlighten at present, and making herself happy with her novel thoughts.

While in the meantime the Colonel and his nephew trudged onward across the moor. The rain had ceased, but the sky was low and the air damp—and evening darkened round the vast blurred circle of the horizon, dropping down among the hills. The scene was dismal enough for anything: the exposed path across the moor—the black furze bushes and withered crackling heather—the slender saplings cowering together here and there in a little circle, where attempts had been made to naturalize them—and the great, monotonous, unbroken stretch of desert soil around, inspected from the lower heights by gaunt clumps of fir-trees, savage and melancholy anchorites, debarred from the change and variety, the autumn and the spring of common nature. Colonel Sutherland threw a shivering glance round him, and drew his cloak close about his throat. We will not say that even at that moment, when his thoughts were occupied with more important things, an involuntary patriotic comparison did not occur to the old soldier, who was native to the rich fields of Lothian, and might be disposed to wonder complacently whether this were indeed the sunnier south. He had, however, a more immediate subject of observation in Horace, who trudged beside him with the stoop and slouch, and heavy irregular step, of a neglected and moody youth. He was well-looking enough, and not deficient in any bodily quality, but the lad's physique had been totally unattended to, and he had never been in circumstances which could have led himself to perceive his faults of bearing and carriage. The Colonel's soldierly eye could not help regarding him with manifest dissatisfaction. We will not take it upon us to affirm that Colonel Sutherland at the head of his regiment might not be something of a martinet, or the least thing in the world particular about stocks and cross-belts. He looked at Horace, and could not help looking at him as he might have done at an awkward recruit. How he held his sullen head down against the wind, as if he butted at an invisible enemy; how he swung his hands in the pockets of his shooting-coat; how he dragged his heavy feet as if there was a clod at each heel. The Colonel did not quite understand how it was that his nephew's person inspired him with a vague distrust, and, somehow, contradicted his nephew's face; but the fact was that Horace could change the expression of his countenance when he had sufficient motive, but could not alter the habits into which neglect, and indolence, and sullen temper had thrown his outer man. And he himself was entirely unconscious of the clownish walk and ungracious demeanour which gave the old officer so much annoyance. Colonel Sutherland respected everybody's amour propre. He could scarcely find it in his heart to wound any one, on the virtuous principle of doing them good; but, between professional sentiment, and that family pride which is wounded by being obliged to admit the imperfections of those it is interested in, he never exercised more self-denial in his life than that which he showed during this walk, in restraining an exhortation to his nephew in respect to his bearing and deportment; while his kind imagination went to work directly, to contrive expedients, and inducements, and hints for Horace's benefit, to lead him to perceive his own deficiencies and adopt means to correct them, without wounding his feelings or his pride.

While Colonel Sutherland occupied himself with these reflections, Horace, totally unconscious of criticisms upon himself, which would have stung his self-love deeply, pondered, in his turn, the best means of bringing his uncle over to the length of helping him, by any means or in any way, to escape from Marchmain. The most palpable mode of entering on the subject—that of lamenting his father's want of hospitality—had been made impracticable by Colonel Sutherland, who laid all the weight of the arrangement upon his own convenience; and his simplicity and straightforwardness made a sidelong approach to it equally out of the question. Horace was compelled, accordingly, to bring in his subject all at once, and without introduction. Colonel Sutherland, without meaning it, said something half consciously about the dreary country, and his nephew seized upon the chance.

"Dreary, indeed!—and nothing else do we see, uncle, from year's end to year's end!" cried Horace. "Is it not enough to kill a man?—without a human face to break it, either; and here am I, strong and young, condemned to this life, and kept from any information—any advice—which can direct me what to do. Uncle, you are the only friend I have been able to see with freedom and confidence, and I am almost glad you don't stay at Marchmain—for there is no freedom there. Tell me, I beg of you, what can I do?"

"My dear boy!" cried the Colonel, grasping his nephew's hand in sudden sympathy, and with a little gasp of earnest attention—"you take away my breath. Solitude has not diminished your energy, at all events. Do? Why, to be sure, a boy like you can do anything. We must look for an opening, that is all—but you should have begun before now."

"My father," said Horace, with unconscious bitterness, "has stopped that. I don't know anything about the world, except this paltry little world here, of gamekeepers and poachers, and sporting farmers' sons—for gentlemen, of course, don't associate with me. What are we, uncle?—nobodies? I can't tell—my father keeps up habits which look like the relics of a better time—and at the same time I know we're poor; but he throws no light upon our unhappy circumstances. He keeps me shut up in this horrible house, till I think all sorts of horrors: that he's a returned convict, or something like that—that our name's a disgrace. What is it?—of course there must be some cause for this seclusion—and you must know."

Colonel Sutherland was much embarrassed. He fumbled with his cloak in the first place to gain time, and then, finding no other resource, fell back upon the shelter of his deafness.

"I'm a little hard of hearing," said the Colonel. "I partly lost your last observation—but what's that about the poachers and gamekeepers? Bad company, Horace!—unfit associates, except in the way of sport, for any gentleman. I've known lads of good family ruined just by an inclination that way. Not that they meant ill to begin with; but what's mere fun at first comes to be liking before long—and a gentleman's son of course is flattered and courted among them. It's a pernicious thing, Horace—attend to me!—it's been the ruin of many a man."

"What is ruin, uncle?" shouted Horace, with a wild and bitter smile, which somehow mingling congenially with the wind and the chill, carried into the Colonel's mind a singular identification of that landscape and scene which gained their climax in this moment. He was startled, he could not explain how. He turned round to look into his nephew's face, with a sudden consciousness of depths in the heart and in the life of Horace undecipherable and mysterious to himself.

"My dear boy," he said, with a little tremble in his voice, "ruin is such a destruction as can be accomplished only by a man himself."

Horace made no answer. His face subsided gradually, out of that self-revelation, into the assumed good-humour which he had put on for his uncle's benefit. Colonel Sutherland, however, continued to regard him with concern and apprehension. The Colonel's mind was not enlightened up to the pitch of modern times. When his imagination uncomfortably pictured Horace seated, perhaps, in the alehouse they had passed, with the gamekeeper or sporting men of the village, it was not the knowledge of life which the young man might acquire, but the old-fashioned horror of "bad society," which moved the thoughts of the uncle, who secretly in his own mind began to attribute something of the slouching gait and unsatisfactory bearing of his nephew to his unsuitable companions. He could not give up the subject, but partly in natural anxiety, and partly to evade the youth's troublesome questions, recurred to it immediately again.

"I am your oldest relation except your father, Horace," said the Colonel. "I have some experience in life. You know what the proverb says: 'A man is known by the company he keeps.'"

"Had he better keep no company?" said Horace; "very possibly; but then I can't help being young, poor devil that I am. I can't make a woman of myself, or be a child all my life. I must have something out of my prison—and you are not the man to blame me, uncle. The fellows you blame are those who have society in their favour. As for those country blockheads, whom I see in the woods or in the alehouses, do you think I care for them? Do you care for a set of dancing dogs or a wandering monkey? You laugh at them. If you have nothing else to think of, they amuse you for the moment. I despise the louts!—they are no more than bears on exhibition to me!"

Once more Colonel Sutherland looked at his young companion. It was not in his kindly human heart, which despised nobody, to like this manner of expression; but somehow the force with which it was uttered, and the implied superiority of tone, had a certain effect on the simple-hearted old man. He still retained his uneasiness, his want of comprehension; but he began to change his ideas of Horace, and to think him intellectual and clever—not a youth dangerously falling into "bad company," but a man whose talents were lost to the world for want of "opportunities." He fixed his gaze anxiously upon his nephew, and longed for the candid eyes which told all Susan's sentiments and emotions; but that doubtful face said nothing of itself. There might be "talent," but there was no candour in the countenance of Horace—what the lips might say, was the only index to what the head conceived or the heart felt. Colonel Sutherland turned away from him again with a little sigh. He was interested, his curiosity was awakened, and his paternal anxieties in full exercise; but somehow under all his heart whispered hesitations and inarticulate warnings to him. He had no experience in this unknown development of human nature. His own instincts said as much. But a man does not always give attention to those instinctive intimations. Colonel Sutherland was accustomed to believe that he had rather a natural gift for the guidance of young men—his sympathies with youth were warm—his heart young—his kindness unbounded. Many a youth ere now, charmed by the natural benignity and freshness of his character, had opened his soul to the old Colonel, and given to him that full, youthful confidence seldom bestowed by halves, which harsher fathers had failed to gain—with great advantage to themselves; for the old man was wise, as old men come to be who are not clever, but only humble, candid, religious, fearing God, and slow to make themselves judges of men. The habit of counsel, of assistance, of kindly attention, and regard to the self-revelations of his young companions, was accordingly strong upon Colonel Sutherland—yet, though he would scarcely acknowledge it to himself, a certain conviction of being out of his depths, and in a world altogether new to him—among elements which he was unable to handle—was present with him now.

"I am glad you have no inclination towards such society," he said, in his perplexed tone; "but, Horace, my boy, even for sport you must not continue it. It sticks to a man in spite of himself; and, indeed, the young fellows now are very different from what they were in my time. I don't bid you despise your fellow-creatures—there's a long distance between despising them and preferring their society—a man of your condition should do neither the one nor the other, as you will learn when you come to know life."

"What is my condition, uncle?" asked Horace, suddenly, interrupting the slow and hesitating general sentiments, which were the only things which the perplexed Colonel could find ready to his hand in this embarrassing case. It is to be feared that Colonel Sutherland heard this question, which was asked in a high tone, for his face became gradually flushed over with a painful heat and colour; but once more he put his hand to his ear.

"Yes; what are your own inclinations?—that is really the question, Horace—if we knew that, we could look out for you. There are many openings now to honourable ambition; but what do you wish yourself for your manner of life?"

"Uncle," said Horace, with a force which would be heard, "I have no inclinations, thanks to my manner of life hitherto—I have only one wish, and that is, to escape from Marchmain. Get me away from that wretched house. I don't care if I turn a shoe-black or a scavenger—get me away from here!"

The Colonel once more looked at his nephew, but with less respect—"On these terms, could you not get yourself away? You are not confined by locks and bars," said Colonel Sutherland, disapprovingly; "why have you no inclinations? That dear child yonder, who has nobody in the world to speak to, has kept her heart as fresh as a May flower."

"Susan?" said Horace, growing red; "you don't compare me with Susan?—Susan's a girl—she's content—she's very well off, so far as I can see—she's in her natural vocation. Would you have me put on petticoats and sit down to patchwork?—As well do that as compare a man with a girl!"

"Susan," said the Colonel, with a little hauteur and heat which became him, "is the only woman of the family. You are not aware, I daresay, of the indulgences and pleasures that are natural to girls of her years. I don't wonder so much either that you think of yourself first—but why have you no inclinations?—she has, and you think yourself her superior, I perceive."

"Don't be displeased, uncle," said Horace, changing his tone, and suffering only a little impatience, to testify to the fury with which he heard himself reproved. "You know better than I do, that women are tame creatures, and content themselves easily in their own sphere, when they don't know any better. Susan has leisure to form little plans and fancies, I believe. I have no such thing—the pain of years has brought me to one point of desperation. I know nothing of the world: I don't know what I am—my position—my prospects—my birth, are all a mist to me. My mind is not sufficiently disengaged to form projects; therefore I say I have no inclinations—the air stifles me—I must get out into the world, where there is room to breathe!"

"Then, why," said the Colonel, "have you not gone away before?"

Horace was silenced—he fumed with silent rage within himself, wounded in the tenderest point of his self-love and pride—it was, perhaps, the only suggestion which could have made him feel a pang of humiliation. It was one which Susan herself, in her simple and practical intelligence, had made more than once. Why had he borne and brooded over his wretchedness? Why had he not gone away?

"Many young men," said Colonel Sutherland, "have left home of their own accord on a less argument than that of desperation. I don't mean to say I approve of it—but—there are some things that one could not advise, which, at the same time, being done, cut a difficulty which might be hard to solve. I say all this, my dear boy," added the Colonel, moved by Horace's gloomy face, "to show you that it is foolish to use such strong expressions: if your desperation had been so great as to deprive you of all choice or inclination, depend upon it you would have gone away."

And having delivered himself of this kindly bit of logic, totally inapplicable as it was to the person whom he addressed, and attributing the silence of his nephew to the natural confusion of a young man detected in the use of undue heroical expressions, the Colonel was himself again.

"And this, I suppose, is my resting-place for the night," he said, as a church-spire and the roofs of a village became dimly visible before them at the end of the road. "I will remain here three or four days, and during that time, Horace, you must find out your inclinations, my boy, and let us discuss them and see what is to be done. You must stay and dine with me in the first place, and be with me as much as possible while I am here—that is to say, unless your father makes any positive claim upon you during the time."

"Positive claim! I wish you had dined with us one day, uncle, to see what these claims are!" cried Horace, with a laugh of bitterness; but the Colonel, who had been thinking of something else for the moment, inclined his ear towards him with a little start and a smile, before which bitterness fled. Horace could no more comprehend his uncle than his uncle could understand him. This smile discomforted him strangely—he could not stand against that kind prompt attention, the ear so solicitous to catch what he said, and the face so guileless and benign. The young man was of a crafty intelligence, and could have detected wiles—but this sunshiny simplicity put him out. It went deep into the primitive truth, sincerity, and honesty of nature—things which Horace Scarsdale had small acquaintance with in the secret spring and fountain of his life.

CHAPTER IX

That evening was an epoch in the life of Horace. The people in the little country inn to which he took his uncle were not unacquainted with the young man. For a year or two past, ever since the bitter independence of manhood had begun to possess him, he had spent much of his waste unoccupied time in this and the other humble houses of entertainment of the district. With a sensation of superiority, which he owed principally to his natural temper—for there was in reality very little distinction of breeding or character between himself and the society he frequented—he held a scornful dictatorial place among the humbler convives of the villages, and observed and amused himself with the peculiarities he saw, very much as if he had been a man of the world, trained to that odious criticism which is dignified by being called "the study of mankind." The coarse enjoyments of the public-house company did not tempt him—he threw his violent decisions into the hum of drowsy talk when it suited him, and at other times looked on, noting, with contemptuous amusement, the dull jollity of the place. His father's singular solitude imposed a certain respect upon the imagination of the district; and between Horace and the country lads around there remained always that inexplainable, undefinable difference which, independent of education, wealth, and every tangible advantage, separates those who are born in different classes of society, especially in rural places. He had accordingly a strange kind of popularity in the district—not the popularity of common love and esteem, but an attraction perhaps more remarkable; his careless rudeness, his bitter humour, the harsh philosophy which contrasted with his youth and inexperience, gave him a certain singular hold upon the imagination of his companions. The very certainty that he did not care a single straw for them attached the little crowd to his footsteps. Dominant and imperious self-regard, like all other regnant qualities, has a wonderful influence upon the common mind. No other person within the immediate knowledge of this rural community assumed the same tone, or showed the same spirit—and the vehement and forcible language, more refined than their own, the utterance of a gentleman, which Horace had acquired involuntarily, the arrogant sentiments he expressed, the unconcealed consciousness of superiority which belonged to him, united to impose a certain allegiance upon the inexperienced minds, which found him unique and singular, the sole development known to them of a kind of intelligence and a manner of man widely differing from their own.

But this night everything was changed. The landlady of the inn, amazed into a flutter of perturbation, appeared herself, at the astounding information that young Mr. Horry, as he was called, had arrived with a gentleman. The good woman supposed it must be his mysterious father, and hastened with all the speed of curiosity to receive them—but lost in amazement to find "the gentleman" a stranger, who required the best accommodation of her house for a few days, and desired to dine as soon as that was practicable—found it only possible to curtsey and retire, more curious than ever, without being able to show her previous acquaintance and familiarity with Mr. Horry, who turned his face with an arrogant blank of unrecognition full upon her, and added to his uncle's orders a request that some one might be sent to Marchmain immediately for the carpet-bag.

"Something's agoing to happen," said the landlady, as she returned to her own domain. "A strange gentleman as wants the best o' everything—an ould sodger lord with musstaches—egh, lad!—a lord I'll warrant, at the very least o' him—and I'll lay you a sixpence he's coom to set a' things straight; for yonder's Mr. Horry, he looks me in the face as broad as I look at you, and says, says he, 'Send a man to Marchmain for a carpet-bag immediantly,' as if he never set eyes on me in his born days afore. Like him! I would ne'er goo starving to his door in hopes o' meat."

Great preparations ensued for the hasty dinner, which was to be ready in an hour; but even the landlady's conviction that her guest could not be less than a lord was not sufficient to work impossibilities. While it was getting ready, Colonel Sutherland and Horace sat together over the new kindled fire. The best room of the inn, which did not receive a guest twice in a year, was a dingy parlour hung with old portraits of famous horses, winners of the cups of antiquity, with a county map, and a print of George IV. to vary the embellishments, and two small windows looking out upon the village street. The Colonel placed himself as close as possible to the fire, not without dreadful apprehensions of the rheumatism, which already sent flying twinges into his spare limbs, and made him wince; and thought with a little natural indignation of his repelled kindness, and the cold reception which had forced him to seek this place, and substituted the accommodation of a poor little country inn for the hospitality he had expected. Silence and these recollections, and the startling twinges of his rheumatism, changed the expression of his face almost into sternness, and seemed to develop in him another phase of character. Horace watched him in the doubtful light, more and more puzzled. The indulgent, tender kindness and forbearance of the fatherly old man had disappeared with the animation of their talk and intercourse—the whole face had a loftier and more rigid expression. Horace, drawing back his chair out of the firelight, gazed and pondered with knitted brows. He began to think more elaborate approaches were necessary, and plans better laid. He had not found it possible hitherto to get much information from this kind old uncle touching the family secret, if there was one. Was Colonel Sutherland a kind old uncle merely? Horace began to suspect he must be something more, and that the task of persuading him and winning him over to his own interests might not be so very easy after all.

The Colonel sat long in meditation, as if he were in full consideration of the whole knotty subject; when he made a little stir in his chair as if about to speak, a sudden burst of anxiety ran over Horace. "I wonder," said the Colonel, with the gravest face, "how long it is since a fire was lighted in this room before. Speak of England, Horace! I don't believe there is anything so dismal from Berwick to John o'

Groats as that moor of yours, and no attempt at cultivation or improvement, so far as I can perceive. You should see our high farming in Lothian! I have not felt the cold so severe since I came home."

Horace had almost laughed aloud in his sudden relief and contempt. These were the thoughts, so deeply ruminated, which had brought gravity to Colonel Sutherland's face. The young man, who now less than ever comprehended the old man, went to stand at the window, not without a certain satisfaction in being seen there by the evening frequenters of the place, who were sure to hear of his companion, and of the different position he occupied for this night at least; and passed another half hour of waiting before the dinner appeared, in strange calculations, at once cunning and foolish—the wiles of a subtle mind, and the inexperience of a young one—thinking with himself how long his uncle's simplicity could withstand his attacks—how soon he should be able to worm all the secrets of the family out of him, and how easily he could work the old man to do what he would. Then, if such a man as Colonel Sutherland had reached to a respectable position and command, what might not such a man as Horace Scarsdale do? The young man's spirits rose—he imagined himself making a stepping-stone of his uncle, to push his way into the arena—and then—.

Considering the height and imaginative character of this ambition, which at the outset gave it a certain refinement, it was astonishing, notwithstanding, to perceive into what almost vulgar elation his spirits rose during that dinner. It was no great things of a dinner, being too ambitious by far for the occasion; but it was perhaps the very first meal in his life, at least since he came to years of self-knowledge, which Horace had eaten with freedom and pleasure. He thought of Marchmain, and the scene in the dining-room at that moment, where Peggy, in the ordinary course of events, would be about removing the cloth and setting on the table his father's solitary glass and jug of claret, and smiled to think of Mr. Scarsdale's silent rage at seeing his vacant place. He was pleased and flattered by the respectful manner of the landlord who waited on them, and could not refrain from talking rather big to his uncle, and assuming a confidence and frankness quite unusual to him, and foreign to his nature, for the advantage of that individual. He was too young to conceal this first gratification, and betrayed himself unawares. Simple and unsuspecting though the Colonel was, he perceived this. However, it was natural, and instead of a hard laugh at it, Uncle Edward smiled and grew kinder, and loved Horace better and trusted him the more for his weakness' sake. They seemed growing friends gradually and surely—the old man believed they were, and rejoiced in it, and could not have believed, had anybody told him that the cold passion of self-regard, to the entire exclusion of warmer feelings, filled his nephew's heart.

When they were left alone, Horace, a little stimulated by the wine he had taken, commenced his attack with boldness:—

"Uncle," he said, "you must think of me—you must help me. I have never been able to speak my mind before to a single individual who could comprehend or assist me. I must know what are our circumstances. It is needless to say that my father's past life does not affect me. It does affect me—everything affects me that I am kept in ignorance of. What are we?—what is he?—why are we here?"

Horace had hit by chance and unawares upon the means really most likely to attain his end. Colonel Sutherland could not return anything but a true answer to a plain and straightforward question; and evasion was so strange to him that he managed it in the clumsiest manner. He retired on his deafness in the first place—a defence from which Horace drove him out triumphantly by a repetition of the question in tones that could not be mistaken. Then he faltered over it a little, with common-places of hesitation too palpable to deceive anybody.

"Your true circumstances—your father's past life? Your father's past life has always been virtuous and honourable," said the Colonel. "What is he? You ought surely to know better than I do, who have not seen him for fifteen years. He is, if you wish my opinion, a man of very peculiar temper. Horace, I do not wonder that you find him rather hard to get on with sometimes, but he is your father; and therefore, my dear boy, whatever others may do, impatience and a harsh judgment do not become you."

Horace shook his head.

"This is not what I want to know. You know it is not," he said, with a rising colour. "Say no, if you will, but don't treat me like a child. Look here, uncle: I am assured there is a secret—I know it, no matter how—tell me what it is."

Horace put the whole force of his voice and mind into the question. He made it not as one who asks, but as one who demands what he has a right to know, feeling convinced that his gentle relative could not now evade him, and had no strength to resist; and with this conviction strong upon him, the young man stared into the Colonel's eyes, with the thought of overawing him and compelling his answer thus.

Colonel Sutherland looked at him steadily, withdrew his eyes a moment, looked again, and at last spoke.

"If you think," said the Colonel, coldly, "that by this persistence and demand you can persuade any man of honour to betray to you a secret with which another has entrusted him, you show only your ignorance of gentlemen and want of belief in your fellow-creatures. If there is a secret in your family circumstances—though, mind you, I do not admit that there is—can you suppose that I will tell you anything which it is your father's desire that you should not know?"

Horace shrunk for a moment in mingled rage and amazement from the tone. It was inconceivable to him that anybody could feel even an instant's contempt for him; but the feeling was momentary.

"Then he does desire that I should not know it!" he exclaimed, with a certain triumph—and set his teeth over the admission, as if this at least was something gained.

"I did not say so," said the Colonel, with some embarrassment. "I said if—No, Horace, if you wish to investigate into all the secrets of your family, go to your father, and ask him—he is the proper judge of what should or should not be told you. At least, if you don't admit that, he is at least the most proper person to be asked; and till he has refused to satisfy you, you have no right to apply to any one else. Take my advice—be honest and straightforward—it is the shortest way and the clearest: ask himself."

"Ask himself! Do you know the terms we are on, uncle?" said Horace, with a smile.

"So much the worse for you both—and long enough that has lasted, surely," said the Colonel. "The past is no man's, the future is every man's: I say to you again, that has lasted long enough! Ask himself, and let the mystery and the strife end together. It is the only honest way to clear your difficulties up."

Once more Horace smiled—a smile of disappointment and anger—baffled and furious; while the Colonel went on with his honest, simple advice, exhorting the young man to candour and openness—he might as well have exhorted him to be Prime Minister—while Horace, for his part, kept silent, perceiving, once for all, that whether it was from mere foolishness, or some principle of character unknown to him, his uncle was impracticable, and that the only way to find anything out from him was to lie in wait for the unguarded admissions which, in spite of himself, might fall from his lips.

"After all," said Colonel Sutherland, when he had concluded his good, honest advice to his own satisfaction, "what has all this to do with it? You are tired of inactivity and quiet, as a young man ought to be; you want to set out upon the world. Of course, your father cannot object to this; and as for me, all that I can do to forward it I will, heartily. But, Horace, setting out on the world does not mean anything vague, my lad. It means doing, or aiming at, some special thing—some one special thing, my dear boy. We can't go out to conquer the world now-a-days—it must be a profession, or business, or a place, or something; so I'll tell you what to do. Think it well over—what you said to me about having no inclinations. Sit down by yourself, and find out if there is not a special turn one way or other in some corner of your heart, and let us hear what it is. After that the way will be clear; we must look for an opening for you, and," added Colonel Sutherland, after a little pause, and speaking with hesitation, "if you should then—wish for—my services with your father, why then, Horace—though we are not the best friends in the world—I'll try my best."

"Thank you," said Horace, with sullenness, which he tried vainly to repress—"thank you, uncle. I will do as you say."

The conversation then came to an end, Horace fuming over it secretly as a failure—and the young man had so high an idea of his own powers, that the thought galled him deeply. Then, after an unsatisfactory interval of indefinite conversation, which Horace could not keep up, and which the Colonel—tired, disheartened, and perplexed—sustained but dully, the young man got up and bade him "good night." Colonel Sutherland went down to the door of the inn, half with a simple precaution to see him safely out of the "temptation" of that "low company" which Horace had owned to seeking, and half by suggestion of that kindness which could not bear to see any one discouraged. "Think it well over," urged the Colonel once more, "and expect me to-morrow; and be cheerful, and keep up your heart, Horace. There's plenty of room for you in the world, and plenty of force in yourself. Good night, my dear boy—good night."

CHAPTER X

When Horace Scarsdale left the lights of the village behind him, and took his way through the black roads towards Marchmain, he carried with him a burden of thoughts rather different from those which accompanied him here. Though his was neither a noble nor a sweet development of youth, still youth was in him, as in others, heroical and absolute. It is impossible to reduce to description the kind of fortune he had planned for himself; for, indeed, he had planned nothing, except a general self-glorification and domination over the world.

His uncle's advice to him, to ascertain how his likings inclined, and make choice of some profession or employment precise and definite, humiliated and offended him unawares. His fancies had not condescended to any such particularity. He had an impression on his mind, how acquired he could not tell, that his father wronged him, and that it was only necessary for him to be aware of their true circumstances to set him at once beyond the common necessities of life. This conviction, however, he had never betrayed to any one; and Colonel Sutherland's recommendation, which implied the restraints of labour and something to do, was not over-palatable to the young man brought up in idleness.

He was too old to begin the study of a profession, and when he thought of the laborious days and confined existence of men who have their own way to make in the world, secret rage and mortification took possession of Horace. Was this all that remained for him?—was this the life which he must look forward to?—was there nothing better in the future than this? He had no desire to choose his means of living, his manner of work—his thoughts eluded the subject when it was presented to him—it was easier to brood over a mysterious wrong, and dream of sudden revelations which should change everything in a moment. At the same time, his intellect was sufficiently clear to show him that contempt was likely to follow any exhibition of these feelings of his—he himself, as he reflected on it, fumed at himself with silent disgust.

Then he had failed to influence Colonel Sutherland as he expected—everything had failed in the absolute fashion—he could no longer carry matters, even to himself, with the high hand of dominant youthful unreason and disregard of things and men:—even things that pleased him took a definite, particular, and limited form, and came under conditions which made them distasteful. Already he began to perceive that the language and manner, which did very well for his alehouse companions, was not practicable in such society as that of his uncle; and unaware as yet how to acquire a more successful tone, fell into deep and angry mortification on the subject. He had not impressed upon Colonel Sutherland a high idea of his spirit, his energy, and his intellect, as Horace had intended to do; but had only conveyed the idea of a presumptuous and ignorant youth to the mind of his uncle. He felt this with a humiliation out of which he drew no humility. It was not so easy as he supposed, to see through and dominate over even so simple a character as that of Colonel Sutherland.

But it did not occur to Horace that his uncle's plain simplicity and truthfulness was, in fact, the only thing in the world which could not be dominated over by the most splendid superiority of intellect. He supposed it was only his own ignorance, and inexperience, and want of address—deficiencies mortifying enough to acknowledge certainly, but not so mortifying as the entire incapacity either to comprehend or to influence. He had time enough to think over all these things, as he made his way through the lonely, dreary country roads, and across the moor.

This day, and this meeting, and the opening of his close heart even so far, had flashed into life the smouldering fire in the mind of Horace. He strode on with long, rapid steps, thinking it scarcely possible that he could contain himself within the miserable hermitage of Marchman, even for a night. He went along pondering schemes to surprise the secret from his uncle, in spite of this first failure; and, intoxicated by the first realization of freedom, to imagine himself altogether free, his own master, triumphing over the world. But among these fancies there mingled neither a desire nor any attempt to ascertain, as Colonel Sutherland said, "his own inclinations," or to decide upon what he should do. He said quite truly, when he reported of himself, that he had no inclinations which concerned labour or a profession, and even in his own thoughts he evaded that question. He could think closely, when the matter was to find out, from his uncle's unsuspicious temper, his father's secret; but not when the thing to determine was the needful labour of his own life.

Meanwhile, Susan sat silent in her father's presence, longing for the return of Horace, picturing him to herself seated opposite to her uncle, free to say what he would, opening his heart under those genial looks, bringing home kind thoughts and kind messages, sunned and mellowed by that unsuspected love which had developed all the wonderful possibilities of a new life to herself. Even Susan could not sit still to-night—her patchwork had lost its attraction for her—her thoughts rose too fast, and were too numerous, to make her ordinary quiet possible. In spite of herself, and even unawares to herself, she was no longer the noiseless girl who sat hushed for hours, opposite to that rigid figure with the little reading-desk and open book. To her own amazement, she caught herself once humming an incipient tune as she sat over her work; and after a while found it impossible to sit still, and moved about with an involuntary restlessness, finding little matters to arrange in all the corners of the room, chairs to place differently, the curtains to be drawn closer, the fire to be stirred, something to keep her in motion, and express, by that only means permitted to her, the unaccustomed stir and commotion in her own heart. And what was even more remarkable, Mr. Scarsdale himself seemed to have an instinctive perception of this, and to be somehow moved in his own calm. A close observer might have perceived that he no longer travelled by mechanical accuracy from beginning to end of his page—that the leaves were tamed less regularly, and that his eyes were fixed upon the upper margin of his book, sometimes for half an hour together, while he watched, without looking at her, his daughter's movements, and heard the faint rustle of her hushed motion about the room. He divined the cause, and knew the emotion in her heart, with a strange and bitter certainty. He was aware by intuition that all the affection, and confidence, and filial warmth which he had never sought, had sprung up in an instant to meet the touch of another who had not the same natural claim as he; and the forlorn man grew more forlorn by the knowledge, and perhaps even once for an instant hesitated whether he should not, at this last moment, open his heart to his child, his wife's daughter, the only woman of the family. Somehow these words returned to him unawares. Mr. Scarsdale was not of the kind of man who is much influenced by women. Sympathy was an offence rather than a pleasure to him—he had none to bestow and he sought none. Consolations of affection he scarcely distinguished from intrusions of impertinence, and there was no soil on which tenderness could grow in his rocky nature. But if he had little affection, he had a perennial envy in his heart. He could not bear that another man should obtain anything which seemed by right to belong to himself. The idea that his wife's brother had already possessed himself of Susan's heart, more than he, her father, had done during her whole life, galled him bitterly; so much, that in that moment of indecision, while he held his book in his hands as though he would have closed it, the impulse had actually come upon him to put confidence in Susan, and so win her over, once for all, to his side, and shut out the less legitimate claimant on her affection.

The only woman of the family! It was his daughter whom Edward Sutherland made this claim of affection on—it was a piece of his property which the new comer appropriated; and Mr. Scarsdale had almost been moved out of himself to secure the filial heart which he cared not for, yet which it galled him to see claimed by any other. But nature conquered the sudden thought; he set his book once more steadily open upon his little desk—he made his heart bitter and hard—a forced and painful smile came upon his lip; within himself he recalled, half unawares, some of those words of contemptuous sarcasm against women, by which some men revenge themselves for some woman's misdeeds. But it made him colder, harder, more forlorn and solitary, in spite of himself. His son, whom he had always treated as an enemy, was with his brother-in-law; his daughter, though here in bodily presence, was with that intruder also in her heart. He was alone, alone—always alone; a jealous, envious, morbid rage deepened the shade upon his face; the love was nothing to him—but he gnashed his teeth to see it enjoyed by another.

When Horace returned—and they could hear his summons at the door, and Peggy's tardy opening—he did not come into the dining-room, but went upstairs at once; sending a message to Susan, to her great disappointment, that he was tired with his walk from Tillington, and was going to rest. Mr. Scarsdale did not retire till a much later hour than usual that night; and when he did, made Susan precede him by a few minutes, that he might see her shut up in her own room, and prevent all communication with her brother. He persuaded himself that they were in a conspiracy against him, and roused his temper with the thought; he spoke more harshly to Susan than he had ever done before in her recollection, and sent her to her own room in tears. Tears!—miserable woman's play of pretended suffering!—at least he was beyond the weakness of being deceived by it; and he smiled bitterly to himself, as he went to his own comfortless rest, thinking on the smiles which would greet her uncle. Unjust fate! unnatural nature!—for these smiles were his, and belonged to him—yet he could not prevent the kind looks of a stranger from stealing this property away.

And Susan cried herself to sleep, with hopes and happy anticipations taking the bitterness out of the tears; and Horace sat in his room, where he had hastily extinguished his candle on hearing approaching footsteps—as little inclined to see Susan as his father was that he should; pondering his wiles for overcoming his uncle. Only last night the house had been undisturbed in its unchanging life; now everything was commotion, disturbance, new efforts and hopes, a changed aspect of existence: and all from the advent of that guileless old soldier, who, waking in the night with his twinges of rheumatism, his fears that his bed had not been aired, and his deeper perplexity and pain about his sister's children, mixed these different troubles altogether, with a hazy mist of oppression and distress in his mind as he turned his head towards the wall, and sank into a heavy sleep.

CHAPTER XI

Colonel Sutherland was out of doors early next morning, as was his wont. The weather had improved, the sun was shining, the fells rose dewy and fresh through the air and distance, the whole face of the country was changed. The Colonel strayed along the country road, with his unusual burden on his mind, yet making such minute, half-conscious observations of external nature as were usual to him; pausing to examine the hedges, to pinch a bud upon a branch, and make involuntary comparison between the progress of the spring at home and here; noting the primrose-tufts which began to appear in the hedgeside herbage, soft green leaves still curled up in their downy roll; and making unconscious memorandums in his mind of the early notes of birds already to be heard among the branches. Everything was early this year, he thought to himself, as with a calm and placid pleasure he enjoyed the air, the light, and the cold yet dewy and sparkling freshness of the morning. In the calm of his age this old man had recovered the sweet sensations and susceptibilities of childhood; life with its passions and struggles was over for him, or seemed so; all was well with his boys; and the many and sharp sorrows of his manhood had left upon him that feeling of happiness in the mere freedom from acute and immediate pain, which only those who have suffered deeply can feel. The sunshine warmed and cheered him to the heart. It was true that trouble, anxiety, and doubt were in that innocent and tender soul; a strong desire to help and deliver his young relatives, with still no perception of the means for doing so; but this was no urgent distress, enough to break in upon that sacramental morning hour. There might be difficulty, but everything was hopeful; and the Colonel wandered along the lonely rural road, where the wet grass sparkled in the sunshine, and the buds on the hawthorn-hedge basked with a secret growth and invisible expansion in the tender warmth and light; and in his age, and the quiet of his soul, was glad as they.

As he approached the corner of an intersecting road, voices came to the ear of the Colonel, or rather one voice, which seemed familiar to him. The speaker was addressing some one who made little reply; and Colonel Sutherland heard, to his great astonishment, a glowing description of the advantages and pleasures of a soldier's life in India, splendidly set forth by the odd, familiar accents of this voice, as he approached. Half amused, half amazed, he listened—the words being, evidently, not of any private importance, and delivered in a tone too loud for confidential communications. He thought to himself that it must be some old soldier beguiling the innocence of some rustic lad, whom want of employment or youthful disappointment had prompted to try the expedient of "soldiering," and went forward with a wrinkle on his forehead, but a smile on his lip—divided between sympathy for the supposed victim, and a professional reluctance to balk the voluntary recruiter, if the recruit should chance to be a promising one. But, to his surprise, when he had gained the corner of the road, instead of a young ploughman or country bumpkin, his eye fell upon a young man of extremely prepossessing appearance, with all the look of a gentleman, who listened with dilated nostrils and eyes fixed upon the distant hills—listened as a man listens whose thoughts are already too many for him, and who has but little attention to spare for what is said—but who, nevertheless, has a serious intention of hearing what is addressed to him. The Colonel was so much startled by this, that he scarcely observed the other person present, till an astonished exclamation of his own name, and the sudden motion of a military obeisance, aroused him. Then the smile returned, though with a difference, to his lip. The speaker was a sergeant of his own regiment, a veteran nearly as old as himself, who now stood before him, between joy and reluctance, eager to make himself known, yet not perfectly satisfied to be found in this exercise of his vocation; with confusion in his face, and his mouth full of excuses.

"What, Kennedy!" cried the Colonel; "my good fellow, what brings you here?"

"It's far enough out of the way, to be sure, Cornel," said the sergeant, rather sheepishly; "and neyther my oun place, nor like it. Sure it's a bit of a flirt of a girl's brought me, that's come to be married here."

"Married! What, you? You old blockhead!" cried the Colonel, inclining his deaf ear towards the voice, "what do you want with such nonsense at your age?"

"Na, Cornel, ne'er a bit of me—the Lord forbid!" said the old soldier; "but a daughter it is, brought up within five mile of ould Derry, but seed a lad o' the fells as took her heart; and sure she's all in wan, as ye may say, the whole stock o' me familly; and according, Cornel, I'm here."

"And at your old trade, I perceive," said Colonel Sutherland—"hey, Kennedy?—you will never forget your cockade and bunch of ribbons; but I rather think you're out a little here."

"Ay, sir, ay—I said as much mysel' wan moment afore. The young master, Cornel, he's aboove my hand," said the sergeant, promptly; "but youth, sir, youth will not hearken to a good advice. So I bid to tell him as he desired; he's all for the cap and the feather, Cornel, and it's not for an ould sodger to balk a gentleman, in especial as it was information Mr. Roger sought; and I well rec'klet, Cornel, that ye aye liked a lad of spirit yoursel'."

"This is a mistake, however," said the young man, hurriedly; "I'm not a gentleman seeking information. Go on, Kennedy; I want pay and bread—don't be afraid, sir, there's nobody belonging to me to break their hearts if I enlist. Let him say out what he has to say."

The Colonel cast kindly eyes upon the young man, and saw his nervous haste of manner, and the impatient way in which he roused himself out of his half abstraction to deny the inferences of the sergeant—which, indeed, were entirely foreign to the address which Kennedy had just been delivering; and his benevolent heart was interested. "I also am an old soldier," he said, with his kind stoop forward, and his smile; "perhaps I am a safer adviser for a young man of your appearance than Kennedy. Eh? Do you prefer the sergeant? Very well! But you must understand that the good fellow romances, and that rising from the ranks, even in India, is not so easy as he would have you suppose. Very true, I have nothing to do with it; but don't be persuaded to enlist with such an idea. I wish you good morning, young gentleman. You can come to me, sergeant, at the inn in an hour or so. I am here only for a few days."

And Colonel Sutherland had turned away, and was once more descending the road, wondering a little, perhaps, that the young fellow did not eagerly seek his offered advice on a subject which he knew so much better than the sergeant, when he heard himself called from behind, and, looking back, found the youth following. As he came up, the Colonel remarked him more closely. He was of brown complexion and athletic form, though only about twenty—already a powerful though so young a man. He was dressed entirely in black—a somewhat formal suit, which almost suggested the clerical profession, though, in fact, it meant only mourning, and had a mingled look in his face of grief and mortification, sincere sorrow, and a certain affronted, indignant, resentful aspect, which raised a little curiosity in the mind of the Colonel. He came up with a bold, firm, straightforward step, which Colonel Sutherland could not help contrasting unawares with that of Horace, and with the colour varying on his cheek.

"I ought at least to thank you, sir, for the offer of your advice," he said hurriedly; then came to a pause; and then, as if vainly seeking for some explanation of the reason why he rejected it; "I am, however, only a recruit for the sergeant, not for the Colonel," he added, with sudden confusion. "It is because of this that I appear churlish and ungrateful in declining your offer. My dress is a deception. I have no right to be treated as a gentleman."

"These are strong words," said the Colonel. "I presume, then, that you have done something by which you forfeit your natural rank?"

A violent colour rushed to the young man's face—"No!—No!—twenty times No!"—he cried, with a sudden effusion of feeling, half made up of anger, and half of the grief which lay in wait for him to catch him unawares; "and will not, if I should starve or die!"

"It seems to me," said Colonel Sutherland, looking round in vain for Kennedy, who had taken the favourable moment to escape, "that you are in a very excited condition of mind; if you will take my advice, you will not do anything in your present state of feeling, and, above all, don't enlist. Kennedy's story is the common recruiting fable, dressed up to suit your particular palate. The old fellow cannot forget his old successes in that way, I suppose. It is as foolish to 'list in haste as to marry in haste, my young friend. It is a thing much easier to do than to undo. Keep yourself out of temptation, and consult your friends."

Having said so much, the Colonel gave a slight kindly bow to his companion, and was about to pass on, but, looking at him again, waited to see if he had anything to say.

"Is it better to take the plough-stilts than the shilling?" exclaimed the young man; "you know nothing about me—but you look at my distress with a kind face. You know the world and life as they really are, and not as they appear to us here, becalmed on the shores of the sea. I have no friends to consult, no one to be grieved for me whatever I do. I have not much wit, and less education; I have only what the brutes have—strength. What shall I do with it. Is it best to be a ploughman or a soldier?—I will abide by your decision—which shall it be?"

"Walk down with me to my inn," said Colonel Sutherland, "and tell me who you are, and how this has happened to you."

The young man turned with an implicit, instantaneous obedience. He made no preface, no explanation. He had reached to that extreme agitation of mind in which a listener, interested and friendly, is salvation to the self-consuming spirit, when that spirit is of the kind which can disclose itself; as in this case it happened to be.

"My name is Roger Musgrave," he said; "I have been brought up as heir to my godfather, a man supposed rich. With him I have lived most of my life—we two. He was more than a father to me: but he is dead, and died poor. There is nothing left of the supposed inheritance—worse than that; but that is all that relates to me," he cried, suddenly pausing with a gasp of restrained grief. "The people here exhaust their kind feelings to me in reproaches upon him who has left me unprovided for. False reproaches!—insults to me as much as to him! He is gone, and all control of me, all love for me, have died in his grave. I have myself to support, and his honour to reclaim. I ask you how I am to do it best—must it be as a labourer at home, or as a soldier abroad?"

"But you have given me no reason why your choice should be limited to these two trades," said Colonel Sutherland; "there are many things besides which such a young man as yourself can do better than either. Come, you are very young—you are arbitrary and impatient. The profession of arms can only carry a man on and forward in time of war. You are thinking of Napoleon's soldiers, those men who might possibly carry a marshal's baton in their knapsacks; but you forget that the first thing required is not the soldiers, but the Napoleon—and things were never so in the English army, my young friend. Even in times of war, not one man in a thousand rises from the ranks—no, not even in India—not in the Company's service. Don't deceive yourself. Don't you know that even the old women in the village break their hearts when their sons enlist, and declare that anything would be better? I don't say that. I am a soldier myself; but they are nearer the truth than you."

"Is it then only the alternative of despair?" cried the young man.

Colonel Sutherland curved his hand over his deaf ear, and begged his pardon, and had not heard him. The excellent Colonel was at home in his capacity of adviser: he could understand this lad who came with his heart on his lips ten times better than he could understand Horace, and took up his case with lively zeal and interest. He took him to the inn with himself, and made him sit by while he breakfasted, and grew into friendship with the young stranger almost against his will. On the whole, the encounter pleased the Colonel: he made Roger promise to come to him in the evening, when they could talk over his affairs at leisure, and warned him with fatherly kindness to do nothing rashly, and to entertain no further thought of enlistment. Perhaps it was very foolish of the Colonel to comfort the youth's heart after this rash fashion; perhaps it was "raising expectations which could never be justified." The old man never thought of that: he had kindness to give, and good counsel, and some knowledge of the world. He said to himself that this was all an old man was good for, and so shook hands with poor Roger Musgrave as if he had known him all his life, and occupied himself on the road to Marchmain with contrivances for serving him. It was his "way"; there are people who have a worse "way" to be met with in this world.

CHAPTER XII

Before Colonel Sutherland left the inn on his expedition to Marchmain, he had another visitor in the sergeant, who took care, however, to make sure that Musgrave was gone before making his appearance. He was not unlike the Colonel himself in his outer man; tall, spare, and brown, with a weather-beaten face and a grizzled moustache, Kennedy had at least sufficient resemblance to his old Colonel to mark their connection as comrades in arms. But the sergeant was neither deaf nor to any remarkable extent benevolent; abstract kindness did not influence him much: he flattered himself that he "knew what he was about" under all circumstances, and was somewhat pragmatical and dogmatic on most matters. His extensive experience and knowledge of the world had made him the cock of the village for a year or two past, where everybody believed his big stories, and most people were disposed to indorse his own opinion of himself. He was from the north of Ireland; a violent Protestant and Orangeman—tendencies sufficiently innocent in him; but the place of his birth, mingling a little of the fire and vehemence of the Milesian with all the obstinacy, dogmatism, and self-opinion of Scotland, had sufficient influence on his character to be noted. He was a rigid Presbyterian—one of the pillars of one of those little churches which, lingering near the border, prove that the national faith of Scotland has pushed her colonies more effectively into the sister country than England has been able to do in return; but this did not prevent Kennedy from making himself the oracle of the village ale-house, where he might be seen three or four nights a-week, sometimes in a very lofty and dignified state of haziness, freely bestowing the most grave advice upon everybody, and disposed to take rather a melancholy view of the degradation of the times, and of things in general. But this was the worst that anyone could say against him. He was fond of his little grandchildren, and was always busy with something for their amusement; good to his daughter, whom he often helped out of his own little funds; and in general friendly and serviceable. He presented himself to his old commander with a little awkwardness, fully expecting, as it seemed, to be taken to task for his morning's exploits; and his expectations were not disappointed. Colonel Sutherland was too much given to advising youth himself to have any patience with the advice of the sergeant. It was an invasion of his own domain which he could not forgive.

"I am glad to hear you are so comfortable," said the Colonel, "and that you manage to live in peace with your son-in-law, which, I confess to you, I would have thought rather doubtful; for I know you're rather strong in your opinions—eh! is it your daughter that keeps the peace?"

"Na, Cornel, na," said the sergeant; "I'm no so onexperienced as that; faothers and moothers are best in their own place. I have a cot to mysel', and a' my traps about me—next house to Mary, poor thing!—and she's kept a' goin' since I've come, and the childer they keep back and forard; and so far as the husband goes, it never was said, among a' slanders, that I was ought but a peaceable man—"

"Oh! a very peaceable man," said Colonel Sutherland, with a smile. "That, to be sure, is the last thing one could think of doubting; but come, you have your faults, my good fellow—what do you say to me, now, for such an account as I heard your giving, this morning, to the young man?"

"Well, Cornel!" exclaimed the culprit, keeping up his boldness, though a little abashed—

"Well! It does not appear to me to be well at all," said the Colonel; "how often have I told you, when on recruiting duty, to tell the truth? You pour a parcel of lies into a poor blockhead's head, and blow up his pride with thoughts of what's going to happen to him; and you expect, when he has found out that it's all lies, as he must do, that he will believe the rest of what you say to him! That's bad enough; but to go into it con amore—I mean for pure love of romancing—when there was neither necessity nor business in it—I admit to you that's something that beats me."

"Ay, Cornel, it's easy for the like of you," said Kennedy, "that have your pensions and commands; but what's a man to say to the poor devils? Hard service and poor wages, barracks and boiled beef, and sixpence a-day! Truth's a grand thing for the army, Cornel, but it does not bring in no recruits; and where's the harm done? If Johnny Raw is deceived wance in a way, it's soon tooken out on him. At the worst, did I ever tell a man he could rise to be Cornel but by a steedy life and doing his duty? Sure, and if he minds himself, he can come to be sergeant, and that's next best; but the biggest lot of them, Cornel, as you know as well as me, never try, and get no honour at all, at all, as may well be proved; for them that strive not, win not on, as I've told them till I was hoarse myself, many's the day."

"You never wanted an excuse," said the Colonel, shaking his head; "however, we'll leave the general question; did you ever know a man in the 100th rise from the ranks?—did you ever hear of a sergeant sent on a political mission?—and how could you venture to begin the day, you old sinner, with such a pack of lies?"

"Well, well, Cornel—aisy, sir," said the sergeant; "sure he was a gentleman, and know'd what was what as well as me!"

Colonel Sutherland laughed in spite of himself at this original excuse, on seeing which Kennedy recovered his courage, and took a higher tone.

"And if ye'll believe me, the best thing for him yonder is just to 'list, Cornel. If he wance 'lists, friends'll come in and buy his commission; for sure they are well off and in plenty, Yorkshire ways—and the disgrace, sir, the disgrace, that's what will make them draw their purse-strings. I would not desire a prettier man, either for parade or battle-field. He's a soldier born!"

"They! who are they?" said Colonel Sutherland; "he has no friends."

"Maybe, Cornel, maybe—I say little of friends—friendship's neither here nor there," said the sergeant, waving his hand; "but the faother and moother I can speak to. Them that heeds not love, heeds shame."

"You are oracular, Sergeant Kennedy," said the Colonel, with a very little peevishness; "but I tell you the lad told me he had no friends."

"Faother and moother, Cornel, as I say," answered the persistent sergeant, with a little nod of his dogmatical head.

Colonel Sutherland got up and fell to pacing the room with great annoyance and agitation. After a little while, being somewhat obstinate himself, he seized Kennedy by the shoulder and shook him.

"You're deaf!" said the Colonel, with a whimsical, half-angry transference of his own defect to the other; "you're hard of hearing! I tell you the lad says he has no friends."

"And I tell you, Cornel, he has faother and moother, if it was my last word!" said the sergeant once again.

"Your last word!—ay, you will always have the last word," cried Colonel Sutherland, this time indeed hearing imperfectly; "there must be some mistake, I suppose. Never mind, we'll inquire into it later. You must see me again, sergeant—I am going now to my young people. Good morning to you, my friend—ask for me here to-morrow."

"Are the young gentlemen in these parts, Cornel?" said Kennedy, rising with a little reluctance; "I said to mysel' the Cornel behooved to have his own occasions here."

"Not my boys—my niece and nephew, people you never heard of," said the Colonel, quickly. "Now, my man, good morning—I am pushed for time—you'll come again to-morrow."

Thus urged, Kennedy had no resource but to obey, which he did, however, very slowly, running over in his mind immediately all the "gentlemens' families" of the district, with which he had any acquaintance, in a vain endeavour to ascertain who could be the niece and nephew of his "old Cornel." Kennedy, as it happened, had not been at his usual post in the public room of the little inn on the previous night, and had consequently no intimation of any dawn of new fortune on Mr. Horry, whom he knew perfectly well, and at whose hands he had suffered contradiction enough to give him some interest in the young man's fate. This information, however, he would have been pretty sure to receive, but that Colonel Sutherland had already sent for the landlady to give her his orders for the day.

The Colonel was extremely frugal, almost parsimonious so far as his own manner of living was concerned, but having set himself to devise some pleasure for poor Susan, shut up all her life in Marchmain, the extremest liberality which the circumstances would allow, was not too much for his inclinations. The only vehicle possessed by the little inn at Tillington was a double gig, a very homely conveyance, which the Colonel had already ordered, and in which he proposed to take Susan "somewhere," bringing her back to lunch with him. The kind old man entered into the most minute directions about this lunch. He put elaborate leading questions, in order to ascertain what the cuisine was capable of, and consulted over puddings and tarts with the zeal of a connoisseur. A sentimental French chef who would have entered into the sentiment of the occasion, would have delighted the Colonel. He wanted a dainty meal of pretty little dishes, sweet and savoury, as much in honour of Susan, as to please her youthful palate, and endeavoured so earnestly to impress his wishes upon the homely innkeeper, that the idea of some secret grandeur belonging to Mr. Horry and his sister impressed itself more and more deeply upon that good woman's mind. She promised to do her very best; with the greatest awe and impressment she left the innocent and too trustful Colonel to study her cookery-book with devotion, and to conceive impossible triumphs of culinary art. But art, even in the kitchen, avenges itself upon those who neglect it. Poor Mrs. Gilsland lost three or four hours of valuable time, and her temper—which was still more valuable—over trifle which sunk dead into the bottom of her dish, and cream which would not "whip;" and dratted the Colonel at the conclusion of it with hearty good will and much vexation. While the innocent Colonel, secure of having done all that man could do to procure a satisfactory collation for Susan, drove the innkeeper's steady old horse across the moorland road, and combated manfully the vexation which rose stronger and stronger in his mind, as he recollected the discrepancy between young Musgrave's account of himself and that given by Kennedy.

The Colonel had a little pride in his own discernment, and could not bear to be taken in; but besides that, was grieved in his kind old heart at the thought of finding his new protegé unworthy; and yet his manner was so sincere, his face so honest and candid! Would that Horace had as clear a countenance! Colonel Sutherland touched the horse with his whip, and went forward with a little start, as if he would rather escape from that last thought, and so dismissed young Musgrave from his mind as best he could, and began to think with simple pleasure of Susan and the unusual holiday which he was bringing to her. He had ascertained that it was possible this fine morning to drive her to the little country town, where it was market-day, and where the little stir and bustle of life would be new to her. The idea of the pleasure she would have exhilarated himself, as he approached nearer to the house. He meant to buy her some books, and anything else that might amuse her in her solitude, and smiled to himself, with a tender and simple satisfaction, as he tried to anticipate her likings and wishes. Thus thinking, and thus smiling, he came in sight of the solitary house upon which at the moment the sun shone.

There it stood in its dark reserve, with the windows buried deep in the wall, sending no responsive glimmer to the light which shone full upon the blank gable, and slanted along the front of the house. There was no projecting point to make a break of shadow in the featureless brightness, nothing but the dull wall and the cold slate-roof; and all around the black moor, without a tree, intersected by long deep cuttings full of black water. Colonel Sutherland pulled up in spite of himself, both in his pace and his thoughts, and went softly over the remaining way. Could he hope to penetrate when the very sun was baffled? A chill of disgust, a throb of impatience, the intolerance of a fresh and upright nature for this unnatural mystery and gloom, possessed him in spite of himself. He said to himself that it was contemptible, that he had no patience with it. It needed all the smiles of Susan looking out from the window to restore him to his pleasanter thoughts, and to throw the least light of feasibility upon his simple expedients for softening and healing the harms of this unnatural life.

CHAPTER XIII

Susan had been at the window for nearly two hours, though it was still only eleven o'clock. She said to herself that Uncle Edward would not certainly come before the middle of the day, but still could not leave the window in case she might possibly lose the first glimpse of him on the road. When she had satisfied herself, to her great disappointment, that the homely country vehicle which she saw approaching contained him, poor Susan nearly cried with vexation. There was not even anybody in the gig with him to take charge of it. It appeared that he must only mean to remain a moment, and Susan withdrew from the window in the first shock of her disappointment, feeling that Uncle Edward had deceived her, and that there was no longer anything to be depended on in the world.

At that instant Horace, who had no desire to subject himself to the inquiries of Susan, and had hitherto kept rather out of her way, entered the room abruptly.

"Here is my uncle!" he exclaimed. "What! you don't care for him to-day, don't you? He's no novelty now?—that's famous, certainly! But, do you hear, Susan, I want something of you. While he's here, make him talk all you can; ask him about my mother; how they used to live when we were babies; what happened about the time she died; everything you can think of. I want to hear what he says, and of course all that's very interesting to you; you want to know."

"Don't you want to know, Horace?" asked Susan, half alarmed by his tone, and yet half pleased with the idea that he was becoming interested about their dead mother, and the life which was connected with her. She looked at him with dubious, uncertain looks; she did not know what to make of him. She could not comprehend any secondary or evil motive which he could have, and yet he did not seem to speak quite honestly, or in good faith.

"To be sure; why else should I bid you ask?" said Horace, throwing a book down on the table and seating himself by it, as if he had been pursuing his morning studies there.

And indeed Susan had said the same thing to herself. She ran to the window again as the wheels began to approach audibly, and could no longer feel disappointed when she met Uncle Edward's smile, and saw him uncover his grey head in the sunshine, in his antique affectionate gallantry. Susan was quite unaccustomed to the common tokens of respect which belonged to her womanhood. The salutation made her blush, and yet pleased her wonderfully; she could no longer believe that her uncle was coming only to call as if they had been strangers. She stood smiling and waving her hand to him till he was quite near, and then ran to the door. John Gilsland's mare was the soberest beast in the district—she stood still as a statue when the Colonel descended, and looked so perfectly trustworthy, that he did not hesitate to leave her to herself for a few minutes. He took both Susan's hands in his and kissed her forehead with a fatherly grace, then drew her arm into his own to lead her back to the dining-room. His whole manner, with its protecting, tender, indulgent kindness for her youth, and its chivalrous respect for her womanhood, had in it the most exquisite sensation of novelty for Susan. She laughed to herself secretly, yet with tears coming to her eyes—she felt a new pride, a tender humility in her own heart. She was flattered, and touched, and stimulated at the same moment. Wonderful was this love, this new influence, this unknown soul of life; it might have been more romantic had it dawned upon her through a young man instead of an old one—a lover rather than an uncle; but in that case the revelation would have been very different, and perhaps the revolution scarcely so complete.

"Call Peggy, my dear child," said Uncle Edward, "and put on your bonnet, I want you to go with me as far as Kenlisle—not too far for a drive this fine morning; it is cold to be sure, but bright and pleasant; tell Peggy you must have on your warmest wraps; tell her I want you to see something else than the moor, for one day at least—tell her—ah, here she is herself! Peggy, I want my niece to drive with me to-day to Kenlisle—will there be any objections, do you think?"

"The master never sets eyes on Miss Susan, from ten o'clock in the day till six at night," said Peggy. "He can scarce complain, and as for me I give my consent willing. Ay, honey! you may look, with your eyes dancing in your head—I said new times was coming. Would you keep the Colonel waiting? and the mare at the door like a douce wife, taking great notice on the bits of green grass agrowing amidst of the stones. There, Colonel, she's off like a hare athwart the moor—the poor child! from a baby, she's ne'er had a holiday before."

And Peggy hastened upstairs after Susan, who, gazing from one to another for a moment of bewildered and doubtful delight, had at last burst from the room, seeing that nobody opposed the extraordinary, delightful suggestion, to get ready for her drive. When the old woman disappeared following her, the Colonel turned to Horace, who had listened with a good deal of discomfiture, resentment, and contempt, unable to comprehend the bad taste which could contrive pleasures for Susan, to the neglect of himself. It gave Horace a worse opinion of his uncle than he had yet entertained. He could scarcely help sneering at him, and calling him an old woman to his face.

"Will you walk over to Tillington and meet us, Horace?" said Colonel Sutherland, who, for his part, exhilarated by the sight of Susan's delight and wonder, was now full of smiles and satisfaction; "I have ordered some luncheon between two and three, which will leave you time to bring your sister home. You will come?—you look a little pale, my boy—you have been thinking too much over-night!"

"It is possible—I have not slept since I saw you, uncle," said the young man.

"Too much—too much," said Colonel Sutherland, resting his hand kindly upon his nephew's shoulder. "Important as the question is, I am sorry you lost your sleep—it is only old people who can do that with safety. And you have come to a good conclusion, Horace?—that is right! Already, I am sure you feel the pleasure of decision. But I will not ask you what you have resolved on now. Eh, Susan?—what, not dressed yet, you fairy?—what is it now?"

"Oh, uncle!—I only wanted to ask, if you won't be angry," cried Susan, out of breath, "whether I should be too grand if I wore my shawl?"

The old man's face brightened, and expanded all over with the simplest pleasure.

"Too grand!—you don't drive with me every day, do you?" he said with a laugh, as he patted her cheek. "No—I should be quite mortified if I did not see you in your shawl; but make haste—think of the mare, and in a winter's day remember there is no daylight to lose."

Susan ran off again with flying feet, and the Colonel turned once more to his nephew. He could not help recognizing then something of the amazement, contempt, and derision which filled the mind of Horace. Uncle Edward was a little struck by his look—perhaps, even a little offended. He paused unconsciously to defend himself.

"You think that very trivial—eh, Horace?" said the Colonel. "Ah, my boy! one is heroical when one is young—one feels it grand to be superior, and despise the smaller matters of life; but at my age one learns that happiness itself is made up of trivial things."

Horace's eyes fell under his uncle's look; he was half ashamed—not of his sentiments, but of having betrayed them.

"I am sure it is very good of you to take so much trouble for Susan," he said, with his uncomprehending, half-resentful voice.

Colonel Sutherland supposed Horace to be jealous, and was a little pained, but yet acknowledged a certain amount of nature in the feeling. He had no conception of the true state of the case—of the entire contempt his nephew felt for himself, and the angry and derisive wonder with which he perceived the importance given to Susan. It was not jealousy: Horace only could not comprehend how any man in his senses could resign his conversation and society for that of his sister—Susan! a girl! who knew nothing, hoped nothing, desired nothing—a tame, contented woman! He found it hard to restrain himself under these circumstances, and called his uncle an old fool and an old trifler in his secret heart. Then Susan came downstairs, smiling and happy—her India shawl contrasting, perhaps, rather too strongly with her simple bonnet and dark merino gown, standing before her uncle to be admired, and turning round that he might see his present in all possible aspects. What trifling! what folly! what miserable vanity! But it pleased the two wonderfully, who stood there making a little sun-bright group of their own, the old man stooping over the girl, with his tender, indulgent smile, and the girl looking up to him in her unusual flutter of happy spirits. Perhaps it is true, after all, that common, every-day happiness—that dear solace of common life, which comes, when it does come, without asking—is made up of very trivial things; at all events, it was much more agreeable to look at them than at Horace, who loured behind them like a dark cloud, and turned away his head in disgust, and felt that it was all he could do to keep the sneer of scorn from his lip. In much the same condition he attended them to the door, and saw them drive away. Susan, wrapped up and covered over with shawls and cloaks of every description by her uncle's careful hands, and with Peggy's great black veil, embroidered with great flowers, like gigantic beetles, fastened over her bonnet; from the midst of all which unusual coverings the pretty face, smiling and blushing, radiant with pleasure and gratitude, looked out in its sweet colour and expression, with a simplicity of happiness quite beyond Horace's frown to stifle or prevent. Somehow his sister's face disgusted him that day: he stood looking after them, suffering his sneer to take form and remain, long after they were out of sight. He rose over them in his own mind with a contemptuous superiority, yet felt himself humbled and envious at sight of the happiness with which he had no sympathy, and which he did not understand. He did not wish to share it—it was something beneath his level. Yet the very power of being exhilarated by such trifles, and finding pleasure so independent of reasonable grounds, filled the young man with a certain envy, and humiliated his pride. Susan's happiness did not give him a single throb of pleasure, yet it brightened his uncle's face into quite a kindred light: it was altogether incomprehensible to Horace. He took refuge in silent contempt and sneers of unacknowledged mortification, disdaining the pleasure, yet galled in himself not to comprehend how it was.

CHAPTER XIV

Meanwhile Colonel Sutherland and his niece drove along the bare and exposed moorland road with very different sentiments. Susan could not feel any cold, could not allow herself to suppose that any landscape more delightful or weather more entirely satisfactory was to be found anywhere in the world. She pitied the poor people shut up in a close carriage, whom they passed at a little distance from Marchmain. She appealed to her uncle if a gig was not of all other kinds of conveyance the most delightful. She listened to his stories of travel in India, with all its elephants and camels, and of the still more miraculous railway at home, with equal admiration and wonder, as things equally unlikely to come under her own observation, and enjoyed her present extraordinary felicity all the more from thinking how unlikely it was to occur again.

Everything concurred to put Susan in the highest spirits—her freedom, her kind protector, the novelty of her position, the wondering looks cast at her from the cottages they passed, the involuntary respect excited by her companion, the air, the sunshine—even the fine shawl, though it was entirely covered by her other wrappings and nobody could see it—all contributed towards the full and joyous satisfaction of her young mind. She put Peggy's great old-fashioned veil, with its big beetles, up from her face—she was not afraid of the wind, or of taking cold, or of anything else in the world; and as the horizon gradually widened, and the road extended out of the immediate vicinity of her home, Susan's delight increased. She declared the hills went faster than they did, and kept continually receding, and every new opening of the landscape increased her pleasure. The Colonel listened to all her admiring exclamations with a smiling face; he told her of his own neighbourhood, a fairer and richer country. He spoke of the visit she must make him shortly, and of all the places he should take her to. The wind blew cold in their faces, with by no means a balmy or genial breath; but then their hearts were so fortified with warm affections and honest happiness, that the cold did not hurt them. Little by little they fell into more particular conversation. Colonel Sutherland was interested and concerned about Horace, anxious to know how to help him; but he was not and could not be confidential with his nephew, whereas his heart flew open to Susan as at a touch of magic. He could not help speaking of everything which moved when he had gained her ear, and had her to himself alone. He had told her all about young Roger Musgrave before he was aware, and about Kennedy's story, and his own vexation and annoyance to find that the young stranger had not dealt quite truly by him.

"But, uncle!—oh, Peggy knows all about him," said Susan; "Peggy did not know he had any friends till just the other day. Perhaps he did not know himself—perhaps—I think, Uncle Edward, I would not believe he was wrong till he told you of it himself."

"But if he is in the wrong, Susan, will he tell me of it himself?"

"Some people would not," said Susan, gravely, "I know that; but yes, uncle, oh, yes, I am not afraid."

"Perhaps you know him better than I do, my love," said Uncle Edward, observing with a little curiosity the expression of Susan's face.

"Yes, I think I saw him once," said Susan. Then she added, with a little laugh—"I was very much frightened—I am afraid it was very wrong of him—he was actually fighting, uncle."

"Fighting?—it was certainly very wrong," said the Colonel; "but you laugh, you wicked little fairy—what was it about?"

"It was not so much fighting either," said Susan—"it was punishing. It was gipsies, uncle—what the people here call muggers, you know. One of them was driving his little cart along the road with a poor wretched donkey, lashing it like a savage, and his poor wife came trudging after him, with her baby tied in a shawl on her back—and twice over he gave her a cut with his whip, to make her go faster. I could have beaten him myself—the great beast!" cried Susan. "Roger Musgrave was coming down the road; and, just as he met the muggers, that fellow pushed his wife out of the way so rudely, that she fell down, poor creature, and hurt herself. Mr. Roger had been watching them like me—he came up just then with a spring, and caught the mugger by his collar and his waist like this; and, before he had time to say a word, tossed him over the hedge—right over—where he rolled head-over-heels on the grass. You should have seen his face when he got up! I clapped my hands—I was so pleased. And Mr. Roger took off his hat to me," said Susan, after a little pause, with a rising colour, "as you did, uncle, to-day."

"It was very well done, I don't doubt," said Colonel Sutherland; "but, my dear child, that was not fighting."

"Oh, no—not that!—but I liked it better than what came after," said Susan. "The mugger scrambled through the hedge, and swore at Mr. Roger; and he took off his coat in a moment, and told him not to be a coward, to flog women and beasts, but to come on—and I was very much frightened; then the mugger's wife, she came forward and swore too, and it was all very dreadful. I did not want to see them fight, and ran into a cottage—I rather think they did not fight at all, for the mugger was frightened too; but, however, that was the only time I ever saw Roger Musgrave; the people in the cottage told me who he was, and I liked him for punishing the man."

"I daresay the fellow punished his wife and the donkey all the more, when they were out of sight," said the Colonel; "but I confess I should have done it myself. Very well! I will put down in my books—my little Susan in favour of young Musgrave versus Sergeant Kennedy against. And so you only saw him that one time? Do you know anybody at all, you poor child?—have you ever had a companion in your life?"

"Not a companion," said Susan; "but"—and she looked up in her uncle's face—"you won't be angry, I know, uncle. Peggy goes to the meeting, and sometimes in the morning, when papa does not go out, I go with her. It is dreary to go to church all alone."

"So it is," said the sympathetic uncle; "and what then?"

"Then," said Susan, blushing a little more, and looking up shyly in his face—"I am sure I do not know how we got acquainted. We used to look at each other, and then we nodded, and then, at last, one day we spoke; and now, sometimes, we meet when we are out walking, uncle—and once I have been in their house—only once. I did not mean it—I was there before I knew what I was about."

"But you have not told me yet who this mysterious person is," said the Colonel, a little disappointed and troubled, if the truth must be told, at the thought of some young and no doubt perfectly unsuitable lover who met his little girl in clandestine walks, and whose house even, the inexperience of Susan had been persuaded into visiting. He said the words rather coldly, in spite of himself—he was mortified to find the virginal quiet of her mind already thus disturbed.

"Uncle, are you displeased?" said Susan, with a little fright and surprise. "Oh, I never thought you would be angry; for even Peggy said that to be friends with Letty would be for my good. She is the minister's daughter at the meeting, and the only child; and she has learned so much, and knows a hundred things that I know nothing of; and, uncle, sometimes I want somebody to speak to—oh, so much!"

"My dear child, forgive me! I wish you knew a dozen Letties," cried the repentant Colonel; "that you should have to blush over an innocent friendship, my poor dear little girl; but your confusion, Susan, made me think it something very different. Why should you be ashamed of knowing Letty? I am very glad to hear it, for my part."

Susan did not answer just immediately. She said to herself, with a little quickening of her breath:—

"I wonder what was the something very different that Uncle Edward thought of," and a little inclination to laughter seized the little girl. Who could tell why? She did not know herself, but felt it all the same.

"Does Horace spend much of his time with you, Susan?" said Uncle Edward; "does he tell you what he is thinking about? Do you know that your brother is tired of an idle life, and wants to be employed, and to make his own way in the world?"

With that question Susan was brought back to her home, and separated as if by magic in a moment from all her individual involuntary girlish happinesses; she shrank a little into herself and felt chilled and contracted, without knowing how. She could not even be so frank as she would have been a little while ago—Uncle Edward's love had opened the eyes of the neglected girl, and developed all at once in her heart the natural instincts of "the only woman in the family." She could not bear to convey an unfavourable impression of Horace to her uncle; but, unskilled in her new craft, she betrayed herself even by her reticences and reserves.

"I know he wants to go away," she said, faltering a little; "and I am sure you would not be surprised, if you lived with us only for a day;—for," added Susan, blushing and correcting herself, "it is very dull at Marchmain, and boys cannot put up with that as we can. Horace has always felt it a great deal more than I have."

"I am not surprised," said Colonel Sutherland; "if Marchmain was the happiest home in the world, still the young man must go away—it is in his nature. He must make his own way in the world."

"Must he, uncle?" said Susan, looking up with a little surprise into his face.

"I was only sixteen, my love, when I first went to India," said the Colonel; "the boys, as you call them, must not stay at home all their lives—they must do something. My Ned will be on his way to India, if all is well, in a year or two. The sooner a young man gets into his work the better—and now Horace would set about it too."

"But he cannot do anything, uncle," said Susan, seriously; "what is he going to do?"

"Has he never told you?" asked Uncle Edward.

The question seemed to imply blame, and Susan was troubled.

"Horace is not like you, uncle," she said, recovering a little boldness; "he does not tell me things; he knows a great deal more than I do—he has almost learned German—and he thinks a great deal more. I am afraid I do not always understand him when he does speak to me. It is my fault; so he thinks over everything all the more, and I am afraid sometimes gets angry in his heart, because no one can understand him at Marchmain!"

Colonel Sutherland shook his head, but did not say anything. He began to tell Susan what he did when he was a lad.

"There were a great many of us at home, to be sure," said the Colonel; "but we were all scattered before the youngest was fifteen—the sisters married, and the brothers making their own career. They are all dead, Susan, every one—but you have quantities of cousins, my dear, in India and elsewhere, whom you never heard of, I daresay. Your Uncle William was puisne Judge of the Saraflat, John was Resident at Cangalore, both of them very much respected. I was the youngest but one. I could not bear the thought that all my brothers were independent but myself. I gave them no peace at home till I got my cadetship. Unless one has the good fortune to get an appointment, it is quite as hard work getting on in India as at home, my dear; and all our influence had been used up for my elder brothers, and exhausted before it came to my turn. I was but a subaltern when I married, Susan. Your aunt was—ah, I can't describe her, my love. I am very happy on the whole and contented, but sometimes I think on what might have been, and make myself wretched, which is very sinful, considering how much I have to thank God for. Yes, Susan, I was a rich man once. I had wife and daughters, and my house full. We had not very much money, but we were very happy; and now, my dear child, you are the only woman of the family—that is, here."

Susan could not have spoken a word to save her life—she sobbed silently under her heap of warm wrappings, looking with a wistful, youthful sympathy into the grave face beside her. The Colonel shed no tears;—he guided his horse with the same quiet caution as before, turning the animal aside from a sudden obstacle in the way, with a steady promptitude, which showed his perfect attention to what he was about, even in the midst of these recollections; yet he was not looking at the road, nor at her, nor at anything; but had his eyes fixed on the far-away horizon, which yet he did not see. Susan sat beside him in silence, wondering with youthful awe and reverence over the indescribable yearning, with which some instinct told her this brave old heart longed for the heaven which held his departed; but she could not say anything—she would have felt it sacrilege.

However, they shortly approached the town, which recalled Colonel Sutherland from his graver thoughts. It was a comfortable country town, pleasantly placed at the opening of a valley, with the gray fells ranging themselves on either side, and the great gray tower of the old Abbey church reigning over the little crowd of houses. The market-place was still busy and bright, though the more serious merchandize of the morning was over; cosy country-women, in cloth pelisses, made promenades round the open square, where the best shops in the town displayed their riches, to see "how things were wore," and make stray purchase of a kerchief or ribbon; and still the notable housewives of the town bought vegetables, and rabbits, and country eggs, and chickens, from the remaining stalls in the market-place. And still heaps of dark-green vegetables—winter greens and savoys, purple flowers of broccoli, and tiny red lines of carrots, illustrated some boards, close to the white eggs and yellow butter, the hapless decapitated poultry, and butter-milk pails of the others. Susan and her uncle walked through the throng, attracting no small degree of observation; for there were not many such cavaliers as Colonel Sutherland in Kenlisle, and very few such shawls as that one which, relieved of all her other wraps, Susan displayed upon her shoulders with no small degree of pride. The scene was quite extraordinary in its animation to her eyes. She looked at the ruddy winter apples and crisp greens with the most perfect interest. She longed, with a natural housewifely instinct, to make purchases herself, to the confusion and amazement of Peggy. She could scarcely conceal her unbecoming curiosity about the booths of toys and sweetmeats, the cases of coarse ornaments, brooches, and rings, and ear-rings, which Susan could not believe to be paltry and worthless. The glamour of her ignorance brightened everything; and when her eyes, as she looked up unconsciously, fell upon the gray mass of the Abbey tower withdrawn into a street which led off from this busy space, Susan felt awed and ashamed to think of her own vanity and extreme regard for "the things of this world." But she could not school herself into righteous indifference; above all, when Uncle Edward, indifferent to her morals, took her into shop after shop, buying a little parcel of books in one place, some pretty ribbons in another, a cap for Peggy, which captivated the old man in a window; and, last of all, patterns and materials for work of various kinds, canvas and Berlin wool, and an embroidery-frame. This last purchase raised Susan into a paradisiacal condition, for which it is to be hoped nobody will despise her. She was not very intellectual, it is true—it might very well happen that she preferred her needlework to her book sometimes. She saw herself rendered completely independent, as she supposed, of ennui and domestic weariness by that ecstatic parcel. She longed to take it in her arms, and run all the way home with it, that Peggy might see, and half regretted for a moment the luncheon at Tillington, which, however, would give her still another hour or two of her uncle's company. Then Susan looked at that uncle with a great compunction, thinking of what he had told her; but Colonel Sutherland was happy in her happiness, delighted to see her so delighted, and entered with fresh, natural pleasure into the scene for his own part. It was quite a work of art to pack the gig with all the parcels, and wrap Susan up again into all her cloaks. Then they went off at a great pace to Tillington. So far it had been a most successful day.

CHAPTER XV

Horace had been waiting some time in the little inn before Colonel Sutherland and Susan arrived. This had not much improved the young man's temper; but the result of his cogitations on the way here, and while he waited, had been, that it was necessary to be no longer critical, but that he must assume the virtue which he had not, and secure his uncle's assistance in his own way. Horace had settled at last to his own satisfaction upon his version of his uncle's character. He concluded the Colonel to be a well-meaning, superficial old man, most at home among women and children, finding pleasure in trifles, strongly prejudiced in favour of some old-fashioned virtues, which he recommended not so much from conviction as from custom. Industry and honesty, and straightforwardness, a homespun and sober interpretation of all human laws—Horace decided that his uncle lauded and urged these virtues on others just as he might recommend cod-liver oil or Morison's pills, and that he was unable to comprehend anything higher than that old code of respectability. But granting this, it was all the more wise to humour and yield to the old man, and permit him to maunder on in his own way. Horace resolved to profess himself ready and anxious for employment, the choice of which he meant dutifully to leave to his uncle; and having thus settled summarily the more important issue, set himself with all his might to observe and entrap the unsuspicious Colonel in his confidential and unguarded talk. It suited him a great deal better to do this, than to consider honestly how he should provide for his own life, and establish his individual position in the world; and it was significant of his character that he dismissed the former question at once, but lingered with inclination and zeal upon the crafts of the other, laying his ambuscade with all the cunning and precaution possible.

He sat by the fire in the inn parlour, while the maid and mistress bustled in and out laying the cloth and preparing for the Colonel's arrival. Mrs. Gilsland having recovered her temper, and remembering the embellishments of her master's table, in the days when she professed herself a cook, had been at pains to gather a handful of laurustinus, with dim, pinky, half-opened blossoms, to adorn the table, upon which sparkled the best glass and whitest linen of the establishment. The worthy woman would fain have insinuated herself into the confidence of Horace as he sat by the fire, and wanted only the very smallest encouragement to break forth in praises of the Colonel, and to hint her fear that they would not see much of the young gentleman at Tillington now that "his grand friends had turned up at last, and he was nigh coom to his fortune." But Horace did not give the slightest opening to any such familiarity. He kept possession of the room with an insolent unconsciousness of the landlady's presence and her hesitating glances at him, which enraged and yet awed her. It was Mr. Horry's "way," and this arrogance imposed upon the village people even while it offended them; but it was very different from "the Cornel." Mrs. Gilsland, who had been much disappointed at first to learn that her guest was no lord, and had not the shadow of a title, was by this time entirely captivated by the old man, and zealous to serve him; but still she turned to Mr. Horry with the interest which attaches to mystery. He took no more notice of her than if she had been a piece of furniture. She was angry but reverential—there was "a power o' thought" in the young man.

When the gig arrived with the two travellers, Horace hastened to the door to meet them with a novel amiability. He lifted Susan down, and gathered her parcels together with a good-nature that astounded her. They were all equally pleased, it seemed, as they went in together and met Mrs. Gilsland, curtseying and cordial, ready—half from goodwill and half from curiosity—to attend Susan herself, and help her to take off her bonnet. Then Susan carried a passport to respect wherever she went in that wonderful shawl; the landlady touched it with reverential ignorance, knowing only that it was "Indae," and ready to believe in any fabulous estimate of its value. Then, for the first time, Mrs. Gilsland remembered her unlucky trifle, with, not anger, but a pang of mortification. The wearer of such a shawl did certainly deserve something better than apples and custards, to which familiar dainties she had fallen back in despair. However, the luncheon was so far satisfactory, that it was eaten in perfect freedom, with a lively flow of conversation on all sides, which exhilarated even Horace, and raised Susan into a little paradise. What a difference it made to the common table, when Uncle Edward sat at the head instead of papa!—what an extraordinary revolution life would undergo, if the bread of every day were sweetened by such domestic intercourse as this! While her brother rose into a certain glow of personal exultation in the freedom he experienced, Susan, thinking less of herself, and feeling more deeply, found herself, unawares, surprised by the sudden mortification of a comparison. Involuntarily tears came into her eyes, and as she grew more grateful and affectionate towards her uncle, her heart ached more and more for her father. She saw now all the unnatural misery of their life. Why was it? But these thoughts did not take possession of the girl—they only came over her mind in a sudden, painful overflow as the tears came to her eyes; and then she thought of Horace's instructions to her; and, moved by strong curiosity and anxiety of her own—of a very different kind from her brother's—proceeded to obey him.

"Uncle," said Susan, with an honest, enquiring look, "did you see very much of mamma after she was married? But ah, I forgot—you went to India so soon."

"I saw her only when I returned, my love," said Uncle Edward—"when you were a baby, and Horace a bold boy of five—yes, and before that, when I had to come home on business, when your other uncles in India made me their commissioner to look after the family affairs. At that time I lived with my sister; that is five-and-twenty years ago."

"And where did we live then, uncle?" asked Susan. Horace did not say a word; he did not look at his uncle, but preserved such a total stillness from all motion, almost from breath, that a suspicious observer must have been alarmed by it. He was listening not for words only, but for tones, inflections—all those unconscious betrayals by which people, who do not suppose themselves watched, naturally disclose a certain amount of feeling with the facts they tell.

But Uncle Edward did not hear—he stooped over towards his niece, and put his hand to his ear. Then he laughed, and patted her hand upon the table. "Nowhere, so far as I am aware," said the Colonel; "there was no word of you, in those days, for all such important grown-up people as you are. My sister was little more than a bride; a gay young wife, full of spirits, pretty, much sought after, and loved everywhere. We were a large family, you know, and had been accustomed to a good deal of society at home. She was a happy young creature, and did not deny herself natural pleasures. Poor Mary!—it did not last very long!"

"Why did it not last very long, uncle?" cried Susan.

"Did you say it never lasts very long, my dear?" said Colonel Sutherland, who perhaps did not hear exactly what she said. "That is a very wise observation for you, Susan; and it is quite true to be sure, for when one begins to have a family, you know, one prefers happiness to pleasure—so that, after all, what the wiseacres say about the change from youth to sober age is true; and it isn't true like most things in this world, for it is by no means a melancholy change. When I came back fifteen years ago there was a great difference. I think she must have been ill of her last illness then, though we did not know of it. She had lost her pleasant spirits, and her pretty colour, and was anxious and desponding, as sick people grow. That made all the house melancholy. I daresay Peggy has told you as much as that."

"Oh! Uncle," said Susan, "when Peggy has told me there has always seemed to be something which she did not tell me. I always fancy something dreadful had just happened—some misfortune, or something wrong, or—I cannot tell what—but she never would say any more. Did mamma break her heart?"

The colour rose in Colonel Sutherland's cheek in spite of himself. Horace watching him, though he never looked at him, and though at this present moment he seemed intent on balancing a fork upon his finger, to the exclusion of all other concerns, found, or fancied he found, a certain irrepressible resentment mingled with his reluctance to answer. The Colonel spoke shortly, and with an embarrassed tone:—

"She was leaving her children young, without a mother; she did not know what might happen to you; she died anxious, troubled about you. I don't know this for certain, Susan, but I can believe it. It is hard to die in the middle of life, my dear child—yes, harder than in youth, for one's children seem to have so much need of one. I have no doubt, before all was over, the Lord showed her something of his purpose in it, and comforted her soul; but I don't wonder she seemed heart-broken. We will not speak any more of this, Susan. Horace is silent, you see, and is not interested, like you. He is thinking of his own concerns, as is natural to a young man—and all that is far and long past."

"On the contrary, I am very much interested, uncle," said Horace.

"I have no doubt of it, my dear boy, at a more suitable time. Of course I don't suppose you to be indifferent about your mother," said the Colonel; "but I understand your feelings perfectly. It is not selfish nor egotistic, as you fear, but simply natural; you must think of your own plans and intentions; you would be to blame if you did not."

If the Colonel could have known how far astray he was! If anything could have made him comprehend how little place in Horace's thoughts these same plans and intentions bore, and with what a stealthy watchfulness his nephew had been "interested" in his own recollections! But Uncle Edward comprehended his nephew quite as little as his nephew comprehended him; and the old soldier was not without a little strategical talent of his own; he found himself getting on dangerous ground; he feared saying too much, a thing which, if he allowed himself to get excited, he was only too likely to do—and Horace's plans were a famous diversion. Disappointed thus again, just at the very point of the story which seemed most likely to elicit something, Horace could scarcely be otherwise than sulky; but once more he put force on himself.

"I have decided, uncle," he said—"but only that it is you who must decide. You know the world, you know life. I am unacquainted with everything that could guide me. I have made up my mind to leave it in your hands. I must provide for myself, it appears," said Horace, sliding into these two words an involuntary interjection of bitterness, in a tone too low for his uncle to hear. "Take it into your consideration, and I will adopt whatever you decide upon. You know a hundred times better than I."

Colonel Sutherland was partly gratified, partly annoyed, for this was not at all what he wished. When at that moment the landlord came in to announce that the gig was at the door again, ready to take the young people home. Susan went away immediately to get her bonnet: then Uncle Edward had leisure to express his sentiments:—

"I daresay it is very probable that I know life better than you do," he said; "but, my boy, I don't know your inclinations, nor your tastes, nor your particular abilities, half, or a hundred part, so well. I'll consider the matter as long as you like, but how shall I be able to determine what you will like best?"

"Uncle, don't be annoyed," cried Horace, starting up—"can I have inclinations?—do you think it is possible? Do you suppose I don't understand what it means, all that you have said, and all that you have not said, about my mother? I would not grieve Susan with such words, but I know, as well as if you had spoken it, that it was my father who broke her heart."

"No, no, no!" cried the Colonel, rising likewise, and lifting his hand in earnest deprecation. "No, it is a mistake—no, you are unjust to him, Horace! I cannot excuse him to you as I might, but beware how you think ill of him. There are excuses—there are reasons. Listen to me, Horace Scarsdale: your father is a man as much to be pitied as blamed."

"And why?" said Horace, with a sceptical smile.

"My dear boy, sometime you will see all these circumstances more clearly," said the Colonel, a little agitated; "take it for granted in the meantime, and remember that he is your father—and really this has little to do with the question after all. You must like something: he has not been kind, I grant; but even where the most perfect love exists between parents and children, a father is never all in all, either for good or evil, to his son."

"No, uncle, but constant hate and enmity may kill the heart out of a man," said Horace. "I am not a fool; I could learn anything if I set myself to it: do you decide for me."

"I will then, my dear boy; and you will come to me to-morrow?" said the Colonel, faltering a little. "Come early, and I will walk back to Marchmain with you. Here is Susan ready. Are all the parcels safe? And you have spent a pleasant day, you fairy? Take care, Horace, that she does not catch cold."

"Pleasant day? Oh, uncle, the very happiest day of all my life!" said Susan.

The old man led her out well pleased, involuntarily solacing himself, after her troublesome brother, with the sight of her fresh face. And Susan's happiest day was quite over when she caught the last glimpse of his gray, uncovered head bowing to her from the inn-door. Horace had no kind talk or affectionate cares for his sister. The wind blew cold, and the evening began to gather damp over the fells. The two young people fell into perfect silence as they pursued the monotonous road, and there was no great comfort to be had in the idea of the welcome which waited them at home.

CHAPTER XVI

When Horace and Susan had left Tillington, the Colonel wrapt his great cloak round him, and went out to take a pondering, meditative walk, and think over all these concerns. This last conversation he felt had rather complicated his position, and changed a little the posture of affairs. It was now he who had to take the initiative—he who seemed to be sending Horace away, and deciding that it was his duty to follow a path of his own, and make his own career. This idea was the last which had occurred to him, when he met his nephew's passionate complaints with his own good, sober, kind advice. Horace had, however, completely turned the tables upon him. He was no longer engaged to give merely a friendly assistance to the young man's exertions, to help him by representing the case to his father, or by using such influence as he possessed to further his nephew's wishes. Horace had skilfully managed to make it appear, even to Colonel Sutherland himself, that it was he who had suggested the necessity for leaving home—that it was he who must decide the manner of doing so, and that the whole responsibility of the matter would lie upon his shoulders. This was far from pleasant to the Colonel; he thought over the whole matter with a very troubled brow: why should he draw upon himself all the trouble and blame of such a proceeding?—undertake the painful task of an interview with Mr. Scarsdale—most likely fail to satisfy Horace himself, and possibly meet with severer reproach hereafter, when the young man came to know that secret which he made vain inquiries after now? The Colonel did not relish his position as he thought over it. It was not of his making. He had but replied, as his kindly nature could not help doing, by offers of assistance to the outcry of Horace's impatience; and behold here was the result.

The very fact that something did exist which he knew, and which Horace did not know, embarrassed and straitened him further. But, at the same time, he had promised. Nothing but the agitation into which the young man had thrown him, by his sudden suggestion that the Colonel meant to accuse his father with breaking his mother's heart, could have led Colonel Sutherland to make so rash an engagement. He had no reason to believe that this was the cause of Mrs. Scarsdale's death. He knew she had been restrained, overruled, and chidden—but he knew also that to the end she loved, and made no complaint beside. For his own part, the circumstances of his sister's death, which followed very quietly upon a singular misfortune to her husband, had filled Edward Sutherland with the deepest compassion and sympathy for his brother-in-law; and accordingly he was more shocked than he could explain by Horace's sudden supposition, that it was Mr. Scarsdale's unkindness which had killed his wife; and in the eager anxiety with which he entreated the youth to believe that this was not the case, he consented unawares to make himself the arbitrator of Horace's fate—so far, at least, as that could be determined by its beginning. He had promised—that was indisputable; yet what right had he to take the first step in such a matter, or to urge upon a young man, in the very peculiar circumstances of Horace, the same personal labour which was necessary to his own sons? When the Colonel had come so far in his thoughts he paused with a sudden effort, and resolutely turned to the other side of the question.

"Ought I to stand by for fear of responsibility, or for the sake of my own pride, or for the risk of ingratitude, and see my sister's son sink into ignorance and debasement, and end in being the autocrat of an ale-house?" he said to himself, and did all that was possible to change the current of his own thoughts. But it was not much easier to choose a profession for Horace, or to fix on what he ought to be. Colonel Sutherland had come to perceive that he did not understand his nephew, and that not a single feature of resemblance existed between them. He marched on upon the road with his steady soldier's step, not perceiving how far he was going, nor how the night darkened—marching gradually into a more and more bewildering mist of thought. The village lay sheltered in a shallow valley, with low slopes ascending on every side towards a higher level of country, slopes much too gentle and gradual to have much affinity with the distant fells. Colonel Sutherland had nearly reached the top of one of these banks, when the toil of the ascent, which just there was steep, awakened him to a consciousness of where he was. He might have wandered for miles over the open country, but for the failure of wind and sensation of fatigue which seized him upon that brae. When he came to himself, wheeling about suddenly, he saw the lights of the village twinkling into the twilight a long way beneath him, and perceived, for the first time, how far he had come.

"The wind being on my back all the time," he said, with a kind of involuntary apology to himself half-aloud, as he commenced his return.

The Colonel's ears were sharper out of doors than in. He recognized that somewhere near, somebody had made a sudden start at the sound of his voice. There was no one to be seen—the Colonel beat the hedgerows with his stick, and called "Who's there?" with soldierly promptitude. He had no idea of being attacked from behind, in case a highwayman lurked behind those bare thorns. After a little interval, during which Colonel Sutherland continued his examination minutely, a voice gruff but subdued, answered somewhat peevishly—

"Cornel, it's me."

And the gaunt figure of Kennedy came crushing through a gap of the hedge to the Colonel's side.

"You!—why, what the deuce are you after here?" said the Colonel, his extreme amazement forcing that mysterious adjuration from his lips, he could not tell how.

"Weel, Cornel, watching the sport o' them living craetures," said Kennedy, with a little hesitation. "I seed the rabbits whisking in and out as I took my walk, and says I to myself—they're as diverting as childer, I'll take a look at them. And that's how it was—I'm rael fond of dumb craetures, Cornel, and there's sich a spirit in thae wild things."

"Do you mean to tell me, you old humbug, that you could see rabbits, or any other moving thing, at this time of the night?" said the Colonel. "If I did not know you to be an Orangeman I would think you were a Jesuit, Kennedy, with a dispensation for telling lies. Man, do you ever speak the truth?"

"Oh, ay, Cornel—always when it's to any person's advantage," said Kennedy; "and as for the Papishers, I hate the very name to my last drop of blood, as is nat'ral for a man of Derry born. I'm none ashamed of my lodge, nor my principles nouther. When I was a young lad, Cornel, the great Castlereagh, sir, he belounged to the same—and as for my eyes, a better sight, barring for the small print, does not beloung to a man of my years within twenty mile."

"I've seen the day," said Colonel Sutherland, softening unconsciously towards his old fellow-soldier, "when neither small print nor half-light would have bothered either you or me; but we're getting old, Kennedy, and Providence has given us both rest, and comfort, and leisure to think before our end comes—a blessing that falls to but few."

"Ay, Cornel, that's just what I say," echoed the ready sergeant; "not that I would even myself with my commanding officer, but a man that has seen the world is a great advantage to the young and onexperienced. Begging your pardon, Cornel, but I knowe your nephew, sir—I knowe Mr. Horry well."

"And what do you know of him, pray?" cried the Colonel, turning sharp round upon his companion, who, startled by the sudden movement and sharpness of the tone, swerved aside a little, and in doing so made visible for a moment a mysterious something, hitherto concealed with great skill, which he swung from his further hand.

"Eh?—what was it you were saying, Cornel?" said Kennedy, with confusion, drawing back his hand. "What do I knowe of him?—a fine young lad, sir, and very affable when he's in the humour, and a dale of judgment, and an oncommon reliance on himsel'. Many's the time, Cornel, he's said 'No' in my face, as bould as a lion, with no more knowledge of the matter, sir, nor a babe unborn. That's what I cal' courage, Cornel. Though he comes and goes in a rale friendly manner, there's ne'er a man in the village will use a freedom with Mr. Horry; but it's poor society for him, as I have seen many a day; and he said to me wance, says he, 'Sergeant, you're a wise man among a set of fools,' he says—'if it warn't for you the blockheads would have it all their own way; and as for me,' says the poor young gentleman, 'I've no business here.' I could see that, though I little thought he belounged to my honoured Cornel of the ould Hunderd, and a credit to his relations and al' his friends."

During this speech, Kennedy keeping wary eyes about him, was guarding the Colonel off with the utmost skill, and contriving that he should neither get sufficiently in advance or behind to have a chance of discovering again the burden he carried. However, the sergeant betrayed himself by a momentary impulse of vanity: he looked round in Colonel Sutherland's face to read the success of his last compliment, and in that moment of incaution the Colonel slid a step in advance, and, thrusting his stick to Kennedy's other side, caught by the feet a hare. The sergeant made the best of it, finding himself caught. He fixed his eyes on the Colonel's face after the first start of discovery with a comical half-defiance, half-deprecation, which, however, the light was too dim to show.

"You old sinner!—you romancing old humbug!—what do you call that thing there, eh? That's what takes you behind the hedge in the gloaming, with your wisdom and your experience! What do you call that thing there?"

"Call it, Cornel?—sure and it's a bit of a leveret, sir," said the sergeant, twisting it up by the legs with pretended carelessness. "I picked the poor baste up, that was laid, with its leg broke, upon the grass."

"And so that's how you take your walks and show your love for the dumb creatures, you old leasing-maker!" cried the Colonel. "Throw it down this moment, sir—carry it back to where you got it, or I'll make an information against you the moment we get to Tillington—I will, by George!"

"Oh, ay, Cornel, at your pleasure," cried the sergeant; "I'm not the man to withstand my commanding officer when he takes to swearing. I'll put it down, lookye, sir, where we stand; or I'll take it back beyant the hedge, and the first labouring chap as comes by, he'll get the baste, and link it hoam in his clumsy hand, Cornel, and be spied upon and given up, and a snare proved to him, and clapped in jail. He'll goo in innocent, Cornel, and he'll come out wroth and ruined, and all because my own officer seed an ould sodger pick up a bit of meat that was useless to any mortal beyant a hedge, and informed on me. And it shall never be said that William Kennedy transgressed discipline. There it is, sir—I'm blythe to be quat of it; pitch it from ye furder than I can see."

The Colonel poised the hare on his stick for a moment, shaking his head, then laughed aloud, and tossed it at Kennedy's feet.

"There's reason in what you say, you poaching old sinner; keep your spoil," he said, "but march on, sergeant, and keep out of my sight till we can take different roads. I don't keep company with stolen game. There, there, that's enough. I've heard your best excuses already. Good night, my man; and I advise you, for the sake of the old Hundred, to have nothing to do after this either with hares or snares."

CHAPTER XVII

Colonel Sutherland did not find much leisure that night. He had scarcely returned from his walk, a little indignant and vexed at the conduct of Kennedy, but less than ever inclined to believe him, when young Musgrave made his appearance. The Colonel was seated by the fire with his spectacles on, and the latest newspaper to be had in these regions laid on the table beside him—but he had not begun to read, having thoughts enough to keep him occupied. The room, with its dark walls and low roof and the indistinct prints hung round it, was left in comparative darkness by the little light of the two candles on the table. The Colonel himself had his back to the light, and, with his elbows resting on the arms of the chair, rubbed his hands slowly together, and pondered in his heart. He had almost forgotten the young stranger in the closer and nearer interests which moved himself; and what with his thoughts and his deafness, and his position with his back to the door, did not perceive the entrance of Roger, who stood undecided and shy when the door had closed upon him, half inclined in sudden discouragement to turn back again, and feeling for almost the first time, with a sudden painful start of consciousness, that he had no claim upon the friendship of this old man, whose kind interest in him this morning had cheered his forlorn young heart, but whom, after all, he had seen for the first time this day. A mind which is elevated by any one of the great primitive emotions, ceases for the moment to feel those secondary impressions of surprise and singularity with which in ordinary times we regard any departure from the ordinary laws of life. Had he been happy, Roger would have wondered, perhaps would have smiled, at the interest which this stranger expressed in him; but it had not even astonished his pre-occupied mind until now: now, as he stood behind the Colonel in the dim apartment, and saw him sitting thoughtful by the fire, unconscious of the presence of any visitor, the young man's impulse was to steal softly out again, and make no claim upon a sympathy which he had no right to. Yet his heart yearned for the kind look, the paternal voice which had roused him this morning out of the quick despair of youth. He approached slowly towards the table: when he reached it the Colonel turned round with an exclamation of surprised but cordial welcome, and pointed him to the chair opposite his own, which had been placed in readiness for his young guest. This little token that he was expected cheered the young man involuntarily; it was another of those trivial things which, as Colonel Sutherland said, make up so much of the happiness of life.

When he saw Roger opposite to him, with his eager, ingenuous face, and a world of undisguised youthful anxieties and disquietude shining in his candid eyes, the old man fell into a momentary pause of silence and embarrassment. It seemed impossible to impute any want of truthfulness to those honest looks, or even to cast upon them the momentary stain of a suspicion. And the same young eyes were quick to perceive even this pause, and remarked immediately that the Colonel was embarrassed, and did not know how to begin what he had to say. Grief in its immediate presence does not bring patience—the pride of the young man took alarm instantly—he half rose, with hasty words barring any apology, and a declaration of proud humility, that he had no right to trouble Colonel Sutherland, or to intrude upon his privacy, rising to his lips. Before he had spoken, the Colonel perceived what he meant, and stopped him. "Wait a little—hear what I am going to say—sit down," said the old soldier, laying his hand upon Musgrave's arm; "I cannot have you quarrel with me so soon—sit down, and let us talk it out."

"Nay, sir, there can be no occasion," cried Musgrave, in his disappointment and offence, his voice faltering a little; "I have but to thank you for your kindness this morning, and beg your pardon for intruding on you now."

"That cannot be," said Colonel Sutherland, with a momentary smile, "because you come by my own appointment; and, besides, I am very glad to see you, and you are a very foolish youth to be so impatient. Sit down quietly—have patience a little, and listen to me."

Roger obeyed, with some haste and reluctance. He was almost overcome by wounded pride and feeling, and yet he had nothing whatever to ground his mortification upon, but the Colonel's pause of embarrassment and confused preliminary tone.

"You thought I hesitated, and did not speak frankly enough," said the Colonel. "Perhaps it is true, for I had something on my mind. But now I mean to speak very frankly. My young friend, I believe I can be of but little service to you, but I can give you my best advice and such encouragement as an old man owes to a young one; while, on the other hand, you must be frank with me. After you left me this morning, I was told you had still parents alive. Is that true?"

"Did you think I had deceived you?" cried Musgrave, quickly.

Mortification and shame and sudden resentment flushed his face. "But you don't know me, to be sure!" he exclaimed, with a passionate tone of pain; "and yet, though I don't know you, I care for your opinion. I have not come to ask anything from you, Colonel Sutherland—I have already made up my mind what to do; but, at best, you must know that I have not deceived you. I have a mother, and yet I have not a mother—that is the only entire bond of nature remaining to me. She made a second marriage, and gave me up to my godfather so long ago, that I scarcely remember the time—her husband made my only visit to her so disagreeable, that I have never repeated it, and I believe never shall. She has a family of whom I know nothing, and has forgotten and forsaken me. I appeal to you, then, whether I was not right in saying that I had no friends?"

"I felt sure it would turn out something of the kind," said the Colonel, heartily. "What, my boy, are you affronted with me? Come, that is foolish—sit down and forgive me. Perhaps you think a stranger like myself has no right to ask such explanations; but I am old, and you are young—that is, after all, the most primitive principle of authority. I assure you, though you may not be quite pleased with me at this moment, I am a much safer counsellor than the sergeant—the old rogue! Draw your chair to the table, take a glass of wine, and let me hear what you are going to be about. I heard of an old exploit of yours from my niece, Susan Scarsdale, to-day."

"From whom?" asked Musgrave, with a little surprise.

"From my niece—you don't know her, I daresay," said the Colonel, whose object was to put his visitor at ease; "but some one told her your name, she says. An adventure of yours with a gipsy—do you recollect it—on some of the roads near Lanwoth Moor?"

"Oh!—the young lady from—" Musgrave paused only in time to prevent himself saying "the haunted house," which was a name very commonly appropriated to Marchmain. The young man blushed a little, partly from the mistake, partly from a very distinct recollection of the flattering applause with which Susan clapped her hands at his achievement. He might not have noticed her at all but for that sign of approbation; but it is pleasant to be approved, especially in a rash and unorthodox proceeding; and it is true that Roger had taken several occasions to pass Marchmain after that occurrence, with a lingering inclination to improve his acquaintance with that face; he never had any success in his endeavour, but still, under the eyes of Susan's uncle he blushed in spite of himself. "I recollect it very well," he said.

The Colonel saw his colour rise, and had not the slightest inclination to pursue the subject.

"Yes, it was very natural, whether it was wise or not," said the Colonel, with a smile, words which might refer equally well either to the encounter with the mugger, or the curiosity about Susan, and which his young companion unconsciously applied to the last. "I remember what I should have done myself at your age; but you say you have made up your mind. Will you let me ask how? for I think you might take more leisure to do that at your age."

"The steed would starve in the meantime," said Musgrave, with a little unnecessary vehemence. "Yes, I have made up my mind—but only as I had done before seeing you, sir, this morning. You spoke very wisely, very kindly. A man who had money, or friends, or skill, or anything in the world to fall back upon ought to have listened to you. I feel grieved that you should think, after so much kindness on your part, that I have not considered your advice. I did consider it, Colonel, believe me, but I have no alternative—I know nothing that I can be but a soldier. Don't say anything to me, it will only increase my disgust at myself to be fit for nothing else; and then, sir," said the young man, attempting to smile, "there is no necessity for thinking of the barracks and the sixpence a-day. I will take this other side of the question: young fellows like me, they say in novels, never did better long ago. I'll be a defender of my country, a servant of the Queen; a general is no more."

"My poor boy!" said the Colonel, whom this "other side of the question" had a pathetic effect upon, "you don't know the life of a common soldier; and do you mean to tell me that in our days, with all our progress and civilization, a young man with your advantages is fit for nothing but this?"

"I might be a gamekeeper," said the youth, with a slight tremble of his lip, "or I might be an emigrant—the last I should certainly choose if I had anything to set out upon; but I don't care to run the risk of blacking shoes or portering at the other side of the world, as the newspapers say the penniless emigrants are reduced to often enough. No, Colonel, I should not sit here, opposite you, a poor fellow, who will never have the right to meet you on equal terms again; but I must 'list, I have no alternative—I can only be what Providence and my education have qualified me for. If I am nothing else, I can be honest, at least. This is the only thing I am good for, and can reach to, therefore I have given up grumbling about it. And if," said Roger, with the fire blazing out of his eyes for a moment, one glance of youthful hope through the darkness, "if chance or war should ever put it in a man's power to rise, then look for me again!"

"My brave fellow!—my excellent lad!" cried the Colonel, "that is the spirit for a soldier! A regiment of ye would subjugate the world! Give me your hand, and keep your seat, boy! If you had 'listed already, does that make you less a gentleman? But is there no help for it, think you? Must you carry this soul to the ranks? By my word, I grudge it sorely!—and that is much for an old soldier to say. Have you no friends—I don't mean relatives—people that have known you in better days, that would help in this pinch? In my young days the very neighbours would have been moved to interfere, whether you would or not. Yes, I believe you're proud; the noble spirit comes very seldom without its attending demon. But look here, man—a heart that would be quick to offer help should not be above receiving it. I am but a poor man myself, or I warrant well you should not escape me, however loth your grandeur might be. Here's the question; I speak to you boldly, as your friend, offence or no offence. Had your godfather never a dear friend that would stand by his heir? Tut! don't interrupt me—if you are heir to little money, all the more reason you should be heir to the love. Is there never a man in this country that for the kindness he bears your late friend, or for affection to you, would hold you his hand to mount you fair in your saddle, ere you set out on the world? Answer me plainly and truly, young man—is there no such person in country or town, within twenty miles of the place where you have lived all your days?"

Musgrave had changed colour several times during this address, and evidently hesitated much to answer. After close questioning, the Colonel at last drew from him that one such friend did exist, but not within twenty miles, in the person of a county baronet, a very dear friend of his late godfather, who had, however, been absent from the district for more than a year, and of whom, during that time, Roger had heard nothing. He could not tell where he was to be found, and it was with extreme reluctance that he confessed even his name, which was one unknown to Colonel Sutherland. Having gone so far, the young man set himself with all his might to combat the Colonel's idea of asking help from anybody. He would not—could not—accept a service which he had no prospect of ever being able to repay. He was determined not to enter the world weighed down by a burden of obligation. Was it not better to enter life a common soldier, with only himself to depend upon, he asked vehemently, than to reach a higher level by the help of another, and live with the shadow of assistance and patronage upon all his life?

"Would you choose to go through your life without assistance?" said Colonel Sutherland, calmly, making a note in his pocketbook, and going on with the conversation without looking up—"would you reject kindness and friendship, and the hand of your neighbour? Have a care, young man—the next step to receiving no help is giving none. Would you live without the charities of life, you foolish boy? And what's to hinder you entering life with a feeling of obligation? I would like to know a nobler and a kindlier sentiment than honest manful gratitude. Can you tell me a better? And how do you know you will never be able to repay it? Do you debar yourself from ever helping another, when you accept help yourself? Go away with your nonsense. I trust I am not the man to advise any youngster against his honour. What do you say—a man is the best judge for himself? No such thing, boy. Not when the man is twenty. I will tell you what to do in the meantime—keep quiet for a week or two, and leave the affair in my hands."

"But you do not know me. I may be deceiving you—telling you lies—working on your goodnature, for my own advantage," exclaimed Musgrave, with a voice which, between vexation and gratitude, and the new hopes which, in spite of himself, began to gain ground upon him, was almost inaudible.

"Eh?—I'm rather hard of hearing. I did not quite catch what you said," said Colonel Sutherland, bending towards him his deaf ear, with that look of anxious, solicitous kindness and earnest attention which nobody could resist.

The effect upon poor Roger was almost laughable in its pathos. He turned red—he turned pale—he could hardly keep the tears out of his boyish eyes; and, with a voice broken with emotion, shouted out his words so loud and harsh, that the Colonel started back in alarm and surprise.

"You don't know me—I may be deceiving you!" cried the young man, with a hurried and abrupt conclusion, singularly like a sob; and so hid his face in his hands, unable to contain himself, disturbed out of all the self-possession which thinly veiled the quick susceptibilities of grief.

The Colonel patted him gently on the arm with his kind hand.

"That is true," he said, with the simple wisdom of his pure heart, "very true—you might be deceiving me—but you are not."

CHAPTER XVIII

It is possible that Colonel Sutherland might have perhaps experienced a little annoyance at himself next day, for having so completely taken up and taken charge of the fortunes of his new protegé. That, however, did not give him half so much thought and perplexity as the other question which this morning presented itself to him more immediately, and demanded a settlement—How to meet, and what to decide upon for Horace. This was a very different matter from the simple help which he could offer frankly to the straightforward Musgrave; and all his doubts of the previous night returned to him with fresh force, as he considered the subject once more. He had not still an idea upon the matter. His own thoughts as to the choice of occupations for a young man ran in rather a circumscribed channel. The first thing which occurred to him involuntarily was, of course, his own profession; and India naturally associated itself to the old Indian officer with all hopes of advancement—but there was something in Mr. Scarsdale's secret, whatever it might be, which made Colonel Sutherland shake his head. "No, that would never do," he said to himself; "he must be on the spot whatever happens."

After that the Colonel thought of the learned professions of Medicine, and the Church, which his acquaintance with Edinburgh kept foremost in his mind—and shook his head over these also, concluding his nephew to be too old to begin an elaborate course of study. Lagging a long way after these, a faint and vague idea of "business" loomed through mists upon the Colonel's mind; he was very well aware of all that it is common to say of British commerce and enterprise—the vast concerns of our trade, and the princely wealth of our merchants; but, notwithstanding, knew as little about these great realities as it is possible for a man brought up in a society innocent of trade, and occupied all his life with the duties of an exclusive profession, to know. He had not the slightest idea what it would be proper to do to introduce a young man into "business." He had no influence to rely upon, nor friend to turn to for enlightenment upon the matter. He began to turn over in his mind the long roll of his allies and acquaintance—to think who he could best apply to; when suddenly finding himself pass in that review name after name of Scotch lawyers, in all their different grades, from the "writer" to the advocate, a brilliant idea burst upon him—the law!—it was evidently of all others the profession which Horace Scarsdale was best fitted for. How strange that he should not have thought of it before!

Somewhat reassured by this idea, the Colonel sat down to breakfast with increased comfort. It was again a drizzly, uncomfortable day—by no means the kind of day which one would choose to spend away from the resources and solaces of home, in the dreary little parlour of a country inn, with the Fool of Quality on the table, and defunct winners of the Oaks and Derby upon the walls. The Colonel stirred the fire, and returned to his pink rasher of country bacon with a sigh. He thought of his cosy sitting-room, warmly-curtained and carpeted, where all the draughts were carefully extinguished with mats, and list, and sand-bags, and from the windows of which he could see the noble Forth and the Fife coast, always bright, attractive, and full of beauty to his eyes. He thought of his books, companions of his life, and of the Times, which was one of his very few personal indulgences, and which at that very moment, all fragrant from the press in its post envelope, would be lying on his table; and the Colonel, munching his bacon with teeth which were not so perfect as they used to be, shrugged his shoulders as he glanced out of the low parlour-window upon the wet houses opposite, and the dim drizzle of rain. If it must be confessed, he thought of his proposed walk to Marchmain, through five miles of that dreary, damp, and dismal road, with a shiver, and terrible imaginations of rheumatism; yet this room and the Fool of Quality were not much more entertaining. And he could not bear the idea of disappointing Susan, who, the old man was pleased to think, would be watching for and expecting him. Then he pleased himself with the thought of carrying Susan home with him, and making her mistress and housekeeper of the house of his old age. He was glad to escape from his perplexities about Horace by thinking of Susan. There was no vexation nor doubt in the remembrance of the candid, honest, affectionate girl, who answered so warmly to his fatherly affections. Would her father give her up, even for a time, to her uncle? Colonel Sutherland, remembering his interview with Mr. Scarsdale, did not think it was likely; but he was young enough at heart, in spite of probabilities, to take pleasure in the thought.

He had just finished breakfast, and the room was beginning to brighten under the influence of a good fire, between which and the Fool of Quality the Colonel felt more drowsy than he thought it creditable to be in the morning, when Horace made his appearance. The young man came in with drops of rain shining all over his rough coat, and with muddy boots, which he had taken no pains to clean before entering, and which offended the Colonel's professional and natural fastidiousness. The rain-drops flew over into his uncle's face as Horace threw off his coat. The Colonel looked on with a mortified displeasure, wondering over him;—he could not understand how it happened that so near a relation of his own should have so little natural grace of manner or perception of propriety. Accordingly, he looked very grave as he shook hands with Horace. He could not enter immediately on the more important subject between them; he could not help criticizing these lesser matters, and thinking how he could manage to suggest an improvement without wounding his nephew; for the Colonel, like other people, had his weaknesses, and in his opinion a disregard of the ordinary proprieties showed a dulness of heart.

As for Horace, he on his part showed no particular anxiety about the question of the day—he was more inclined a great deal to draw his uncle into conversation on general subjects connected with his past life, his former visits to England, and the intercourse he formerly had with his sister and her husband. To this conversation Horace himself contributed a little description of their dinner-table on the previous evening, which was indeed a very dismal picture, and could scarcely be exaggerated. The Colonel shook his head over the story with pain and distress, grieved for the facts, and still more grieved to know that they rather gained than lost in bitterness by his nephew's recital. This stimulated him to introduce the real subject-matter of the present conference.

"It is natural enough, under all the circumstances, and I daresay advisable as well," said the Colonel, "that you should wish to get away as soon as possible. Then as to what you are going to do, Horace, I come to the question under great difficulties. In the first place, when you leave me to choose for you, it almost appears as if I were the person sending you away, and not your own desire; and I have no object in sending you away, you must be aware."

"What does it matter, uncle, how it appears, when we know exactly how it is?" said Horace, with apparent impatience and real craftiness.

"That is very true, and the most sensible thing I have heard you say," said the unsuspecting Colonel. "Well then, Horace, my boy, there's business. I don't know very well how to set about it, but no doubt we could inquire; and I believe, for a man who desires to get on, there is nothing equal to that."

"If a man has money to begin with, sir," said Horace. "No, uncle, I detest buying and selling—that will not do for me."

"Then you detest what many a better man than either you or I has practised, Horace," said the Colonel, a little affronted. "And there is my own profession. I have some little influence to serve a friend; but to be a soldier—a real soldier—I don't mean a man of parades and barracks, for at present you are not rich enough for that—requires a strong natural inclination. No—I see your answer—that will not do either; and indeed I think you're right. Then—I speak to you frankly, Horace—I would not advise you, for instance, to think of the Church."

"Because I am not good enough," said Horace, feeling his pride wounded by the suggestion, yet laughing with a contempt of the goodness which could conform itself to that level; "and also, uncle, because I have no education and no influence—that of course is impossible."

Colonel Sutherland could not help making an involuntary comparison between Roger Musgrave's humble declaration of want of wit and want of teaching, and this confession, which sounded the same in words. But Horace made his avowal with all the egotistic confidence of a young man who knew nothing of the world; and having never met his equals, in his heart thought education a very trivial circumstance, and believed his talent to be such as should triumph over all disadvantages. The Colonel gave a little suppressed sigh in his heart, and said to himself that nothing would show the boy his mistake—nothing but life.

"Well then, Horace," he cried, with sudden animation, remembering his own brilliant idea, "what do you think of the Law? So far as I can see, that is exactly the thing which is best suited to your genius—eh? My wonder is that it should never have occurred to yourself. What do you think of that, my boy?—the very thing for you, is it not?"

"The Law?" said Horace—"do you mean to make me an attorney, uncle?"

"I mean that you should make yourself anything that you may prove yourself to have a talent for," said the Colonel. "What, boy! you must have some idea as to what you're good for—attorney, solicitor, advocate—I am not particular for my part, but let it be something. It's an honourable profession when it's exercised with honour: in my opinion, it's the thing most suitable to your manner of mind. Eh?—don't you think so now yourself?"

Horace leaned over the table with his elbows on it, and his chin supported in his palms. It flashed upon him as he gazed into the air, and thought with little goodwill over this project, that the practitioners of the Law were men who knew everybody's secrets; that the power of the profession lay in its craft, and the skill with which it laid things together; that to lawyers, of all the different grades, belonged especially the task of finding out, and of concealing everything which it was for the interests of the rest of the world to discover or to hide. This idea sent a little animation into his face; he began to feel that this might really be congenial to the habits of his mind, as his uncle said; and, at all events, he might thus be in the way of discovering those secrets which affected his own life.

"The Law, like every other profession, requires study and time," said Horace, with, at last, a sincere sigh; "and I have no chance of being able to wait or to learn, uncle. No! it is impossible—my father will do nothing for me. If I could be a clerk, or something, and pick up what information I might," he continued, warming to the idea, as it seemed more and more impracticable; "but, as for study, what can I do?"

"My dear boy," said the Colonel, warmly, "if you really feel that you can go into this with all your mind, I will not hesitate to speak to your father. I believe he has not been kind to you—but no father in the world will sacrifice the future of his son for the sake of a trifling sum of money, or a little trouble. No, Horace, you do your father injustice. If you really can go into this—if you feel yourself ready to give your whole might to it, and make thus a deliberate choice of your profession, I feel sure he will not deny you the means. No, my boy—you are wrong; trust to me; I will see him myself."

"I shall be very glad, uncle, if you will make the experiment," said Horace; "but I know him better—he will do nothing for me. No!—he'd rather see me an errand-boy or a street-sweeper, than help me to the profession of a gentleman. I have known it for years; but still, if you will take the trouble, and undergo the pain of asking him, of course I can only be thankful. Try, uncle—I will not be disappointed if you fail, and you will be satisfied. I can only say try."

"Yes; but my condition of trying is that you are resolved to go into this, and think it a thing in which you can succeed," said the Colonel, fixing his eyes anxiously on his nephew's face.

Horace did not look at him in return; but there was an animation and eagerness unusual to it in his face—he was following out in imagination, not a young man's vague, ambitious dreams, but a chain of elaborate researches after the one secret which he could not discover, and which haunted him night and day. "I do!" he exclaimed, with an emphasis of sincerity and earnestness which delighted the Colonel, who seized him by the hand, and promised, over and over again, to leave no exertion untried which could obtain him his wish. Horace responded to this with the best appearance of gratitude and cordiality which he could manage to show, but with, in reality, a great indifference. He had no hope whatever from his uncle's mediation, and was forming other and secret plans in his own mind for his own object, which was not the same as Colonel Sutherland's; for he did not dream of success in the profession which he was about to choose, or of "scope for his talents," or any of those natural ambitions which occurred to the old soldier—but had entirely concentrated his underground and cavernous thoughts upon this new and unthought of mode, of carrying his personal inquiries out.

Having settled this matter to his great satisfaction, Colonel Sutherland walked to the window and contemplated the weather: it had ceased to rain, but the chill, damp, penetrating atmosphere was as ungenial as ever; the roads were wretched, and he shuddered involuntarily to think of that bare and miserable moor. However, the Colonel had already been three days at Tillington; and did not admire his quarters sufficiently to remain longer than he could help. Then this interview with his brother-in-law, being eminently disagreeable, would be well over. He hesitated, looked wistfully at his good fire, and with melancholy eyes at the dark sky without; but, at last, taking courage, buttoned on his great-coat, threw his cloak round him, took his stick in his hand, and thus defended from cold and violence, took his way once more, Horace by his side, to Marchmain.

CHAPTER XIX

The walk was not more agreeable than Colonel Sutherland foresaw it would be—the return the old soldier actually failed of courage for. He directed the gig to be sent for him, and so trudged upon his way without the dreadful thought of retracing all his steps in an hour or two. When they reached Marchmain there was no welcome vision of Susan at the window to solace her uncle's fatigue. When Peggy admitted them it was with an exclamation of surprise and half-indignation. "To think of walking such roads, five miles on a day like this!" she cried, as she bustled into the dining-room after them to refresh the smouldering, half-dead fire. Peggy was by no means rejoiced that day to see Colonel Sutherland. To the shame of her housewifery she remembered that she had nothing in her larder which could be cooked readily for the visitor's luncheon; and Peggy, like most other women of her years, country-bred, was overpowered by shame at the idea of having "nothing to offer" to the chance guest. Susan had gone upstairs, up to a garret room, the highest of the house, to fetch Peggy some apples which were stowed there; and as she was too high up to be able to hear the arrival of her uncle, Horace went to seek her. Peggy gazed after him, pausing in her cares for the fire, with a singular vexation.

"If that lad would but tell the truth—and all the truth," said Peggy; "but he wunnot, Cornel—it's somegate in his blood. I warrant he never told you a word how Miss Susan begged and prayed him to say you were never to think to come; that you would catch cold and wet, and do yoursel' an injury, as it was just like her to say, the thoughtful thing. Na, says I to myself, as I saw him march away with his shut-up face, the Cornel'll come or no come as his ain will bids, but Mr. Horace has no mind to stop him; yet if ye'll believe me, he never said a word, but let Miss Susan believe he would tell her messages every one."

"Never mind," said Colonel Sutherland—who, however, did mind a good deal, as people generally do who use that expression—and who could not help thinking that Susan's messages, had he ever received them, would have turned the scale and kept him under cover that miserable day. "Never mind, Peggy; I ought to take it as a compliment that Horace likes my society so much. I wish I could carry my niece home with me, poor child—eh? do you think her father would be likely to consent?"

"Eh, Mr. Edward, run not the risk of asking!" cried Peggy; "I'm no the person to speak an evil word of him, no me—but he's unhappy himself, as how do you think he can be other?—and he will not have happiness come near his house. Eh, Cornel, honey, if ye could but beguile him to open his heart! I knowed him a boy, and I knowed him a young man, and I knowed him in the mistress's time, but, sir, though he had his faults, and I would not deny them, all the days of his life, you would not reckonise him now; and all along o' that weary ould man!"

"Hush, Peggy! we must not blame those that are gone," said the gentle Colonel; "they are in other hands than ours; but it has been a melancholy business altogether. Horace, do you know, wishes to leave home and begin the world for himself."

"And the sooner the better, Cornel!" cried Peggy; "the lad will be clean ruined, root and branch, if he bides here. I would give all the pennies I've gathered all my life to see him safe out of that door, though he's a strange lad, is Mr. Horace. Hoosht, they're coming—listen, Cornel," said Peggy, stretching up to the Colonel's ear, that she might whisper this last communication—"Don't you be afeard about Miss Susan. I've that confidence in the Lord, I believe the poor chyild will fall to your hands, Mr. Edward, when the time comes; but, Lord bless you, Cornel, she's no more like her brother nor the tares is like the corn. Her heart's as sweet as a rose—nothing in this world can kill the good that's in that unfortinate infant, but Death itself. Hoosht, here they are coming!—she's just the delight of an ould woman's eyes—ay, there she is!"

The Colonel heard this speech very imperfectly, understanding just enough of it to know that Susan was commended, and nodding his kind head in pleased acquiescence; but when Peggy ended her oration by crying "There she is!" Uncle Edward turned round to greet his niece, who came running up to him out of breath. Susan was sorry, shocked, surprised, and delighted—but underneath all her flutter the Colonel, whose vision was quick when those whom he loved were concerned, saw at a glance that her eyes were red, and that even her joy in seeing him was made half-hysterical by some other sentiment lying under it, which she did not wish him to see. This contradiction of feeling, new and unusual to her, made Susan unlike herself. Her manner was hasty and agitated—she laughed as if to keep herself from crying. Colonel Sutherland looked at her with silent distress and sympathy. What new development of trouble had appeared now?

"Why did you come?" cried Susan. "I wanted Horace to carry a note, and he would not; but he promised to tell you what I said. And your rheumatism, uncle—I am so distressed to think you should have come all this way for me."

"But suppose I did not come all this way for you?" said Colonel Sutherland. "Don't you think my visit is too important to be all for a little girl? No, my love, I should have come for you whether or not—but to-day, I mean, if possible, to see your father."

Peggy had left the room, and Horace had not yet entered it: the two were alone together.

"To see papa!" cried Susan, with a look of dismay, clinging suddenly to her uncle's arm, and looking up in his face. "Oh, uncle, not to-day!"

"And why not to-day, my dear child?" said the Colonel, tenderly; "what has happened to-day? You have been crying, Susan. Can you tell why that was?"

With his kind eyes searching into her face, and his tender arm supporting her, Susan could not keep up her feint of good spirits; she faltered, cast down her eyes, tried to speak, and then fell unawares into a passion of youthful tears—hot, angry, indignant, rebellious tears—the first overflow of personal mortification, injury, and wounded feeling—tears too warm and too plentiful to blight or kill. The Colonel soothed her and bent over her with alarm and anxiety—he was almost too much interested to be a good judge of the depth of her suffering, and for the first moment thought it much more serious than it was.

"Papa called me into the study to-day; he said that you—I mean he said that I was careless of him, and did not do what I ought," said Susan, who had evidently changed her mind, and substituted these words for some others injurious to her uncle. "He said I loved you better in three days than I had loved him for all my life. Oh, uncle, can I help it?—is it my fault?—for nobody until now ever loved me!"

"Hush, my dear child!—is that all?" said Colonel Sutherland. "Come, come, do not cry—I daresay you were thinking of something else at breakfast, and forgot what you were about—perhaps Letty. He will soon forgive you, my love. Sometimes I have a row with my Ned when he is at home. Don't cry, my dear child."

"Ah, uncle, but you don't understand it," cried poor Susan, rather disappointed to have her sorrow undervalued; "he wanted me not—not"—and here with a great burst the truth came out—"not to keep your presents—nor to see you—nor to write to you—nor anything: he said he would not permit it; he said I belonged to him, and so I think he believes. I do, uncle," cried Susan, with fire and indignation, "like a table or a chair!"

"Hush, my child! I wonder why he objects to me, Susan," said the Colonel, with a little grieved astonishment. "And what did you say?"

"I said I would not, uncle—I could not help it!" cried Susan, with another burst of tears. "I never disobeyed him in my life before; but I was very obstinate and stubborn. I know I was. I said I would not do what he told me. I can't! I will not! I will stay in Marchmain, and never seek to go away. I will do everything else he tells me. I will work like Peggy, if he pleases; but I will write to you, uncle, and see you whenever I can, and love you always. Oh! uncle, uncle, do not you be angry with me too!"

"I!" said Uncle Edward, his voice faltering, "my poor dear, child!—I!—if I only could carry you home with me, Susan! It is hard to think I have given you more, instead of less to suffer. Ah, Susan, if I could but take you home with me!"

Susan dried her eyes, comforted by the words. "I must not hope for that, uncle," she said, with more composure; "and indeed I could not leave papa, either. He is very unhappy, I am sure. If I only knew what to do for him! And I don't want him to think me stubborn and undutiful. He is angry, and disturbed, and strange this morning. I never saw him so before. Do not speak to him to-day."

"Would it be better to-morrow?" said Colonel Sutherland. "No, Susan, especially after what you told me. I must not stay here longer than I can help, and I must see your father before I go; it is about Horace, my love. I have promised to speak of his wishes. I did not know," cried Colonel Sutherland, with a little mortification, "that I should hurt his cause by pleading it; but I ought to see him at anyrate. No, I cannot submit to this without any appeal. I have lived in his house, and eaten his bread, and had never a moment's dispute with him. It is impossible; there must be some mistake."

And Colonel Sutherland went to the window, and stood looking out, with his eyebrows puckered, and his hands behind him; while Susan, drying her eyes again, went to stir the neglected fire. Everything was cold, meagre, uncomfortable, and the poor girl's restless curiosity, eager to prove her devotion to himself, yet glancing now and then with terror at the door, as if she feared her father's appearance, and a scene of strife, was not lost upon the Colonel. He stood for some time in silence, considering the whole matter, vexed, and mortified, and indignant, yet feeling more of honest pain for the position of the household, and for unfortunate recluse himself, than offence in his own person. Then, without saying anything to Susan, the old soldier marched silently towards the study-door. It was necessary now, to say what had to be said, at once.

CHAPTER XX

Mr. Scarsdale was alone in the study, where he passed his recluse life. The fire burned low in the grate, the red curtains hung half over the window, the atmosphere was close and stifling. He sat in his usual seat, with the invariable book before him. But though it was hardly possible for him to be more pale, there was something in the colour of his face, in the rigidity of his attitude, which betrayed a smothered passion and excitement exceeding his wont. When Colonel Sutherland knocked at the door, he got up with a kind of convulsive haste, stepped towards it at one hasty stride, and opened it. He thought it might be Susan, returned to make her submission. When he saw his brother-in-law, Mr. Scarsdale gazed at him with undisguised amazement and a sullen rage. He stood facing the Colonel, holding the door, but without inviting or even permitting him to enter. "I have something important to say to you," said the old soldier—"permit me to come in. I shall not detain you." Then the recluse stepped back suddenly, opening the door wide, but without uttering a word. Colonel Sutherland went in, and the door was closed upon him; they stood opposite each other, looking in each other's faces. The Colonel, with a grieved surprise and appeal in his look, the other with his head bent, and nothing but sullen, smothered passion in his face. Two men more unlike never stood together in this world. For the first moment not a word passed between them, but their looks, full of human motion and painful life, made the strangest contrast in the silence, with the motionless, dreary quiet of this stifling room.

After this pause, natural wonder and impatience seized the Colonel; he could not resist the impulse of trying to right himself—to right his brother-in-law—to recover if possible a natural position. "Robert!" he exclaimed, suddenly, with unpremeditated warmth and emotion, "why is this?—what have I done to you?—is there any reason why you cannot receive me as of old?"

"I beg your pardon," said Mr. Scarsdale, with a formal inclination of his head. "My life and all my habits differ very widely from yours. I have long made a rule against admitting strangers into my house. My circumstances are peculiar, as you are aware—perhaps my dispositions are peculiar too."

"But, for heaven's sake!" cried the Colonel, who found this repulse not so decisive as he had feared—"why shut out me?"

Once more the solitary man bowed, with a sarcastic respect. "Again, I beg your pardon; but it does not follow," said Mr. Scarsdale, with a smile, which would have been insulting, but that it trembled with unreasonable passion, "that a man's own favourable opinion of himself is shared by all the world."

The Colonel looked at him with a hasty, astonished glance, a look of compassion and surprise, which wounded the pride of his companion to the quick.

"Well, then," cried the master of Marchmain, "I decline to receive you—your society is disagreeable to me. Is not that enough?"

"That is perfectly enough," said Colonel Sutherland; "now, I have only my commission to discharge, and I am grieved I should have made so unfavourable a beginning. I come to you on behalf of your son."

"Of my son!—oh! and of my daughter also, I presume! You would wish me to bring her 'out,' and give parties for her—perhaps you would like her to have a season in London?" said Scarsdale, with his trembling lip, and the forced smile of his passion—"is there anything else I can do for you?—for, as it happens, I choose to take Susan into my own hands."

"I say nothing of Susan," said the Colonel, gravely; "if you choose to debar the poor child from all the pleasures of her youth, it is not for me to interfere. She is in God's hands, who will guide her better than either you or I. I come to you from your son. Horace is a man grown, very nearly of an independent age, clever, ambitious, and at that time of life when youths would fain see the world and act for themselves; do you think it right to keep him here without occupation or training, in the most precious years of his life? I come to you with a humble entreaty from the young man, that you will give him your permission and help to set forth upon the world for himself."

"That is admirable!" said Mr. Scarsdale—"my permission and help? This is the first time I have heard of the faintest desire on his part;—nay, I do not believe that he does desire it—you have made it up among you; and no doubt you have settled the manner as well as the fact. What profession, pray, does my clever son mean to devote himself to?"

"He wishes to study law," said the Colonel, laconically.

"Law?—to read for the bar, I presume?" said the father; "to have chambers in the Temple, and the pleasures of his youth. It is vastly well, Colonel Sutherland—I admire your project greatly—he has my permission by all means; as for my help, I do not need to inform you what kind of claim this young man has upon me. Is it likely I should take my straitened means, from my own comfort and my daughter's, to support him in luxury and idleness?—is it probable, do you think, that I will make a sacrifice for him? Can you look me honestly in the face and ask it of me?"

"I trust so," said the Colonel, with a little sadness. "Scarsdale, we are both fathers—we ought to be able to understand each other; is it necessary to weigh the nature of claims, the probabilities of temper, when one appeals to a father for the future life of his son?"

"My son's future life," said Mr. Scarsdale, vindictively, "is quite independent of me. Had there been any nature left in our mutual position things might have been different. No! my son has no need to betake himself to a profession—he is quite above the necessity. Should I accelerate the time when he shall come to his fortune? Should I beg your prayers—for I remember you are pious—that he may enter speedily upon his inheritance? I thank you. I do not profess to be quite so disinterested. No, let him wait!—let him take his share of the evils of mankind. Must I deny myself to smooth his path for him, and give him roses for my thorns? It would be the conduct of a fool. No, I repeat he has no need for a profession—let him wait! I support him—is it not enough?"

"Too much!" cried Colonel Sutherland; "you must perceive that it would be ten times better for him to support himself, to labour for himself, instead of embittering his life in this forced idleness here. Why should he be a burden on you at all, at his years? Though he does not ultimately require a profession, to have one would be his salvation now. You are a hale and healthy man, in spite of all you do to yourself—you have twenty years to live before you attain the limited age of man. Can you think of this unfortunate boy living here as he lives now, in utter ignorance of the fortune which waits him, till he is forty? Think of it, I implore you! It has lasted long enough—too long, Scarsdale. Think, if you have human bowels, human mercy in you, of the extraordinary fate to which you destine your only son. Suppose him growing into maturity, into full manhood, to years in which you had the world at your feet and children at your knees; yet kept in darkness, kept in bitterness, idle, solitary, able to think of nothing but of the injury that has been done to him; until, all at once, you are struck down in extreme desolate old age—and wealth, which is no longer anything to him, wealth which will disgust him, falls into his hands. What! you turn away—you will not have that event even mentioned? What are you thinking of? Is a miserable heap of money of more importance to you than the welfare of your son?"

"Upon my word," said Mr. Scarsdale, turning away with a violent colour on his face, and an exclamation of disgust, "I see no reason in the world why I should study the welfare, as you call it, of my son."

"You do not—and you can say so?" cried the Colonel, in loud and stern astonishment.

"I do not, and I can say so, and without raising my voice," said the other, with a sneer. "My son, I beg to tell you once again, is provided for. I give him food and clothing—he has nothing else to hope or to expect from me."

"This is all then that you have to say?" said Colonel Sutherland; "you will not assist him to make his life honourable and useful? Will you explain to him why you decline doing so?—will you tell him that his future is so secured, that a profession is unnecessary to him? Do the boy some justice—let there be a natural explanation between you. You cannot expect him to go on in this way for years. Could you wish it? I beseech you, either tell him how matters stand, or help him to carry out his most lawful and virtuous wish! Will you do one or the other? I beseech you, tell me!"

"I tell you no!" said Mr. Scarsdale. "Let the dog wait! I will neither put myself in his power, nor help him to the best means of spying out my secret. No! Have I spoken distinctly?—he shall have neither confidence nor assistance from me!"

"Is it possible?" cried the Colonel, driven to an extremity of mingled wonder, indignation, and pity; "for the sake of your own exasperated feelings, can you make up your mind to revenge yourself, by ruining this unhappy lad, your only son, for ever?"

"I beg your pardon—this unhappy lad is very well off," said his extraordinary father; "so well off, that I certainly do not find myself called upon to do any more for him—although," said Mr. Scarsdale, with a glance of bitterness upon the kind, anxious face which bent towards him, "I am aware that to help a man who does not require help is understood to be the way of the world."

The Colonel's weather-beaten face flushed high with angry colour; he was surprised and grieved and wounded to his heart, but he had still and always this advantage over his adversary, that the unkindest insinuation which Scarsdale could make made his brother-in-law only the more sorry for him, and wrought more grief than passion in his mind. After the first moment he looked wistfully into the face of his former friend, with a compassionate and troubled amazement, which, little though the Colonel intended it, roused his companion to fury. "How you must be changed!" he said, sadly, "to be able to say such words to me;" and Colonel Sutherland sighed as he spoke, with the hopeless patience of a man who sees no means of bringing good out of evil. The sigh, the tone, and the look wound up the recluse into the utmost rage; he made a wild imperative gesture and exclamation—for his voice was choked with fury—and opened the door violently. It was thus that Colonel Sutherland's appeal and hopes for Horace concluded; he left the study without another word.

CHAPTER XXI

"Yes, Susan, I am going away presently, and I fear I shall not see you again either," said Colonel Sutherland, with a cheerfulness which he was far from feeling—"that is, not this time, my love; but there is plenty of time, if it be the Lord's will, Susan. You are very young, and I am not very old. We are tough, we old Indians; we wear a long time, and we shall meet, my dear child, I don't doubt, many happy days."

Susan looked up to him with inquiring eyes—with eyes, indeed, so full of inquiry that he thought she must have spoken, and put his hand to his ear. "No, uncle, I did not say anything," cried Susan, touched by that gesture almost out of her self-possession. The poor girl turned away her head and rubbed her eyes with her trembling fingers, to send back the tears. When might eyes so tender shine in that forlorn solitude again? It was impossible to look at the old man, with his solicitous kindness, his anxious look of attention, and even the infirmity which threw a tenderness and humility so individual and characteristic upon his whole bearing, in the thought of, perhaps, never seeing him again, without emotion. It was to Susan as if the sunshine was departing. He might go away, she might never see him again, but nothing could obliterate the effect of that three days visit; nothing in the world could make Susan what she was when this week began. She did not know how it was, but the fact was indisputable; her undisturbed and unsusceptible content was over for ever. Was it good for Susan? She did not ask the question, but rubbed back the tears, and stood close to her uncle, intent upon hearing the last words which he might have to say, and vowing to herself that she would not grieve him by crying—not if she should faint or die the moment he was gone.

Such resolutions are hard to keep. When the Colonel laid his kind hand upon her head, Susan trembled over her whole frame. Her unshed tears—the youthful guilty anger provoked by her father, which still palpitated in her heart—which the poor child could not overcome, yet felt to be wrong; and the unusual agitation of this crowd of diverse feelings, very nearly overcome her. Her cheeks grew crimson, her lips and her eyelids trembled, yet she controlled herself. And Uncle Edward was still making light of the injury to himself—still accepting his repulse as something natural and spontaneous; it moved her to an indignation wild, impetuous, and unlike her character; but there was no blame on the Colonel's lips.

"Some time or other you will come to my little house, and see the country where your mother was born," said Uncle Edward; "we shall not know what to make of you when we get you there—you will be queen and princess, and do what you please with us. Yes, I hope after a time your father will consent to it, my love. He is rather angry just now, but time will soften that down. And remember, Susan, you must make the best and not the worst of everything. Horace does that last, you know, and 'one wise body's enough in a house,' as we say in Scotland; you must be the foolish one, my little Susan, and always hope; everything will turn out well, under the blessing of God."

"I hope so, uncle," said Susan, with an involuntary sob.

"Perhaps, my dear child, I ought to say you must obey your father, and not write to me," said Uncle Edward—"but I am not quite virtuous enough for that; only always do it honestly, Susan—never conceal it from him—and stop if it should make you unhappy, or you find it out to be wrong in your own conscience. However, I shall write to you in any case. My boy Ned will want to come and see you, I fear, before he leaves the country. You must always remember that you are of great importance to us, Susan, though we have not the first claim on you. You are the only woman in the family; you represent all those who are gone, to me, my little girl. Hush! do not cry—you must be very strong and courageous, for all our sakes."

"I am not crying!" cried Susan, with a gasp of fervent resolution, though she could scarcely articulate the words.

"That is right, my darling," said the Colonel. "Now, don't let us think any more about it, Susan. We shall hear from each other constantly, and some time or other I'll show you Inveresk, and Edinburgh, and your mother's country; and in the meantime, you will be cheerful and brave like yourself. Now tell Peggy to bring me some bread and cheese, my love—I am going to be grand to-day; my carriage is coming for me presently. Where is Horace? I must see him before I go—call him here, Susan, and order me my bread and cheese."

Susan was very glad, as her uncle suspected, to run out of the room for a moment, and deliver herself of the sob with which she was choking. When she was gone, Colonel Sutherland looked sadly round him upon the dreary apartment, to which the agitation of this day had given a more than usually neglected and miserable appearance. He shook his head as he glanced round upon those meagre walls, and out to that bare moor, which was the only refuge for the eye. He thought it a terrible prison for a girl of seventeen, unsweetened by any love or society. He thought that even the departure of Horace, though he was not much of a companion to his sister, would aggravate her solitude; and involuntarily the old man thought of his own bright apartments at Inveresk, and wondered, with a natural sigh, over the strange problems of Providence. Had Susan been a child of his own, saved to him from among the many dead, what a different lot had been hers!—but here was this flower blossoming in the desert, where no one cared for its presence—and his hearth was solitary. He did not repine or complain—ingratitude had no place in his tender Christian soul, but he sighed and wondered at the bottom of his heart.

In a few minutes Horace joined him. Horace did not care to form the third of a party which included his uncle and his sister. Their friendship annoyed him, he could not tell how; it was an offence to Horace that they seemed to understand one another so entirely; far superior as he thought himself, he was conscious that neither the one nor the other was intelligible to him. He came, however, with a little excitement on hearing that the Colonel had been with his father, expecting little, yet curious, as he always was about everything, done and said, by his perennial and lifelong antagonist. When he entered the room Colonel Sutherland held out his hand to him with an affectionate sympathy, which he accepted with astonishment, and not without a passing sneer in his mind at the idea of being consoled, either for such a supposititious disappointment, or in such a manner. It was with a feeling very different from a young man's anxiety to know his fate, or expectation of a decision which should influence his life, that he waited to hear what his uncle had to say.

"I am sorry to tell you, Horace, you have judged more correctly than I did," said the Colonel, with hesitation; "I find, to my great disappointment, that your father is not disposed to assist you, my dear boy. I don't know what to say about it—it appears that he has taken some erroneous idea into his mind about myself. I'm afraid the advocate hurt the cause, Horace. If some one else spoke to him, perhaps—; but however that might be, to my great concern and astonishment, he has quite refused me!"

"Don't trouble yourself about it, uncle; I knew how it would be," said Horace, his eyes lighting up with the unnatural contention which had pervaded his life. "It was not the advocate, but the cause which was hopeless. What did he say?"

"He said—some things which had much better remained unsaid. He was affronted with me," said Colonel Sutherland; "but he gives his permission, Horace—not assistance, remember, but still permission—that is always something; he seems to have no objection that you should follow your own course, and do what you can for yourself."

"That is very kind of him," said Horace, with a smile; "but I rather think I never should have asked his leave, but for your hopes of help from him, which I never shared. I suppose he was amazed at the idea that I should expect anything from him. I daresay he appealed to you why he should take his own narrow means to support an idle vagabond like me. Ah! he did!—I could have sworn he would!"

"Nay, Horace," said the Colonel, who had been struck unawares by the correctness of his nephew's guess; "what is the use of imagining unkind words, which most likely were neither spoken nor intended? The fact is simple—your father does not think a profession is essential to you; he thinks that—that you will most probably have enough without. In short, he does not feel called upon to assist you; but at the same time, remember, Horace, he puts no obstacle in the way. All is not lost yet, my boy: I must try whether I can do anything. I am not rich, I have little to spare, but I have friends, and there are some people who might be interested in you. Wait a little, Horace—leave it to me, and we will see what can be done. I would not be discouraged; there are more ways than one of doing everything in this world."

"You may trust to me, uncle, that I certainly will not give up my own intention because my father declines to assist it—everything is safe enough so far," said Horace; "as for anything great, you know, study and that sort of thing, I give that up as impossible—I did so from the first. I will never be a great lawyer, uncle; but I daresay I'll learn enough for my own ends."

"Your own ends!—I don't understand you, Horace," cried the Colonel, somewhat alarmed at the expression of his nephew's face, and for perhaps the first time in his life suspecting something of double meaning in the words he heard.

"Have I not to work for my own living?—to support myself, uncle?" cried Horace, turning round upon him with a bitter emphasis.

"Very well, my lad, what then?" said Colonel Sutherland, with dignity—"is there anything very terrible in that? The best men in the world have had to work for their living. I am sorry for you that you cannot get the freedom of using your powers, and proper advantages for their cultivation; but I assure you, Horace, I am not sorry for you on the ground that you must support yourself."

"To be sure not," said Horace, with a little secret mortification; "but it is therefore I say that I will learn law enough for my own ends."

Once more the Colonel looked at him doubtfully, pondering the peculiar and unnecessary emphasis with which the young man pronounced these words. Colonel Sutherland perceived, in spite of his unsuspicious nature, that there was a gleam in the eye, and a sudden animation in the manner of Horace, which referred to something different from the calm means of sustenance, or the knowledge sufficient to secure it. Something vindictive and eager was in his look. The Colonel probably thought it better not to inquire too closely into it, for he turned away from Horace with a sigh.

Perhaps it was a relief to them all when the gig arrived at last, and Colonel Sutherland bade farewell to Marchmain. The old man was troubled because he trusted his niece, and knew that she would not deceive his expectations; and he was troubled because he could not trust his nephew, and did not feel at all warranted in undertaking for him. While Horace, for his part, brooded with renewed anger, though he professed to expect it, over his father's refusal of assistance, and was tired of amusing Colonel Sutherland by a show of good humour, all the more when his uncle seemed unlikely to be of much service to him; and the difficulty with which Susan kept her composure, and the unusual tumult of personal feeling in which the poor child felt herself, made the continued effort almost too much for her. The gig arrived at last. The Colonel said his last good-bye, and drove away from the inhospitable door which he had seen for the first time three days ago, leaving Susan, Horace, and Peggy outside, watching his departure, and waving farewells to him; and leaving, besides that external demonstration, a revolution in the house, and, for good or for evil, the germs, to these two young people, of a new world.

CHAPTER XXII

The Colonel drove away, out of sight of Marchmain and its moor, with thoughts many and troubled. This visit, which he had undertaken with so much simplicity of intention, had already thrown a disturbing influence into his life; he went away, bearing on his own very heart and conscience the burden of an unmanageable boy, and a girl neglected and suffering. An unmanageable boy! The Colonel summed up his non-comprehension of the character of Horace in these uncomplimentary words, and it was his first experience of the kind. He had never learned to doubt the honest common-places about youthful openness and candour which good hearts, like his own, receive and repeat so authoritatively. He could have laid down rules to any one, with a little mild dogmatism, and a world of kindness, for the management of "the young;" and would have told you, with affectionate complaisance, and not without an idea that judicious training had much to do with it, that his Addiscombe cadet had never given him a moment's anxiety. That was very true of honest Ned, to whom nature had given, not her fairy wealth of genius, but something safer; her gift of competency, if one may use the expression—a sincere, straightforward, sagacious soul—a judgment wise without knowing it, and true by instinct, to which craft or concealment were things impossible. Colonel Sutherland, "with his experience," as he said, did not believe in the youthful mystics, the Manfreds and Werters. He smiled in his kindly superiority and said, "Youth at bottom was very consistent in its inconsistencies, and very manageable if you took pains enough, and knew the right way." The Colonel was a little mortified, accordingly, to be obliged to conclude that he knew very little of Horace, and that his nephew baffled him. It put him out in his calculations—it spread a certain doubt over the whole fair face of nature, and left an ache in the old man's unsuspicious heart. He could not persuade himself to condemn, and therefore troubled his mind with the idea that he could not possibly understand.

It was early evening when the little vehicle reached the top of the slope from which the road descended to the village; and the twinkling lights in the shallow vale beneath, the hum of sound, the twilight calm through which the Colonel, whose eyes were equal to any practicable distance, though "small print" somewhat troubled them, recognized the different points of his morning and evening walks—filled the old man with a strange sensation of familiarity and friendship. Already, though he had been here so short a time, he knew the place, remembered the hedge-rows and the trees, could tell where was the best point of view, was able to distinguish from a distance the principal houses in the village, and could even recollect where the green primrose leaves lay warmest, and were likely to be first unrolled and spread into the light by the spring sun. Somehow, unawares to himself, the kind old man, with his warm natural sympathy, had established a certain connection with this unknown place. Here was Kennedy, his old companion-in-arms; here was young Musgrave, whom the Colonel seemed to have somehow adopted, in spite of himself, as the type of what Horace should have been, and in whom he had interested himself with an inexplicable rapidity and rashness which appeared very odd when he thought of it, though it was extremely natural. He recollected now that this second protegé must be looked after and seen this evening. The Colonel had become quite a man of affairs since he came to Tillington. All this time, occupied as he was by his own thoughts, the drive had been a very silent one—so much so, that honest John Gilsland, who had driven the gig himself in hopes of an opportunity of displaying his wisdom to "the Cornel," had been much disappointed of his expectations. John was supposed to play second fiddle in his own house; the "missis" had not so much respect for his talents and sagacity as became a wife, and the good man proportionately esteemed the chances of letting loose his opinions out of doors; and was especially anxious that "the Cornel" should not leave Tillington without being aware of his host's superiority. The honest fellow had been maundering on for some time about the houses which they passed before some chance words caught the Colonel's attention. He turned round rather sharply with the sudden "Eh!" of a mind pre-occupied. John Gilsland started so much, that he startled the mare, who tossed her head and winced, and showed inclinations "to mak' a boult of it," as her master said. This occurred, as it happened, near the spot where the Colonel had discovered Kennedy and his hare on the previous night. He raised himself with a little alarm, and peered into the darkness over the bushes, doubting that some concealed movement of the old poacher must have been the occasion of the mare's start. However, there was nothing to be seen behind the hedge, and John Gilsland recommenced his monologue, to which the Colonel now gave his ear, with a flattering attention which won his landlord's heart.

"As far as you can see—not that that's so far as might be wushed at this hour o' the nicht," said John, "was th' ould Mr. Musgrave's land, Cornel. Yon'er's the house, sir, amidst of a bit of wood—guid tim'er and ould, and a credit to the place. D'ye see the pair bit dribble o' smoke, Cornel?—th' ould chimneys puffed i' another fashion when the Squire was to the fore. There wasn't six days i' the twelve-month but there was coompany at the Grange, and a sight of fine folks wance or twicest in the year, like in September and the shooting saison. But ye cannot both eat your cake and have your cake, Cornel. There's this coom of it, that the siller's a' puffed away; and the young heir, poor lad, he's left destitute; and the more's the pity; for a more affable gentleman than Mr. Roger never carried a gun. That's him that coom to see yourself, sir, the last nicht—ye would be a friend o' his family, it's like?—for he's no of this parish born."

"Was the young man related to the Squire?—his godfather, I know—but they seem to be of the same name," said the Colonel; "he is a fine young fellow—he will have many friends, I presume, in the families hereabout."

"Ye see, Cornel," said John Gilsland, dropping the reins upon the mare's neck, and suffering her to fall into almost a walking pace, as he saw himself at last appreciated, "it makes an uncommon difference when a man gets shot of his siller. There was a time when Mr. Roger was foremost favourite mony's the place; but wan house ye see, there's a parcel o' young ladies, and what if wan o' them took a fancy to him? They're tender-hearted, them girls—they're just as like as no to fa' in love with a man, for the reason that's he's misfortinate. I've seen a young lad myself that lost a' he had, and was prosecooted by the women for ne'er anither reason that I could see. Then anither place you see there's a regiment o' sons, and my leddy wants a' the influence she can wun, fair means or foul, for her owen prodgedy; and another place, they've little enough themsels, and cannot afford to keep friends with wan that has not a penny—and that's how it stands, Cornel, on the whole. If he had th' ould Squire's estate, he'd ha' loads o' friends."

"Poor fellow!" said the Colonel, shrugging his shoulders, half with compassion, half with disgust—he was not very well acquainted with this phase of human nature. Nobody had ever suspected him of being rich, and he remembered, with a half smile, quickly followed by a sigh, the gleeful opposition to established authority, with which young Edward Sutherland, ensign or lieutenant, returned to the charge, when repulsed by a prudent mamma from the vicinity of her daughters. But he soon reverted with ready sympathy to the woes of the disinherited. "This Squire must have been a very imprudent man," he said, "or a very heartless one. Had he no regrets to leave the young man penniless?"

"Hoosht, Cornel!—Mr. Roger, sir, he's wild if a man dare whisper a word. He's broke with his acquaintance that he had, and the common sort o' folks, sir, that were sorry for him, and ready to make friends if he wushed—he's quarrelled with half the county, Cornel, because this wan and the tither said their mind o' th' Squire. He wull not have a reproach of him, not a word. He took even mysel' down as fast, I thought the nose was off my face, for saying, in an innocent way, that th' Squire was very free with his money when he had it, and so was seen on him. I would not say, but it's all the better of him, to stand up for wan as cannot stand up for himself no more. And I ne'er knew a man as was deceived in Mr. Roger, Cornel—he's hasty, but he's true. He'll gang in o' the auld wives' cots, and give the children pennies, but never put an affront on a lass, or refused satisfaction to a man, as far as ever I heard, all his born days."

"I am glad to know it," said the Colonel, with a little shiver,—"but we are surely making very slow progress. What's happened to the mare? She surely forgets that this is the road to her own stable. Eh?—a beast of her good sense seldom does that."

"She's fresh, sir, fresh—she minds no more for her own stable nor I do, Cornel. She's good for twenty mile and more, if there was the occasion," said John, caressing the animal with the end of his whip, but prudently increasing her pace.

"And, by-the-bye, I have a question to ask you—Sir John Armitage? What sort of a place has he?—is it near?—is he rich?—and where do you think he is to be found?" said the Cornel rapidly, as they approached near Tillington.

Once more the mare, much against her will, slackened her pace. "Ye see, Sir John Armitage, Cornel," said John, raising his hand in explanatory action, "he's wan of the great squires o' th' county. He wasn't born tull't, as ye may say. He was an army gentleman, sir, such like as yourself, and th' ould Sir John was as far off as his second cousin, a dissolute man, without neither chick nor child. This wan, he's grey and onmarried likewise—the title will gang, as it came, slantlike, to a nevvy or a cousin. It's the park, Cornel, a grand mansion as is his sait—but a desolate place, and him no more enjoyment in't nor me. Sir? The mare? Oh ay, she's jogging on."

"It's rather cold for this pace, it appears to me," said the Colonel, whose face, so much of it as was visible out of the cloak, was blue with cold. "Hey? Halt then! Do you mean to upset us? What's the matter with the beast now?"

"Na, Cornel, she's gane fast and she's gane slow, and nouther pleases—it's none of her blame, puir brute," said John, with affected humility. "I give her a taste o' the whip, and ye say I'll upset ye. Me! I'm the safest driver in ten mile; and as for my mare—there she is—she kens her gate hoam."

Where accordingly they arrived in a few minutes, and where the Colonel got down frozen, and limped into the little parlour, where the blazing fire comforted his eyes. But having been frozen stiff in the first part of the road, and then jolted almost to pieces in the concluding gallop, it was some time before his numb fingers had vigour enough to unloose his cloak, and his lips to speak. The landlady brought in wine, pushed it aside with a mild feminine imprecation upon the "cauld stuff," and came back presently with a steaming goblet of brandy and water. The Colonel was the most temperate of men, and had not had his dinner; but the siren seduced him—and the first words he uttered, when the frost in his throat began to melt, was an inquiry, which startled Mrs. Gilsland out of her propriety, for an "Army List," if such a thing was to be had.

"An 'Army List!'—eyeh, Cornel, what's that?" said the good woman in dismay.

"Are there any old officers about Tillington, Mrs. Gilsland? An 'Army List' is simply a list of the army," said the urbane Colonel. "Do you think you can manage to borrow one for half-an-hour from anybody in the village—eh? Consult with your husband, it is of importance to me."

"Him, Cornel? What does he know?" said the landlady. "Officers, na—unless it was th' Ould Hundred, begging your pardon, Cornel, for he's nothing but a sergeant; but that's the byname he goes by in my house."

"The Old Hundred? I'm an Old Hundred man myself," said the Colonel, laughing. "Kennedy, is it? No, he will not do, the old humbug—I suspect he tells the lads a parcel of lies about the regiment, and brings discredit on as fine a body of men as there is in the service. Eh?—is the sergeant a great man among ye here?"

"Oh, Cornel!" cried Mrs. Gilsland, "I'll go down to you on my bended knees if you'll say to my Sam, sir, what you say to me. He's wild for the sodgerin', is that lad! and th' Ould Hunderd he lays it on till him as if it was Paradise!—and an only son, Cornel, and a great help in the business, and if he 'lists, and go to the bad, what will I do?"

"But if he 'lists, he need not go to the bad," said the Colonel. "I'll speak to him if you like; but in the meantime, my 'Army List'? Is there nobody in Tillington who has a son an officer? Nobody who—"

"Bless my soul, what am I thinking on? To be sure, there's the Rectory!" cried the landlady, rushing out of the room in the fervour of her discovery. And the Cornel heard her immediately commission her son, who seemed to be at a distance, at the top of her voice, to run this moment to the Rectory, and ask if there was such a thing about the house as a list of all the regiments and officers, for a gentleman that was an officer himself, and a Cornel, and that was staying at the "Tillington Arms." "And thou'll take it in thyself, Sam," shouted the good woman, "with thy best manners, and never tarry on the road. The Cornel wants to speak to thee himself. Now, mind what I say!—he's something to tell 'ee lad, will put 'ee out o' conceit with th' Ould Hunderd—run, as if thou hadst wings to thy heels!"

The Colonel, sitting by his fire, gradually thawing, laughed to himself, and shrugged his shoulders as he heard this adjuration. Was he to be elected impromptu adviser of all the adventurous youth of Tillington? He sat in his chair, by the fire, wondering whether the 'Army List' could be had—whether Sir John Armitage would turn out to be Armitage of the 59th—and chuckling quietly over the Sergeant's nickname, until, in the warmth and the silence, the old soldier nodded over cheerily into a half-hour's sleep.

VOLUME II

CHAPTER I

Sam returned victorious, with an Army List, and the Rector's compliments, who would call upon Colonel Sutherland presently, in time to wake up the excellent Colonel, who was a little amazed, and a little amused at himself, to be made aware of that unusual indulgence. Sam had his own word of advice and warning against the deceitful blandishments of the "Ould Hunderd," with which he went away, flattered and ashamed, but by no means cured of his passion for "sodgering." To the questions of his mother, the hopeful young man only responded, that "the Cornel said th' army was a noble perfession," and appended thereto a vow to "break the head of that thundering 'Ould Hunderd'" at the first opportunity, neither of which conclusions was satisfactory to Mrs. Gilsland. The Colonel had scarcely put on his spectacles, and begun to turn over the leaves of the professional beadroll, when the proprietor of the same made his appearance, very cordial and anxious that the Colonel should dine at the Rectory, where the mother and sisters of "my boy in India" were already preparing themselves with a hundred questions to ask the old Indian officer. Colonel Sutherland, however, had already tasted quite enough of the damp, out-of-doors air for one day. He made the most of his threatening rheumatism by way of apology. He was fatigued with a long drive, and taking leave of friends. The Rector was politely curious; he had no doubt that he had the pleasure of knowing Colonel Sutherland's friends?

"I think not," said the Colonel, decidedly; "my brother-in-law is a recluse, and, I fear, keeps his family in the same retirement; besides, it is five miles off."

"Five miles is nothing in the country," said the courteous and persistent Rector.

"My relations live at Marchmain," said Colonel Sutherland, who had still the "Army List" in his hand—"I want to find out if the Sir John Armitage of this neighbourhood is an old friend of mine—Captain Armitage of the 59th—do you happen to know?"

"The very same," said the Rector; "he succeeded six or seven years ago, but he has not been at the Park for a year back. Bad health, I believe, an unsettled mind—he has never taken kindly to his new position; he thinks it is his duty to marry, and is extremely nervous about it. I thought it proper to pay him a good deal of attention when he was here. Poor man, his anxiety about the young ladies of the neighbourhood, and his terror of them, is something ludicrous to see."

"You are so fortunate as to have daughters of your own," said the Colonel, without perceiving the inference, which the other, possibly from a little disagreeable consciousness, applied instantly.

"My daughters were very young at that time," said the Rector, quickly—"almost children; besides, there are many points in which, though I think it right to show him attention, I do not approve of Sir John. His opinions are not what could be desired, and the father of daughters requires to be very careful whom he commits them to, as perhaps you are aware, Colonel Sutherland."

Colonel Sutherland bowed very gravely; the appeal touched on griefs too profound to be exposed to the compassion of a stranger. "He was a very good fellow when I knew him," said the Colonel; "I hear he was on terms of very intimate friendship with a Mr. Musgrave—he who died lately—is that true?"

"Ah, Mr. Musgrave?—yes, I knew him very well; an unfortunate, imprudent man, lavish and foolish," said the Rector. "He had a very good fortune to begin with, but lived with the most entire recklessness, like a man of three times his means. He brought up a young man, a sort of distant relative, as his heir. Poor man, when the affairs were examined it turned out that the heir had nothing but debt to enter upon; a very sad business altogether. Ah, yes, to be sure, Sir John, now that I recollect, had been to school with him, or something—there was a friendship between them."

"And does no one in the neighbourhood feel disposed to do anything for the young man?" asked the Colonel.

"For—Roger? Well, it is a very difficult question," said the bland Rector; "men with families of their own are so circumscribed in that way. There are no very wealthy men in our neighbourhood; and really, no one has felt warranted in incurring so great a responsibility. Sir John, indeed, might have done something for him; but then he is abroad, and of course no private individual likes to step forward, and perhaps excite expectations which could never be realized; besides, he has, no doubt, relatives of his own."

"And so, I presume, there is an end of him, poor fellow," said the Colonel, with the least outbreak of impatience; "is there anything known against the young man?"

"Nothing in the world," said the Rector, readily; "we all received him with pleasure, and found him really an acquisition; a young man not of much education, to be sure, but perfectly unobjectionable in a moral point of view. I remember urging strongly upon the late Squire the propriety of sending Roger to Cambridge, when my own boy went there, for we had no suspicion then of his unfortunate circumstances. He would not, sir; he was an unreasonable, old-fashioned person—what you call a John Bull sort of man. He said his Nimrod had no occasion to be a student. Poor man!—he would have acknowledged the wisdom of my counsels had he been living now."

"Is the young man, then, a Nimrod?" asked Colonel Sutherland.

"I understand—for of course such exploits are a little out of my way," said the gracious Rector—"that he is one of the best shots in the country; and I know from my boy, who was fond of athletic sports, that he excels in most of them. So much the worse for him now. It is a very sad thing, and one unfortunately too common, to see young men brought up to no other habits than those of a country gentleman, and then launched upon life with the sentiment of the unjust steward, 'To dig I know not, and to beg I am ashamed.'"

There was a little pause after this solemn and somewhat professional utterance, the Colonel not perceiving exactly how to answer this calm regret and sympathy, which never conceived the idea of helping, by a little finger, the misfortune it deplored. After a little silence, the Rector added, "You were acquainted with Mr. Musgrave, perhaps?—you feel an interest in the young man?"

"I do, certainly—though I had no acquaintance whatever with his former circumstances; he has been thrown accidentally in my way since I came here," said Colonel Sutherland.

"Let us never say anything is done accidentally," said the Rector, rising to take his leave with the most ingratiating smile—for he was low church, and evangelical in theology, however he might be in his actions; "everything has a purpose, my dear sir. Let us hope that it is providentially for poor Roger that he has been thrown in your way."

So saying, with many regrets that he should not have the pleasure of entertaining the stranger at the Rectory, the excellent incumbent of Tillington left him. The Colonel shrugged his shoulders when he was gone. The authoritative, insinuating professional manner with which his reverence corrected the expression of the old Christian stranger, who, coming "accidentally" to a knowledge of Roger's trouble, was after all the only neighbour whom the poor youth found in his extremity, made the Colonel both smile and sigh. "Right enough to correct me," said to himself the Scotch soldier, whose ideas of Providence wanted no enlargement by such advice; but once more the Colonel shrugged his shoulders, and remembered involuntarily the priest and the Levite who passed on the other side. He could not comprehend this entire want of all neighbourly and kindly feeling among the inhabitants of the same locality. The old man had been so long absent from home, and was so much accustomed to attribute the want of human kindness, which of course he had seen many times in his life, to the deteriorating effect of a strange country, and the entire want of home influences, that it amazed him now to perceive how even the primitive bosom of an English rural village held sentiments of self-regard as cold and unneighbourly as anything he had met with in the faraway world to which he was accustomed. Why could not this Rector, the friend and consoler of his parish by right of his office, a man who (undeniable inducement to all tenderness in the Colonel's tender heart) had children of his own—why did not he take the matter in hand, and appeal to Sir John Armitage, if the baronet alone was to be expected to do anything on Roger's behalf? The Colonel shook his head over it, and took refuge in his dinner. No repetition of instances would make the generous old man adopt or believe in this as the way of the world; he had only stumbled unfortunately upon cold-hearted individuals. Heaven forbid that he should put such a stigma on his brethren and his kind!

CHAPTER II

He had scarcely finished his dinner, when young Musgrave came to him, full of excitement and emotion, with a letter in his hand. The Colonel received him with all the more cordiality, that he had not yet quite lost the impression of the Rector's visit. The young man had evidently something to tell, and that something as evidently was of a nature to move him much.

"You are the only individual who has shown any interest in me," cried poor Roger; "I could not rest till I had come to tell you: I am not so entirely alone as I supposed I was. Look here, sir, a letter from my mother—my dear mother, whom I have never been able to forget, whom I have never ceased to love. I have done her injustice, Colonel; though she has only written it for my eyes, I bring it to you, because to you I have accused her unjustly. My mother has neither forgotten nor forsaken me!"

And with honest tears in his eyes, the young man thrust his letter into the Colonel's hands, half reluctant, it is true, to show his mother's expressions of love, but eager, above all, that she should be done full justice to, and acquitted of all unkindness. The Colonel took the letter with grave sympathy. It was not by way of conquering Roger's heart entirely that he put on his spectacles with so much serious attention, and applied himself to the hurried and half-coherent letter as if it were something of the gravest importance. He did naturally, and spontaneously from his own heart, this, which was the most exquisite compliment to the young man; and the Colonel's glasses grew dim as he read. It was the letter of a weak, loving woman, with too little strength of character to assert for herself any right of protecting or succouring her first-born, who was alien and strange to her husband and his family. One could almost see the gentle, broken-spirited woman over-ridden even by her own children, uncertain of her own mind, in weak health, and with nerves which everything affected, as one glanced over those hurried lines, which seemed to be written in absolute fear of discovery. There was little in them but the mother's yearning for her boy—her dear boy, her first-born, her own Roger, whom she prayed for on her knees every day, and thought of every hour. There was neither wisdom nor reason in the epistle—the poor woman had nothing to advise, nothing to offer. A cold observer might have thrown the whole away as affectionate nonsense, and desired to know what benefit that could be to the young man in his troubles. The Colonel knew better. "Therewithal the water stood in his eyes." He knew, without a word from Roger, how this tender touch had stanched the wounds of the young man's heart.

The only thing which he did not understand was a blurred and hasty postscript, to the effect that the enclosed was her own, and that her dear boy need have no hesitation in using it. This Musgrave explained to him by holding up, as he received back the letter, a twenty-pound note.

"And my mother enclosed this, sir," he said, looking up with an honest eagerness which twenty twenty-pound notes could not have produced—the poor lad was so proud to be able to show this evidence of his mother's concern for him. "I know she must have saved it up—spared it from her own necessities for me; I know she must, for she knows very well I would never receive an alms from him," cried poor Roger. "I—I daresay you think it's not very much to talk about, Colonel, but I could not rest till you had seen that I was wrong. To think I should have done her such injustice!—and you perceive, sir, that I can indeed take a week or two's leisure before I decide upon my future now."

"I am very glad of it," said the Colonel; "and still more glad that you have your mother's letter to comfort you. Take a lesson by it my boy, and never think you're forsaken. If we could know exactly our neighbour's circumstances, and see into their hearts, we would be slow to judge them, let alone dear friends. 'Can a mother forget her child, that she should not have compassion on the son of her womb?' Ah! my young friend, God knows better than we do the nature he has made. Here are two things come at once—your heart is comforted, and you are content to wait?"

Roger hung his head for a moment at the last proposition; he felt a little ashamed of giving in to the dawn of expectation which his last interview with Colonel Sutherland had excited in him in spite of himself; but the Colonel's unlooked-for kindness, and the affection of his mother, had warmed the young man's heart, and put him once more on good terms with the world. He began to believe in friendship and kindness, and to think that, after all, matters were not hopeless with him; but still his high spirit revolted from the idea of waiting till an application for aid had been made on his behalf, and doing nothing on his own account till that had been granted or refused.

"I can wait, and think it all over again for a few days," he said, with a little hesitation, "though indeed there is little to think of; for the case is not at all changed; but because you wish it, Colonel—you who have been so kind to me. I would be a poor fellow indeed, if I could not wait for a time for your pleasure."

"Very well," said Colonel Sutherland, with a smile; "we will let it stand on these grounds—it will please me. I have made a discovery also to-day. I find that your Sir John Armitage is an old friend of mine. I shall be very glad to seek him up for my own sake; they tell me he is invalid, and unsettled; but that should not make him less cordial to his fellow-creatures. We have been under fire together, and under canvas. He is an older acquaintance of mine than of yours. It will be odd if two old soldiers, when they lay their heads together, can do nothing to help on a young one. I have a little influence myself, and my own boy is secure. Some day you two may stand by each other when we old fellows are gone. I daresay, if you were together, you would not be long of making friends with my Ned. He is an honest fellow, though his father says it, and I think never gave me an hour's pain."

"But what can I say? I who have no claim whatever on your kindness, why are you so good to me?" cried Roger, astonished; "thanking you is folly; I have no words for it; it is beyond thanks; why are you so generous to me?"

"Tut, boy, nonsense!—I have sons of my own," said Colonel Sutherland; "and what is the good of an old man in this world? By-the-bye, tell me—have you ever sought or admitted the friendship of your neighbours since your grief? There are various families hereabout, I understand; your Rector for example—I am afraid you must have repulsed that good man in your first trouble—eh?—remember I am hard of hearing; you were too melancholy, too miserable for sympathy, and you have taken it into your head since that they had ceased to care for you?"

"I was thankful for all the sympathy I got; I trusted everybody then," said Roger, simply; "but—it does not matter," he said, after a little hesitation; "I found out the difference afterwards; no—it was not me."

"But the Rector—he has children, a son—was not he very friendly?" asked the Colonel, with persistence; he wanted to ascertain, as closely as he could, what was the real state of the case.

"Ah, Willy!"—said Roger; he paused a little, and grew red, and shook his head with a slight, involuntary motion, as if to shake off some disagreeable thoughts. "We were very good friends once," he said—"pah! why should I care—you will not think worse of me, Colonel Sutherland? I had rather not think of Willy. It is the greatest folly in the world, but I cannot help it; when I think of meeting him, perhaps, in my changed circumstances—I who used to be almost, if there was any difference, superior to him—I feel it painful; I don't like the idea; this is the plain truth. I had rather not go to India for the risk; forgive me! I had rather you knew the worst of me."

"If that is the worst I am glad to know it," said the Colonel. "It is a very natural feeling; to have been without it, would have proved you a different person from what I supposed. Now, tell me again; shall you stay here? you are still in your late friend's house—what is to be done with it?—who does it belong to?—and during this little interval shall you stay here?"

"The Grange is mine," said Roger, with a little pride; then he continued, with a slightly bitter smile—"next week everything is to be sold—everything—if they leave a wooden stool for poor old Sally in the kitchen, I will be grateful to them; but they cannot sell the Grange. It is entailed—I cannot sell it. Poor, dear old nest, it is the last wreck of all that ever belonged to the Musgraves; everything but that is gone already; yes, though it is empty and desolate I shall stay, till I leave all, in my own house."

"Then you are heir, not only of love, but at law," said the Colonel, gravely.

Somehow that changed the aspect of affairs a little. Useless though it was, that old house, empty and desolate, it gave still an indisputable point of inheritance and ancestry, upon which the young outcast could set his foot. It seemed more and more impossible to the Colonel, whose mind was not free of romantic prejudices, and upon whose imagination this circumstance made a great impression, that the young man should be left to his own forlorn devices; and he grew more and more angry at the neighbouring people, who could suffer not only "a worthy youth" to enter the world under circumstances so unfriendly, but could also permit the total extinction of an old family, whom such a young man, once aided to begin, might well resuscitate. However, he wisely kept these thoughts to himself. He exacted a promise from Roger to do nothing without letting him know, and to wait until he should be able to obtain an answer from Sir John Armitage; but, above all, to keep him advised of where he was, and what he was doing—a promise which the youth gave with a slight reluctance. Then a cordial farewell passed between them. They parted like old friends—the young man with grateful affection, the old man with interest and kindness quite fatherly. They had never met till three days ago, yet however long they lived, neither could ever cease now to feel the warmest interest in the other. In the meantime, the Colonel put up this matter of Roger Musgrave in the bundle with his most particular concerns, and gave himself, with the most earnest gravity, to his voluntary task of aiding and helping this stranger, nothing doubting to succeed in it; while Roger, on the other hand, went home to his solitary Grange, not knowing well what to make of it, struggling against the renewed hopes of his mind, fortifying himself against renewed disappointment by recalling his brief but sharp experience of the friendship of the world, and wondering whether he did right to trust, as he could not help trusting, the sincerity of his new friend. The young man paced in front of his house, among the dark trees, revolving over and over these questions which were of so much importance to him, and stimulated in all his hopes, without being aware of it, by that letter of his mother's, which he prized so much; and Colonel Sutherland sending out for paper, pens, and ink, and receiving in answer a dusty inkstand, a rusted steel pen, and two sheets of post paper highly glazed and with gilt edges, wiped his spectacles, lighted his low bedroom candle, that the light might suit his eyes, and sat down to write.

CHAPTER III

Colonel Sutherland was not very much addicted to correspondence: he wrote kind, wise, fatherly letters to his boys, but, except on extreme occasions, he wrote to nobody else, and was not easily moved to the exercise even in case of his oldest friends. It was therefore with a little importance that he opened out his gilt-edged paper before him, and smoothed the crumple, which Sam Gilsland's hand, not used to such delicate burdens, had left in the sheet, and, beginning with a most particular date, "Tillington Arms, 15th February, 184—" made a pause, after having achieved that, to think what he should say. We need not linger over all the Colonel's cogitations and pains of production. Here is at last, in the best language he could think of, the most wise and careful statement of his case which he found it possible to make:

"My dear Armitage,—I congratulate you very cordially upon the accession of rank and fortune which I have just learned has fallen upon you. Living, as you know I used to do, very much engaged with my own duties, and hearing scarcely any news except what occurred in our own branch of the service, I had never heard of this till to-day, when I suddenly found my old comrade in the Sir John Armitage of a district quite unknown to me, but with which I have managed to establish a connection rather surprising to myself, by dint of a few days residence here. I came home six months ago, after more than thirty years' service, exclusive of leave and former absence from duty, and had the happiness to find my boys well and hearty, and making progress to my entire satisfaction. Ned, you will be pleased to hear, is already provided for, and goes out the summer after next, to enter upon active life, with, I trust, if the boy works as he promises to do, an appointment in the Engineers. My other boy, I think, will very likely take to the Church, and be the solace of my old age. He makes very good promise for it, at least now. These, you will be sorry to know, are all that God has been pleased to spare me out of my flock.

"You will think it odd, perhaps, that I should hasten to tell you this the very moment of hearing your whereabouts and discovering your identity; but, to tell the truth, I have another reason more urgent, which, in point of fact, made me aware that you now belonged to this neighbourhood. I have accidentally" (here Colonel Sutherland paused, looked at the word, remembered the Rector's reproof, and made a half movement of his pen to draw it through; but, stopping himself, he smiled and shook his head, and went on without changing the expression) "met a young man called Roger Musgrave in the village, a very fine young fellow, to the best of my judgment. I understand that you were intimately acquainted with his godfather, whom the people here call Squire Musgrave, of the Grange. He died lately—when it was found that all he had was insufficient to meet his debts, and that this poor youth, whom I don't doubt you remember, was left entirely unprovided for. I found the boy in conference with a romancing old rogue of a sergeant of my own regiment, who was filling his head with all kinds of ridiculous accounts of a soldier's life in India. You may suppose I made short work of the sergeant, but found the young man, on entering into conversation with him, entirely bent upon enlisting. He had evidently been treated very shabbily by your gentry here; and, having no money, and being too proud to seek help from any one, the lad had made up his mind that the only thing left him to do, was to go for a soldier, and never be heard of more. By dint of questioning, I discovered that you were his relative's (I don't know what is the degree of kindred—the boy calls him his godfather) closest friend, and made up my mind at once, believing you to be a stranger, to take upon myself the task of making an appeal to you, to prevent this sacrifice. To-day I have discovered who you are, which you may suppose does not diminish my inclination to claim your assistance for this young fellow, who has captivated me, and gained my warmest interest. I have some little influence myself, which, now that my boy is provided for, I have no personal occasion to use. Don't you think you and I together could get him a pair of colours without any great difficulty? You know him better than I do, and I am sure you are not the man to leave a youth of good blood and high spirit to throw himself into the ranks in the romantic and vain hope of rising from them. I cannot profess to regret that so few chances of promotion are open to the private soldier, though I remember you have your own views on this subject; but I am most reluctant to see a youth, who would be a credit to the profession, throw himself away.

"I write this without the least idea where it will find you; but earnestly trust you will lose no time in answering. I need scarcely tell you, who I daresay have not forgotten the time when you were twenty, that the boy is very impatient, and quite likely to do something rash out of his own head, if he supposes himself neglected. Address to me at Milnehill, Inveresk, North Britain, where at all times you will find my solitary quarters, and a warm welcome, should you think of straying so far north. My dear Armitage, yours very faithfully,

"EDWARD SUTHERLAND, "Late Colonel, 100th B.N.I."

Having finished, read, and re-read this important epistle, the Colonel put it up, and writing in large characters, deeply underscored, To be forwarded immediately, put it beside him to be sent by express to Armitage Park. Then the old soldier's countenance relaxed. He laid his other sheet of paper lightly before him and dipped his pen in the ink with a smile. This time he was going to write to his boy.

"I have had no small vexation, Ned, since I came here," wrote the Colonel to his son; "you shall hear a circumstantial account of it. First, I was dismayed at the sight of the house—a melancholy place on the edge of the moor, without a scrap of garden or enclosure of any kind, and not a house within sight; fancy your poor pretty cousin Susan, at seventeen, shut up in such a prison, with never a face but her father's and brother's to cheer the dear child in her solitude! You have always heard that your uncle Scarsdale was a man of very peculiar character, and you will remember that I told you the very remarkable circumstances in which your cousin Horace stands. This, my dear boy, if you should happen to have any intercourse with Horace, you must do your best to forget. By some unaccountable perversion of mind, which I can excuse, perhaps, in a man of his character, but certainly cannot explain, your uncle has carefully concealed everything from his son which can throw the least light upon his position; and as he has at the same time refused all special training and education to the lad, and never encouraged or directed him to make any provision for his future life, you may imagine what an unsatisfactory state everything is in at Marchmain. First of all, you know, Ned, I am delighted with Susan. Please God, some day we'll have her at Milnehill, and let her see that there is something in life worth living for. It would make my old heart light to see her pleasant face about the house, and yet, Ned, sometimes I can scarcely look at her without tears. Heaven knows it should be our duty as well as our pleasure to do everything we can to brighten the life of this dear, pure-hearted little girl, who is the only woman in the family now.

"But, to begin at the beginning, I got a very strange account of the family from the man who drove me to Marchmain; then I was startled by the sight of the house; then, though greatly re-assured by the appearance of Susan, I was overcast again by seeing the cloud that came over her at the mention of her father. He never appeared to receive me, but sent for me to his study, where he made the request that I would keep his secret from his children in the most absolute terms, not without reproaches against me, and against—God forgive him!—my poor sister, because I knew it, which I confess rather exasperated me. I resolved at once not to stay in the house, nor to see him again, and accordingly came down here to this little inn—very poor quarters—where I have been for three days. Horace accompanied me here, and on the way broke out into rather extravagant protestations of his wish to leave home, and bitter complaints against his father. You may suppose I was confused enough, longing to let the poor lad know the secret which could have explained all to him, and hindered by my promise. I detest mystery—always abjure it, Ned, as you value my approbation; nothing can be honest that has to be concealed. This miserable, mistaken idea of your uncle's has gone far, I am afraid, to ruin the moral nature of his son. There is a shocking unnatural enmity between the two, which cuts me to the heart every time I think of it. Of course, Horace has no clue whatever to the secret of his father's conduct. He thinks it springs out of mere caprice and cruelty, and naturally fumes against it. This is all very dismal to look at, though I suppose, by dint of usage, it does not seem so unnatural to them as it does to a stranger. Horace himself, I am sorry to say, does not quite satisfy me; with such an upbringing, poor fellow, who can wonder at it? He is very clever, but much occupied with himself, and does not seem to have the honest, spontaneous wishes and ambition of a young man. There is a look of craft about him which grieves me; and I fear he has got into indifferent company, according to his own avowal, and declares to me he despises them, which, in my opinion, does not mend the matter. Altogether, I am very much puzzled in my own mind about him; he is very unlike the young men I have been accustomed to meet with—and that with my experience, in thirty years of active life, is a good deal to say.

"However, with my advice, he has been led to conclude that he will adopt the law as a profession, and is anxious to be put in the way of it immediately, and do what he can to qualify himself for making his own bread in an honourable way. Can you believe it possible, my dear boy, that his father, on my appeal to him, absolutely refused either to help your cousin in his most laudable wish, or to explain to him why he did not? Oh, Ned, Ned, how miserable we can make ourselves when we get leave to do our own will! The man is wretched—you can read it in every line of his face; but he will not yield to open his heart to his boy, to receive him into his confidence, to make a friend of his only son. This miserable lucre—and I am sure in his better days, when your poor aunt was alive, nobody imagined that Scarsdale had set his heart much upon it—has turned his whole nature into gall. God forgive the miserable old man that left this curse behind him!—though, indeed, that is a useless wish, as he has been dead for fifteen years, and his fate determined long ago.

"So you perceive, on the whole, I have had a good deal on my hands since I came here. Now that nothing can be done with his father, I mean to make an appeal on behalf of your cousin to one of the trustees. To tell you the truth, Ned, I am almost afraid now of the secret being made known to Horace. Your uncle has so forgotten that word, 'Fathers, provoke not your children to wrath,' that it absolutely alarms me when I think what may be the consequences if Horace hears it suddenly from any lips but his father's. So, if you should chance to come in contact with your cousin, my dear boy, see that you forget it, Ned. Let never an appearance of knowledge be perceived in you—to be sure, this of itself is a kind of deceit, but it is lawful. If Scarsdale himself could be moved to disclose the whole to his son, a better state of affairs might be brought about—otherwise, I am alarmed to think of any discovery, more than I can say.

"Not content with this business, I have taken in hand, like an old fool as I am, another young fellow, whom I have fallen in with here; a fine, sincere, hearty lad, whom I hope to hear of one day as your brother-in-arms. I have just been writing on his behalf to old Armitage, of the 59th, whom you remember, I daresay, when you were a child, and who knows this young fellow, of whom I'll tell you more hereafter. To-morrow I go home (D.V.), and will post this in Edinburgh, as I pass through, that you may know I have had a safe journey. I had a letter from Tom the day before I left. The rogue has got five or six prizes at the examination; but of course he has told you all about that before now.

"God bless you, my dear boy; never forget the Gospel grace, and all we owe to it—nor your love and duty to our Father in Heaven.

"E. SUTHERLAND."

After finishing this paternal letter, the Colonel leaned his head upon his hands for a little in silent cogitation. He was rather tired of his epistolary labours, and could not help thinking with a secret sigh of the carpet-bag, which had still to be packed up-stairs, and of the chilly journey which he had to undertake early next morning. Had he not better put off his other letter till he got home to Milnehill? "There is no time like the present," said the Colonel, with a sigh, and he rung the bell and commissioned Mrs. Gilsland to procure him another sheet of that famous gilt-edged paper. Having obtained it, and fortified himself meanwhile with a cup of tea, which the landlady brought at the same time, the persevering Colonel thus indited his third epistle:—

"SIR,—It is a long time since I met you at the house of my brother-in-law in London, and it is very possible that you may have forgotten even the name of the writer of this letter. I am the brother of the late Mrs. Robert Scarsdale—late Colonel in command of the 100th Regiment, B. N. I., in the Honourable Company's service, and since retiring from active service have resided at Milnehill, Inveresk, North Britain, where any answer you may think proper to give to this communication will find me. I write to you now on behalf of my nephew, Horace Scarsdale. His father, to my great grief, has kept him entirely ignorant of his very peculiar and painful circumstances; and, at the same time, with a feeling sufficiently natural, but much to be deplored, declines to aid him in studying the profession which he has chosen, being that of the law. Under these circumstances, which, as his nearest relative, I have become aware of, I feel that my only resource is to apply to you. Mr. Robert Scarsdale, as you are aware, is still a man in the prime of life, and, so far as I know, in excellent health. To keep the young man without occupation, waiting for the demise of a vigorous man of fifty, would, even if my nephew were aware of all the circumstances, be something at once revolting to all natural feeling, and highly injurious to himself. I venture to ask you, then, whether you are justified in advancing to him, or, if you prefer it, to me, under security for his use, a sufficient sum to enable him to enter on the study of his profession? The matter is so important, that I make no apologies for stating it thus briefly. This would be of more importance than twice the amount can be when his youth is gone, and the best part of his life wasted. I beg you, for the young man's sake, to take the matter into your serious consideration, as trustee under the unhappy arrangement which has done so much harm to this family. I will be happy to enter into further details, or make any explanation in my power, on hearing from you; and trusting that your sympathy may be so far moved by my story as to dispose you to the assistance of my unfortunate nephew, of whose talents I have formed a very high opinion—I have the honour to remain, your faithful servant,

"EDWARD SUTHERLAND."

This done, the Colonel put his letters together and retired into his arm-chair, with a satisfied conscience; as he sat there silent by the fire, the old man carried his pleadings to a higher tribunal. How could he have kept his heart so young all these years, except by the close and constant resort he made to that wonderful Friend, whom every man who seeks Him must come to like a little child?

CHAPTER IV

Within a week after Colonel Sutherland's departure from Tillington a little flight of letters arrived from him—one to Susan, full only of her uncle's heart, and all the kind devices he could think of to amuse and give her pleasure; and a more business-like communication to Horace, who, during these seven days, had felt Marchmain more and more unendurable, and did not behave himself so as to increase anybody's comfort in the house. "I have appealed on your behalf to a person who ought to feel an interest in you," wrote the Colonel—"and as soon as I hear from him I will let you know immediately whether he can help me to put you in a satisfactory position. If not, my dear boy, we must try what my own means can do; and, in that case, I should propose that you come here to me, where it might be possible enough for a vigorous young man like yourself to pursue your studies in Edinburgh, and at the same time live with me at Milnehill. All this we can arrange by-and-bye. At present there is no resource but to wait, which I must advise you to do, my dear Horace, with as much cheerfulness as possible, for your own, and for all our sakes."

Horace put up this letter with a smile. There was one thing in it which should certainly have made the advice contained here palatable. The Colonel, remembering himself that very likely his nephew was kept without money, enclosed to him, with the merest statement that he did so, a five-pound note—the sight of which did bring a momentary pleasure, mingled with mortification, to the young man's face. But his bitter, ungenerous pride, made the kindness an offence, while it was a service. He never dreamed of rejecting it, but wiped off all necessity for gratitude by feeling the present an affront. It was a strange alchemy which Horace exercised; he made the most precious things into dross, putting them into the fire of his contemptuous philosophy. "Was it to please me my uncle did this, or was it to please himself?" he said, with that smile in which no pleasure was: and so made it out, instead of a natural act of kindness, to be a selfish piece of personal gratification on the part of Colonel Sutherland, who very likely had pleased himself mightily by this little exhibition of liberality and apparent goodness, at Horace's expense. With this miserable ingenuity Horace defended himself from all the influences of kindness, and stood coldly and bitterly superior to the devices which he supposed himself to have found out. Having thrust the note into his pocket with this satisfactory clearance of everything like thanks from his own mind, he turned to the letter itself, which was not at all agreeable to him. He had no more idea of waiting for the decision of the anonymous individual to whom his uncle had appealed, than he had of proceeding to Edinburgh, and living under the eye and inspection of Colonel Sutherland. He had unbounded confidence in himself, in his own abilities and skill in using them; he was not disposed to wait upon anybody's pleasure, or to be diverted from his own purpose, because some one else was labouring for his benefit in another fashion. He smiled as he read his uncle's letter, and thought upon his own scheme; but it never occurred to him to tell the Colonel that his pains were unnecessary, that he himself saw another way, and had resolved upon his own course. That was not Horace's way; he preferred to know of these exertions being made for him, and secretly to forestall, and make them useless, by acting for himself. Then it appeared to him as if he should recover his natural superiority to his uncle, and demonstrate triumphantly that he was not a person to be insulted with favours and kindnesses, or from whom thanks and gratitude were to be expected. With these sentiments he put up the letter in his pocket, and looked with disdainful amusement at Susan, who was still in the full delight of her excitement over hers; and went out, as was his wont, to ripen his own plans in his mind, and, secure in the possession of the Colonel's bank-note, to determine on his own independent movements, and decide when he should leave home.

Emotions somewhat like those of Horace, yet as different as their natures, were roused in the mind of young Roger Musgrave by a communication very similar. To him, afraid of startling the sensitive young man, the Colonel wrote with the greatest delicacy and tenderness. He told him that he had applied to Sir John Armitage for the aid of his influence, and had already put all his own in motion; that he had very little doubt speedily to see his young friend bear Her Majesty's commission, and that all he had to beg of him was a little patience and confidence in his very sincere friend. Roger did not pause for a moment to suggest to himself that Colonel Sutherland was exercising a natural taste for patronage and affairs in thus befriending him. The young man started up in the solitary library of the Grange, where he sat that day for the last time, his cheeks crimson with excitement, and his eyes full of tears. He was confounded, troubled, touched to the heart by the friendship shown to him; and yet, as he thought over it alone in the silent house, felt it overmuch for him, and could scarcely bear it. Should he take advantage of this wonderful goodness, the busy devil whispered in his ear? Was it right to impose his misfortunes—which, after all, were not so bad as many others in the world—as a claim upon the tender compassion of the Colonel? Was it generous to accept services which, perhaps, another had more need of? He could not remain quiet, and resist this temptation; he rushed out, like Horace Scarsdale, into the bare woods, where the wind was roaring, and through the dark plantation of fir-trees, with all its world of slender columns, and the dark flat canopy of branches overhead, which resounded to the level sweep of the gale; and where, by-and-bye, the things around took his practical and simple eye, and won his heart out of the tumult of thoughts which he was not constituted to withstand, and which were very likely, in his unwonted solitude, to drive him into some irresistible but unpremeditated rashness, and make him break his promise before he was aware. Then he returned home, fatigued and exhausted, lost himself willingly, and of purpose, in an old romance, borrowed from the village library, and so kept out of the dangerous power of thought, till it was time to sleep. After that his imagination played strange freaks with Roger. We cannot tell anybody what his dreams were about; for though they seemed to himself wonderfully significant and vivid, he was mortified to find that he could not recall them in the morning so distinctly as he hoped. For he was not a poetical hero, but only a young man of very vigorous health and simple intelligence, whom grief and downfall, and melancholy change of circumstances, had influenced deeply, without making any permanent derangement, either of his mind or his digestion.

He had no need of dreams to increase the real pain of his position next morning. It was the day of the sale; a kind of simple heroical devotion to the memory of his godfather, an idea of being on the spot to repel any slight which might be thrown on his character, impelled him to be present in or near the house during the whole day. Very likely he was very wrong to expose himself to the trial, but in his youthful, excited feeling, he thought it his duty, and that was enough for Roger. The bland Rector, who came with his wife to buy some favourite china ornaments, which the lady had contemplated with longing eyes in the Squire's time, extended a passing hand to Roger, and recommended him, scarcely stopping to give the advice, not to stay. Some young men, warmer hearted, surrounded him with attempts, the best they knew, to divert him from the sight of what was going on, and scandalized the grave people by their jokes and laughter. The humbler persons present addressed Roger with broad, well-meaning condolences: "Ah, if th' ould squire had but known!" one and another said to him with audible sighs of sympathy. The poor youth's eyes grew red, and his cheeks pale; he assumed, in spite of himself, a defiant look: he stood on the watch for something he could resent. The trial was too much for his warm blood and inexperienced heart; and when the great lady of the neighbourhood passed out to her carriage, as the sale drew towards a close, and saw him near the gate with his colourless face and agitated look, she scarcely bowed to poor Roger, and declared, almost in his hearing, that the young man had been drinking, and that it showed the most lamentable want of feeling on his part to be present at such a scene.

Poor Roger! perhaps it was very foolish of him to expose himself unnecessarily to all this pain. When the night came, and the silence, doubly silent after all that din, he went through the rooms, where the moon shone in through all the bare, uncurtained windows; where the straw littered the floor; and where the furniture was no longer part of the place, but stood in heaps, as this one and that one had bought it, ready to be carried away to-morrow; with his heart breaking, as he thought. In a few hours the desolation of the Grange would be complete, although, indeed, emptiness itself would be less desolate than the present aspect of the familiar place. Once more he read over the Colonel's letter, with all its good cheer and hopefulness. Only to have patience! Could he have patience?—was it possible that he could wait here, listless and inactive, while the good Colonel laboured for him?—and once more all his doubts and questions returned upon the young man. Should he accept so great a favour?—was he right to stand by and allow so much to be done for him, he who was a stranger to his benefactor? He buried his face in his hands, leaning on the table, which was the only thing in the apartment which had not been removed out of its usual place. Here exhaustion, and emotion, and grief surprised the forlorn lad into sleep. Presently he threw himself back, with the unconscious movement of a sleeper, upon his chair. The moon brightened and rose in the sky, and shone fuller and fuller into the room. The neglected candle burned to the socket and went out; the white radiance streamed in, in two broad bars of light, through the bare windows, making everything painfully clear within its range, and leaving a ghostly twilight and corners of profound shadow in the rest of the apartment. There he lay in the midst of his desolated household sanctuary, with the heaps of packed-up furniture round him, and the candle trembling and dying in the socket, and the white light just missing his white face—the last of the Musgraves, the heir of emptiness!—yet in his trouble and grief keeping the privilege of his years, and sleeping sweet the sleep of his youth.

CHAPTER V

While the two young men responded thus to Colonel Sutherland's communications, Susan took her letter to her heart, and found unbounded comfort in it. All had not disappeared with Uncle Edward. Here was a perennial expectation, a constant thread of hope henceforward to run through her life. Never before had Susan known the altogether modern and nineteenth-century excitement of looking for the postman. It gave quite a new interest to the day—any day that unknown functionary might come again to refresh her soul with this novel delight. She could see him come across the moor, that celestial messenger! Not a Cupid, honest fellow; but bearing with him all the love that brightened Susan's firmament. She thought it would be quite impossible to be dull or listless now: even to be disappointed was something which would give a point and character to the day; and all was very different from the dead blank of her former life, in which she had no expectation, no disappointment, nothing to look for, and for entertainment to her youth only her patchwork and Peggy's talk, enjoyed by intervals. Her whole existence was changed. Uncle Edward's bundle of books, which had not captivated Susan at first sight, she found, after looking into them, to be more attractive even than her new embroidery frame. They were all novels—a kind of composition totally unknown to Susan. She had been very little attracted by literature hitherto; in the first place, because to obtain a book was a serious matter, necessitating a visit to her father's study, and a formal request for the undesirable volume, which had no charm for a young imagination when it came. But now Susan read with devotion, and amazement, and delight, each more vivid than the other. She entered into the fortunes of her heroes and heroines with a perfect interest, which would have won any story-teller's heart. She sat up almost all night, in breathless engrossment, with one which ended unhappily, and cried herself to sleep, almost frozen, with great indignation and grief at the last, to find that things would not mend. There, too, she found enlightenment upon many things. She learned, after its modern fashion, the perennial fable of the knight who delivers his lady-love. She found out how it is possible for a heroine to come through every trouble under heaven, to a paradise of love, and wealth, and happiness; and Susan's spirits rose, in spite of herself, into that heaven of imagination. Sometime or other nature and youth must come even to Marchmain; sometime it would be Susan's turn; sooner or later there would be some one in the world to whom she too would be the first and dearest. This inalienable privilege of womankind came to every Laura and Lucy in her novels, happily or unhappily; and the novels were not so far wrong either—so it does, to be sure, in life; but Susan did not take into her consideration the sad chance that liberation might be offered to the bewitched princess only by the wrong knight. The wrong knight only came in as a rival to make some complications in the story, as Susan read it; and somehow the girl adopted the tale by intuition, and fell into a vague delight of innocent dreams. Pursuing these at her needlework, after all her novels were exhausted, was almost as good as another romance; and this tale spun itself on inexhaustibly, a story without an end.

This spring in Susan's fresh heart developed itself unawares in her actions and life. She went about the house with a more sprightly step; she caught up Peggy's snatches of song, and kept humming and murmuring them, without knowing it. Sometimes her hands fell idle on her lap, as her new thoughts rose. Often she went out upon solitary rambles, with this pleasant companionship in her heart. It would not be right to say she was bolder, for the contrary was the case—she was shyer, more ready to shrink from any person whom she met; but somehow found a vague, delightful expectation, which gave a charm to everything diffused over her life.

A few days after she received Uncle Edward's letter, Susan had the good fortune to meet her friend Letty, her sole acquaintance—her secret intercourse with whom she had tremblingly revealed to the Colonel. Letty was delicate, and had not been permitted to be out of doors during the bad weather. She was a tall, meagre girl, who had outgrown her strength, and whose sallow cheeks, and prominent light gray eyes, made the greatest contrast possible to Susan's blooming health and simple beauty. Letty was supposed to have received a wonderful education: she could play on the piano, and draw, and speak French—achievements which, in Peggy's opinion, made her a most desirable companion for poor Susan, who was ignorant of all these fine things. Besides her accomplishments, Letty was very sentimental, and wrote verses, and took rather a pathetic view of things in general. Her great misfortune was that in her own person she had nothing to complain of. She was the only child of her parents, who petted and humoured her, as old people are apt to do to the child of their old age, and who were correspondingly proud of her acquirements. Consequently, to her own great disgust, she did very much as she liked, and was contradicted by nobody. She threw herself, with all the greater fervour of sympathy, into the circumstances of her friend, not without a little envy of Susan's trials, and splendid imaginations, had she been in the same position, of what she should have done. After this long separation she flew upon Susan, throwing her long arms round her friend's neck with enthusiasm. Then the two, with arms interlaced, strayed along by the side of the high hedgerow in the winterly sunshine—the young buds opening out on the branches against which they brushed in passing, and the young grass rustling under their feet. There was not a single passenger on the road as far as they could see. They were free to exchange their friendly confidence, without the least fear of interruption.

"Oh! Susan, I have wanted so to see you! I have been so melancholy shut up at home," cried Letty; "and when I wanted to come out, mamma would not let me. I do not mind being ill. Why should not I die young like my cousin Mary? I think it must be very sweet to die young, when everybody will be sorry for you—oh, Susan, don't you?"

"I—don't—know," said poor Susan, who thought this was a great sign of Letty's superiority, and scarcely liked to confess her own worldlymindedness. "No; I should think it rather hard to die if I had a great many people who loved me like you."

"Ah, people may love one—but then, perhaps, they don't understand one," said Letty. "Mamma would not let me go to the Sabbath school, because she thought I might take cold! Ah, Susan, do you think that is an excuse that will do at the Judgment?—perhaps I might have said something to one of the children which she never would have forgotten all her life—and to think of the opportunity being lost, for fear I might take cold! I am sometimes afraid," said Letty, with a deep mysterious sigh, "that God will think it necessary, for poor papa and mamma's sake, that I should die very early; for I am so frightened that they are making an idol of me. We ought not to love anyone so very much, you know."

"I think I would not mind how much anyone loved me," said Susan, with a little boldness; "the more the better, I think; for indeed I am sure, Letty, that the Bible never says anywhere that it is sinful to be very, very fond of one's friends."

"We must never make idols of them," said Letty; "and when I see how mamma takes care of me, I tremble for her. I should not mind it at all myself, but she would be so lonely if I were to die."

"Oh, Letty, for pity's sake, do not speak of it!" cried Susan.

"Why shouldn't I speak of it? I feel quite sure that people who feel like me never live long," said Letty. "I am going to write my will in poetry, Susan—I did one verse the other night. I think it is rather a nice idea—it is about putting flowers on my grave."

"Oh, Letty, do be quiet!—for your mamma's sake!" cried Susan, in terror and dismay, holding fast by her friend's arm, as if afraid to see her vanish into the impalpable air.

Letty was not at all inclined, having made so great an impression, to give up the subject, and was about to resume it in a still more pathetic tone, when Susan, stimulated by her own livelier meditations, made an animated diversion.

"My Uncle Edward has been here!" said Susan; "he is the very kindest, dearest old man you ever saw. I did not think there was anybody like him in the world. He took me to Kenlisle one day in a gig, and bought me books, and I don't know how many things. Oh, Letty, such delightful books!—one is the 'Heiress;' I have just finished it; about a young lady that had a great deal of money left her, and did not know of it, and was brought up quite poor, and a gentleman fell in love with her, and they went through such troubles; and at last they were—but oh, I forgot, I ought not to tell you the end. You don't know how nice it is to get frightened over and over again, and think something dreadful must happen, and yet everything comes all right in the end. I wish, I am sure—oh, Letty, do you think you could come, just come once, to Marchmain?"

"Yes, if you wish me, Susan," said Letty, with a little demureness.

"Wish you! Oh, if I could only have my own will! Would your mamma be pleased?" cried Susan; "and would you promise not to be frightened if you saw papa?"

"Frightened!" exclaimed Letty, repeating the word in her turn. "But if I saw him, it would perhaps be my duty to speak to him, Susan—for very likely if some one spoke to him properly, about being good to you, and about what people say, he would be kinder, I should like very much to see him—perhaps I might be the means of doing him good."

Susan was lost in unspeakable dismay. "Oh, Letty, what are you thinking of?—you don't know papa!" she said with a smothered voice; her desire to show Letty all her treasures fading before her terror at the thought of anybody attempting to "do good" to her terrible father. Unconsciously she quickened her pace, and hurried her companion farther from Marchmain. The idea terrified her out of her discretion. She forgot everything else in that dreadful thought. Lost in her apprehensions, she hurried her companion on towards Letty's own house, where she resolved to deposit her safely out of harm's way, telling meanwhile in elaborate detail the plot of another of her novels. Letty, who had no intention of making an immediate onslaught upon Mr. Scarsdale, turned the matter over in her mind, and thought it was "quite a duty," if she should see him, to remonstrate with her friend's unnatural father. The thought captivated Letty. As for the consequences, instead of being frightened, she would be pleased to be denounced and upbraided. That would be the persecution which she could not possibly find out in any other form in her life, and for which she longed as the seal of her Christianity. Notwithstanding, she inclined her ear to hear of the novel, and was not unmoved by Susan's promise to send it to her. They parted at a little distance from the little manse, which was Letty's home. "And remember, Susan," said Letty, kissing her affectionately, "that whenever you choose to send for me, I shall come."

Susan turned home again alone, with the sensation of having escaped from a great danger. She was quite sick with apprehensions. No wonder her father debarred her from society, when the issue was that a girl of her own age should take it upon her, without warrant from any one, to argue the question of his conduct with papa. She made haste to reach Marchmain, with an odd fear that Letty might possibly take another fancy and get there before her; and what with the fright and the ridiculous thought, Susan, half laughing and half crying, began to run to the defence of her home and her father. Who could the poor child trust if Letty failed her? When she came in sight of Marchmain, Susan stayed her steps; she did not want to betray her panic to any one there, though indeed nobody but herself ever looked out of these gloomy windows. There was some one, a rare event in that road, passing before the house. He went slowly along in front of Marchmain, looking at it. Susan looked at it too, with curiosity, wondering what could interest any stranger in her cheerless home. The sun shone once more on the gable as Colonel Sutherland had seen it, besetting the bare walls round and round, and printing off its naked outline against the moor, which stretched round it on every side. Familiar as she was with the house, Susan's heart sank as her attention fell involuntarily upon the strange nakedness and neglect which its unenclosed condition seemed to show. A bit of cottage paling, a yard of grassplot, the merest attempt at flowers, even a little paved yard, would have made a difference. No such thing was there; the doorstep descended upon the wayside herbage; around, the black whins and withered heather came close up to the walls. Here was no gracious life, active and affectionate, to beguile into verdure the stubborn yet persuadable soil. Nobody cared—that was the sentiment of the place: its unloveliness was of the merest unimportance to those who found a shelter within its walls. Who was this looking at it? When he had once passed the house, he turned back again, made a little pause, and then sauntered along the front of it once more, advancing to meet Susan, who felt a little alarmed at so unusual an exhibition of interest. One of the little clumps of seedling trees in the moss interposed between them before they met. Coming out of its shadow at the same instant, they encountered each other suddenly, and without preparation. Susan half stopped, started, made a suppressed exclamation, for which she could have killed herself, and blushed over all her face. The young man was no less startled; he too grew crimson with a guilty and conscious colour; and as Susan hastened past him, stepped aside out of her way, and took off his hat, without attempting to say a word. Both not only recognized each other, but perceived, with a wondering sensation, something akin to pleasure, that they were mutually recognized. Both hurried off the scene precipitately, without looking behind them, and both somehow discovered that this sudden meeting had given a different direction to their several thoughts. Strange, unexplainable consequence of a natural accident!—why should not these two have met on a public road as well as any other two in the district? Yet somehow this sudden encounter had a certain extraordinary supernatural aspect to them both.

This person whom Susan was so unaccountably startled to see, was, of course, Roger Musgrave, walking here, as he walked everywhere within ten miles, because the poor fellow could not endure himself, and did not venture to battle with his own thoughts, and kept himself out-of-doors and in motion as a kind of safeguard. The only wonderful thing of the whole was that while Susan, without running, reached

Marchmain with an incredible silent speed, and got in with her pulse high and her eyes shining, and the most profound amazement in her mind, Roger scarcely ever drew breath, on his part, till he had reached his own deserted house, though that was five miles off. Why they should have used such prodigious pains to get as far distant as possible from each other, in the shortest conceivable time, remains until this hour the mystery of that day.

CHAPTER VI

That day was an important one to Roger Musgrave. To live in that Grange, a great, empty, deserted house, where every desolate apartment echoed to his footstep as if he were a dozen men, and which contained through all its ample rooms nothing but a rude table and chair in the library, where he took his solitary food, a truckle bed where he slept, and some homely implements for poor old Sally in the kitchen, which the unfortunate young man had redeemed out of his mother's twenty pounds—became at last and once for all impossible to him. That day, setting out for the only refuge of his idleness, a long walk, it had occurred to him to turn his steps in the direction of Marchmain, more from a passing caprice than a serious intention. His kind old Colonel had been there—and there was the Colonel's niece, the pretty frank little girl, who had clapped her hands at his boyish exploit a year ago. The gratified vanity of that moment, his former curiosity to see Susan again, and her friendly mention of him to her uncle, warmed the young man into more earnestness as he approached the house. Seeing no one, and amazed at its utter solitude and sadness, he had turned away disappointed, when their meeting took place. Then, as we have already said, the young man hurried home. When he arrived there he kept walking up and down the empty library, till the old house rung again, and old Sally believed the young squire was "a-gooin' out of his mind." But he was not doing any such thing; he was only repeating to himself that it was impossible!—impossible! that it was against nature, and a discredit to his own character; that he could no longer wait for what other people were doing for him; that this very day he must leave the Grange. What his meeting with Susan had to do with hastening this resolution it is quite impossible to tell; he did not know himself; but the conclusion was beyond disputing. He felt a feverish restlessness possess him—he could not remain even another night, though the morning certainly would have seemed a wiser time for setting out upon his journey. He pushed aside the chop which old Sally, with much care and all the skill her old hands retained, had prepared for him, and began to write. He wrote to his mother, who had recovered all her original place in his affections, a short cheerful note, to say that he was going to London, and would write to her from thence. Then he indited less easily a letter to the Colonel, in which, with all the eloquence he possessed, he represented the impossibility of remaining where he was. He described, with natural pathos, the empty house, the desecrated home, the listless life of idleness he was leading. He said, with youthful inconsequence, strong in the feeling of the moment, that, thrown back upon himself as he had been all these lonely days, he no longer cared for rank, nor desired to keep up a pretence of superior station, which he could not support. "In what am I better than a private soldier?" he wrote, with all the swell and impulse of his full young heart: "worse, in so far that I am neither trained to my weapons, nor used to obedience—better in nothing but an empty name!" And with all that facile philosophy with which young men comfort the bitterness of their disappointments, the lad wrought himself up to a heroical pitch, by asking himself and the Colonel why he should not serve his country as well in the ranks as among their commanders. Why, indeed? The fever of his excitement mounted into his brain. When he finished his letter he was in all the fervour of that self-sacrificing sentiment which is so dear to youth. He went upstairs and packed his clean linen—a goodly store, all unlike the equipment of a private soldier—with some few other necessaries, into a travelling-bag. Then he went down to the great deserted kitchen, where poor old Sally sat "like a crow in the mist" by the chimney corner, her morsel of attenuated fire gleaming faintly across the cold floor. Sally got up and curtseyed when the young master entered. She was a little old woman, bent and feeble, but she had lived there almost all her life, and it would have broken Sally's heart to be sent away from the Grange. She stood before him with her withered hands crossed upon her white apron, wondering in her dim thoughts whether there might be something to complain of in the dinner she had prepared. Behind her spread all the hospitable provisions of the rich man's kitchen, the arrangements which spoke of liberal entertainment, assembly of guests above and crowd of servants below; all black, cold, and desolate, unlighted save by the early wintry twilight from the windows and the superannuated glimmer of Sally's fire; and the emptiness and vacancy went with a chill and an ache to Roger's heart.

"Sally," said the young man, courageously, "I shall not give you any more trouble for a long time. You must keep the house as well as you can, and make yourself as comfortable as possible. Don't make the old place a show for strangers, now that it's desolate. See, Sally, here's for your present needs, and when I am settled I will send you more."

"I allays said it," said the old woman, "ye can ask Betty Gilsland. I said, says I, 'the young maister, take my word, 'll no bide here.' Ay, ay, ay, I allays said it—and you see it's coomed true."

Saying these words, Sally went off into a feeble little outburst of tears, and repeated her affirmation a third time, holding the money he had given her in her hand as if she did not know what to do with it. At last her ideas, such as they were, collected themselves. She made another curtsey.

"And where are you a-gooing, maister?" she said, looking earnestly into his face.

"To make my fortune, Sally," said the young man, with a smile which trembled between boldness and tears.

"And Amen—and grit may the fortin' be!" cried the old woman. "Have ye eaten your dinner?"

This was too much for the young man; he burst into a hysterical laugh, grasped her withered hand, shook it rapidly, and hurried away. The poor old body toiled up the stairs after him, to make sure that "the sneck was in the door—for them young things are that careless!" said poor old Sally; then she went back again to her kitchen, and looked at the money, and, after an interval, perceiving what had happened, fell a-sobbing and crying in her solitude, and praying "the Lord bless him!" and "the Lord be gude to him!" as she rocked herself in her wooden chair. He who, out of all that poverty and sadness, and stupor of old age, heard these ejaculations, is no respecter of persons, and it was not without a true benediction that Roger Musgrave left his home.

When he was out upon the high road he turned back to look at the Grange. The evening was dark and favoured him. The day had been mild, and early spring quickened and rustled among those trees, warming to the very tips of their branches with that invisible and silent life which should shortly make them green. There they stood clustering in mutual defence against the night wind, with the high-pitched gable-roof of the old house looking out from among them, and the black belt of firs behind filling up the breaks in their softer outline. By-and-bye, as Roger lingered in that last wistful look, he could see a small, unsteady light wandering from window to window. It was poor old Sally shutting the shutters, murmuring to herself that it was always so when the family were from home. There was something in the action symbolical and significant to Roger; it was the shutting up of the old house, the closing of the old refuge, the audible and visible sentence forbidding the return which up to that moment had been possible: he turned away with tears in his eyes, slung his travelling-bag over his strong shoulders, and setting his face to the wind, sped away through the dark country roads to the little new-built railway town, with its inns and labourers' cottages. It was quite dark when he got there; the lights dazzled him, and the noise of the coffee-room into which he went filled him with disgust in his exalted and excited state of feeling. Strangely enough as it appeared to him, a recruiting party had possession of the inn; a swaggering sergeant with parti-coloured ribbons went and came between the coffee-room and the bar, where a batch of recruits were drowning their regrets and compunctions in oceans of beer. Roger went out, with a strange mixture of disgust and curiosity, to look at them. He could not observe, and criticize, and despise as Horace Scarsdale could have done; he found no amusement in the coarse self-reproach of one, the sullen obstinacy of another, the reckless gaiety with which a third put off his repentance till to-morrow. The din of their pretended enjoyment was pathetic and melancholy to Roger; but, amid all, he could not help the thought which occurred to him again and again—"Am I to be the comrade of these unfortunate blockheads?—are these my brothers-in-arms?"

And then, quick as thought, another picture presented itself to him. He thought of the Colonel, with his kind solicitous face, his stoop of attention, and the smile which lighted up his fatherly eyes when he spoke of his boy, whom he should hope to see Roger's brother-in-arms. For the moment he saw before him, not the flaring lights and clumsy figures of this rude company, but the dim inn-parlour, with its poor candles, and the benign old stranger with his paternal smile. The young man could not bear it. He said to himself sternly, "This must not be!" and dismissed the contrast which distracted him from his mind with a violent effort. Then he made his way into the half-lighted railway-station, where everything lay dark and silent, a stray porter making ghostly appearance across the rails, and an abysm of darkness on either side, out of which, and into which, now and then plunged the red-eyed ogre of a passing train. In answer to his inquiries, he found that the night-train to London stopped here to take up passengers in the middle of the night. He made a homely supper in the inn, and then came outside, to the station, to wait for it. There he paced up and down, watching the coming and going of short trains here and there, the hurried clambering up, and the more leisurely descent of rural passengers, upon whom the light fell coldly as they went and came. The roar and rustle with which some one-eyed monster, heard long before seen, came plunging and snorting out of the darkness, and all the rapid, shifting, phantasmagoria, of that new fashion of the picturesque which belongs to modern times. The wind blew chill from the open country, with a shrill and piercing concentration of cold through the narrow bar of the little station. By-and-bye the lights diminished, the noises stilled, nobody was left in the place but himself, a drowsy clerk in the little office, and some porters sleeping on the benches. Roger, for his part, could not sleep; he kept in motion, marching up and down the short, resounding, wooden platform, urged by the midnight cold, and by his thoughts, until his weary vigil was concluded by the arrival of his train. Then he, too, plunged like everybody else into darkness, into the mysterious midnight road, with dark London throbbing and shouting at the end; into life and his fate.

CHAPTER VII

On the same day, and in a manner not very dissimilar, Horace Scarsdale left his home.

If that could be called home which had been for years a prison to the young man. With a secret feeling of exultation, he collected everything belonging to him into a trunk, which he confided, without much explanation, into the hands of Peggy. "When I send for this give it to my messenger," said Horace. Peggy was prudent, and nodded in assent, without asking any question. She had divined for some time that he meant to go away, and Peggy, who thought it the best thing he could do, prepared to remain in ignorance, and to have no information to give her master in case he should think of questioning her. Susan had not yet returned from her walk; there was no one in the house but Mr. Scarsdale, shut up as usual in his study, and Peggy looking out anxiously, but stealthily; unwilling to be seen, or suspected of watching her young master, when Horace left the house. He, too, carried a little bag—and he, too, when he had got half-way across the moor, turned round to look at the house in which the greater part of his life had been spent. Looking back, no tender images softened in the mind of Horace the harsh and angular outline of those unsheltered walls; he had no associations to make sweet to him the dwelling of his youth. He drew a long, deep breath of satisfaction. He had escaped, and he was young, and life was bright before him. As he stood there, too far off to be called back, with his bag lying at his feet among the brown heather, he could see Peggy steal out to the corner of the house and look up and down the road to see which way he had gone, with her hand over her eyes, to shield them from the sun: and then another lighter figure came quickly, with an agitated speed, to the door, and stood there in the sunshine, without looking round her at all, waiting for admittance. Horace contracted his eyebrows over his short-sighted eyes, and smiled to recognize his sister—smiled, but not with affection or pleasure. Perhaps it heightened for the moment his own sense of liberation to see that poor little bird going back to her cage; perhaps he imagined her consternation and alarm and amazement on finding him gone. When Peggy had gone in from her corner, and Susan had disappeared into the house, Horace took up his bag and pursued his way. He was not going any great distance; his destination, for this time at least, was only Kenlisle, where he arrived in the afternoon, after a long walk, made pleasant by the sense of freedom, which increased as step by step he increased the distance between himself and Marchmain.

Horace had not frequented the rural alehouses and listened to the rural talk for nothing. He knew, as far as popular report could tell him, all about the leading people of the district: he knew, what seldom comes to the ears of their equals, except in snatches, what their servants said about them, and all the details and explications which popular gossip gave of every occurrence important enough to catch the public eye. All this, long before he thought of making use of it, Horace noted and remembered by instinct; it amused him to hear of the follies and vices of other people; it amused him to distinguish, in the popular criticism upon them, how much of the righteous indignation was envy, and a vain desire to emulate the pleasant sins which were out of that disapproving public's reach. By this means he knew a great deal more about the social economy of the district than anybody who knew his manner of life would have supposed possible. He had heard, for example, numberless allusions made to a notable attorney, or solicitor, as he called himself, in Kenlisle, who managed everybody's affairs, and knew the secrets of the whole county. It was he to whom Horace intended addressing himself; a romantic idea, one would have supposed; for he was a prosperous man, and was not very likely to prefer a penniless individual in young Scarsdale's position to a rich townsman's son, with premiums and connections. However, the young man was strong in the most undaunted self-confidence—an idea of failure never crossed his mind. He made as careful a toilette as he could at the inn, had himself brushed with great care, and, pausing no longer than was absolutely necessary for these operations, proceeded at once to the solicitor's office. Here Horace presented himself, by no means in the humble guise of a man who seeks employment. Business hours were nearly over—the young men in Mr. Pouncet's office had clustered round one desk, the occupant of which was performing some piece of amateur jugglery, to the immense admiration of his colleagues. These accomplished young men dispersed in haste at the appearance of a stranger. Mr. Pouncet was known to be disengaged, and Horace asked for him with a confidence and authority which imposed even upon the managing clerk. After a very little delay he was ushered into the attorney's sanctuary, where Mr. Pouncet himself, business being over, read the papers in his elbow-chair. Mr. Pouncet had none of Colonel Sutherland's objections to Horace's stooping shoulders. He bowed, and invited him to take a chair, without the least unfavourable comment on the appearance of his visitor. Then the lawyer laid down his paper, took off his spectacles, and assumed the proper look of professional attention. Horace saw he had made a favourable beginning, and rose in courage as he began to speak.

"I have come to consult you about some matters of much importance to me," he said. "I am forced to adopt a profession, though I ought to have no need for any such thing. I have determined to adopt yours, Mr. Pouncet. I have a long explanation to make before you can understand the case—have you time to hear me?"

"Certainly," said the lawyer, but not with effusion; for the preface was not very encouraging to his hopes of a new client.

"My father lives not very far off, at Marchmain, on the borders of Lanwoth Moor," said Horace, and made a pause at the end of these words.

A look of increased curiosity rewarded him. "Ah, Mr. Scarsdale? I remember to have heard the name," said the attorney, taking up his pen, playing with it, and at last, as if half by inadvertence, making a note upon a sheet of paper.

"He lives a life of mystery and seclusion," said Horace; "he has some secret which he guards from me; he says it is unnecessary for me to support myself, and yet his own establishment is poor. What am I to do?—life is insupportable at Marchmain. My uncle wishes me to proceed to London, to read for the bar. I confess my ambition does not direct me towards the bar. I see no necessity for losing my best years in labour which, when I discover all, will most likely be useless to me. Here is what I want to do: I wish to remain near; I wish to attain sufficient legal knowledge to be able to follow this mystery out. Such is my case plainly; what ought I to do?"

Mr. Pouncet gave a single, sharp glance at Horace, then resumed his scribbling on his paper, drawing fantastic lines and flourishes, and devoting a greater amount of attention to these than to his answer. "Really, I find it difficult to advise," he said, in a tone which meant plainly that he perceived his client had something more to say. "Take your uncle's advice."

"No," said Horace; "you will receive me into your office."

"I—I am much obliged, it would be an honour; but my office is already full," said Mr. Pouncet, with a little quiet sarcasm; "I have more clerks than I know what to do with."

"Yes, these fellows there," said Horace—"I can see it; but I am of very different mettle; you will find a place for me; wait a little, you will soon see your advantage in it."

"You have a very good opinion of yourself, my young friend," said the lawyer, laughing dryly, with a little amazement, and a little anger.

"I have," said Horace, laconically; "I know what I can do. Look here—I am not what I have been brought up to appear; there is something in my future which my father envies and grudges me; I know it!—and it must be worth his while; he's not a man to waste his ill-temper without a good cause; very likely there's an appeal to the law before me, when I know what this secret is. You can see what stuff I am made of. I don't want to go to London, to waste time and cultivate a profession; the chances are I shall never require it—give me a place here!"

"Your request is both startling and unreasonable," said Mr. Pouncet, putting down his pen, and looking his visitor full in the face. "I have reason to complain of a direct imposition you have practised upon me. You come as a client, and then you ask for employment; it is absurd. I have young men in my office of most excellent connections—each of them has paid me a premium; and you think the eccentricity of your demand will drive me into accepting you, whom I never saw before; the thing is quite absurd."

"I beg your pardon," said Horace, coolly; "I am not asking for employment—I am your client, seeking your advice; here is your fee. I ask you, whether this is not what you would advise me, as the best thing I could do. As for premium, I don't care for that. If I am not worth half-a-dozen of these lads, to any man who knows how to employ me, it is a very odd thing to me. Now, understand me, sir: I have left home—I wish to conclude what I am to do at once; if not in your office, in some other; can you find a place for me here?"

The lawyer took a pinch of snuff, rose up, went to the window, came back, and after a variety of other restless movements sat down again. During this interval he turned over all that Horace had said, and something more: he made a hurried run over the highly-condensed summary of law reports in his brain, in a vain hunt after the name of Scarsdale. "Most probably a will case," he said to himself. Then he turned once more his eyes on Horace. The young man met that inspection without wavering. What the inquisitor found in that face was certainly not candour and openness of expression; he looked not with a human, but a professional eye. Perhaps it occurred to him that his visitor's boast was something more than a brag, and that one such unscrupulous and acute assistant in his office would be worth much more to him than his articled clerks, who teased the life out of his unfortunate manager, and even puzzled himself. Then, "to do him this favour would be to bind him to me in the commonest gratitude," was the inarticulate reflection which passed through the mind of the attorney; forgetting entirely, as the most sagacious men forget, that the qualities which would make Horace a useful servant were not such as consist with sentiments like gratitude. On the whole, the young man's assurance, coupled with the known mystery that surrounded Marchmain, and the popular report of some great law-suit in which Mr. Scarsdale had once been concerned, imposed upon the lawyer. He kept repeating in his mind, Scarsdale versus —Scarsdale against —, but could not find any name which would satisfy him for the other party to the suit. After some indifferent questions, he dismissed Horace, promising him an answer next day, with which the young man left him, calmly triumphant—and, as it appeared, with reason. Mr. Pouncet could not resist the bait of a probable struggle at law, and all the éclat of a prolonged and important suit. He determined over and over again that Horace had a clever face, and might be of the greatest use to him. He found that he had for some time wanted some one who should be entirely devoted to himself—ready to pick up any information, to make any observation, to do whatever he wanted. He concluded at last that this was the very person; and when Horace came in next day he found himself engaged. The following morning he took his place among the others in the office. Thus he too had entered upon his life.

CHAPTER VIII

"Eyeh, man! and that's a' the geed ye've done? If I had but had the sense to ging mysel'! Where's my son? Black be the day ye coom across this door, ye bletherin' Ould Hunderd! Where's my Sam? Eyeh, my purty boy, that was aye handy to a' things, and ne'er a crooked word in his mouth but when you crossed him, and a temper like an angel? Where's my Sam? Do you mean to tell me you've gane and you've coomed, John Gilsland, and brought nae guid news in your hand?"

"The devil's i' the woman!" cried honest John. "Could I lay the lad on the front o' the mare, and bring him hame like a sack o' corn? He's sorry enough and sick enough by this time, if that's a consolation; but do you think it was me to face the sodger officers, and say he bud not to list?—and him had listed, if I preached till the morn. Na, wife, he's fast and sure—as fast as the Ould Hunderd himsel'. If ye'll take my advice, the best thing you can do is to put up his bundle and make him commforable. He's brewed, and so must he drink. It's for better, for warse, like the marriage state itsel'."

"And grand I would be taking your advice!" said the landlady, more from habit than anger; "and a grand joodge you would mak' o' what a mother'll do for her son! Eyeh, away! I've nae pleasure in man nor woman. Oh, my Sammy! and after all the pains the Colonel took to speak a word to the lad himsel'; and after all his schooling and what was done for him; and a new waistcoat and buttons I bought him mysel' but a week agoo; and everything he could set his face to to make him commforable. Oh! Sammy, Sammy! what will ye say when your mother's grey hairs is brought to the grave in sorrow along o' you? I'll tear the een out o' that murderin' Ould Hunderd if he come near this door!—I will! if he was the best customer in twenty mile. What do I care for his dribble of drink and his deceiving tongue? If it hadn't been for him, I would ne'er have lost my Sammy, the best lad, though I say it as shouldn't, and the cleverest, ye could set your eyes on. I could have trusted him with every key in the house, I could; and the modestest lad! Praise him to his face, and he would colour up like a girl. If I had but had the sense to ging and speak to the offisher mysel'!"

"Eyeh, woman, if ye but had!" said John, "ye would have knowed better; yon'er he is fast enough, and no a penny less than thirty pound'll buy him off, and ye know best yoursel' if ye can spare that off of the business in such bad times; but there's mair as bad off as you. And I can tell you I saw greater folk nor our Sam look wistful at the ribbons. As I sat down by the chimney side, who should come in but Mr. Roger, him that should be the young Squire by rights, if the ould wan had done fairly by him. He stood i' the door, as I might be dooing, and gave a look athwart the place. If he warn't envying of the lads as could 'list, and no more said, never trust my word again. I'll bet a shilling he was in twenty minds to take the bounty himsel'. Though he is a gentleman, he's a deal worse off nor our Sam; he'll goo hanging about in London, till the great folk doo somat for him. He durstent set for'ard bold, and into the ranks wi' him. I'm more grieveder like, in a general way, for the sort of him nor our lad. Dry thy een, wife, and set on a great wash, and take it out on th' wench; it'll do thee good, and thoo canst do nae benefit to Sam."

Mrs. Gilsland, though she contradicted her husband as usual, found some wisdom in his advice, and, after doing something elaborately the reverse for a time, adopted it, to the discomfiture of her poor maid-of-all-work, who might not have appreciated her master's counsel had she been aware of it. A good scold did the landlady good; she sought out poor Sam's wardrobe, collected a little heap of articles to be washed and mended for him, and managed, by this means, to get through the day with tolerable comfort, though interrupted by many gossiping visits of condolence, in all of which she renewed and expatiated upon her grief. When the evening arrived, Mrs. Gilsland was in considerable force, with red eyes, and face a little swollen, but strong in all her natural eloquence and courage, lying in wait for the arrival of the unsuspecting "Ould Hunderd," who had not yet been informed, so far as she was aware of, what had taken place. Before he made his appearance, however, there arrived the carrier from Kenlisle, who made a diversion in her excitement. He brought a note from Horace Scarsdale to John Gilsland, enclosing an open one, addressed to Peggy at Marchmain, and requested her to send his trunk with the bearer; a communication which very much roused the curiosity of both husband and wife. While they were considering this billet, Sergeant Kennedy came in as usual, and got his place, and his pipe, in the public room, without calling forth any demonstration of hostilities. When she became aware of his presence, Mrs. Gilsland rushed into the apartment, with the note still in her hand.

"Eyeh, gude forgive me if I'm like to swear!" cried the indignant mother, "you're here, ye ould deceiver! You're here to beguile other folks's sons, and dare to look me in the face as if ye had ne'er done mischief in your days. Where's my Sam? Where's my lad, that never had an ill thought intill his head till he came to speech of you? Well did the Cornel say ye wur an ould humbug! Where's my son?"

"Husht! husht!" said the Sergeant, soothingly—"I have heard on't already in the town. I always said he was a lad of spirit—he'll make a good souldhier, and some day ye'll be proud enough to see him in his uniform. Husht, would you have the onlearned believe he had 'listed in drink, or because of ill-doing? You're an oncommon discreet woman when ye like. Think of the poor lad's credit, then, and hould your peace. Would you make the foulks think he 'listed like a ne'er-do-well? Husht, if any person says so of Sam Gilsland to me, Sergeant Kennedy, o' the Ould Hunderd, I'll knock him down."

This sudden new aspect of the subject took away the good woman's breath; she was not prepared for so skilful a defence, since, to blame her son in blaming Kennedy, was the last thing she could have thought of. After a few moments she recovered herself, but not the full advantage she had started with.

"I said you was a deceiver, and it's proved upon me," said Mrs. Gilsland; "and you think you can take me in with your lyin' tongue as well as my boy! How dare ye speak of drink or ill-doing and my Sam?—a steadier lad was never born; he's no' like you, you ould sponge that you are, soaking in whatever's gooing in the way of liquor. He's no as long-tongued nor as acquaint with ill; and but for coming across of you when the lad knowed no better, and taking a' your stories for Gospel, he'd ha' been here this day. And you sit and lift up your face to me in my own house, you do! Ye ould storyteller!—ye cruel deceiver!—ye onnat'ral ould man! You a feyther yoursel' and make other foulks's house desolate! But what need I speak?—there's wan there forenenst ye, that cares little more nor you do, for all the lad I'm naming is his son as well as mine!"

This sudden attack took the unfortunate John entirely by surprise; he recoiled a step or two, with an exclamation of amazement and injury. He had been standing calmly by, enjoying the unusual pleasure of listening to his wife's eloquence as a spectator, and rather rejoicing in the castigation of the sergeant. This assault took away his breath—nor was it allowed to remain a single blow. Before anyone could speak, an old cracked, high-pitched voice made itself heard from the door of the apartment, where, shivering with cold, and anger, and age, with an old checked shawl thrown over her cap, old Sally from the Grange shook her withered and trembling hand at the unhappy John.

"It's you that's a-spreading tales against the young maister—it's you!" she cried, in her shrill accents; "and it's you, Betty Gilsland, that's puttin' him up to it; you that's eaten the Squire's bread, and married on his present, and thrived wi' his coostom. Fie upon me for a silly ould fool, that thought there was such a thing as thankfulness to the fore in this world! Eh, man! to think ye should have come coorting to the Grange kitchen, many's the day, and eaten your commf.orable supper wi' the rest on us, and yet have the heart to turn again Mr. Roger, like the gentry themsels! I would not have believed it if half the sheer had ta'en their Bible oath—no, not for nothing but hearing on it mysel'. What ill did he ever doo you, that you should raise a story on Mr. Roger? Oh, fie, fie, fie, for shame!"

The husband and wife looked at each other in mutual amazement at this unexpected charge, while Kennedy pricked up his ears and recovered his former boldness. He did not doubt now to come out of the affair with flying colours; for though John Gilsland's reflections on the looks of Roger when he encountered him the previous night had been overheard and carried rapidly to the interested ears of Sally, the sergeant was still unaware both of Roger's purpose and his departure. He inclined his ear with great attention to Sally's complaint; he cocked his cap upon one side of his head, and assumed the part of moderator with a masterly promptitude; he called her in, waving his hand to her, and set a stool for her near the fire.

"It's mortial cowld," said the sergeant, "here's a drop of beer for you, ould Sally. Them good foulks there, take my word, had no ill maening to Mr. Roger. We'll al' hear the rights on it. Many's the talk I've had with him, and many's the good advice I gave the young man. Onexperienced lads they're al'ways the better of a good advice. Take a drop of beer."

Sally made a nervous, frightened curtsey, warmed her icy fingers at the fire, and took the beer in her hand, with her respects to the sergeant; but before she could drink it Mrs. Gilsland arrested her with a sudden exclamation.

"Sally! touch you none on it—it's pisoned—it's Judas—it's a-betraying on you!" cried the landlady; "if there's harm come to your young gentleman, who should it be but him there? He's seduced away my innocent lad. He's led Sam astray, and putten it into his head to 'list and goo for a souldhier. He's nothing but lies and deceits from end to end on him. If there's harm to the young Squire, you take my word, it's him!"

"Lord have a care of us!" cried Sally, emphasizing her exclamation by a violent start, and dropping the glass from her hands; "pisoned!—eh, the cannibal! the murderin' villain!—and what harm did I ever do to him, a puir old body like me?"

Upon which text the excellent Mrs. Gilsland made a renewed onslaught upon the sergeant, referring directly or indirectly to his influence all the accidents of the country side. If he was in some way to blame for the failed crops and the potato disease, he was evidently first cause that Mr. Roger had left the Grange, and her boy had gone away; both were entirely under the influence of the all-conquering sergeant. John Gilsland stood by a little nervous, but secretly enjoying the attack which old Sally, easily diverted from her indignation against himself, and turning her arms upon "th' Ould Hunderd," aided with all her feeble forces. The other spectators encouraged the combatants with vociferous plaudits. As for the sergeant, he gave his cap a fiercer cock, crossed his arms upon his breast, sat back upright as a post in his chair, and puffed mighty volumes of smoke from his pipe. It was impossible to move him. When at last, in sheer exasperation and rage, the women found nothing more to say, Kennedy took the pipe from his mouth, thrust his chair farther back, and made his exculpatory address:—

"If you will listen to me," said the sergeant, stretching forth his arms, and laying down the plan of his discourse with the fingers of one hand upon the palm of the other, "I'll make you my answer under three heads: There's, firstly, Sam Gilsland—and there's, secondly, Mr. Roger—and there's, thirdly, the Cornel. As ye cannot onderstand the first till ye've heard the last, I advise ye to have patience. Then, in the first place, Sam—he's a very fine lad, clean, well-made, a good figure, a good spirit, fond to be out o' doors, and to see the world. I'll say, before a hunder faothers and maothers, it's a disgrace to keep a man like that serving beer. He behooved to serve his country, did a lad like that; thinks I to mysel', there's a figure for a uniform; if the drill-sergeant had his will o' him, there's hands would be clever at their weapons! Was it my fault that his Maker had made him straight and strong? He heard me speak of the service, sure; I'm a man of experience; I see no good reason to hide my light away from the world; and natur' up and spoke. I knowed no more of his going away nor the babe unborn."

The wily sergeant saw with the corner of his eye that Sam's mother, overcome by this eloquence, had fallen to crying—he knew the day was won.

"And I ask ye a'," said the sergeant, "when a man that's served his country sets foot among ye, with the Queen's coat on his back, and a medal on his breast, do ye turn your backs upon him? Is he not as great a man as the Duke till his furlough's done; and I ask you," continued Kennedy, turning boldly round upon his principal accuser, "when the boy comes to end his life in aise and comfort, with a pension to keep him snug, and never to move his hand but when he pleases—would ye rather he was looking after the farmers' horses, good weather and bad weather, and serving beer?"

Mrs. Gilsland was overcome; flattering fancies stole over her mind; splendid visions of a figure in uniform, with honours and rewards heaped upon him by the public gratitude, which should call her mother; she put up her apron to her eyes and sobbed. The sergeant was victorious.

"And as for Mr. Roger, I am not the man to meddle with them that are aboon my hand—I gave him my advice, like any other speerited young man," said the sergeant; "I tould him my mind of the service. I tould him there was glory and fame to be found in the profession of arms. He was very well inclined to lead me on, was Mr. Roger; he asked about this one and he asked me about the t'other one, and I gave the young gentleman what information I could. And then, ye see, al' at once, out of my knowledge, comes up the Cornel. I cannot purtend to say what business he had here. There was some story about a nevvy of his, Mr. Horry, that ye al' knowe. I've no very great faith in Mr. Horry, for my own account. My belief is—for he never spared pains or trouble for his men, as I can well say—my belief is, if ye ask me, that the Cornel heard there was some promising lads here, and came to take a look at them himself. That's just my fixed opinion, if ye ask me. So there's Sam away, and Mr. Roger away, and I'll lay any man here a hunder pounds we'll hear tell of the Cornel again."

"Eyeh, man! d'ye think it's true?" cried Mrs. Gilsland. "I asked the Cornel to speak to my Sam mysel'. Eyeh, sergeant! it's an awfu' misfortune—but it's a great honour! Do ye think it would be that that brought the Cornel here?"

John Gilsland was more sceptical than his wife; but, at the same time, he was more favourable. "Here's Mr. Horry gone his gate also," said John—"I'm strong o' the mind to take the cart mysel', and goo round by Marchmain the morn for his trunk as he bids, and see if I can see owght o' the ould man."

"Thoo'st aye right ready for a ploy," said his wife, "a deal better than honest work. Eyeh, but it's true—Mr. Horry has gane as well—three young men of them out of this wan place! Blees me! its awful like as if the Cornel was at the bottom o't, after all."

"Ay, ay—you'll come into my opinion. I seed him three times mysel'. The Cornel was aye an affable gentleman, and spoke his mind free; I knows what I knows," said the sergeant—"he had his own occasions here."

"Come you with me, Sally, and you shall have a cup o' tea to comfort your heart," said Mrs. Gilsland. "Eyeh, woman, I'm heartbroken; but I'm glad!—three on them, and his own nevvy! That Mr. Horry is a rael queer lad—he takes no more notice of a body nor if they were the dust beneath his feet; but dreedful clever, there's no doubt. I'll make John goo himsel' to Marchmain as he said—maybe there's some news. Keep a good heart about the young Squire, Sally. I would not say but them three they're all together, and the Cornel with them; and they're rael well off, if he's there, that's for certain; such a man!"

CHAPTER IX

The next day John Gilsland and his cart took their leisurely way across the moor, carrying with them the note which Horace had addressed to Peggy at Marchmain.

Horace had now been gone two days. The afternoon of the day on which he left home Peggy confided her suspicions on this subject to Susan, who was struck with alarm and terror, quite out of proportion to the event. Where had he gone?—what would he do?—and what, oh! what would papa say? Susan sat by herself in the dining-room, vainly trying to work; and now that there was so little likelihood of hearing his footstep, watching for it with the most breathless eagerness. Evening came, and the dreaded hour of dinner; exactly at six o'clock Mr. Scarsdale took his seat at the head of the table. Horace's chair was placed as usual, and stood empty by the side. Mr. Scarsdale gave one glance at the empty seat, as he took his own, but said nothing. Susan could not help remembering the only former time when that place was vacant, the day so happy and so miserable, when Uncle Edward first came to Marchmain. As on that occasion, his father took no notice of the absence of Horace; the dinner was eaten in silence, Susan swallowing a sob with every morsel which she ate, and trembling as she had trembled before her father ever since the interview in which he forbade her correspondence with her uncle, and she refused to obey him. That scene had never departed from her mind—her own guilty feeling had never subsided. Bearing on her conscience her first real personal offence against her father, it was impossible for Susan now to have any confidence even in their accustomed stillness. She felt a continual insecurity when he was present—at any moment he might address to her these commands and reproaches again.

But the evening passed as usual, without any interruption; once more Mr. Scarsdale sat motionless at the table, as he had done every evening in Susan's remembrance, with his book set up on the little reading-desk, and the crystal jug with his claret, reflecting itself in the shining table. And there sat Susan opposite him, somehow afraid to-night to bring out her embroidery-frame, or to employ herself with any of the pretty things which Uncle Edward had bought for her—taking once more, with timidity, and half afraid that he would notice even that, her neglected patchwork, out of her large, old work-bag. Susan had been trimming up for her own use, with great enjoyment of the task, with linings of blue silk, and scraps of ribbon found in one of Peggy's miscellaneous hoards, an old, round work-basket, which she had found in the upper room where the apples were kept. But she did not venture to put that ornamental article, so simply significant as it was of the rising tide of her young feminine life, upon the table. She bent over her neglected patchwork, smoothing it out and laying the pieces together, but somehow finding it entirely impossible to fix her attention upon them. She could not help watching her father, shaking with terror when, in putting down her scissors, or her cotton, she disturbed the profound stillness; she could not help listening intently for those sounds outside which betokened to her accustomed ear the approach of Horace. She longed, and yet she feared to see her brother come back again; she could not believe he had really gone away; she wondered, till her head ached, where he could be; and could not bring herself to realize anything more cheerful about him than an aimless wandering through that dreary moor, or through the cold cheerless dark streets described in some of her novels, which two things the poor child connected together with an unreasonable ignorance. Then came the dismal tea-making. The night went on—it grew late, but still Mr. Scarsdale kept his seat. Midnight, dark, cold, solitary night, with the fire going out, the candles burned to the sockets, and Peggy, as all was still, supposed to be in bed. Then Mr. Scarsdale closed his book. "It is quite time you should have gone to rest," he said. "Why do you start?—is there anything astonishing in what I say? Good night!"

Susan got up instantly, stumbled towards the side-table, got her candle, and lighted it with a trembling hand. She went out of the room so quickly, and in such evident trepidation, that the sight of her terror struck another arrow into her father's mind. He looked after her with a pale, dreadful smile. "She is afraid of me!" said the forlorn man. He said the words aloud, and Susan came back trembling to the door, to ask if he called her. His "No!" drove her to her room with hurried steps, and limbs which could scarcely carry her. Susan was so terrified that she could not rest; she put her candle in her room, and came out to look over the rail of the little gallery from which the bed-chambers opened. There, standing in the dark, after a little interval, she saw her father come out of the dining-room, with his candle in his hand, and go to the door, which he barred and bolted, with a precaution Susan had never known to be taken before. Then she heard him securing the shutters of the windows. With an infallible instinct of alarm and terror, she knew that it was against the return of Horace that all these precautions were taken. She stole into her room, closed the door noiselessly, and looked out. Black in its unbroken midnight of gloom lay the moor, a waste of desolate darkness on every side, rain falling, masses of black clouds sweeping over the sky, a shrill gleam of the windy horizon far away, shining over the top of the distant hills. And Horace, if he should be near, if he should still be coming home, remorselessly shut out! Susan sat up half the night, listening with a nervous terror to all the mysterious sounds which creep and creak in the absolute silence of the dead hours of night. Horace was most comfortably asleep in a comfortable room in the "George," at Kenlisle, while his poor sister sat wrapped in a big shawl, trying to keep awake, thinking she heard his footsteps approaching the house, and waiting only to be certain before she should steal down-stairs in the dark to open the door. Poor Susan fell fast asleep at last, and slept till long after her usual time; then she was roused by Peggy to just such another day. Mr. Scarsdale still did not say a word, though his glance at the empty chair was more sharp and eager. And so things continued till the forenoon of the third day, when John Gilsland stopped his cart at the door; and, calling for Peggy in his loud, hearty voice, which could be heard over all the house, informed the entire family of Marchmain that he had come for Mr. Horry's box.

Susan was with Peggy in the kitchen, solacing her anxieties by a discussion of where her brother could be, and what he was most likely to be doing. This summons made her jump, as she stood listlessly by the window. Peggy, without saying a word, made a stride to the side door, and went round to the corner of the house to confront this incautious messenger. Susan, trembling and afraid to join her, sprang up upon the wooden chair, and peeped out of the window. There she saw Peggy in the act of assaulting the unfortunate John, shaking him by the shoulder, and demanding to know if that was the way to deliver a message at a gentleman's house. John scratched his head and shrugged his shoulders: he was too much accustomed to ill-usage from women to feel much resentment; he only looked sheepish, and, patting the mare on the shoulder, came round with Peggy to the side door. There she introduced him on tiptoe, taking elaborate precautions of quietness, which were all intended to impose upon John, and silence his heavy feet and country clogs to the greatest degree of silence possible.

"It's not so heavy but what a man like you can carry it down on your shoulder," said Peggy; "and if ye make a bump on the road, Gude forgive ye, for I'll no, nor the master, if he's disturbed in his study. I would not advise you to rouse up him. Whisht then!—if you have any regard for your own peace, hold your tongue! In the very stairs, and the study no furder off nor yon door! If ye cannot be quiet, it's as much as your ears are worth!"

Thus warned, John went creaking on his tiptoes upstairs, and was introduced to Mr. Horace's room, where the furniture had been specially arranged, and where the good order and trim array of everything made no small impression on his simplicity. John got downstairs again in safety, jealously watched by Peggy, who stamped her foot at him from the foot of the stairs, and produced the "bump" which she had deprecated by her super-caution. However, the business was performed in safety, the cart was drawn up to the side door, and Horace's goods safely deposited in it—Mr. Scarsdale, up to this moment, taking no notice of the proceeding. Then John returned into the kitchen, to have a little chat with Peggy, who was nothing loth. Peggy did all the marketing for the family, and though perfectly impenetrable and deaf to all questions about her master, was rather popular in the neighbouring villages, as a housekeeper and purveyor, who was not sparing in her provisions for her master's table, was like to be. John stood, with his hat in one hand and a glass of beer of Peggy's own brewing in the other, describing to Mr. Scarsdale's factotum the events of the previous days—Th' young squire gone out of the Grange, no one knew where; his own son listed, and gone for a soldier; and Mr. Horry—ah! Mr. Horry was deep, he never let on of his secrets: he supposed the family knew where the young gentleman was.

Susan kept in the kitchen, hovering about the window, very anxious, but afraid, to ask questions, and listening to this volunteer gossip with all her ears. Peggy answered very brusquely to the inferred question of Horace's messenger.

"You may depend the family doesn't need to ask you," said Peggy. "Mak' haste, man, about your ain business—no wonder the wife has little patience if this is how you put off your time. How will ye send on the box?—that's all I'm wanting to hear."

"Oh, just by the carrier—to the 'George' at Kenlisle—it's none so far away either," said John; "if the family wanted word sent particular, I could goo a' the way mysel.'"

As he made this offer he threw an inquisitive glance at Susan, whose restless attention he had skill enough to perceive. Peggy's answer was a violent shake of her head, as she went on with her work. John resumed.

"Our wife, she thinks it's a very strange thing that these three should be away at the same moment, as you may say. Not to compare our Sam to the young gentlemen, but you see Sam had a word himself with the Cornel. As for the young squire, he was coming and going the whole time, and Mr. Horry, he's nevvy to th' ould gentleman, as far as I can hear. It's a rael coorious thing—they all had speech o' the Cornel, and all started off on the same day. Maybe you and the young lady you ken a deal better nor that—but ye'll allow it's an awfu' coorious thing."

While John, pausing, looked for an answer, in calm security of having said something which could not fail to make an impression; while Peggy, with her back to him, vigorously washed her dishes, clattering one upon another with emphasis, which, however, did not drown his voice, and was not intended to do so; and while Susan stood timidly with her work in her hand, startled with this new piece of intelligence, and looking towards the stranger with a face full of wonder, a sudden sound startled the vigilant ear of Peggy. But she had scarcely time to put down the dinner-plate in her hand, and to wave her towel at John Gilsland, commanding imperatively a hasty retreat, when the door of the kitchen suddenly flew open, and Mr. Scarsdale himself, pale, erect, and passionate, his dressing-gown flying wide around him with "the wind of his going," his thin lips set together, and an expression of restrained and silent fury in his face, came abruptly into the room.

John recoiled a step in amazement and awe; then, emboldened by curiosity, kept his place, and made his bow to the master. Mr. Scarsdale stamped his foot on the floor in lack of words, and pointed to the door with a violent gesture; and before he knew what he was about, Peggy rushed against John, thrust him out before her, and closed and bolted the door after him. The amazed and sheepish look with which he rubbed his shoulders, and gazed at the inhospitable door from which he had been so summarily expelled, would have been worth a comic actor's while to see. The honest fellow stood outside, looking first at the house and then at his mare, with a ludicrous astonishment. "The devil's in the woman!" said John. That was a proposition not unfamiliar to him. Then in his blank bewilderment he marched gravely round the house, spying in at the vacant windows. Everything was empty except that kitchen, in which the pale spectre in the dressing-gown might be murdering the women for anything John knew. What should he do? After various pauses of troubled cogitations, John decided that discretion was the better part of valour, and chirruped to his mare. The two went off together, much discomfited, and the landlord of the "Tillington Arms" had full occupation for the rest of the road in amending the circumstances according to his fancy, and bringing himself into sufficient dignity and importance in the tale to make it meet for the ears of his wife.

When John Gilsland was disposed of, Mr. Scarsdale addressed himself to his daughter and his servant.

"I understand," he said, without speaking directly to either, "from his absence at table, and from the articles which I have just now seen taken out of the house, that Mr. Horace Scarsdale has chosen to leave Marchmain; I say nothing against that—he is perfectly welcome to choose his own residence; but I desire you to understand, both of you, that on no pretence whatever must this young man return into my house—not even for a visit; he has placed himself among those strangers whom I decline to admit. I make no complaint," added the recluse, coldly, "that my family conspire against me, and that messages are received, and my property sent away, without my knowledge."

"Master," said Peggy, while Susan stood trembling before her father, her work fallen from her hands, and her womanish fright and anguish falling into tears. "Master," exclaimed his old servant, who was not afraid of him, "you're no to leave that reproach on me. I've conspired against none of you, if it was my last word! Your son's gone, as he should have gone a dozen years ago, if ye had been wise, or ta'en my advice. He's gone, and God's blessing and grit speed be with him! I never was more glad of nothing in my born days; and for his things in his box!—I knowed you a lad and a man, and a better man nor you are this day; but did I ever even it to you to keep back another man's, if it was a servant's claithes?"

"Be silent!" cried Mr. Scarsdale, putting his hand to his ears; "you conspire, you whisper, you hide in corners; there is not a soul in the world whom I can trust; but I beg you to understand, in respect to Horace Scarsdale, that I am master here, and that he shall not return to this house. He may say he wishes to see his sister—he does not care a straw for his sister! Do you comprehend me?—he is never again to enter here!"

Neither at first said a word, but Peggy advanced before her master and dropped him a grave curtsey. "You're master here," said Peggy; "never a word against your will, as has been proved for fifteen years, could wild horses get out of me. I've served you faithful, and I will. Bear your ain blame before heaven, and the Lord forgive you, master. It's my hope he'll never seek to enter these darksome doors again."

Thus concluded the startling episode of Horace Scarsdale's departure from his father's house. Deeply wounded, in spite of herself, by her father's plain and cold statement that Horace did not care a straw for his sister, Susan went back to her now unbroken solitude. Perhaps it was true, but it was not the less cruel to say it; and now that he was gone Susan's heart clung to her brother. She tried to remember that he had been sometimes kind to her; it was hard to collect instances, and yet Horace, too, like other people, had been moved by caprice sometimes in his life, and had done things once or twice contrary to the tenor of his character. And her whole nature revolted against the unnatural prohibition which debarred his return. There she sat, poor child, in that dreary room, certain now that no voice but her father's should ever break its silence—that nobody but he should ever sit opposite to her at table; and if her heart sank within her, as she tried in vain to occupy herself with her needlework, it was not wonderful. She thought of Horace, and Roger Musgrave, and Sam Gilsland, with a sigh—she wondered whether John was right; and with almost a pang of jealousy wondered still more that her uncle should take pains to liberate these three, while yet he did not try to do anything for her. She could not work—she tried her novels, but she had read them all, and in them all there was not one situation so forlorn and hopeless as her own. Poor Susan threw herself on her knees, with her face against the prickly hair-cloth of the elbow-chair—not to pray, but to bewail herself, utterly disheartened, angry and hopeless! Her temper was roused; she was cross and bitter, and full of unkindly thoughts; she felt as if she herself loved nobody, as nobody loved her. By-and-bye, when a sense of her attitude struck her, with its appearance of devotion, and the strangely contrary feelings of her mind, she sprang to her feet in a passion of sobs and tears, feeling more guilty and miserable than she could have explained. After a long time—for there were elements of stubbornness and obstinacy in Susan's nature—she subdued herself, and went upon her knees in earnest. When she was there the second time, thoughts came upon her of Uncle Edward's tender blessing, of his family in heaven, and of the confidence, so calm and certain, with which the old man looked thither. The poor child scarcely knew how to pray out of her wont; but her very yearning for some compassionate ear to pour her troubles into gave her heart expression—and in the act was both comfort and hope.

CHAPTER X

While Colonel Sutherland's plans for everybody's benefit were thus being rendered useless, the Colonel himself, unaware of these untoward circumstances, waited anxiously for answers to those letters which he had written at Tillington. Morning after morning the good man sighed over a post which brought him only his Times, and the letters of his boys. The dining-room at Milnehill, which was breakfast-room and library, and everything to the Colonel, was as unlike as possible to that of Marchmain. One side of it was lined with bookcases, full of the collections of the Colonel's life. There were two large windows, commanding a wonderful view. A Turkey carpet, warm and soft, a low fireplace polished and shining, a great easy-chair, drawn close to the cosy round table, with its cosy crimson drapery falling down round it, just appearing beneath the folds of the snow-white tablecloth. Here the Colonel took his place in the morning, rubbing his chilled fingers, and pleased, in his solitude and the freshness of his heart, by the look of comfort around him. Here he took his solitary breakfast, and looked over his Times, and wondered why there were still no answers to his letters. It was not wonderful in the case of Sir John Armitage, who might be at the other end of the world for anything that was known of him; but why there should be ten days' delay in having a letter from London, the Colonel did not know.

One morning, however, two epistles in unknown hands were brought him; he took the one which bore the London postmark. This is how it ran:—

"DEAR SIR,—Your favour of the 15th came duly to hand, though I confess that I was startled by its contents. My connection with the Scarsdale estate is not what you imagine. I have no control over the money whatever, nor power to draw upon it until the proper period; therefore, of course, I must decline, as you will perceive it is entirely impossible for me to accede to your request. My position is sufficiently uncomfortable at present without further complications.

"You are, perhaps, aware that the trustees were chosen from among young men, for the express reason that they might be expected to survive until the time stipulated. As I have just said, I find my position sufficiently disagreeable already, and should be very sorry to embarrass it further with any unjustifiable proceedings. Your relation has the eye of a lynx, and keeps it constantly upon us. As for the young man, I cannot but think his father is quite right in keeping him ignorant. In such circumstances as his, with the least inclination towards gaiety, and knowing his own position, he would assuredly fall into the hands of the Jews. As for putting him in a profession, I am bound to say with Mr. Scarsdale, that I consider it unnecessary; but as I am unable to render any assistance, I refrain from advice which might not be so acceptable as I could wish."

The Colonel read this over and over again, with concern and attention. After he had fully satisfied himself of its meaning, and discovered that there was not even an inference of help from one end to the other, he folded it up again, and threw it into the fire. "Better leave no chance of its ever coming into Horace's hands," he said, as he accomplished this discreet destruction. He was annoyed and vexed with a renewal of the feeling which had moved him on his interview with Mr. Scarsdale, though without the profound regret and compassion which he then experienced; but he was scarcely disappointed. He held his other letter in his hand, and entered into a little rapid mental calculation before he broke the seal, considering how it would be possible, out of his own means, to make the necessary provision for his nephew's studies—"Unnecessary for him to have a profession? Is it necessary for the boy to be ruined body and soul?" cried the Colonel, unconsciously aloud—"because he has the luck to be descended from a diabolical old—." Here Colonel Sutherland made a pause, restrained himself, shook his head, and said, with a sigh, thinking certainly of his brother-in-law, and perhaps a little of his nephew, "Ah! there's mischief in the blood!"

His other letter was that one which poor Roger Musgrave had written amid all the echoes of his empty house. This agitated and excited the Colonel much more than the other had done. His spectacles grew dim while he was reading it—he gave utterance to various exclamations at the different points of the letter. He said, "Very true!" "Very natural!" "Poor fellow!" "Exactly as I should have felt myself!"—and showed other demonstrations of interest in his restless movements and neglect of his half-finished breakfast. The conclusion, however, threw him into evident distress; he got up and walked about the room, stopping unconsciously to take up a piece of useless paper on one of the tables and tear it into little pieces. Anxiety and doubt became the prevailing expression of his face. Here in a moment were all his plans for Roger deranged and broken to pieces; and yet it was so natural, so characteristic, on the whole so right and honest, that he could not say a word against it. But it did not grieve him the less on that account. Roger was going to London, that was the sole clue to him; and he had no reply from Sir John Armitage—no response to his own appeal from the influential personages whom he believed himself to have influence with.

"He'll be a private soldier by this time; most likely a Guardsman," said the Colonel, and his imagination conjured up the splendid figures under the arches at the Horse Guards with a positive pang, as he thought of Roger Musgrave's ingenuous face turned, crimson and shame-faced, towards the crowd. What could the Colonel do?—nothing but fill his mind with anxious and uncomfortable reflections concerning the life and fortune, and, besides these, the manners and morals, of his young protegé—and wait.

The house of Milnehill stood upon the sunny brae of Inveresk, at no great distance from the square barn-church, ornamented by a pepperbox steeple, with which the taste of our grandfathers has crowned that lovely little eminence. The garden on one side was surrounded by an old wall, mossed and gray, above which you could see nothing but the towering branches of the chestnuts, which in the early summer built fair their milky pinnacles of blossom over this homely enclosure. The garden sloped under these guardian shadows open and bright towards the sea, though at the distance of at least two miles from the immediate coast—and the wall on the lower side was low enough to permit a full view from the windows of that beautiful panorama: the little town of Musselburgh, with its fishing suburb lying snug below; the quiet pier stretching its gray line of masonry into the sea; the solitary fishing-boat hovering by; the wide sweep of bay beyond, with the Bass in the distance lying like a turtle or tortoise upon the water, and all the low, far, withdrawing ranges of the hills of Fife. The house was of two stories, homely and rural, with one pretty bright room on either side of the little hall, which was filled with Indian ornaments, as was also Colonel Sutherland's drawing-room, which the Colonel did not enter once in a month. Behind and on the upper story there was abundant room for a family—though the rooms upstairs were low, and shaded by the eaves. The house altogether was old-fashioned, and much behind its neighbours. Smooth polished stone, square-topped windows, palladian fronts, and Italian villas have strayed into Inveresk as to other quarters of the world. But Milnehill remained red-tiled and picturesque, with eaves in which the swallows built, and lattice windows which opened wide to the sweet air and sunshine, and smoke curling peacefully through the branches over the red ribs of the tiled roof. The Colonel had some family associations with the place—perhaps, in his heart, for he was no artist, the old soldier was a little ashamed of his tiles, and thought the smooth "elevation" next to him, turning its windows to the dusty road, and looking as if it had strayed out from the town for a walk and been somehow arrested there, was a much superior looking place to his nest among the trees. But Milnehill, the Colonel was fond of saying, was very comfortable, and he liked the view; and, indeed, not to consult the Colonel, the fact was, Milnehill was the cosiest, honestest little country house within a dozen miles.

If Susan could but see that paradise of comfort and kindness!—she who knew no interior but Marchmain. When the Colonel had read his paper he put up his glasses, put on his great-coat, took his hat and his cane, and went out through his garden, pausing to see the progress of the crocuses, and to calculate in his own mind when his earliest tulip would bloom—to take his daily walk. Though his mind was engaged, he had all that freshness and minuteness of external observation which some old men keep to the end of their days: he saw, with a real sensation of pleasure, the first big bud upon his favourite chestnut begin to shake out its folded leaves; he noted the earliest tender shoot of a green sheath starting through the sheltered soil, in that sweet nook where his lilies of the valley waited for the spring; and so opened his garden gate and went out into the sunshine of the high-road, to see the light shining upon Arthur's seat, and the smoke floating over Edinburgh, and the country between quivering over with an indescribable sentiment of renewal and life. There was not very much variety in the Colonel's walks—this day, without any particular intention, he turned his steps towards the sea.

The Colonel took his leisurely way, with his hat a little on the back of his head, and his cane in his hand, along the dusty high-road towards Edinburgh. Most of the people who met him on the way knew the old soldier: he got salutations respectful and familiar on all sides; he had something to say to half at least of the people on the road; and at the doors, as he passed along in the fresh sunshine, which gladdened the air without much warming it. Through the breaks in the houses were to be seen glimpses of the broad sands, with the sea breaking upon them in its long rush and roll, ringing through the air like a cannon-shot, though there was nothing beyond a fresh breeze to impel its course. The Colonel, born in this neighbourhood, and carrying its well-remembered sights and sounds in his heart, during all his years of exile, rejoiced in the boom of the Firth with that mixture of familiarity and novelty which makes all the special features of his native locality so delightful to a man who has been absent from it for years. He went along, stopping now and then to speak to some one, recognizing every turn on the road, and curious if he met a face which he had not seen before; happy in his fresh outward eye, his youthful heart, and the natural friendliness and universal interest which covered the sunny surface of this Christian soul. Do not think that what lay below was less profound or less sincere; but for that happy, natural temperament, that involuntary observation of external things, the Colonel would have been a bereaved, solitary, heartbroken man—would he have been better, or more worthy of the love and respect which followed him everywhere?

As he approached the little town of Portobello, the Colonel diverged from his road, and went to make inquiries of kindness for an old friend. It was a prim suburban house, with its little plot of grass and evergreens before the door, at which he entered, on the urgent invitation of the maid, who, with perhaps less apparent deference than such a maid would have had on the other side of the border, smiled over all her fresh face her own welcome to "the Cornel," and took upon herself to assure him that "the mistress was all her lane, and had been baith the day and yesterday, and would be so thankful to see him." On this representation the Colonel entered. This, too, it was easy to gather from a priori evidence, was an Indian house. Indian curiosities ornamented the hall and staircase, by which the Colonel proceeded to the drawing-room, a little faded in colour but very comfortable, where an old lady, wrapped in a large old Indian shawl, of which the colours, like the colours of the room, were rather the worse of years, sat in an easy chair, with a soft footstool, and cushions for her shoulders, the bell within her reach, and a little table with her book and her work close by her side. Her hair was snow-white, but her cheeks as fresh in complexion through their wrinkles as the cheeks of her rosy maid; and her close cap, with its soft white blond and white ribbons, came round her kind old face with a warm and homely simplicity, increasing the natural expression, which was that which we call by instinct motherly. Yet mother as she certainly must have been, she was alone, with nothing near to bear witness of family love or ties, save a half-open letter, written on impalpable pink Indian-letter paper, which lay on her little table. The old lady held out her hand to her visitor without rising from her chair. "Is that you, Edward? I am very glad to see you," she said, with a look of real pleasure. The Colonel drew a chair to the other side of the table, and sat down opposite to her. Then they asked each other about their health, and the Colonel confided his private pangs of rheumatism to the attentive ear of his ancient friend. They were old friends, "close connections," as they said themselves—old people—had lived much the same kind of life, with the difference of man and woman; knew each other's affairs and each other's friends; and had lived for years on those terms of affectionate amity which by-and-by perhaps will be impracticable, and not to be hoped for, between a man and his deceased wife's sister. Such was the relationship between Colonel Sutherland and Mrs. Melrose: they had all the confidence of brother and sister in each other, with perhaps even a touch of more animated kindness, because their friendship had a little of choice in it, as well as of nature.

"You look fashed," said the old lady. "I can see there's some trouble going on behind your smile. What's the matter? Nothing wrong, I hope, with the boys?"

"No, thank heaven!" said the Colonel; "if I had not meddled with other boys, who are less within my control. I have two vexatious letters this morning—one from that trustee I told you I had written to about my nephew: he will not do anything for him."

"I thought as much," said Mrs. Melrose, with a little nod of her head. "Take my advice another time, Edward: never you put any dependence on these business men; what do they care for a young man's heart or spirit, when it's interest and compound interest that's in the question? I saw a great deal of them when I was young. My uncle that we were sent home to was a merchant, you remember: we used to spend our holidays there. I was very near marrying in that way myself, if I had had my own will at seventeen. They're very good fathers and husbands, and the like of that; but put a question of what's good for a man, and what's good for his money, before them, and they aye put the last first. Yes, yes, I had very little hopes from that; but you, you see, you're one of the sanguine kind—you are a man that never will learn."

"So it appears," said the Colonel; "and now, as though that were not enough, here's that hot-headed young Musgrave I told you of—he about whom I wrote to old Armitage, of the Fifty-ninth, and to Sir George—a famous young fellow!—a boy you'd make a pet of, as sure as life; here's a letter from him, informing me that he can't impose upon my goodness, and all that sort of thing, and that he's off to London. I have no doubt in my own mind," said the Colonel, solemnly, "that at this moment the lad's on horseback under the arch at the Horse-Guards, with a crowd staring at him. You may laugh, but it's a very melancholy reflection; a man of birth and manners; the last of an old family; it is extremely vexatious to me."

"And why should the folk stare at him?—is he such a paladin?" asked the old lady, with her merry laugh.

"He is a handsome fellow," said the Colonel, "and carries himself like a gentleman—which is more than can be said of everybody," he added, with a vexed recollection of Horace; "however, these are all my affairs. Is that a letter from Charlie? I certainly begin to forget the time for the mail."

"You'll find it out by-and-bye, when Ned is gone," said Mrs. Melrose; "but look you here, Uncle Edward—here's a sight for you—do ye think that's like Charlie's hand?"

The Colonel made haste to get his spectacles from his pocket, and put them on with a little nervousness.

"Eh?—what?—it's a lady's hand," he cried, peering at the pink epistle, which the old lady held out to him triumphantly at arms length. "Who is it? Eh? What's this? Fanny—no—Annie Melrose? Who on earth is Annie Melrose? Do you mean to tell me the boy's married before he has been out a year?"

"Indeed, and I am very sorry to say it is quite true," said the old lady, shaking her head with a demure and proper regret, which was quite belied by the bright expression in her eyes; "and really the two young fools, they seem so happy, that I have not the heart to blame him; for, after all, he's my only one, Edward, and I know who she is—she's Charlie's Colonel's daughter—you may recollect her; but I doubt if she was out before you came home. It's a very short acquaintance, to be sure, but she was at school here, and used to come and spend the day with me. Her mother and I were great friends at Bintra when my poor General was in command there. The father was just a subaltern then, and no so very discreet either; and she was fighting among her young family, poor thing! I took a notion in my head that she was like one of my friends at home, and grew very fond of her. That time when Charlie was ill, when he was five years old, just before we sent him home, when I wanted poor Mary to go to the hills with me, and she could not—you remember?—I took Mrs. Oswald and her youngest, who was very delicate just then. To be sure, it was only a baby, poor bit thing, but the two bairns had but one ayah between them, and lived for a month or two like brother and sister. They were too young to remember anything about it; but I always think there's a providence in these things. And so the short and the long of it is, Charlie's married, and here's a penitent letter from him, and a loving one from her; and if you believe me, when I got them first, what with Charlie's pretence to be very sorry for doing the rash act, as the newspapers say, out of my knowledge, when it was just as clear as possible the boy was out of his wits with happiness; and what with her pretty bit kindly letter, poor thing! I laughed with pleasure till I cried, and cried till I laughed again. And you may look as grave as you like, Uncle Edward—it was what you did yourself, my man, and what your son will do after you; and you'll no persuade me to make myself wretched because my only son is happy, and has made himself a home."

Here some tears rolled quietly into the corners of the old lady's eyes, and were wiped off with a small, withered, lively hand.

"For you know, Edward," she added, softly, "though I am not the person to say much about that kind of thing, or to deny that there's quite as many bad women as bad men, still, you know, Edward, it wants one of us really to make a home."

"Ay, Elizabeth, I know," said the Colonel, with a suppressed and quiet sigh. Then there was a momentary pause; but these two old people had both come through life and its battles; both knew losses severe enough to be beyond talking of; and over both beneficent age, consciously approaching the invisible borders of another world, had spread his patience and calm. The stream of talk was renewed again with a very little interval.

"But I want to know," said Mrs. Melrose, "what you are going to do about your nephew—is he coming here?"

"I proposed he should; I don't know—very likely he may prefer London; indeed, it is rather difficult to decide for Horace; he has a great opinion of his own judgment," said the Colonel. "However, things are less complicated now; there is only himself to think of, since it appears whatever is to be done for him I must do."

"Mind the boys in the first place, who have the best right, Edward," said the prudent old lady; "and mind, too, that I have a penny in the corner of my purse if you should be put to that; and then about your niece—is there any word of her coming to Milnehill?"

"I fear it," said the Colonel, shaking his head; "but, by-the-bye, that reminds me—if I could persuade her father to let Susan come, will you come to Milnehill, Elizabeth, and take charge of my little girl?"

"For why?" said Mrs. Melrose; "do you think you are not a safe enough guardian for your niece at your age?—or that the young creature wants an old wife to be spying over her for propriety's sake?

Nonsense!—and beside, Edward, if all's true the papers say, I'll want somebody to take care of me, a delicate young person that I am, when I go to your house. You do not suppose I would have gone to see you if I had thought you any less than a brother all this time? But look at the fellow's impudence, venturing to say, in the very Parliament itself, that the like of us are no relations, and might court and marry like strangers. I would just like to have a woman's Parliament for once in a way, to settle them, the filthy fellows!—if they got out of it with a hair upon their heads I can tell you it would be no fault of mine."

"You were always a politician, Elizabeth," said the Colonel, rising with a smile.

"Very true. I had to read up all the news by every mail to let my poor General know what he would be interested in," said the old lady; "little wonder if I came to like it myself; and speaking of that, Edward, go you your ways home and send me the Times. You would have brought it with you if you had been a thoughtful man."

"Wait a wee," said the Colonel, in his kindly Scotch. "I had very near forgot it with your news; here it is, safe in my pocket all this time—and never deliver your judgment, Elizabeth, after this, till you're sure the pannel is duly convicted. Here it is!"

So saying, the Colonel put down the paper, and took his leave of his sister-in-law. As he went downstairs her elder servant, who seemed to be on the watch, came out of the kitchen, followed by the pretty maid, to arrest the Colonel, and ask if he knew Mr. Charlie was married. "And the mistress is as pleased!" said that respectable functionary, "and pretends to be angry, and laughs wi' her heart grit—and him only three-and-twenty, and her eighteen! Cornel! did ye ever hear the like a' your days?"

"Oh, yes, I've heard the like," said Colonel Sutherland, smiling; "and as it was sure to happen some time, Janet, do you not think it's as well soon as syne?"

"Weel, Cornel, that's true," said Janet, going out with grave perplexity to open the little garden gate for him. Janet was more shocked in her propriety than her mistress, and did not find it nearly so easy to reconcile herself to the strange event.

Then the Colonel proceeded homeward in the same leisurely fashion. The day had overcast, the breeze had freshened, the sea rushed with a louder fling upon the sand, and made a sharper report at the height of each successive wave. Rain was coming on, and Colonel Sutherland quickened his footsteps. When he had reached as far as the wayside village of Joppa (Joppie in the vernacular), it was necessary to take shelter till the shower was over. While he stood waiting, with his deaf ear attentive to the entreaty of the good woman at whose porch he stood, to come in and rest, a post-chaise went rapidly past. Glancing out from it, with the momentary glance of a wayfarer, appeared a face which the Colonel recognized without being able to tell who it was; a yellow face, querulous but kindly—a fastidious, inquisitive pair of eyes. Beside the driver on the box was a man with a cockade on his hat, with whose face, too, the Colonel found himself strangely familiar. Who could it be? He watched the vehicle till it was out of sight, persuading himself that it had taken the road to Inveresk, and followed it as soon as the rain was over, without knowing who his visitors might be, but in the fullest expectation of finding somebody arrived before him at Milnehill.

"Somebody has arrived!—who is it?" asked the Colonel of his factotum, who opened to him the garden-door—that door in the wall which admitted you suddenly into all the verdure of the garden of Milnehill.

"Cornel, you're a warlock!" exclaimed the man, with amazement. "This very moment, sir, two carpet-bags and a portmanteau. I reckon they're meaning to stay."

"They—who are they?—is there more than one?" asked the Colonel; "make haste! do you see you keep me in the wet, blocking up the door?"

"The rain's off," said Patchey, dogmatically; "I'm meaning to say there's wan gentleman, and his man, of course—his man. That's maybe no interesting to you, Cornel—but it is to me."

"You provoking old rascal!—who is it?" said the Colonel.

Patchey scratched his head. "If you'll believe me, Cornel, I cannot think upon the name. It's no Arnot—no, that's not it; nor Titchfield neither. I ken him as weel as I ken mysel', Cornel—dash me if ever I thought of asking him his name! Arnold—na—tuts! he was in the Queen's service, this gentleman, up Burmah ways, when there was warm work gaun on; but, bless me, what whimsy's ta'en the Cornel by the head noo?"

This last exclamation followed the Colonel's abrupt disappearance along the garden-path, leaving Patchey amazed and wonderstricken, with his hand upon the door. Colonel Sutherland had heard enough to inspire him with a new hope in respect to his visitor. To be sure, he recognized him!—to be sure, it could be no other person! He made haste into his cozy dining-room, casting a hurried glance as he passed at the carpet-bags and portmanteau, which still encumbered the hall. The dining-room was in confusion, much unlike its usual state; great-coats, and cravats, and wrappings of every kind lay scattered on the chairs; while in his own easy chair by the fire the stranger sat pouring out his tea, and with all the materials for a comfortable breakfast round him. Certainly he had lost no time.

"Armitage!—it is you, then?" cried the Colonel, hastening up to him with the heartiest welcome.

"Ah! yes, it is me—how d'ye do, Sutherland?—delighted to see you again. Here I am in full possession, like an old campaigner," said the stranger, somewhat languidly; "puts one in mind of Kitmudgharee, eh?—the happiest time of my life!"

"And yet I am very glad to hear you have advanced in fortune and the world since then," said Colonel Sutherland, drawing a chair to the other side of the table; "and how is your health? They tell me you have become an invalid of late days—how is that? you used to be the most vigorous of us all. India?—liver affected?—how is it?"

"Humph!" said Sir John, shaking his head; "can't tell—come to my fortune—some people say that's it. Nothing to do but please a man's self is what I call hard lines, Sutherland; and duties of property, and all that. Never had any bad health till I got rich. Here's a nice kind of existence for a man come to my time of life—not married and not intending to marry. Here's a set of men that hunt half the year and shoot the other half—ought to keep friends with 'em—only society in the country, except my Lord Duke, and he's stuck-up. Then, when I'm at home, there's a confounded lawyer with his new leases and his raised rents, and 'Sir John,' 'Sir John,' till I'm sick of my own name. Then there's a fellow of a chaplain pegs into me about an heir. What the deuce do I want with an heir? Says the estates go into another family after me—swears it's a sin to let the name of Armitage die out of the country. What's the consequence?—I can't look a woman in the face without thinking she wants to marry me, or I want to marry her, or something; and the end of the whole concern was, Sutherland, that I ran away—bolted, that's the fact, and got your letter in Paris, where I was bored to death. Thought I couldn't do better than come to you express—and, by George! I haven't enjoyed my breakfast like this for ten years!"

"Very well—here you shall do as you like, and hear not a word of leases or heirs," said Colonel Sutherland, laughing. "We'll have it all our own way at Milnehill—ladies never come here."

"Ah! very sorry," said the new comer, glancing up vaguely, as if to see how far it was safe to go in reference to the past; then returning to his breakfast, proceeded with the perfect inconsequence of a man—not selfish, but occupied with himself, and saying whatever came uppermost. "Very odd thing—the very day I got your letter something came into my head: There's old Sutherland, thought I, got a couple of nice daughters—honest girls—mother a very pretty woman—no doubt they take after her. Then came your letter: 'pon my life, it brought the tears to my eyes!"

This downright stroke the Colonel bore with sufficient fortitude. He held his breath for a moment, and said nothing—then hastened to interest himself in the progress of the stranger's breakfast, which was going on in the most satisfactory manner. Never guest did more honour to hospitality. He repeated that he could fancy himself once more in the Kitmudgharee station, but for the blazing fire, and the Frith haddocks, which were perfection; and repeated over again, with emphasis, "The happiest time of my life!"

"Before then I was a young fellow of ambition," said Sir John, "waiting to get on in society, and all that sort of rubbish. If this confounded fortune had come then, there would have been some comfort in it. Never felt myself a man till I went to India—always kept trying to find out what this one and the other thought of me. Got clear of all that rubbish among your bungalows. Ah! these were the days! But I say, Sutherland, guess how I came here?"

"In a postchaise; I saw you, but could not remember for my life who you were," said the Colonel.

"Eh? Ah! couldn't remember me?—humph!" said Sir John, with momentary mortification; "odd that—I should have known you anywhere. Postchaise from the boat—detestable boat!—rocks like a tub, and smells like an oilshop—came down from London by sea. And, now that I think of it, do you know, I'm mighty sorry about poor Musgrave; a fox-hunter, you know—nothing but a fox-hunter; but a very good fellow—gave me a helping hand myself, when I was young and stood in need of one—what have you made of the poor boy?"

"I am sorry to say he has made something of himself which I don't like," said the Colonel. "Poor fellow! he was too high-spirited, and impatient, and proud, to wait for our influence, and what we should do for him: he's gone off to London, I fear, to enlist. He's a famous young fellow—I grudge the lad putting on a private soldier's uniform even for a day."

"I don't—best thing he could do," said Sir John. "If the service was as it ought to be, that fellow would rise like a shell. If I had sons I'd put them in the ranks, every one, and push 'em, sir—for an example, if nothing else—sons, ah!" Here Sir John shrugged his shoulders slightly, shrank back into his chair, and, in dismal contemplation of that distressing subject, made an end of his breakfast. "However," he said, after a pause of thought, devoted to his own engrossing affairs, "I'll give in to the popular opinion of course here, as I always do. We'll look the fellow up, Sutherland: he shall have his commission; I've got no claims upon me, at present, at least. Musgrave's boy shall not go to the bad if I can help it. I suppose, after all, it's not likely to help a young man's morals to throw him loose on London, out of his own class into a barrack room, eh?—where he don't care a straw for the public opinion, and where the fellows get drunk, eh? Where do you suppose now he'll go?"

"He's six foot one, if he's an inch," said the Colonel, meditatively; "of course into the Guards."

"Guards!—ah! lots of fellows there that have seen better days," said Sir John—"wild fellows, that break their mothers' hearts, and bring gray hairs to the grave, and so on. Regent's Park—nursery-maids—wont do that; he's fit to marry any girl he might take a fancy to, sir, and make it impossible for any man to help him—for a fellow who marries beneath him," said Sir John, falling into the favourite channel of his own thoughts, "is lost—you can do no more for him. To be sure! I never thought of that, odd enough, till this moment; raise a man from the ranks, all very well—but I defy you to raise his wife; that must be looked to directly, Sutherland—don't you know where he is?"

In answer to this question, the Colonel placed before his old comrade Roger's letter. Colonel Sutherland was not at all afraid of the nursery-maids or of young Musgrave's foolish falling in love. The Colonel, who had loved and been married at the natural season, wore no false spectacles to throw this hue upon everything, as did the unhappy old bachelor, hunted to death by his problematical heir, and able to think of nothing else. Certainly lads of twenty are not to be guaranteed against such accidents; but Roger, the Colonel felt very certain, was by no means possessed by that hyperbolical fiend who directed the thoughts of the unfortunate baronet to "nothing but ladies." Sir John read the letter with a little emotion, which he was evidently ashamed of; he held it in his hand for some little time after he had finished reading it, in order that he might be able to look perfectly unsympathetic and unconcerned. Then he put it down and got up hastily.

"With your permission, Sutherland, I'll have an hour's rest," he said. "I tumbled in here—what with the cold and feeling desperately hungry; nothing like sea-sickness for giving a man an appetite afterwards—without ever asking for my apartment. Thank you for your hospitality, old fellow—you see I mean to take advantage of it—and we'll talk this all over after dinner. I say, what a famous snug place you've got! There's another grievance of that said Armitage Hall, which the fellows there would have you believe a paradise. Not a room in the house that does not want half a dozen people about to make it look inhabited; not a chance for a snug chat like what we've just had. Suppose a mite of a fellow like me crouching by a fire that could roast me, shut in by a screen in a room that would hold half the county!—ugh! the thought is enough. Here we are!—famous!—there's a fire!—I'll bet you sixpence my man lighted that fire. He has a genius for that sort of thing. I'll tell him to communicate his secret to your people here."

"I suspect," said the Colonel, with a smile, but a momentary pique, "the fabric was built by the maid; but I hope you'll find the place comfortable. Take care you don't injure your night's rest by resting through the day—dinner at six—nobody but ourselves. You will find me downstairs whenever you please, but don't think you're in the least degree called upon to make your appearance before dinner."

Then the Colonel went downstairs and stepped into a little side-room, in which he sometimes indulged himself with a modest cigar, while the dining-room was being cleared of all the litter brought by his visitor. Colonel Sutherland was an orderly man by nature; he did not like to see the coats and rugs and mufflers lying about on his chairs, and smiled to himself with a little perplexity over that guest, who was so singularly unlike himself. He was not quite certain as yet how they should "get on," though very confident in Sir John's good meaning and his own good temper. Presently Patchey came to consult him about the dinner, and to state that the cook would gladly have an audience of her master, which, with a little reluctance, the Colonel accorded. An arrival so sudden, and of so important a person, was no small event at Milnehill.

CHAPTER XIII

For this first day, it must be allowed, the Colonel did not particularly enjoy the stranger in his house. The establishment of Milnehill consisted of two maids and Patchey, who had been Colonel Sutherland's factotum and personal manager for twenty years. Patchey's name was Paget as it happened, and he was supposed to have noble blood in his veins, as he boasted on certain extreme occasions; but it was only on very grand festivals, and as a name of state, that his noble patronymic was produced, and for the most part he was well content with Patchey, which consisted better with his fortunes. Patchey was Irish by birth, though Scotch to extremity in everything else; but that accident perhaps helped him to rather more blunders than might have been expected from his discreet years and sober mind. At the present moment Patchey was considerably elated by the arrival of his old acquaintance, Sir John's man, who required more entertainment than his master, and made demands upon Patchey's time as host which somewhat interfered with his duties. This travelled gentleman made no less an impression upon the maids, who were also considerably distracted from their proper and necessary occupations, in spite of the anxiety of Betsy, the cook, to produce a creditable dinner in honour of Sir John. These combined causes made great infringement upon the Colonel's quiet comfort during the day. His biscuit and little bottle of Edinburgh ale did not make their appearance till nearly an hour after the proper time. He had to ring three times for something he wanted; and Patchey himself, the soberest of men, shared, by way of encouraging his confrère, in so many little bottles of the said Edinburgh, that he appeared at last in a confused condition of wisdom, which excited to the utmost the wrath of the Colonel. The explosion of unwonted indignation which came upon Patchey's astonished head sobered him effectually, and the house recovered its equilibrium, especially when Sir John's man was summoned to his master, and the maids awoke to an uncomprehending dread of "the Cornel in a passion," which frightful picture Patchey presented to them in colours sufficiently terrible. Afterwards things went on smoothly enough. An unexceptionable dinner made its appearance, with such a curry as would have won the heart and warmed the palate of any old Indian; and Patchey, if he looked a little wiser and more solemn than usual, was all the more rigid in the proprieties, and behaved himself with a dignity worthy of the grand butler at Armitage Park. Sir John, who had not been seen since breakfast, appeared wonderfully refreshed and rejuvenated at the dinner-table. The leading fancy which inspired him at the present moment, though it frightened him, and though he feigned to fly from it, had nevertheless its influence upon his toilette, as well as on more important things. He was about fifty, middle-sized, yellow-complexioned, but, save for a little querulousness of expression, by no means like an invalid. Neither did the shade of Parisian fashion in his dress increase his pretensions to ill health, though it added a certain odd, indefinable something of the ridiculous to his appearance, which Colonel Sutherland could not make out, yet could not help observing. Of this, however, nobody could be more profoundly unaware than Sir John, though no one would have been quicker to perceive the same thing in another. He took his seat at the cosy round table with a sigh of satisfaction, and looked round upon all the comforts of the room; the fire sparkling and manageable and not too large, the crimson curtains drawn, the bright lamp, the well-spread table, and Patchey's solemn face at the sideboard. "Happy man!—you have not been thrust into a gloomy desert of an Armitage Park, and congratulated on your good fortune—you can make yourself as cosy as you will!" said Sir John, who for the moment commiserated himself most sincerely, and thought with a positive shudder of those ghostly rooms from which he had fled, to such cold comfort as could be found in a Parisian appartement, shining with white marble and white muslin, stucco and gold.

"I suppose you could make yourself snug, too, if you preferred it, eh?" said the Colonel, across the table. "I don't think I should have quarrelled with Armitage Park, for the sake of my Ned and Tom."

And as he said these words he put his hand to his ear, and bent across the table for his companion's answer; for the Colonel was not without a spice of mischief in his nature, and rather enjoyed the silent hitch of the unfortunate baronet's shoulder, the pucker on his brow, and the "pshaw!" of disgust which burst from his lips. However, the dinner mollified Sir John—that Indo-British dinner, with its one yellow-complexioned dish, and its general tone, slight but prononcée, of oriental fervor. Had not Betsy been cook to General Mulligatawny, and lived three years with Mrs. Melrose? Paris was nothing to her—Sir John proclaimed his enthusiastic approbation aloud.

When the important meal was over, and the two gentlemen sat by the fire over their wine, they had a long dinner-talk about Scott of the 27th and Wood of the 40th—and that fine fellow Simeon, who was forming the troop of Irregulars, you know—and poor Peter, who lost his majority by that ugly accident, and only recovered to see his juniors passed before him—and Hodgson, who came home on sick leave—and Roberts, who had got cadetships for all his five sons. When that highly interesting and satisfactory talk flagged with the removal of the cloth, and the departure of the servants, Colonel Sutherland began to grow a little anxious about his protegé. Poor Roger, though Sir John might be very willing to befriend him, evidently occupied a very small place in the baronet's memory. The Colonel cracked some nuts very slowly, and fell into silence. His visitor lost in the depths of that easy chair—the Colonel's own chair—which the selfish little man, in the most entire disregard of prescriptive rights, had unfeelingly appropriated, looked round him with perfect comfort and satisfaction. In the momentary silence, the crackle of the fire, the deliberate crack, crack of Colonel Sutherland's nutcrackers, the faint sound of the breeze outside, combined to heighten the tranquillity, ease, and uninterrupted comfort of the scene. "By George!" cried Sir John, suddenly starting up with an action so impetuous that he almost upset his wine, and caused the Colonel to stop short in his occupation, holding out his nutcracker in one hand, putting the other to his ear, and looking with a startled glance over the top of his spectacles.

"This time last night I was tossing on your detestable German ocean, wishing you and your house far enough, and as sick as—as—as an unfortunate traveller could be. I think this a very agreeable contrast. Though you do throw your boys in my teeth, old fellow, here's prosperity and happiness to Milnehill!"

"And a very hearty welcome to my old comrade," said the Colonel, stretching out his kind hand.

Settling down after this little effusion, cost the English temper of the guest a few minutes silence. Then he resumed upon the business of the night:—

"Now, Sutherland, about this boy. I think that was a very proper letter of his, do you know; I like him the better for having written it: I should have done the same thing in his place. The young fellow of course has done something to bring us into mud and bother by this time; of course he has—what's the good of making a bolt if nothing comes of it? I incline with you to think he's gone into the Guards."

"By-the-bye," said the Colonel, "I've been thinking that over. I'm not so sure of that by this time: a man who hopes to rise from the ranks would find that, I fear, about the most unkindly soil he could try. Musgrave, of course, wants to see service—the Guards very rarely leave London. After all, I incline to change my opinion: a marching regiment would be better for him with his views."

"What a fellow you are!" cried the baronet, "you bring a man round to your views, and then cast him off and declare a contrary opinion. Now I'm all for the Guards and the Regent's Park barracks. He's a handsome fellow enough, I suppose, and I know he's not very clever. Of course, he's taken in by the superior corps, and high reputation, and all that sort of thing. I'll bet you something he's a Guardsman. Now, what's to be done? If you want me to start for town directly and hunt him up, I say thank you, my excellent friend, I am exceedingly comfortable here; travelling bad for my health—beginning of March the worst season in the year—and so on, to any extent you please. But I don't want the boy to slip through our fingers, mind you. What's to be done? Don't you think he'll write again?"

"Very doubtful," said Colonel Sutherland.

"Doubtful?—doubtful's something," said Sir John. "It can do no harm, so far as I can perceive, to wait and see. Let's be quiet for a little, and keep on the look-out. Of course, had I known what had happened I might have stayed in town," he added, with a slightly injured air, "and settled that concern before I came on here. But, of course, as I did not know—"

"I did not know either; nobody knew—he only left home the day before yesterday," interrupted the Colonel.

"To be sure; and yet it would have been very convenient could I have been informed of it while in town," proceeded the baronet, still in a tone of injury; "really at this time of the year—and I don't see there can be any damage done by waiting to see if he writes again."

"Only that he might enter a regiment going to India, or Canada, or Australia, and might write on the eve of the voyage, as is most likely, and be lost beyond remedy," said the Colonel, anxiously.

Sir John scratched his head. "That would be a bore," he admitted; "at all events, let's wait—we'll say a week; a recruit can't be off to the end of the world in that time. Then there's a little leisure to think; and I say, Sutherland, keep your interest for your own occasions, old fellow—you may want it yet for one of those everlasting boys of yours. I've a strong confidence Tom will take you in, and go for a soldier like the rest of his race. What would you make the boy a parson for? A Scotch parson too!—whom nobody can be of the least benefit to. Wait a little—he'll change his mind, that fellow will, or he's not the boy I took him for. Let's join the—hum—I forgot—no ladies to join," he muttered, in as low a tone as he could drop his voice to so suddenly. "Play chess still, Sutherland?—let's try a game."

CHAPTER XIV

Sir John Armitage found Milnehill an exceedingly agreeable habitation. He fell into the routine of the Colonel's habits as a man long accustomed to a life and duties similar to those of his host only could have done. Day by day he recovered of his querulousness and invalidism. He even forgot the dreaded heir who had driven him from his new inheritance, and began to be able to speak on ordinary subjects without much allusion to the dreadful subject of marriage, and his own perplexities in respect to it. Then Sir John, when once delivered from himself, was a little of a humorist, and enjoyed the peculiarities of the society in which he found himself. Numberless old Indian officers, members of the Civil service, families who, without being of that origin, had two or three sons in our oriental empire, and people more or less connected with India, were to be found in the neighbourhood. Indeed, with the mixture of a clergyman or two, a resident landed proprietor, linked to the community by means of a son in the B.N.I., or a daughter married in Calcutta, and one or two stray lawyers from Edinburgh—this formed the whole of Colonel Sutherland's society, and no small part of the general society of the neighbourhood.

These excellent people, to the greater part of whom the world consisted of India and Edinburgh, whose associations were all connected either with the kindly and limited circle of home, or with the bizarre and extraordinary life of the East, and to whom the rest of the world came in by the way, a sort of unconsidered blank of distance between the two points of interest, were as original and agreeable a community as one could wish to meet with; experienced, for years of travel, of intercourse with primitive people, and of universal command and authority, had given a certain decision and authority to their judgment; yet so singularly simple in respect to this European world and its centres of civilisation, and so innocent of all public sentiment other than the dominant Anglo-Saxon instinct of sway and rule over an inferior race, that their views on general subjects had a freshness and novelty which, if sometimes a little amusing, was always racy and original. Knowing very little, except in words, of the races who contest with us the supremacy of the modern world; of those powers so equally balanced whose slightest move on either side sets all the kingdoms of Christendom astir, and threatens contests bigger and more ominous than any conquering campaign of the East; this community was good-humouredly contemptuous of the incomprehensible ignorance of those dwellers at home who knew no difference between Tamul and Hindostani, who innocently imagined that a man at Agra, being in the same country with his brother at Madras, might have a chance of meeting with him some day, or who could not be made to comprehend the difference between a Dhobi and a man of high caste. These strange ignorances they laughed at among themselves with a pleasant feeling of superiority, and contested Indian appointments and the new regulations of the Company with far greater interest than the state of Europe could excite them into. One and another had charge of a little troop of children, "sent home" for their education. Somebody was always returning, somebody always "going out." There was great talk, especially among the ladies, of outfits and their comparative cheapness, and of the respective advantages and disadvantages in travelling overland or by the Cape. Sir John, who was Indian enough to find himself much at home in this society, was at the same time man of the world enough to be amused by its characteristics. He found it more entertaining to listen to a lady's troubles in a journey to the hills, to the adventures of the dàkh, or the misbehaviour of the Syces, than he had found it in recent days to bewail the afflictions of a continental tour, the impositions of the inns, and the failure of the cooks. Palanquins and howdahs were unquestionably more picturesque than travelling carriages and vetturini, and the Dakh Bungalow ten times more original than the Hôtel d'Angleterre or the Römische Kaiser. Sir John, for the moment, found himself so famously entertained, that he showed no inclination whatever to abridge his stay at Milnehill.

He liked his host, he liked the society, he liked the quarters; the dinners were good, the curry superlative, the house extremely cosy. Then the freedom of the bachelor life, free from any disagreeable claim of duties, suited the baronet exactly. His room was exactly the size he preferred, his fire always burned cheerfully, the Colonel left him to himself with perfect good breeding and discreet kindness, forcing his inclinations in nothing. General Mulligatawny, whose "policy" touched one side of the humble enclosure of Milnehill, had two unmarried ladies at present resident in his house, in whom the baronet felt a certain interest, both bound for India, and consequently not to be seen or treated with after a certain date, which greatly increased their attractions. One of them, the General's granddaughter, a pretty girl of eighteen, to whom Sir John seriously, but secretly, inclined, and who, he rather more than suspected, was pretty certain to laugh in his face at any avowal of his incipient sentiment; the other, a handsome woman of thirty, youngest of all the said General's dozen children, "going out" to keep house for a brother, who had already got through two wives, and preferred a little interregnum before looking for another. This latter lady, Sir John felt with a little terror, was what people call "extremely suitable," and the very person for him. Consequently, he conceived a great dread of her, mingled with a little anxiety to look well in her presence. With these attractions to the neighbourhood, is it wonderful that Sir John showed little inclination to leave Milnehill?

The week passed, and another week followed it. There was still no news from Roger Musgrave, and the Colonel grew at once impatient and anxious. These feelings, struggling with his punctilious and old-fashioned hospitality, made him exceedingly uncomfortable. He could no longer enjoy the presence of his guest, while at the same time it was against all his traditions of friendliness to suggest anything to him which should shorten his stay, or make him feel himself unwelcome. The Colonel, to whom all the varied sentiments of life had come in their due season, could not see the baronet's perplexities and pre-occupations in presence of womankind without secret amusement and wonder; and Sir John's regards, divided between Miss Mulligatawny and her niece, surprised his host into occasional accesses of private laughter; but this by no means sufficed to divert the Colonel, as it diverted his visitor, from the important object which had originally brought him here. Colonel Sutherland never entered his cosy dining-room in the morning without the dread of finding a letter from Roger, telling of some step which was irrevocable, and carried him quite out of their reach. He went to rest with that thought in the evening, and took it up on waking the next day: he began to be quite restless and full of discomfort; he even meditated setting out by himself to London to find the young man: he wrote to various old friends in town, begging them to make inquiries. Then he repeated to himself, "Make inquiries! look for a needle in a bundle of hay!" Yet, nevertheless, sent off his letters. On the whole, nothing had so agitated and disturbed the Colonel for years. He pictured to himself the lingering hope of being yet sought after and aided, which would dwell in the youth's mind unawares: he imagined the hope sickening, the expectation failing: he thought of the bitter enlightenment, which has ceased to believe in words and promises, growing round the boy: he felt his own word losing its meaning, and his own earnest desire frustrated. Then, unable to keep silence, in spite of his reticence as host, he spoke to Sir John on the subject. Sir John made light of his troubles: "My dear fellow, what can they do with a batch of new recruits in a week—three weeks, is it? Very well, then, three weeks; what do you suppose could be done in that time? Besides, have you any certainty that troops are being sent abroad at all? I don't know of any; and for the Queen's service, you know, I ought to be almost a better authority than yourself. No, no, have patience—we'll hear from the boy presently, I have not the slightest doubt of it. Give him up?—no, not a bit! but a little knocking about will do him good—always does young men good! If you look so very serious, I shall believe you want to get rid of me."

This last address was unanswerable. The Colonel closed his lips with a sigh. As for his own influence, from which he at one time hoped a good deal, he found it conclude in a courteous letter and a ready promise. The Colonel was extremely discomfited and discouraged; for the first time in his life he repented of kindness. Had he, after all, "raised expectations which could never be realized?" The matter gave him a great deal more pain than Sir John could have thought possible. He, with all the carelessness of a man who has commonly found the world go well with him, put this affair aside lightly. Why should anything happen to disconcert their plans? As soon as the boy should turn up he was ready and eager to help him. He had no apprehension of any romantic contretemps, such as the Colonel feared; such things only occurred in very rare cases. What harm could it do to wait?

Thus still another week passed on. A month after hearing from Roger, Colonel Sutherland found another letter on his breakfast table; it was dated "Ship 'Prince Regent,' in the Downs, March 21st." With a gasp of excitement the Colonel ran his eyes over it, and then thrust it into the hand of Sir John, who was calmly eating his breakfast. The baronet started, read it over, jumped from his seat, and called for his man in a voice of thunder. Then he flew to a writing-table which stood in one corner, wrote something hurriedly in gigantic characters, shouting aloud at the end of every word for "Summers! Summers!" Summers made his appearance hastily, amazed and fluttered by the imperative demand.

"Fly!—horseback, railway, anything that's quickest—telegraph-office, Edinburgh! To be sent this instant; return directly; here's your money; I tell you, fly!" cried the excited baronet.

Summers made an astonished bow, looked at the paper, and demanded where? His master took him by the shoulders and thrust him out of the door, following him through the rain along the garden, and shouting, "Telegraph-office, Edinburgh!" in his ear, with sundry stimulating expletives. Then Sir John returned much more slowly. He found the Colonel marching about the room, very grave, and very much excited.

"It's not your fault, old fellow," said the baronet, hastily "bolting," to use his own expression, the remainder of his breakfast; "here's the man that's to blame; come down upon me, it'll do you good. I don't give this up yet. How's the wind? Dead south-west for a miracle—can't go a step down the Channel in a sou'-wester! Come along—put up your traps, brighten your grave face, and let's be off by the first train!"

"We'll be too late!" said the Colonel, whose mortification and distress were great.

"Not a bit of it," said Sir John. "Telegraph reaches the ship in half-an-hour—'Young man, Roger Musgrave, enlisted among the troops on board the "Prince Regent," to be detained. To the officer in command.' We shall be there by noon to-morrow all right. Why do you suppose now that Fortune should make up her mind to spite us? Why shouldn't the wind stay for twenty-four hours in that quarter, and all be well?"

"Why, indeed?" said the Colonel, with a sigh; "why should not everything serve our caprice when we lose the true opportunity, and then make a fictitious one?—but they don't, Armitage. I shall never forgive myself; however, while there is still a hope let us go."

For the Colonel's fears had been literally fulfilled. Roger had enlisted in a regiment about to sail for the Cape, where there was at present raging one of the many Caffre wars. He wrote to take leave of his friend, believing well to be out of reach before any late succour could reach him. A certain shade of proud and forlorn melancholy was in his farewell. The young man felt to his heart a pang which he would not confess—he had been taken at his word.

CHAPTER XV

By the same evening train—for they were too late for any other—which had carried the Colonel not very long before to that little rural world which included Tillington and Marchmain, Horace Scarsdale and Roger Musgrave, the two gentlemen that night rushed to London. As they went their darksome way in the dimly-lighted carriage, which, as it chanced, they occupied alone, each leaned back into a corner, occupied with his own thoughts. Sir John, totally refusing to accept the uncomfortable chance of being too late, looked out at every station with an anxious eye upon the wind, and cried, "Hurrah for the sou'-wester!" as they dashed into London in the cheery spring morning which brightened the grimy face of even that overgrown enchantress. Colonel Sutherland said nothing; his interest in the wind was very limited; he had made up his mind to misfortune, and blamed himself deeply. The old man understood, as by a revelation, the mind of the youth who had addressed to him that letter. The feeling of secret disappointment, without anything to complain of, the forlorn success of his experiment, the perfect acquiescence which everybody seemed to have given to his self-disposal; while, at the same time, it was quite true that he had put himself out of everybody's way, and "that nobody was to blame," as people say, all shone through his melancholy leave-taking. If they did succeed in finding him, would he return? the Colonel asked himself. If they came to the rescue at last, after he had made his plunge, and had borne the bitterest part of it, would he consent to be bought off, and owe his improved rank to Sir John's tardy benevolence? The message itself—was that judicious?—might not its only effect be to leave a certain stigma upon the character of the young soldier? Thus one subject of reflection only more painful than another had quick succession in the Colonel's thoughts. He vowed to himself he should never again wait for the co-operation of another in anything which was necessary to be done; and so only shook his head as Sir John hurra'd for the "sou'-wester," and, looking behind him as he descended from the carriage, shook his head still more, and felt the cold whisper of another wind rising upon his cheek. Sir John perceived it also, and grew pale. "It is only a current—there are always currents of wind under these archways," he explained, hurriedly. Then they drove across London in a cab to the Dover railway, snatched a hasty breakfast of boiling coffee and cold beef, for which they had not above ten minutes time, and so rushed on again to make sure of poor Roger's fate. Even Roger's uncertain fate, however, and all his self-reproach on this occasion, could not hinder the Colonel's eyes to brighten as they whirled past almost in sight of Addiscombe, and saw some distant figures in the Cadet's uniform on a distant road. Could one of them perhaps be Ned?—and the Colonel thought of seeing his boy to-morrow with a cheerful warmth at his heart, which, in spite of himself, made him more hopeful—thinking of Ned he could still believe to find the wind unchanged, the ship unsailed, the young man's mind unembittered. As the miles and the moments passed, as the green country sloped upward into grassy hills, and showed here and there its little precipice of chalk, the Colonel's courage rose. Not from any reason; he was a man to be above reasons sometimes, this tender old soldier; the comfort and the courage came, an inexplicable genial breath from the neighbourhood of his boy.

While, in the meantime, a result perfectly contrary was produced on Sir John: he shuffled about in his seat with an incontrollable impatience; he gazed out of the window; he closed his eyes with disgust when he turned from that; he could have got out and pushed behind like the Frenchman, so eager was his anxiety. The express train was too slow for him—the wind had changed!

The wind had changed! When they came in sight of the sea these stormy straits were specked with ships liberated from their prison, with white wings spread, and impatient feet, making their way out to the ocean. Cold and shrill, with its whistle of ungracious breath, the gale hissed with them through the narrow tunnels; pennons fluttering to the west—bowsprits pointed seaward, clouds flying on the same cold track, and as much as these an increase of cold, an acrid contradiction of the sunshine, bewrayed the east wind which drove invalids to their chambers, but carried ships down channel. Often before had Sir John Armitage anathematized the east wind—perhaps he never cursed it in his heart till now, as he watched with envious impatience a large vessel covered with sail making her way out of the Downs. "That's her for a wager!" said Sir John to himself; "the very thing they'd send troops in—a round, shapeless, horrid old hulk, warranted the worst sailer on the station. To be sure!—there she goes, bobbing like an apple in a posset—ugh, you ugly old beast!—couldn't you have waited another day?"

"Eh?—you were speaking—what's the matter, Armitage?" said the Colonel, roused by the sound.

"Nothing," said Sir John. To tell the truth, he did not feel himself quite the hero of the position at this moment; he did not care to disclose his fears until hope was proved vain; perhaps, after all, that was not the "Prince Regent"—perhaps the officers were still not aboard, or some happy accident had prevented her from taking the earliest advantage of the change of wind. The baronet dragged his companion along with him to the "Ship" before he would suffer him to ask any questions. There the obsequious attendants who received the strangers were startled by the impatient outcry and gesture, almost wild, of the excited baronet. "The 'Prince Regent,' lying in the Downs, with troops on board for the Cape—who can tell me if she has sailed?" This inquiry was somewhat startling to the innkeeper and his vassals. "We can send and see," suggested timidly one of the waiters, "directly, sir." Sir John rushed out again, and started off almost at a run towards the pier. "Sailed two hours ago," said a "seafaring" individual, of questionable looks, who stood on the steps of the hotel smoking his cigar. "Hallo there! sailed two hours ago, I tell you—d'ye think you can make up to her, hey? I'd back you against the precious old tub if you're in that mind—but she's got the start, look you, by two hours—all sail and a fresh wind!"

Sir John came back much discomfited and crestfallen. He could not make up his mind to the disappointment. It was quite intolerable to him. He consulted everybody round as to the chances of overtaking the ship—was he likely to do so if he hired a steamer? The nautical bystander took up this idea with great zeal; but before Sir John committed himself a better informed waiter volunteered the information that there were still some officers to join the vessel at Portsmouth, and that she might be overtaken there. The Colonel shook his head. To him the chances of success seemed so small, that the further journey was scarcely worth the while, and some hours would still elapse before there was a train. Sir John however, still sanguine, found out with a telescope the vessel, which he still held to be the "Prince Regent," exhausted himself in contemptuous criticisms on her build and sailing qualities, and declared that they were certain to be at Portsmouth hours before the unwieldy transport. The Colonel said nothing; he paced about the room with serious looks and a grieved heart, sometimes pausing to look wistfully out from the windows; a week earlier and Roger might have been saved—a day earlier and they could still have seen him, have tried the last chance for his deliverance, and made him aware of their real intentions and regard for his welfare. The Colonel could not forgive himself. For perhaps the first time in his life he judged his companion unfairly, felt disgusted at Sir John's exclamation of self-encouragement, and secretly blamed as levity his eager special pleadings and arguments with himself. Presently they started again for Portsmouth, fatigue and vexation together proving almost too much for Colonel Sutherland, who was the elder by several years, and the most seriously affected in the present instance. As for Sir John, he still kept himself up by expectations: of course, they must reach Portsmouth in time—of course, there could be no difficulties in the way of buying Roger off—he would return with them, get his commission, and then follow his pseudo-comrades, if he had still a hankering after the smell of powder. He was thus flattering himself, when they reached the busy seaport. Sir John, for once forgetful alike of dinner, rest, and toilette, with yesterday's beard, and no better provision for the fatigues of the day than a couple of biscuits, rushed at once into the hubbub of the port. Some time was occupied in these inquiries; he ran from place to place, the Colonel marching gravely by his side, putting his hand to his anxious ear when any one addressed them, listening with his solicitous stoop forward to every word of every answer. But it was again in vain—the "Prince Regent" had only signaled in passing, and had neither paused nor taken in any officers at Portsmouth: by this time, heavy transport as she was, the vessel was at sea.

Heavily and in silence the two travellers sought an hotel, marched up the stairs side by side, without saying a word to each other, and threw themselves, with a simultaneous groan of fatigue and disappointment, into chairs. This last performance elicited a short, hard laugh from the baronet, now thoroughly out of sorts. "I've been a confounded fool!" cried Sir John—"I'll never forgive myself. Why the deuce don't you come down upon me, Sutherland?—I'm an ass—I'm an idiot—I deserve to be turned out of decent society! Hang me, if I did not mean to be a father to that boy!"

The real sincerity and penitence of his tone woke once more all the kindly feelings of the Colonel. "It cannot be helped now," he said with a sigh; "by this time it's providence: and I don't doubt it'll turn out for the best."

"Ah, it is easy for you to speak," said Sir John, who perhaps did not quite understand his companion's simple, practical reference to a disposition beyond the power of man; "you are not to blame: to think, with my confounded trifling, I should have let Musgrave's boy throw himself away!"

This led the Colonel to soothe his friend, and take the guilt upon himself, a proceeding which the baronet, after a few minutes, did not object to. After a while his spirits rose. He began to be reminded of a vigorous appetite, and to recover the exhaustion of fatigue. With a little assumption of languor on his own part, and a tender regard for the necessities of the Colonel, Sir John took upon himself at last to order dinner. Then the travellers separated, to make their most needful ablutions. When they met again at dinner Sir John was himself again.

"After all, Sutherland," he said, "nothing can be more absurd than to disturb ourselves about this, though it is very vexatious. 'Twill do the boy good, after all—nothing I should have liked better at his age; and won't harm his prospects a bit—everybody likes adventurous young men. Here's a health and a famous voyage to the young fellow. I'll take care there's a welcome waiting for him when he lands—for of course every ship that sails the passage will outstrip the transport. To be sure, he's melancholy enough now, I believe. Do him good—teach him to be careful how he runs away from his friends another time. What's the good of breaking our hearts over it?—he'd be just as sea-sick if he were Colonel; and I warrant the 'Prince Regent' gives him quite enough to think of for eight days. What can't be cured, you know—here's good luck to him!—the end of his voyage will make up for it all."

The Colonel drank his luckless protegé's health very gravely: he thought of him all night, travelling with the forlorn lad over the darksome sea; and sent better things than wishes after him—remembering his name, in every break of his sleep through that long night, before God, who saw the boy; and so, unseen, unaided, and ignorant of the disappointed efforts which had toiled after him, and of the one tender heart which ached over its failure, and was his bedesman, nothing else being possible, the young adventurer went away deeper into the world and his life, further into the night and the distance, and the black paths of the sea.

CHAPTER XVI

The two gentlemen returned next day to Dover, to make inquiries after the fate of Sir John's telegraphic despatch, which, it appeared, had been delivered without doing any good. Roger had enlisted in a regiment of rifles: he was a famous shot, young, strong, and active—by no means such a recruit as a commanding officer concerned for the credit of his regiment would relinquish readily; and, so far as the travellers could ascertain, no notice had been taken of their communication. Then they went back to London, where Sir John, feeling himself considerably discomfited, hurried to the Horse Guards, to see what could be done at last for his unfortunate protegé. Having ascertained, with difficulty, the regiment in which Roger had enlisted, he discovered, with no difficulty at all, that this regiment was quite complete in its number, and that at present there were no vacancies among the officers. At present! The chances were that a few months of a Caffre war might show some difference in those full lists; but a man could not purchase a prospective commission on this grim possibility. The only thing Sir John could do in the circumstances he did. There was no lack of kindness at the bottom of his heart: he wrote a kind letter to Roger, enclosing a bank-bill for a considerable amount, confessing his mortification at the consequences of his own delay, and ordering the young man, with an imperative cordiality which he felt quite justified in using, and which Roger was not likely to resist, to use the money and come home directly—at least, whether he came home or not, he was not to serve the campaign in the ranks. "If he comes home, he's not the boy I took him for," said Sir John; but he dispatched his letter, and with it a note to the major who led the detachment, and with whom he had some slight acquaintance. Having done this, the baronet's conscience was clear: he did what he could to persuade Colonel Sutherland to remain for some time in town; he himself, after what had happened, having no particular inclination to return to Milnehill. When he found the Colonel was not to be persuaded, Sir John remained by himself, finding refuge, alike from Armitage Park and the grave looks of his friend, in the London season. He had been long out of the gay world. After a week or two in town, he gradually warmed to its fascinations, and forgot all about his failure very speedily, in a modest amount of fashionable dissipation and the comforts of his club.

The Colonel stayed only to spend a day with Ned, and hastened home; and as everything there went fair and softly, and nothing else within the limits of this history requires immediate attention, let us spare a moment to glance after poor Roger, forlorn and alone among his comrades upon the monotonous sea.

Among his comrades, and yet alone—more alone than the young man had been during all his life. He had never supposed—he had no means of imagining—the humiliations of this new life. He could gulp the inferior rank, the mortifications of his humble position—he could manage to salute as superiors, totally above him and out of his sphere, the young officers who a year ago would have been too happy to accompany him into the preserves of the Grange, or sit by his side at his godfather's hospitable table. These things he could bear; what Roger could not bear was the perpetual society from which he could not free himself—the constant presence of his "mates," and entire lack of anything like privacy in this existence, of which he had not conceived half the pangs. If he had been able to seek the meanest possible retirement of his own, he could have borne all other grievances cheerfully—but this was impossible; and the life of which every hour sleeping or waking was spent in the rude companionship of men of a class much inferior and a breeding totally different from his own, grew bitter to the young man. He became unnaturally grave and self-absorbed. He attended to the minutest details of his duty with the most scrupulous and rigid care: but the sunshine and the glow of youth died away from him—life spread around him full of vulgar circumstances, unceasing noise, unceasing mirth, a perpetual accompaniment which made his heart sick. He did everything he could to recall his courage—he tried to flatter his imagination with pictures of future distinction; but Roger had not the imagination of a poet; his fancy was not strong enough to carry him out of the midst of the reality which vexed his soul; the pictures grew languid, the hopes feeble. His whole nature retreated within itself, and had to summon its uttermost forces to bear the trial. An experience which he had never looked for deepened his thoughts, and gave a painful development to his mind. His nearest approach to solitude was when he leaned over the side of the ship, and lost the talk of his comrades in the sweep of the waves. Then many a melancholy fancy possessed poor Roger: sometimes he could fancy he saw the face of his godfather gazing at him with a melancholy compunction; and the loyal heart rose, and his own looks did their best to brighten, as if even the departed spirit should not blame itself while he had power to say No. Sometimes it was the good Colonel who looked out of Roger's imagination, with a kind and grieved reproach, "Why did you not wait a little?—could you not trust me?"

Sometimes for an instant the face he had seen upon that moorland road beside Marchmain—the young face troubled and blushing, which knew and recognized him, in spite of itself, flashed for a moment before Roger's dreaming eyes; and then he turned away from the water and the heavens with a quick sigh, and turned back to the little world which made its passage over that sea—the noisy world between those wooden bulwarks, lounging here and there, playing cards, sleeping in the sun, jesting, quarrelling, talking unprofitable talk, and laughing loud laughter. This was his world, where Roger had to live.

At the same time an incident occurred to trouble him. A detachment of a regiment of infantry shared the comforts of the same transport; and one day, shortly after they sailed, Roger was startled to meet Sam Gilsland, who for his part came to an amazed stand before him, and sheepishly put up his hand to his forehead in respectful salutation. Nothing could persuade Sam that "th' young Squire" was, like himself, in the ranks. A hurried conversation ensued, in which Roger made strenuous endeavours to knock the fact into the thick head of his countryman; and Sam went away with a confused idea that he was not to touch his cap any more to this unexpected shipmate, or to address the rifleman as Mr. Roger, or to speak of him as the young Squire. This incident at once grieved Roger and comforted him. Somehow there was a certain consolation in the idea that one individual, at least, in that little community knew what and who he really was. But the annoyance overbalanced the comfort. Sam after this could not come in contact with his former patron but with a ludicrous and embarrassing consciousness, which would have made Roger laugh if it had not pained him; the simple lout felt himself alarmingly on his good behaviour whenever he suspected Roger's neighbourhood, and made a hundred furtive errands and clumsy attempts to do something for him, which at once disturbed his mind and touched his heart. He was by no means a bad fellow, this Sam—a certain gleam of chivalrous sentiment warmed his opaque spirit at sight of the sad equality with himself to which, in appearance, never in reality, the young Squire was reduced. The honest clown felt a certain mortification and downfall in his own person to think that Roger in his crowded cabin was cleaning his own accoutrements like "a common man!" Sam made stealthy private expeditions into the rifleman's quarters to do it for him, moved by an indescribable mixture of compassion and respect, and those tender home-associations which never had been so warm in the simple fellow's heart as now, and could not comprehend the burst of mortified gratification—the mixture of pain and pleasure, wrath and gratitude, with which Roger sent him away. After that he had to content himself with touching his cap stealthily when he could have a chance unseen, to the young Squire, and confiding, when he had the opportunity, his own private troubles to him, not without a secret conviction that Mr. Roger, by-and-bye, if not immediately, would be able to right and avenge his humble follower. Sometimes Roger was disposed to think Sam's presence an augmentation of his own downfall, but in reality there was a certain solace in it unawares.

All this time, however, a third person, totally unsuspected by the unfortunate youth, observed him narrowly and closely, losing nothing, not even the clownish services which Sam would fain have rendered to the young rifleman. The Major was one of the most unsentimental of men. Abstract benevolence would never have suggested to him any special interest whatever in a recruit of superior rank. "His own fault, of course—best thing the fellow could do," would have been the only comment likely to fall from the lips of the Major; and no indulgence had any chance to drop from his hands upon the head of the unhappy volunteer who had been "wild," or "gay," or "unsteady," and who had lost himself in the ranks.

But from the day of their embarkation the face of Roger had caught his eye. A puzzling consciousness of knowing these ingenuous features troubled him; he felt certain that he had seen them, and seen them under very different circumstances, somewhere. Then came the telegraphic message of Sir John Armitage, which, abrupt and unauthorized as it was, made the Major wroth. He tore it through and sent the fragments overboard in the first flush of his indignation. After a while, however, he repented of his wrath. He had scarcely noted the name in his hurried glance upon the paper—he forgot it in the flush of passion with which he tossed the presumptuous missive overboard; but as soon as he came to himself an uneasy idea that it concerned the young man whom he began to note, troubled the Major. The thought riveted his attention more and more upon the melancholy and grave young rifleman, who seemed to spend all his leisure time leaning over the bulwark watching the waves sweep by the vessel's side. Gradually, and unawares to himself, the Major grew more and more interested in this solitary soldier; his interest grew into a pursuit; he could no longer help observing him, and so strongly had the idea entered his mind, that to find it mistaken would have been a personal mortification and disparagement of his own wisdom. Then the Major, in his quick, quarter-deck promenade, was witness to the amazed recognition of Sam Gilsland, and of various other private encounters between the two young men, in which Sam's furtive salutation of respect spoke more than words to the sharp eye of the old soldier. How to act upon his suspicions was, however, a more difficult matter than how to pursue them; and if he was right, what then? Sons of gentlemen before now had dropped clandestinely into the green coats of the Rifle Brigade, about whom the Major had given himself no manner of trouble; and he scarcely liked to acknowledge to himself how much that unregarded message lay on his conscience, or how glad he would have been now to have paid a little more attention to it.

However, the time slipped on, and the voyage progressed, while the commanding officer busied himself with these fancies, finding himself strangely unable to dissociate the melancholy young private soldier in his green coat from a certain radiant young huntsman "in pink," whom his fancy perpetually conjured up before him as the hero of some north-country field, but whom he could not identify by name. The Major even tried the unjustifiable expedient of discovering Roger in some neglect of duty, that he might have a plausible motive for calling him into his judicial presence. But not the most sudden and unlooked-for appearance of his commanding officer could betray the young rifleman into forgetfulness of the necessary salute, and in every other particular his duty was done rigidly and minutely, beyond the chance of censure. This circumstance itself piqued the Major's curiosity further. Then his interest was aided by the interest of others. Somebody discovered the "superior education" (poor fellow! he himself, in sincere humility, was ready to protest he had none) of the young man, and suggested his employment apart in those regimental matters which required clerking. Strange occupation for the old Squire's Nimrod! Recognizing that he was not what he seemed, the first impulse of assistance thrust the young huntsman—the child of moor, and fell, and open country—into a little office, and put a pen into the fingers which were much better acquainted with gun and bridle. This odd conclusion of modern philosophy contented the projectors of it mightily, and by no means discontented Roger, who, sick at the heart of his humiliated life, was glad of anything which separated him from his comrades, and gave him at least his own society, if not that of anybody higher; though he knew very well, if no one else did, that his rôle of rifleman was much more natural and congenial to him than the rôle of clerk, of which he knew nothing whatever.

The fact, however, which everybody knows perfectly well, yet few people acknowledge, that all the nameless somethings which distinguish between the lower and the higher—and build most real and palpable, though indescribable, barriers between class and class, do by no means necessarily include education, was not a fact taken into account by the good-natured subaltern who interested himself in Roger's behalf, while the Major only watched him. So the young man, whose penmanship was not perfection, sat by himself over the regimental business, puzzling his honest brains with accounts which were sometimes overmuch for his arithmetic, yet encouraged by the consciousness that even this irksome business, totally unsuitable for him as it was, was a step of progress. And the Major now and then appearing across his orbit, tempted him with wily questions, to which Roger was impenetrable; and Sam Gilsland, with a grin of satisfaction, tugged his forelock and whispered his conviction that Master Roger would ne'er stand in the ranks when they came to land—which conclusion, however, and the hopes of his subaltern patron to get permanent employment for him of this same description when they reached the end of the journey, were anything but satisfactory to Roger. It began to be rather hard for the young man to keep on the proper respectful terms with this honest subaltern, whom yet he did not choose to confide in. "No!" exclaimed Roger, "I am fit for a soldier, not for a clerk;" and a flush of his old sanguine conviction, that on the field and in actual warfare there must still be paths to distinction, swept across his face and spirit for the moment. The next minute he was once more puzzling over his papers, with his head bent low and his frame thrilling, his emotion and enthusiasm all suppressed; though they would have made a wonderful impression on the young officer who patronized and took care of him, and who was convinced that Musgrave was not a common fellow, and had a story if he would tell it. This, however, was the very last thing in the world which Roger, totally hopeless now of any deliverance, and too proud to accept the pity of men who were no more than his equals, had any mind to do.

Their arrival at the Cape, however, made a wonderful difference in the prospects of the young rifleman. Sir John Armitage's letter, put into his hands before they landed (for the baronet was correct in his supposition that the "Prince Regent" was of course the slowest sailer on the seas), threw him into a sudden agitation of pride, gratitude, shame, consolation, and perplexity, which it is impossible to describe; in the midst of which paroxysm of mingled emotions he was summoned to the presence of the Major. The Major received him with outstretched hand. "Thought I knew you all along," said that unagitated functionary; "could not for the life of me recollect where—made up my mind it was a peculiar case—eh?—Sit down and let me hear at once what you mean to do."

"What I mean to do?" asked Roger, in amazement.

"To be sure—you've had your letters, I suppose? This here is a delusion," said the Major, tapping upon the coarse sleeve of the young man's uniform; "found it out, haven't you?—knew it myself all along; meant to interfere when we came to land, whether or no, and inquire about your friends. Here's old Armitage spared me the trouble; recollect as well as possible the meet with the Tillington hounds—your uncle's, eh?—and the old boy was extravagant, and left you unprovided for? Never mind! a young fellow of pluck like you can always make his way. Now, here is the question—Are you going home? What are you going to do?"

These questions were easy to ask, but impossible to answer. Roger had scarcely read with comprehension Sir John's letter, and his mind was in the utmost agitation, divided between his old ideas of entire independence and the uneasy consciousness, of all that his experience had taught him. He scarcely knew how he excused himself from immediate answer, and managed to conclude his audience with the Major. The rest of the day he spent in the most troubled and unsatisfactory deliberations; but a little later, delayed by some accident, a letter from Colonel Sutherland came into his hands. That letter persuaded and soothed the young man like an actual presence; he yielded to its fatherly representations. That voice of honour, simple and absolute, which could not advise any man against his honour—Roger could scarcely explain to himself how it was that his agitation calmed, his heart healed, his hopes rose with all the rebound and elastic force of youth; he no longer felt it necessary to reject the kindness offered him, or to thrust off from himself, as bitter bonds, those kindly ties of obligation to which it was impossible to attach any mean or sordid condition. Why should he be too proud to be aided? But he had no mind to go home and lose that chance of distinction and good service which would be his best thanks to his friends. A few days after, Roger Musgrave had rejoined his regiment as a volunteer, money in his purse, a light heart in his breast, and everybody's favour and goodwill attending him. He who was the best shot within twenty miles of Tillington was not far behind at Cape Town; and there we leave him for his first enterprise of arms.

In the meantime the life of Horace Scarsdale had made progress, according to his own plan, in his new sphere. His uncle, at first annoyed and disturbed by the summary settlement which the young man had made for himself, was perhaps, after all, rather pleased than otherwise to be thus freed from the charge of arranging for one whom he understood so little; and no opposition of friends hindered his establishment in the office of Mr. Pouncet, where the lawyer, half out of admiration for the abilities which speedily developed themselves in his new clerk, and half in tender regard for the suit which he possibly might have to conduct for him, was very gracious to Horace. Everything promised well for the new comer: his prodigious knowledge of the private affairs of everybody in the county, their weaknesses and follies—knowledge acquired, as we have said, from the outdoor servants and humble country tradesmen in the village alehouses, but of which Horace was skilful enough to veil the origin—amazed his employer, who found these gleanings of unexpected knowledge wonderfully useful to him, and could not comprehend how they had been gained. The young man had now an income, small in reality, but to him competent and satisfactory, and sweetened by the consciousness of freedom and of knowing it was all his own. He was eminently cold-blooded, and "superior to impulse"—a man who could calculate everything, and settle his manner of life with an uncompromising firmness; but he was not a stoic. He stepped into all the dissipations of the little country town—stepped, but did not plunge—with an unlovely force, which could command itself, and did not. He was not "led away," either by society, or youthful spirits, or by that empire of the senses which sometimes overcomes very young men. What he did which was wrong he did with full will and purpose, gratifying his senses without obeying them. He carried his cool head and steady nerves through all the scenes of excitement and debauchery of which Kenlisle was capable—and it had its hidden centre of shame and vice, like every other town—sometimes as an observer, often as a partaker; but he was never "carried away"—never forgot himself—never, by any chance, either in pleasure, or frolic, or vice more piquant than either, ceased to hold himself, Horace Scarsdale, closer and dearer than either sin or pleasure. He was the kind of man to be vicious in contradistinction to being a victim or a slave of vice. He was the man to pass triumphantly through hundreds more innocent than himself, strong in the unspeakable superiority of being able to stop when he found it necessary, and of having at all times that self-control and self-dominion which belongs to cold blood and a thoroughly selfish spirit. Secure in this potent ascendancy of self-regard, Horace could do many things which would have destroyed the reputation of a less cool or more impressionable man. Yet his entry into independent life, and those pleasures hitherto unknown to him—mean and miserable as were the dissipations of the little country town—occupied Horace, though not to the exclusion of his own interests, enough to make him slower than he had intended to be, in his searches after his father's secret. True, there was no case of Scarsdale versus Scarsdale, or versus any other person, in any of the law reports he could reach, any more than there was in Mr. Pouncet's brain; and he knew no means at the present moment of entering on his inquiry, and had obtained no clue whatever as to the manner of this secret, or which was the way of finding it out. But he did not chafe under this, as in other circumstances he might have done: for the present he was sufficiently occupied, and not at all discontented with his life.

At the same time, in spite of the deportment which displeased the Colonel, there were some traces of breeding, unconsciously to himself, in the speech and manner of Horace, which gained him acceptance among the people around him. He was not refined nor cultivated, nor accustomed to society; but though his sentiments might be vulgar enough, he himself was not so. His very rudeness was not the rudeness of a Kenlisle townsman; he was ignorant of that extraordinary junction of rural vanity and urban importance, which goes towards the making of the fashionable class of such a place. His father, whom Horace would not have imitated consciously on any account whatever, and who certainly bestowed no pains on his instruction, had notwithstanding known in his day a society and breeding much superior to anything in the little north-country town, and the atmosphere lingered still about Mr. Scarsdale, an imperceptible influence which had affected his son unawares. Then his very position, outcast from society as he had been brought up, gave him a certain superiority over the limited people to whom a local "circle" was the world, and an introduction to some certain house the highest point of ambition. Horace laughed aloud among his new associates at the idea of society in Kenlisle, and smiled to the same import with a silent contempt which was extremely superior and imposing in Mrs. Pouncet's drawing-room, to which he was speedily admitted, in right of his mysterious "prospects."

By dint of this contempt for the community in general, which everybody of course understood to bear exception for themselves, and of the singular and mysterious circumstances of his family, which began to be remembered and talked of; by his own arrogant philosophy, which imposed upon the inexperienced youths about him, and the subtle talents to which his employer bore witness, he grew rapidly into an object of interest and curiosity in the little town. No one could tell what sudden eminence he might spring into, upon some sudden discovery; nobody knew anything of him—no one was admitted to his confidence; he was the inscrutable personage of the place, and left the fullest ground for fancy, which, in the form of gossip, occupied itself mightily about the singular young man. All this involuntary homage was incense to Horace; he sneered at it, yet it pleased him. He was elated to find himself a person of importance, though he despised the community which honoured him; and between the honours of the little Kenlisle society, the pleasures deep down below the surface, which gave a black side to the humanity of even that secluded place, and the new sense of freedom, solitude, and self-government in this new life—the whole put together effaced from his mind for the time all that eagerness for his father's secret which had preyed upon him when his life was idle and unoccupied, and when he sat by that father's table every day. He had no responsibilities, no "ties," and no heart to feel the want of affection. He abandoned himself, so far as he could abandon that self which was the only thing he never forgot, to all his new enjoyments. He was still young, absolute, and highflying, though his youth was neither innocent nor lovely; he forgot his deeply-laid projects for the moment, and stood still on his way, contenting himself with an importance, a mysterious superiority, a license of pleasure unknown to him before.

He was not an experienced schemer, bent upon the success of his plans, and deaf to the voices of the charmers. He was young, and, according to his fashion, he stood still and forgot his object in the pastimes of his youth.

This state of things went on for a longer time than Horace himself was aware of. He had no correspondence with Marchmain, nor indeed with any one. For though he wrote once to Colonel Sutherland, he had no present motive sufficient to keep up a correspondence with his uncle; and nearly a year had passed over his head before he recollected this unrecorded passage of time. At the end of this period, however, business brought a visitor to Kenlisle, and to Mr. Pouncet's office, who was destined to have a most serious part in Horace Scarsdale's future life.

This was Mr. Julius Stenhouse, the principal solicitor of an important county town in Yorkshire—a man who had been bred in Mr. Pouncet's office, had suddenly, to everybody's amazement, become his partner, and who, as suddenly, a few years after had left Kenlisle for his present residence. These events had all happened before Horace had any cognizance of the news of the district, and were consequently unknown to him until Mr. Stenhouse appeared. The stranger was a man of about fifty, with what people called an "extremely open manner," and a frank wide smile, which betrayed two rows of the soundest teeth in the world, and gave a favourable impression to most people who had the honour of making Mr. Stenhouse's acquaintance. This prepossession, however, as might be ascertained on inquiry, was not apt to last—everybody liked, at first sight, the candid lawyer; but he had few friends. Unlike the usual wont of a country town, nobody appeared anxious to claim the recognition of the new arrival. Far from being overwhelmed with hospitality, Mr. Pouncet had so much difficulty in making up a tolerable number of people to meet him at the one little dinner-party given in his honour, that Horace Scarsdale, for the first time, though he had long assisted at Mrs. Pouncet's "evenings," had the distinguished honour of an invitation.

Before this time, however, various circumstances had concurred to attract the attention of Horace towards Mr. Stenhouse. The extreme difference between his manners and his reputation, the mixture of repugnance and respect with which Mr. Pouncet treated him, the great reluctance which he showed to enter upon any private business with his visitor, and the mystery of the former partnership which had existed between them, roused the young man's curiosity. Altogether, these new circumstances brought Horace to himself; he remembered that he was still only in an inferior position, with no avenue open as yet to fortune or importance. Running over everything in his mind, he perceived that he stood farther than ever from his father's secret, and that no other means of advancing himself had as yet appeared; and with a certain instinctive and sympathetic attraction, his thoughts turned to Mr. Stenhouse. He bestowed his best attention upon him on every opportunity—he sought all the information he could procure about him, and about the connection subsisting between him and Mr. Pouncet. It appeared they were joint-proprietors of some coal-mines in the neighbourhood. What might a couple of attorneys have to do with coal-pits? Horace scented a mystery afar off, with an instinctive gratification. Did the mystery lie here?—and what was its importance, could it be found out?

Without knowing anything whatever on the subject, except the sole fact that Pouncet and Stenhouse were partners in this valuable piece of property, Horace set out very early one spring morning to inspect the ground, and see if anything could be discovered on the subject. It was, as it happened, the morning of the day on which he was to dine at Mr. Pouncet's. Horace had been late, very late, the previous night. This early walk was of two uses—it restored his unsusceptible nerves to the iron condition which was natural to them, and it gave him a chance of finding out in his old fashion anything that there might be to find out. Horace neither knew the extent nor the value of the land possessed by Messrs. Pouncet and

Stenhouse: he knew they drew very considerable revenues from it, but did not know how they had acquired it, nor from whom. He pushed briskly along the long country road, winding downwards to a lower level than that of Kenlisle, where once more the hawthorn hedges were greening, and the primrose-tufts unfolding at their feet.

The country looked cheerful and fresh in the early morning, with its few clumps of early trees here and there, in the tender glory of their buds, diversifying the deeper green of the fields. The smoke rose from the cottages, and the labouring men came trudging out from their doors, greeting one another as they passed with remarks upon the weather. By-and-by he came in sight of the village, with its irregular line of thatched and red-tiled houses, with the one blue-slated roof rising over them, which marked the place where an enterprising publican had swung his "Red Lion," in well-justified dependence upon the "pitmen's drouth." Beyond, several tall shafts here and there scattered over the country gave note of the presence of the pits and their necessary machinery. Horace slackened his pace, and went sauntering through the village, keeping a wary eye around him. He had not gone very far when he perceived an old man limping out of a miserable little house near the end of the village, with a poor little cripple of a boy limping after him, in the direction of the coal-fields. Their lamps and the implements they carried pointed out clearly enough their occupation; and a certain dissatisfied, discontented look in the old man's face made him a likely subject for Horace, who quickened his steps immediately to overtake the wayfarers. It required no great exercise of speed. The querulous, complaining jog with which the old man and his shadow went unsteadily across the sunshine, told its own tale—the very miner's lamp, swinging from his finger by its iron ring, swung disconsolately, and with a grumble and crack, complaining audibly of the labour, which, to say the truth, was sufficiently unsuitable for the two who trudged along together, the crippled childhood and tottering age, to whose weakness belonged a milder fate. The old man's face was contracted and small with age—the nose and chin drawn together, the cheeks still ruddy from a life of health, puckered up with wrinkles, and the very skull apparently diminished in size from the efforts of time. On he went, with his feeble limbs and stooping shoulders, the "Davy" suspended from his bony old fingers, and a complaint in every footstep, with his shadow all bent and crumpled up, an extraordinary spectrum moving before him along the sunny road. Horace, who gave him the usual rural salutation of "A fine morning," received only a half-articulate groan in reply. The old pitman was not thinking of the fine morning, the sweet air, or the sunshine; but only of his own troubles and weaknesses, and himself.

"To them as has the strength it's fine and fine enow," he mumbled at last; "but an ould man as should be in his commforable bed—eugh-eugh! Needcessity's sore upon the ould and frail."

"How is it that you have to get to work so early?—you're not a new hand," said Horace, with the rough and plain-spoken curiosity which often does instead of sympathy.

"A new hand!" groaned his querulous interlocutor; "an I was as I hev been, my young spark, I'd gie you a lesson would larn you better than to speak light to an ould man. I've bin about the pit, dash her, since ever the first day she was begoud, and mought have broke my neck like the rest if it hadn't a bin for good loock, and God A'mighty—eyeh, eyeh! I was about the very ground, I was, when the first word was giv there was coal there; but I'll never believe there was ought let on o' that to the ould Squire."

"Eh!—the pits here are not old pits then, aren't they?" said Horace; "who was it found the coal? I daresay the landlord made it worth his while."

"The Lord make me quat of a parcel o' vain lads, that ken no more nor as many coodies!" cried the old man; "haven't I as good as told you my belief?—and will ye pretend ye ken better than me, that was born on his very land?"

"That's a bad cough of yours," said Horace, who had good practice in the means of extending information; "what do you say to a dram this sharp morning, to warm you before you go underground?"

"Eyeh, eyeh, lad, we're owre near the border," said the old pitman, shaking his head; "if ever there was a deevil incarnate on this earth it's the whiskey, and makes nought but wickedness and misery, as I can see; but to them as knows how to guide themselves," he added, slowly, "it's a comfort now and again, specially of a morning, when a man has the asthmatics, and finds the cowld on his stomach. If you're sure you're able to afford it, sir, I've no objection, but I would not advise a brisk lad like you, d'ye hear, to partake yoursel'. Ye haven't the discretion to stop at the right time at your years, nor no needcessity, as I see. Robbie, I'm a-gooin' on a bit with the gentleman—see you play none on the road, nor put off your time, and say I'm coming. Eugh, eugh! as if it wasn't a shame and a disgrace to them as has the blame, to see the likes of me upon the road!"

"At your time of life they ought to take better care of you," said Horace; "see, here's a seat for you, and you shall have your dram. Why don't your sons look to it, eh, and keep you at home? It doesn't take very much, I daresay, to keep the pot boiling; why don't you tell them their duty, or speak to the parson? You are surely old enough to rest at your age!"

"Eugh, eugh! I haven't got no sons," said the old man, with a cough which ran into a chorus of half-sobs, half-chokes. "The last on 'em was lost i' the pit, two year come Michaelmas, and left little to his ould father but that bit of a cripple lad, poor child, that will never make his own salt. It's the masters, dash them! as I complain on. There they bees, making their money out on it, as grand as lords; and the like of huz as does it a' left to break our ould bones, and waste our ould breath for a bit of bread, after serving of them for a matter of twenty year. Eyeh, eyeh, lad, it's them, dash them! If it had been the ould Squire, or ony o' the country gentlemen, an ould servant mought hev a chance. No that I'm saying muckle for them, more nor the rest o' the world—awl men is for their own interest in them days; but as for mercy or bowels, ay, or justice nouther, it's ill looking for the like of them things in a couple o' 'torneys, that are born and bred for cheating and spoliation. I never had no houps of them mysel'—they'll sooner tak' the bit o' bread out atween an ould body's teeth, than support the agit and the orphant—ay, though it was their own wark and profit, dash them! that took the bread from Robbie and me."

"Ah!" said Horace, "that's hard; so the pits here don't belong to the Armitage property, nor any of the great landlords? But what have a couple of attorneys to do with them—they manage the property for somebody, I suppose?"

"My respects to you, sir," said the old pitman, smacking his thin lips over the fiery spirit, which he swallowed undiluted; "and here's wishing us awl more health and better days; but I wouldn't advise you, a young lad, to have ony on't. There's guid ale here, very guid ale, far better for a young man of a morning. You may weel ask what has the like o' them to do concerning sich things; and there's few can tell like me, though I say it as shouldn't. I was a likely man mysel' in them days—a cotter on the ould Squire's land, and serving at Tinwood Farm, and had my own kailyard, and awl things commforable. It's like, if you knaw this country, you've heard speak of the ould Squire?"

"To be sure—old Musgrave, of the Grange," cried Horace, with a certain malice and spite, of which he himself was scarcely aware; for Roger Musgrave's honest simplicity, which he scorned, yet felt galled and disconcerted by, had often humiliated and enraged the son of the recluse, who could take no equality with the young relative of the fox-hunting Squire. He listened more eagerly as this name came in—not with a benevolent interest, certainly; but the mystery grew more and more promising as it touched upon the history of a ruined man.

"About twenty year ago, I would say, as near as moight be, there was a couple o' young chaps comed about here, for their holiday, as I aye thought to mysel'. The wan o' them was uncommon outspoken in his manner, wan of them lads that's friends with every stranger at the first word, with a muckle mouth and teeth—dash em!—that would crunch a man's bones like a cannibal. T'other he was some kind of a student, aye fiddling about the grass and the rocks, and them kind o' nonsense pastimes. I heard the haill business with my ain ears, so it's no mystery to me. I was ploughing i' the lang park belonging to Tinwood then, with the two o' them somegate about the ploughtail, having their own cracks, with now and again a word to me—when all of a suddent the student, he stops, and he says out loud, 'There's coal here!' I paid little attention till I saw them baith get earnest and red in the face, and down on their knees aprying into something I had turned up with my plough; and then I might have clean forgot it—for what was I heeding, coal or no coal?—when the t'other man, the lad with the muckle mouth, he came forrard, and says he, 'Here's my friend and me, we've made a wager about this land, but we'll ne'er be able to settle it unless awl's quiet, and you never let on that you've heard what he said. He's awl wrong, and he'll have to give in, and I'll be the winner, as you'll see; but hold you your peace, neighbour, and here's a gold guinea to you for your pains.' Lord preserve us, I never airned a goold guinea as easy in my life! I wush there was mair on them coming a poor body's way. I held my whisht, and the lads gaed their way; but eugh, eugh! eh, man, if I had but knawn! I would ne'er have been tramping this day o'er the very grund I ploughed, to work in that pit, dash her! and me aughty years of age and mair."

"How, then, did it happen?" cried Horace, eagerly.

"But I'll hev to be agooin," said the pitman, lifting himself up with reluctance and difficulty—"the timekeeper yonder, he's a pertickler man, and has nae consideration for an old body's infirmities: though I'm wonderful comforted with the speerits, I'll no deny. Eyeh! eyeh! the old Squire, he was a grand man, he was, as lang's he had it, and threw his siller about like water, and was aye needing, aye needing, like them sort o' men. Afore mony days, if ye'll believe me, there was word of his own agent, that was Maister Pouncet, the 'torney in Kenlisle, buying some land of him, awl to serve the Squire, as the fowks said; but when I heard it was this land, 'Ho, ho!' says I to mysel', 'there's more nor clear daylight in this job,' says I. So I held my whisht, and waited to see; and sure enow, before long came down surveyors and engineers, and I know not all what, and the same lad, with the muckle mouth, that was now made partner to Mr. Pouncet; and that was the start o' the pit, dash her! that's cost me twenty years o' my life and twa bonnie sons; and them's the masters, blast them! that take their goold out o't year after year, and wunna spare a penny-piece for the aged and frail. Eyeh, that's them!—but it's my belief I'll see something happen to that lad with the muckle mouth before I die."

"And what did your old Squire say, eh, when the land was found so rich?" said Horace; "did he try to break the bargain, and take it back again?"

"Him!" cried the decrepid old labourer, now once more halting along in the fresh sunshine, with his shadow creeping before him, and his "Davy" creaking from his bony finger—"him! a man that knawed neither care nor prudence awl his born days; and to go again his own 'torney that had done for him since ever he came to his fortin',—not him! He said it was confoonded lucky for Pouncet, and laughed it off, as I hev heard say, and thought shame to let see how little siller he got for that land. He never had no time, nor siller nouther, to goo into lawsuits, and his own agent, as I tell you; besides that he was a simple man, was the Squire, and believed in luck more nor in cheating. Eyeh! eyeh! but I blamed aye the chield with the muckle mouth. He was the deevil that put harm into the t'other lawyer's head; for wan man may be mair wicked nor anither, even amang 'torneys. It wasn't lang after till he left this country. Eh, lad, yon man's the deevil for cunning. I wouldna trust him with his own soul if he could cheat that—dash them a'! I mought have keeped on my kailyard, and seen my lads at the tail of the plough, if, instead of his pits and his vile siller, them fields had still been part o' Tinwood Farm!"

And the poor old man relapsed out of the indignation and excitement into which the questions of Horace, his own recollections, and, above all, his "dram," had roused him, into the same querulous discontented murmurs over his own condition which had first attracted the notice of his young companion. Horace sauntered by him with a certain scornful humour to the mouth of the pit—untouched by his misfortunes, only smiling at the miserable skeleton, with his boasted wisdom, his scrap of important unused knowledge, and his decrepid want and feebleness. He set his foot upon this new information with the confidence of a man who sees his way clear, and with a strange, half-devilish smile looked after the poor old patriarch, who had known it for twenty years and made nothing of it. The idea amused him, and the contrast: for pity was not in Horace Scarsdale's heart.

CHAPTER XIX

As he started on his rapid walk back to Kenlisle at a very brisk pace, for the distance was between four and five miles, and business hours were approaching, Horace put together rapidly the information he had obtained. Perhaps a mind of different calibre might have rejected the pitman's inference, and benevolently trusted, with the defrauded Squire, that Pouncet and his partner were only "confoonded looky" in their land speculation—such things have happened ere now honestly enough. Horace, however, was not the man to have any doubt on such a subject. His mind glanced, with a realization of the truth, quick and certain as the insight of genius, along the whole course of the affair, which appeared to him so clear and evident. How cautious, slow Mr. Pouncet, in most matters a man of the usual integrity, had been pounced upon by the sudden demon which appeared by his side in the shape of his clever clerk: how his mind had been dazzled by all the sophisms that naturally suggested themselves on this subject: how he had been persuaded that it was a perfectly legitimate proceeding to buy from the needy Squire these lands which at present to all the rest of the world were only worth so little, and which concealed, with all the cunning of nature, the secret of their own wealth. The Squire wanted the money, and was disposed to sell this portion of his estate to any bidder; and even if he were aware of the new discovery, had he either money or energy to avail himself of it? Horace knew, as if by intuition, all the arguments that must have been used, and could almost fancy he saw the triumphant tempter reaping the early harvest of his knavery, and stepping into a share of his victim's business, and of the new purchase which was made in their joint names. These coal-pits were now a richer and more profitable property than the whole of Mr. Pouncet's business, satisfactory as his "connection" was; but Horace was very well able to explain to himself how it was that the career of Mr. Stenhouse at Kenlisle had been very brief, how all Mr. Pouncet's influence had been exerted to further the views of his partner elsewhere, and how it happened that the stranger's reception showed so much ceremonious regard and so little cordiality. With a certain sense of envy and emulation, the young man regarded this new comer, who held another man, repugnant and unwilling, fast in his gripe, and had him in his power.

It is chacun a son gout in matters of ambition as well as in other matters. There was something intoxicating to the mind of Horace in this species of superiority. To have command secretly, by some undisclosable means, of another individual's will and actions: to domineer secretly over his victim by a spell which he dared neither resist nor acknowledge; this was something more than a mere means of advancement; independent of all results, there was a fascination indescribable in the very sensation of this power.

And it was this power which he himself had acquired over these two men, so totally unlike each other, who would see him to-day, unsuspicious of his enlightenment, and this evening meet him at the social table, which already won such influence, put under a painful constraint. Horace exulted as he thought of it, and brushed past the early Kenlisle wayfarers with such a colour on his cheek, and a step so brisk and energetic, that not one of them believed the tales to his disadvantage, and furtive hints of having been seen in unnameable places, which began to be dropped about the little gossiping town. He had only time to make a hurried toilette, deferring to that more important necessity, the breakfast, which he had no leisure to take, and to hasten to "the office," where he sat punctual and composed at his desk, for full two hours before his companion of the previous night appeared, nervous and miserable, at his post, with an aching head and trembling fingers. Horace glanced across with cool contempt at this miserable as he entered. He was conscious that he himself, in his iron force of youth and selfishness, looked rather better and more self-controlled than usual under the inspiration of his new knowledge, and he looked at his weaker compeer with a half-amused, contemptuous smile. This very smile and disdain had their effect on the little circle of spectators, who all observed it with an involuntary respect, and forgot to think what might be the heart and disposition of this lofty comrade of theirs, in admiring homage to the coolness of his insolence and the strength of his head.

Meanwhile, thoughts at which they would have stood aghast mingled in the busy brain of Horace with the drier matters of daily work which passed through his hands. Upon which of these two men who were in his power should he exercise that unlooked-for empire? Should he frighten Mr. Pouncet out of his wits by disclosing to him his new discovery? He was certainly the most likely person to be frightened with ease; but this did not suit the ideas of Horace. He was tired of Kenlisle, and found no advantage in a residence there, and he felt in Mr. Stenhouse a kindred spirit with whom he could work, and under whom his fortune was secure. Thus the virtuous young man reasoned as he sat at his desk, the bland object of his thoughts passing him occasionally with smiles upon that wide mouth which the old pitman remembered so well. It might not be possible for Horace to refrain from waving his whip over the head of his present employer, but it was the stranger upon whom for his own advancement he fixed his eyes. Mr. Stenhouse was a man much more able to understand his gifts, and give them their due influence, than Mr. Pouncet would ever be; and in the excitement and exaltation of his present mood Horace thrust from his mind more consciously than ever before that anxiety about his father's secret which had moved him to so much eagerness ere he began to have affairs and prospects of his own. He became contemptuous of it in his youthful self-importance and sense of power. He was dazzled to see how his own cool head and unimpressionable spirit, the undeviating iron confidence of his supreme self-love, had imposed upon his comrades in the town—if comrades they could be called, who won no confidence and received no friendship from him; and he was elated with the new power he had gained, and ready to believe himself one of those conquerors of fortune before whose promptitude and skill and unfailing acuteness every obstacle gives way.

In this mood he filled his place in Mr. Pouncet's office during that day, meditating the means by which he should open proceedings in the evening. Mr. Pouncet, meanwhile, as it happened, by way of diverting his conversation with his former partner from matters more intimate and less manageable, had been pointing out to his notice the singular qualities of Horace, his remarkable position and subtle cleverness. Perhaps Mr. Pouncet would not have been very sorry to transfer his clever clerk to hands which could manage him better; at all events, it was a subject ready and convenient, which staved off the troublesome business explanations which had to be made between them. Mr. Pouncet had committed himself once in his life, and betrayed his client; but he was a strictly moral man notwithstanding, and disapproved deeply of the craft of his tempter, even though he did not hesitate to avail himself of the profits of the mutual deceit. Twenty years had passed since the purchase of that "most valuable property," but still the attorney, whose greatest failure of integrity this was, remained shy of the man who had led him into it, reluctant to receive his periodical visits, and most reluctant to enter into any discussion with him of their mutual interest. So Mr. Pouncet talked against time when necessity shut him up tête-à-tête with Mr. Stenhouse, and told the stranger all about Horace; while Horace outside, all his head buzzing with thoughts on the same subject, pondered how to display his occult knowledge safely, and to open the first parallels of his siege. For which purpose the young man made his careful toilette in preparation for Mr. Pouncet's dinner-table, where the attorney's important wife, and even Mr. Pouncet himself, received the young clerk with great affability, as people receive a guest who is much honoured by their hospitality. How he laughed at them in his heart!

CHAPTER XX

Horace laughed at the condescension of his hosts, but not with the laugh of sweet temper or brisk momentary youthful indignation. There was revenge in his disdain. It fired his inclination to exhibit the power he had acquired, and make the most of it. The party was few in number, and not of very elevated pretensions; a few ladies of the county town, in sober but bright-coloured silk and satin, such as was thought becoming to their matronly years, who had plenty of talk among themselves, but were shy of interfering with the conversation of "the gentlemen"; and a few gentlemen, the best of their class in Kenlisle, but still only Kenlisle townsmen, and not county magnates. Even the vicar was not asked to Mr. Pouncet's on this occasion; the show was very inconsiderable—a fact which Horace made out with little difficulty, and which Mr. Stenhouse's sharp eyes were not likely to be slow of perceiving. Nothing, however, affected the unchangeable blandness of that wide-smiling mouth. Before the dinner was over, Horace, by dint of close observation, became aware that there was a little bye-play going on between the hosts and their principal guest, and that Mr. Stenhouse's inquiries about one after another of the more important people of the neighbourhood, and his smiling amazement to hear that so many of them were absent, and so many had previous engagements, had an extremely confusing effect upon poor Mrs. Pouncet, who did not know how to shape her answers, and looked at her husband again and again, with an appeal for assistance, which he was very slow to respond to. Horace, however, permitted Mrs. Pouncet and her accompanying train to leave the room before he began his sport; and it was only when the gentlemen had closed round the table, and when, after the first brisk hum of talk, a little lull ensued, that the young man, who had hitherto been very modest, and behaved himself, as Mr. Pouncet said, with great propriety, suffered the first puff of smoke to disclose itself from his masked battery, and opened his siege.

"Did you see in yesterday's Times a lawcase of a very interesting kind, sir?" said this ingenuous neophyte, addressing Mr. Pouncet—"Mountjoy versus Mortlock, tried in the Nisi Prius. Did it happen to strike you? I should like extremely to know what your opinion was."

"I was very busy last night. I am ashamed to say I get most of my public news at second hand. What was it, Scarsdale? Speak out, my good fellow; I daresay your own opinion on the subject would be as shrewd, if not as experienced, as mine; a very clever young man—rising lad!" said Mr. Pouncet, with an aside to his next neighbour, by way of explaining his own graciousness. "Let us hear what it was."

Mr. Stenhouse said nothing, but Horace saw that he paused in the act of peeling an orange, and fixed upon himself a broad, full smiling stare; a look in which the entire eyes, mouth, face of the gazer seemed to take part—a look which anybody would have said conveyed the very soul of openness and candour, but which Horace somehow did not much care to encounter. Mr. Stenhouse looked at him steadily, as if with a smiling consideration of what he might happen to mean, glanced aside with a slight malicious air of humour at Mr. Pouncet, gave a slight laugh, and went on peeling his orange. The whole pantomime tended somehow to diminish the young schemer's confidence in his own power, which naturally led him to proceed rather more vehemently and significantly than he had intended with what he had to say.

"The case was this," said Horace, with somewhat too marked a tone—"Mortlock was a solicitor and agent among others to a Sir Roger Mountjoy, a country baronet. Sir Roger was very careless about his affairs, and left them very much in his agent's hands; and, besides, was embarrassed in his circumstances, and in great need of ready money. Mortlock somehow obtained private information concerning a portion of his client's land which more than tripled its value. After which he persuaded the baronet to sell it to him at a very low price, on pretence that it was comparatively worthless, and that he made the purchase out of complacency to meet the pressing needs of his patron. Immediately after the sale a public discovery was made of a valuable vein of lead, which Mortlock immediately set about working, and made a fortune out of. A dozen years after, when the baronet was dead, his heirs brought an action against the solicitor, maintaining that the sale was null and void, and demanding compensation. Only the counsel for the plaintiff has been heard as yet. What do you think they will make of such a plea?"

Mr. Pouncet set down upon the table the glass he was about raising to his lips, and spilt a few drops of his wine. He was taken by surprise; but the momentary shock of such an appeal, made to him in the presence of Stenhouse, and under his eye as it was, did not overwhelm the old lawyer as Horace, in the self-importance of his youth, imagined it would. His complexion was too gray and unvarying to show much change of colour for anything, and the only real evidence of his emotion were these two or three drops of spilt wine. But he cleared his throat before he answered, and spoke after a pause in a very much less condescending and encouraging tone.

"It depends altogether on what the plea is," said Mr. Pouncet; "the story looks vastly well, but what is the plea? Can you make it out, Stenhouse? Of course, when a man acquires a property fairly at its fair value, no matter what is found out afterwards, an honest bargain cannot be invalidated by our laws. I suppose it must be a breach of trust, or something of the sort. You are very young in our profession, my friend Scarsdale, or you would have known that you have stated no plea."

"The plea is, of course, that the solicitor was bound to his client's interest, and had no right to make use of private information for his own advantage—and they'll win it. There, my young friend, I give you my opinion without asking," said Stenhouse; "purchases made by an agent for his needy client are always suspicious, sure to create a prejudice to start with, and against the honour of the profession, Mr. Pouncet? Attorneys can't afford to risk a great deal—we don't stand too high in the public estimation as it is. It's a very interesting case, I do not wonder it attracted your attention. The baronet was a gouty, old spendthrift, perfectly careless of money matters—the solicitor, a sharp fellow, with an eye to his own interests; which," continued Mr. Stenhouse, with his frank laugh, and a humorous roll of his eye towards his former partner, "is a thing permissible, and to be commended in every profession but our own."

A general laugh followed this proposition. "You manage to feather your nests pretty well, notwithstanding; better than most of those other people who are encouraged to look after their own interests, and do not pretend to nurse their neighbour's," said one of the guests.

"Accident, my dear sir, accident!" said Stenhouse, laughing; "to be truly and sublimely disinterested, a man must be an attorney. It is the model profession of Christianity. Here you must see innumerable personal chances slip past you, at all times, without a sigh. Why?—because you are the guardian of other men's chances, perpetually on the watch to assist your client, and forgetting that such a person as yourself is in the world, save for that purpose. That is our code of morals, eh, Pouncet? But it is high, certainly—a severe strain for ordinary minds; and as every man may follow the common laws of nature, save an attorney, it follows that an attorney, when he is caught tripping, has more odium and more punishment than any other man. Mr. Pouncet, you agree, don't you, with all I say."

And Mr. Stenhouse, once more with his broad laugh of self-mockery and extreme frankness, directed everybody's attention to his old partner, who by no means relished the conversation. Mr. Pouncet's glass remained still untasted before him on the table—he himself was fidgety and uneasy—the only answer he made was a spasmodic attention to his guests, to encourage the passing of the bottle, and a sudden proposition immediately after to join the ladies. Not one individual at his table had the slightest sympathy with the old lawyer—every man chuckled aside at the idea that all these arrows were "in to old Pouncet;" not that he was generally disliked or unpopular, but sublime disinterestedness was so oddly uncharacteristic of the man, and unlike the ordinary idea of his profession, that everybody was tickled with the thought. Next to Mr. Pouncet, however, the person most disconcerted of the party was Horace, whose "power" and menace were entirely thrust aside by the jokes of the stranger. The young man went in sulkily, last of the party, to Mrs. Pouncet's drawing-room, dimly and angrily suspecting some wheel within wheel in the crafty machinery which he had supposed his own rash hand sufficient to stop. Perhaps Mr. Pouncet, after all, was the principal criminal, and Stenhouse only an accomplice—certainly appearances were stronger against the serious and cautious man, evidently annoyed and put out by this conversation, as he was, than against the bold and outspoken one, who showed no timidity upon the subject. But Horace's ideas were disturbed, and his calculations put out. He had no knowledge of the character of Stenhouse, when he exulted in the vain idea of having him "in his power." If things were really as he suspected, this was not an easy man to get into anybody's power; and Horace began to inquire within himself whether it would not be better to have a solemn statement made by the old pitman, to send for authority from Roger Musgrave, the old Squire's heir-at-law, and to come out on his own account in the grand character of redresser of injuries and defender of rights. That at least, stimulated by the influence of Mountjoy versus Mortlock, was in Horace's power.

While the young man hung about the corners of the drawing-room, turning over Mrs. Pouncet's stock of meagre Albums and superannuated Annuals, and pondering over his future proceedings, Mr. Stenhouse came up to him with his usual frankness. He was ready to talk on any subject, this open-minded and candid lawyer, and spoke upon all with the tone of a man who is afraid of none.

"Well, Mr. Scarsdale! so you are interested in this Mountjoy and Mortlock business," said his new acquaintance—"a curious case in every way, if they can prove it. Want of legal wisdom, however, plays the very devil with these odd cases—it may be perfectly clear to all rational belief, and yet almost impossible to prove it. Perhaps something of the kind has fallen under your own observation—eh?"

"I have," said Horace, a little stiffly, "become suddenly acquainted with a case of a very similar kind."

"Aha, I thought so—I daresay there's plenty," said Stenhouse. "Capital cases for rising young barristers that want to show in the papers and get themselves known. Famous things for young fellows, indeed, in general—that is to say," he added, more slowly, "if the heir happens to be anybody, or to have friends or money sufficient to see the thing out. In that case it does not matter much whether he loses or wins. Thinking perhaps of striking off from my friend Pouncet and establishing yourself, eh? Could not do better than start with such an affair in hand."

"I should be glad of more experience first," said Horace; "and, to tell the truth, I don't care for beginning by betraying old friends. Mr. Pouncet has behaved very liberally by me, receiving me when I had very little qualification."

"Pouncet!" cried Mr. Stenhouse—"you don't mean to say that Pouncet has been burning his fingers in any such equivocal concerns. Come, come, my young friend, we must be cautious about this. Mr. Pouncet is a most respectable man."

"Mr. Stenhouse," said Horace, "I was, as it happens, at Tinwood this morning—perhaps you know Tinwood?"

"A little," said the other, with his most engaging smile.

"There I met, partly by chance," said Horace, feeling himself provoked into excitement by the perfect coolness of his antagonist, "an old man, who gave me an entire history of the first finding of the coal."

"Ah, it was a very simple business. I was there myself, with a scientific friend of mine; a blind fellow, blind as a mole to everything that concerns himself—feeling about the world in spectacles, and as useless for ordinary purposes as if he had moved in a glass case," said Mr. Stenhouse; "extraordinary, is it not? It was he who found the first traces of that coal."

"And found them," said Horace, pointedly, "before the land was purchased by Mr. Pouncet and yourself from Squire Musgrave of the Grange."

"Ah, we had better say as little as possible about that in the present company. Pouncet mightn't like it—it might look ugly enough for Pouncet if there was much talk on the subject," said Mr. Stenhouse, sympathetically glancing towards his old partner, and subduing his own smile in friendly deprecation of a danger in which he seemed to feel no share.

"And how might it look for you?" said Horace, with his rough and coarse boldness.

Mr. Stenhouse laughed, and turned round upon him with the most candid face in the world.

"My dear fellow, Squire Musgrave was no client of mine!" said the good-humoured lawyer. "The utmost punctilio of professional honour could not bind me to take care of his interests. I was a young fellow like yourself, with my fortune to make. You put it very cleverly, I confess, and it might look ugly enough for Pouncet; but, my excellent young friend, it is nothing in the world to me."

"Yet you were Mr. Pouncet's partner," said Horace, with a certain sulky virulence, annoyed at the small success of his grand coup.

"After, my dear sir, after!" cried Mr. Stenhouse, with another of his éclats de rire.

Horace made a pause, but returned to the charge with dogged obstinacy.

"I know Roger Musgrave," he said, "and I know friends who will stand by him as long as there is the slightest hope—"

"Ah, very well, as you please, it is not my concern; and it is quite likely you might make a good thing out of Pouncet," said Mr. Stenhouse. "By-the-bye, now I think of it, come and breakfast with me to-morrow, when we can speak freely. I have no particular reason to be grateful to him, but Pouncet and I are very old friends. Come to the 'George' at eight o'clock, will you? I'd like to inquire into this a little more, for old Pouncet's sake."

So they parted, with some hope on Horace's side, but no very great gratification in respect to his hoped-for "power."

CHAPTER XXI

It was with a slightly accelerated pulse that Horace went next morning to the "George" to keep his appointment. He seemed to have put his own fortune on the cast, and temper and ambition alike forbade his drawing back. Either he must secure Stenhouse as an ally and coadjutor, bound to him by secret ties of interest, or else he must establish his own career upon the charitable and Christian work of restoring to Roger Musgrave such remnants of his inheritance as it might be possible to rescue from the hands of Pouncet and Stenhouse. This last alternative was not captivating to Horace. It was not in his nature, had he been the instrument of such a restoration, to do it otherwise than grudgingly. He was too young as yet to have added any great powers of dissimulation to his other good qualities, and his own disposition sided much more with the clever operator who served his own interests by means of some unsuspecting simpleton, than with the simpleton who permitted himself to be so cheated. Accordingly, his thoughts were very reluctant to undertake that side of the question—still, it was his alternative, and as such he meant to use it.

Mr. Stenhouse entertained his young visitor sumptuously, and exerted all his powers to captivate him. He, too, was ignorant of the person he had to deal with, and did not suspect how entirely uninfluenceable by such friendly cajoleries was the young bear of Marchmain, who had scarcely heart enough to be flattered by them, and had acuteness sufficient to perceive the policy. He began, at length, cautiously enough, upon the subject of their last night's conversation—cautiously, though with all his usual apparent candour and openness of tone.

"Let us have a little talk now about this business, this hold which you think you have got over poor old Pouncet," said Mr. Stenhouse. "Do you know, my dear fellow, Pouncet has been established here some thirty years, and the people believe in him; do you think they will take your word, at your age, against so old an authority? I advise you to think of it a little, my friend, before you begin."

"My word has very little to do with it," said Horace; "of course, I know nothing of the transaction except by evidence, which has satisfied my own mind; and Squire Musgrave was quite as well known, while he lived, as Mr. Pouncet. Besides, it is your own opinion that the public verdict is always against the attorney; and then," said Horace, with a slight irrepressible sneer at his own words, "we have all the story in our favour, and the sympathy which everybody feels for a disinherited heir."

"But then, your disinherited heir has not a penny in his purse, nor the means of raising one—a private in a marching regiment," said Stenhouse, with a laugh; "you yourself are one or two-and-twenty at the outside, have spent a year in Mr. Pouncet's office, and do not assert yourself, so far as I am aware, to have any command of capital. How are you to do it?—your father, eh?—your father has a place in the country, and perhaps influence—you mean to seek support by his means?"

"My father," said Horace, rudely enough, "has no influence—and, if he had, would never use it for me; my father is my greatest enemy, or takes me for his, which is the same thing."

"That is very extraordinary," said Stenhouse, with a sudden appearance of interest; "takes you for his enemy?—how is that?—there is surely some mystery here."

"I don't see that it matters at all to what we were speaking of," said Horace. "Look here, Mr. Stenhouse, I'll speak plainly: Pouncet and you are in the same boat—if you don't actually lose money by having this brought to a trial, you'll lose reputation—I know you will. I know well enough the thing was your doing. I don't pretend to be very clever," continued Horace; "but I think I know a man when I see him. It was you who found out the secret about that land—it was you who put the affair into Pouncet's head—it was you who managed it all along—the success of the undertaking belongs to you, and you know it. Now, look here—perhaps there's no legal hold upon you; but you are a flourishing man, with people who believe in you, as much as some other people believe in Mr. Pouncet. If this matter should come to a trial, how would your reputation come out of it? I ask you boldly, because you know better than I do the whole affair."

"And am not afraid of it, I assure you, my dear fellow; go on as briskly as you please, so far as I am concerned," said Stenhouse; "but though I don't care for this, I care for you. You have a natural genius for this kind of work, not often to be met with. Pouncet would not understand it, but I do. I'll tell you what, Scarsdale—you can't do me any harm, but it is quite likely you might do me service. Another man most probably would send you off with a defiance, but I am not so liable to offence as most people; I never found it pay, somehow. You can't do me any harm, as I tell you; but you are bold and capable, and might be extremely useful to me: whilst I for my share could probably advance your prospects. Pouncet was telling me something about you yesterday, but I did not hope to have so clear a specimen of your powers. I want a confidential man in my own office. What do you say to leaving Pouncet and transferring your services to me?"

"I should have perhaps a few questions to ask, in the first place," said Horace, who, elated with this sudden success, the first fruits of his "power," though his antagonist concealed it so skilfully, was by no means disinclined to be insolent; "about remuneration and prospects, and how I should be employed; for I do not hold myself a common clerk, to be hired by any man who pleases," added the young man, with something of the rude arrogance that was in him. It was a new phase of his character to his observant new friend.

"So I understand," he said gravely, but with a twinkle of sarcasm in his eye, which disconcerted Horace. "I shall be glad to hear the facts of your own private concern from yourself, and you may reckon on my best advice. As for the terms of your engagement, if you enter upon one with me, these, of course, you must consider on your own account, without suffering me to influence you. I shall look after my interests, to be sure," added Mr. Stenhouse, with that charming candour of his, "and you must attend to yours; and if you make up your mind afterwards to attack Pouncet on behalf of your friend Musgrave," he continued, with a pleasant smile, "why, well and good—you must follow your fancy. In the meanwhile, I have no doubt I can employ you to good account, and give you more insight into business than Pouncet could. Time for the office—eh? I thought so. Well, you must consider my proposal; no hurry about it—and let me know how you have decided; I'll mention it to Pouncet, that there may be no difficulty there. Good morning, my young friend; you have a famous spirit, and want nothing but practice; and there is no saying what light you and I together may succeed in throwing on your own affairs."

Thus dismissed, Horace had no resource but to take his hat, and shake the smooth hand of Mr. Stenhouse, which grasped his with so much apparent cordiality. The young man went to his business with a strange mixture of sensations: humiliated, because he had suffered a seeming conquest, and his antagonist had clearly borne away the victory, so far as appearances were concerned; and flattered and excited at the same time by the substantial proof he had just received that his threat had not been in vain. Advancement greater and more immediate than to be made the "confidential man" of a solicitor in excellent practice, after one brief year of apprenticeship in Mr. Pouncet's office, he could not have hoped for; and his ambition was not of that great and vague kind which is always startled by the pettiness of reality. Then that last hint gave a certain glow of eagerness to his excited mind: light upon his own affairs!—light upon that mystery which shrouded the recluse of Marchmain, and made his only son his enemy and opponent! Horace had managed to content himself with inevitable work, and even to excite himself into the ambition of making a fortune and his own way in the world; but that was a mere necessity, to which his arrogance bowed itself against its will; and the thought of leaping into sudden fortune, and the bitter long-fostered enmity against his father which continually suggested to his mind something which that father kept him out of, remained as fresh as ever in his spirit when they were appealed to. These thoughts came freshly upon him as he hastened to his daily occupation, and again began to revive the dreams of Marchmain. Twice he had succeeded in his private essays towards self-advancement. After an hour or two's reflection, with returning confidence he exulted to see his present and his future employer equally in his power, and made himself an easy victory in his own mind over the plausibilities of Mr. Stenhouse. Why should he not succeed as well in "his own affairs," and with equal pains overcome as easily the defences of his father?—and what if Stenhouse had actually some light to throw upon these concerns? Horace revelled within himself with a secret arrogance and self-esteem as he pondered. What if it remained to him, in as short a time as he had taken to achieve these other successes, to dress himself in the grander spoils of imagination from which his father's enmity or interest kept him at present shut out.

CHAPTER XXII

Horace did not require to reflect much over the offer of Mr. Stenhouse; but, a singular enough preliminary, went out once more that evening to Tinwood, and again saw his old pitman, from whose lips he took down in writing the statement which he had previously heard. The man was old and might die, and though Horace dared not make the deposition authoritative by having the sanction of a magistrate, and thus letting daylight in upon the whole transaction, he received the statement, and had it signed and witnessed, as a possible groundwork of future proceedings—a strong moral, if not legal, evidence. With this document in his pocket-book, he saw Mr. Stenhouse, accepted his proposal, and consented to his arrangements; then had an interview with Mr. Pouncet, more agreeable to his temper than anything he could extract from the more practised man of the world, to whom he had now engaged himself; the Kenlisle lawyer, it is true, was most deeply "in his power." Mr. Pouncet was very serious, uneasy, and constrained, disapproving, but checking the expressions of his disapproval by a certain anxious politeness, most refreshing and consolatory to his departing clerk.

Horace could not for his life have behaved himself generously or modestly in such circumstances. He took full use of his advantage, and was as arrogant and insolent as a man could be, quietly, who suddenly finds himself in a position to domineer over an older man who has employed and condescended to him. That half-hour was sweet to Horace. Mr. Pouncet's secret flush of rage; his visible determination to restrain himself; his forced politeness, and uneasy, unnatural deference to the studied rudeness of the young bear before him, were so many distinct expressions of homage dear to the young victor's soul. He could strip the respectability off that grave, uneasy figure; he could hold up the man who had betrayed his trust to the odium of the world, and force out of his stores the riches he had gained so unjustly. Did he ever dream of doing it, or of suffering any one else to do it, honestly, as a piece of justice? Not he: but it delighted him to see the conscious culprit quail, and to recognize his own "power."

However, before setting out for his new sphere, a less comprehensible motive determined the young man to pay a parting visit to Marchmain. Perhaps he himself could not have explained why. Not, certainly, to see his sister; for Susan had no great place or influence in her brother's thoughts. To see his father, much more likely; for steady opposition and enmity is almost as exigeant as affection, and loves to contemplate and study its object with a clear and bitter curiosity, more particular and observing even than love. He reached Marchmain on a spring afternoon, when even Lanwoth Moor owned the influence of the season; when solitary specks of gold were bursting on the whin-bushes, and purple stalks of heather-bells rose from the brown underground. Under that sunshine and genial spring stir the very house looked less desolate. The moor, spreading far around and behind, was sweetened and softened by the light and shadow of those changeful northern heavens; the sunshine brightened the windows with a certain wistful, outward warmth, as if the very light was cognizant of the blank within, and would have penetrated if it could. The low hills which bounded the horizon had greened and softened like everything else; and even the wistful clump of firs, which stood watching on the windy height nearest to the house, were edged and fringed with a lighter growth, touching the tips of their grim branches into a mute compliment of unison with the sweet movement of the year. Perhaps the most human token of all was a row of two or three homely flower-pots, outside the dining-room window of Marchmain: that was a timid evidence of the spring sentiment in Susan's solitary young heart, and it was something in such a desert place. Horace observed it as something new, with a little ridicule in his smile. Perhaps his father, now that he was gone, had changed the manner of his sway over Susan: perhaps it was only he, the son, who was obnoxious to Mr. Scarsdale, and had to be put down. Horace was not jealous, nor troubled with any affectionate envy; he smiled with superiority and contempt. He, a man not to be trifled with, was quite indifferent how any one might choose to behave to such a trifle as a girl.

But Susan, it appeared, was out, when Horace, going round by the back of the house, startled Peggy out of her wits by his sudden appearance; and, what was more, his father was out, an unexampled incident.

The old woman screamed aloud when she saw who her visitor was, and put out both her hands with an involuntary movement to send him away.

"The Lord help us all!—they'll come to blows if they meet!" cried Peggy, in her first impulse of terror. Then she put out her vigorous hand and dragged Horace in, as impatiently as she had motioned him away. "You misfortunate lad! what's brought ye here?" said Peggy; "them that gangs away of their own will should stay away. Bless and preserve us! do ye think I dare to receive you here?"

She had not only received him, however, but fastened the kitchen-door carefully after him as she spoke. The very look of that kitchen, with Peggy's careful preparations going on for her master's fastidious meal—preparations so strangely at variance in their dainty nicety with the homely character and frugal expenditure of the house—brought all his old thoughts back to Horace as with a flash of magic. He had begun to forget how his father lived, and the singularity of all his habits. His old bitter, sullen curiosity overpowered him as he stood once more under this roof. Who was this extraordinary man, who preserved in a retirement so rude and unrefined these forlorn habits of another life? The dainty arrangements of the table, the skilful and learned expedients of Peggy's cookery; the one formal luxurious meal for which Mr. Scarsdale every day made a formal toilette; the silent man with his claret-jug and evening dress, in that homeliest of country parlours, flashed before him like a sudden picture. Who was he?—and what had driven him here?

"So my father's out," said Horace; "why should not I come to see you, Peggy? Has he forbidden it? He can shut his own door upon me, it is true; but neither he nor any man in the world can prevent me if I will from coming here."

"Hush, sir! hold your peace!—the master says he'll have none of you here again, and I'm no the woman to disobey the master!" said Peggy. "And what do you mean by staying away a year and never letting us hear word of you, Mr. Horry? Is Miss Susan nobody?—nor me?—wan would think your love was so great for your father, that you never thought of no person in the world but him!"

"So it is—perhaps," said Horace, with a momentary smile; "and he's out, is he?—what is he doing out in daylight and sunshine? Gone to walk with his pretty daughter, Peggy, like a good papa? Ah! I suppose these amiable little amusements would have begun sooner if I had but been wise enough to take myself away."

"To walk with Miss Susan?—alas!" cried Peggy; "but ye allways had a bitter tongue as well as himsel'. Na, he's out of a sudden at his own will, or rather at the good will of Providence, Mr. Horry, to prevent a meeting and unseemly words atween a father and son. What would ye have, young man?—and where have ye been?—and what are you doing? But come in here, for pity's sake, if ye'll no go away, and let me hear all your news, and I'll keep a watch at the back window against the master's coming in."

"My news is nothing, except that I am about to leave Kenlisle," said Horace, impatiently; "but, for heaven's sake, Peggy, who is this father of mine? You know, though nobody else knows—who is he? what does he do here? why does he hate me? why can't you tell me, and make an end of these mysteries? I'm a man now, and not a child; and here is your chance while we're by ourselves—tell me, for heaven's sake."

"You're very ready with your 'heaven's sake,' Mr. Horry," said Peggy, severely; "do ye no think another word might stand better? Heaven has but little to do with it all. The Lord help us! Who is he? 'Deed and he's a man, none so vartuous as he ought to be. And what does he here? Live as it pleases him, the Lord forgive him! without heeding God nor man—that's all about it. And as for hating of you, how much love is there lost, Mr. Horry? Do you think I could kep it on the point o' my finger? You never were wan to waste your kindness. How much of it, think you, gos to him?"

"It is well I can equal him in something," said Horace, with a careless but bitter tone. "However, Peggy, you'll tell nothing, as I might have known. I suppose I may wait to see Susan; there's nothing against that, is there? So, with your permission, I'll go and wait for her. Don't be afraid—only to the dining-room."

"The Lord preserve me!—and if he comes in!" cried Peggy, half addressing herself, and half appealing to her unwelcome visitor.

"Let him come in. I am in my father's house," cried Horace, with that cold, hopeless smile. Peggy knew it of old, and had seen it on other faces. She put out her hand with a fierce impatience, shaking it in his face.

"Oh, man! go away, and make me rid of ye! Go where ye please; if ever mortal man has a devil incarnate in him, it's when ye see that smile!"

Smiling still, Horace went coolly away to the dining-room, as he said; and Peggy, at her wit's end, as she was, found no better way of averting the evil she dreaded than by fastening the doors, so that they could not be opened from without, and clambering upstairs to watch at the elevated window of the storeroom, from whence she could see her master's approach. Horace had never felt himself so entirely in command of the house. He paused at the door of the dull apartment in which he had spent so many hours and years, and where Susan's needlework, more ornamental now than of old, made a little unaccustomed brightness on the dark mirror of the uncovered table; but no sympathy for his young sister, shut up here hopelessly during her early bloom of life, warmed his heart, or even entered his thoughts. He thought of himself—how he used to waste and curse the days in this miserable solitude, and what a change had passed upon his life since then. Listening, in the extreme silence, he heard Peggy go upstairs to her watch. He smiled at that, too, but accepted the safeguard; and, without any more hesitation, turned round, and went across the hall to his father's room.

The study; that dreaded, dismal, apartment;—with its dull bookcases set at right-angles, the hard elbow-chair standing stiffly before the table, the big volume laid open upon the desk, the stifling red curtains drooping over the window; his heart beat, in spite of himself, as he entered; he could scarcely believe his father was not there, somehow watching him, reading his very thoughts. With a sudden "Pshaw!" of self-contempt and temerity, he hastened forward to the table. There was no lock upon the little sloping desk which sustained the volume Mr. Scarsdale had been reading. Without hoping to find anything, but with a vague thrill of curiosity and eagerness, Horace lifted the book, and opened the desk. It was full of miscellaneous papers—Peggy's household bills, and other things entirely unimportant; but among these lay some folds of blotting-paper. He opened them with a trembling hand; the first thing he saw there was a letter, which fell out, and which Horace grasped at, half-consciously, and thrust into his pocket; another fold concealed, apparently, the answer to it, half written, and hurriedly concluded. The young man ran his eyes over it with burning curiosity. It was addressed to Colonel Sutherland, and chiefly concerned an invitation from her uncle to Susan, which Mr. Scarsdale peremptorily declined. Then his own name caught his eye; the last paragraph abruptly broken off, as if the writer had thrown down his pen in impatience, and could continue no longer. These words, which conveyed so little information to him, burned themselves, notwithstanding, upon Horace's memory with all the vehement interest of unnatural hate:—

"As for my son, I do not choose to answer to any man for my sentiments and actions in respect to him. I held all natural ties as abrogated between us from the period you mention, when, as you say, he seems to have ceased to appear to me as my child, and I have only viewed him as a rival, unjustly preferred to me. I do not object to adopt your words; they are sufficiently correct; but I will suffer no question on the subject; let the blame be upon the head of the true culprit. As to the will—"

Here the letter ended, with a dash and blot, as if the pen had fallen from the writer's fingers; it was this, evidently, which had driven him forth in wild impatience, stung by his subject. Horace read, and re-read the sentence, devouring it with his eyes of enmity. Then he restored it rudely to its place, put back the book, and left the room. He thought he had discovered something in the first flush of his excitement. It did not seem possible that he could have looked thus directly into his father's thoughts without discovering something. He no longer cared to risk a meeting with him. In the tumult of his imaginary enlightenment he called to Peggy, hastily, that he was going away, and went out, as he entered, by the back door. Nobody was visible on the moor; the whole waste lay barren before him, under the slanting light of the setting sun. He put up the collar of his coat, set his hat over his eyes, and plunged along the narrow path among the gorse and heather, to Tillington, thinking still in his excited mind, and feeling in his tingling frame, that he had found out something; and knew more of the secret of his life than he had ever known before; deluded by his eagerness and enmity, and the excitement caused in him by the first stealthy investigation it had ever been in his power to make.

CHAPTER XXIII

The little inn at Tillington, to which Horace betook himself for his night's lodging, had suffered little change from the day when he conducted his uncle there. Sam, it is true, was fighting the Caffres in Africa, far enough distant; but his mother had recovered her bustling good spirits, and his father his philosophy, and even Sergeant Kennedy, great and pompous as of old, dominated over the little sanded parlour, and fired the village lads with martial tales, unabashed, under Mrs. Gilsland's very eye. It was not to the sanded parlour, however, that Horace now betook himself. He was no longer the sullen country lad, whole idler and half gentleman, whose deportment had distressed Colonel Sutherland; and his old gamekeeper acquaintances and alehouse gossips scarcely knew him, in his changed dress and altered manner. He was the nephew of "the Cornel," a name which Mrs. Gilsland and Sergeant Kennedy had made important in the village, and he was flourishing in the world and likely to come to higher fortune, circumstances which mightily changed the tide of public opinion towards him. Mrs. Gilsland received the young man with her best curtsey, and with profuse salutations. She opened the door of "the best room" for him, and suggested a fire as the evenings were still cold, and offered a duck for his supper, "or dinner, I was meaning," added the landlady, as Horace shrugged his shoulders at the chilly aspect of the room, and tossed his great-coat on a chair with lordly pretension and incivility. The good woman was daunted in spite of her indignation. "The Cornel," it is true, had shown no such scorn of her humble parlour, and she was not disposed to overestimate the comforts of Marchmain. Still, there is something imposing to the vulgar imagination in this manner of insolence. The room had never before looked so mean to its mistress. She stopped herself in her unencouraged talk, and began to displace the faded paper ornaments in the fireplace, which concealed a fire laid ready for lighting, and kindled the wood herself with a somewhat unsteady hand. "It's just as it was when the Cornel was here, and he was very well pleased with everything," she said, half to herself. Horace took no notice of the implied apology and defence.

"Send me candles, please, and I'll see about dinner later," he said, loftily; "lights in the meanwhile, and immediately; never mind the fire—I want lights, and at once!"

Mrs. Gilsland withdrew, awed, but deeply wrathful. "I would like to know how many servants he had to wait upon him at Marchmain!" she exclaimed to herself as she left the room—"with his candles, and lights, and his immediantely! Immediantely, quotha! Eh me, the difference of men! Would the Cornel, or young Mr. Roger, order a person that gate? I would just say no!—but the like of an upstart like him!"

However, the candles did come immediately, in Mrs. Gilsland's best candlesticks, and in elaborate frills of white paper; and the duck was killed, as a great gabble in the yard gave immediate notice, and all the preparations which she could make set on foot instantly for her fastidious guest. Clean linen, snowy and well-aired, was spread upon the bed which "the Cornel" had once occupied; and greater commotion than even the advent of the Cornel himself would have caused diffused itself through the house. Meanwhile Horace addressed himself at his leisure to his immediate business. He had come thus far without being able to perceive that he had gained nothing by his inroad into his father's privacy. He was still possessed by the excitement of the act. All the way, while he walked as if for a race, he had been going over these unfatherly words, and they moved him to an unreasoning and unusual amount of emotion, rather more than a personal encounter would have done—confirming all his own sentiments, and adding to them a certain bitterness; but in the haste and fervor of his thoughts he still imagined himself to have acquired something, and now took out the letter which he had seized and crumpled into his pocket, only in the idea that it might supplement and confirm his visionary information. It was, as he supposed, from Colonel Sutherland, and chiefly occupied with that earnest invitation to Susan which her father had declined. What concerned himself was brief enough, and was to the following effect:—

"You will probably say that I have very little right to address you on subjects so intimate and personal. I merely throw myself upon your indulgence, pleading our old acquaintance and connection. I have no right whatever to say a word, and I trust you will pardon all the more kindly what I do say on this account. Your son Horace is a very peculiar and remarkable young man. That miserable circumstance that happened when he was a child seems to have had an effect upon the boy unawares, little as he knows of it. And you, my dear Scarsdale, have you forgotten that this boy is your own child, and not a rival unjustly preferred to you? I acknowledge the wicked and desperate injustice of the whole proceeding, but Horace was not to blame. Would it not have been better, I appeal to you, to make an open effort to overthrow this iniquitous will, than to suffer it to produce results so deplorable? Hear me, I beseech you: receive the boy into your confidence before it is too late. It is your only means of really defeating and forestalling the evil objects of that posthumous punishment and vengeance. Suffer me to speak. I have no interest in it, save that of natural affection; let your own heart plead with me, as I am sure it will, if you permit it. Let him know his singular and unhappy fortune, and I am grievously mistaken in human nature if the attempt does not prove to you how little you need to apprehend from the temper and disposition of your son."

Horace read this over with an interest only more intense than the contempt which it produced in him. "The old twaddler!" he exclaimed to himself, in the first impulse of his disdain. That feeling moved him, even before curiosity. He could not take time to think what it was which his father was urged to reveal to him, in his scorn of the anticipated result, the natural affection, the generous response, which his innocent old uncle believed in. Then he put the letter back into his pocket, and set his mind to consider what information he had really gained. What was it? Some vague intimation about a will, which Mr. Scarsdale had better have tried to set aside: some mysterious hint at posthumous punishment and vengeance, and his own singular and unhappy fortune; and on his father's side a declaration of dislike and enmity, but nothing more. That was what he had discovered—this was the information which had sent him in nervous haste out of Marchmain, and quickened his solitary walk over the moor—and this was all. He ground his teeth together when he perceived it, with savage disappointment and rage. He had been deceived—he, so boldly confident in his own powers, had allowed himself to be blinded and circumvented by his own excitement and childish commotion of feeling. For a moment he had enjoyed such command of his father's house as a midnight thief might have gained, and had sacrificed all the results of that precious instant by a piece of involuntary self-deceit and ridiculous weakness, an indulgence absurd and contemptible. His feelings were not enviable as he sat in Mrs. Gilsland's dark little parlour, with the two faint candles burning, and the damp wood hissing in the grate. He might have borne to be deceived, but it was hard to consent to the humiliating idea of having deceived himself. However, he could make nothing better of it, and grinding his teeth did no harm to anybody, and certainly could do little service to himself. So he swallowed his mortification as he best could, put Colonel Sutherland's letter in his pocket-book, and addressed himself with what content he might to Mrs. Gilsland's duck. He was not without appetite, in spite of his disappointment. Then he sauntered into the public room, and opened his heart so far as to bestow a pint or two of ale upon his old acquaintances. Even this divertissement, however, did not withdraw his thoughts from his own affairs—he lounged at the door of the sanded parlour, doing a little grandeur and superiority as he loved to do, but turning over his secret strain of thought without intermission, notwithstanding. A will!—then there was a will which concerned himself, and lay at the bottom of all these hints and mysteries. Wills are accessible to curious eyes in this country, in spite of all the safeguards which the most jealous care can take. The young man started when that idea interposed the flicker of its taper into the darkness. He raised his head again and renewed his courage: after all, his invasion of his father's private sanctuary had not been entirely in vain. There was comfort to his self-esteem, as well as a definite direction to his efforts, in the thought.

CHAPTER XXIV

Mr. Scarsdale had left his room and the house in a sudden flush of impatience beyond bearing, as his son had imagined. The very idea of the will to which Colonel Sutherland referred plainly in his letter was maddening to the solitary man. He could not bear the name, much less any discussion of this fatal document; and when he found himself constrained to mention it in his own person, a violent and angry petulance overpowered him; he dashed his pen to the ground, threw his paper into the desk, and rushed out of doors into the spring air, which had no softening effect upon him. Half consciously to himself, he had lived with more freedom since the departure of his son, and felt himself relieved of a certain clog upon his movements; and it was not now so extraordinary an event as Horace had supposed that he should be out of doors in daylight and sunshine. Mr. Scarsdale had strayed deep into the moor in an opposite direction to Tillington, with thoughts even more bitter than those of Horace—thoughts which the well-meant intervention of the Colonel only raised to a passionate virulence. He, too, like his son, scorned, with a deep contempt, the tender simplicity of the old soldier, which neither of them comprehended; and coming back over that desolate waste of moorland to see his own desolate house standing out solitary and wistful in the bosom of the wilderness, Mr. Scarsdale realized, with a bitter superiority, the kind of house which was likely to call his brother-in-law master—the house full of warmth and kindliness, at which he sneered dismally, with the disgust of an evil spirit. The very desire which her uncle showed to have Susan with him increased the scorn of Susan's father. What did he want the girl for? To make an old man's pet of her, and amuse himself with the fondness of dotage? Thus the recluse returned to his house to conclude his letter, and to intimate, in words few and strong, as befitted his present temper, his desire to receive no further "favours" in correspondence from Colonel Sutherland. He went in unsuspicious, where there seemed nothing to suspect, seeing, as he passed, Susan seated near the window with her work on her knee, and her wistful young eyes gazing across the moor. She had come in from her walk and her stolen interview with the one sole companion whom she ever had any intercourse with. She was leaning her head upon the pretty hand, which had dimpled into womanly roundness and softness, thinking over some stray thoughts put into her mind by the romantic Letty, and dispersing, with her own honest womanly good sense, the boarding-school absurdities of the half-educated girl whom Susan so devoutly believed to be her own superior; and perhaps wondering a little wistfully, as girls will, when, if ever, her fate and fortune would come to her over that blank of moorland. She was not discontented, little as she had to content her; she was only a domestic woman—a household creature; word of flattery or voice of compliment had never sounded in her ears all her life. She could still brighten her dull firmament not a little with a new pattern for her muslin work, or a new story privately borrowed from Letty, though perhaps only out of the Sunday School library, and nothing remarkable in point of literature; but still wandering ideas will float into minds of nineteen, and eyes that have grown weary even over a new pattern might be pardoned if they searched the horizon with a little wistfulness, and wondered if nobody ever would appear again on the purple blank of Lanwoth Moor.

Susan, at least, was thinking so secretly to herself when her father entered, running over in her own mind the few, very few, people she had ever known. She did not count the turnpikeman and his wife and children upon the road, nor the chance cottager whom she knew by sight. But who were the others? The Rector, and Letty's father, the poor Presbyterian minister, the first of whom she had heard preach, and the latter had spoken to her when she gave him a chance, which was seldom; Letty herself, who was older now, and had ideas of lovers, and made Susan, a little to her own confusion, shame, and amusement, her chosen confidante; Uncle Edward, dearest of friends, whom, alas, it was like enough she might never see again; and, yes—among so few it was impossible to omit him—Mr. Roger, who had thrown the gipsy's husband over the hedge, and had taken off his hat to her, and who was lost in the distant world and unknown mists of life. Which of them had Susan a chance of seeing across that moor? Nobody, poor child; not even the postman, the one messenger of brightness to her life; for it was too late for that emissary; but she sat at the window, with her work in one hand, leaning her head upon the other; perhaps dreaming of some figure which it would have lightened her heart to see, appearing in the evening light on the road across the moor.

She was still seated thus, and the light was failing, giving an excuse for her sweet wistful idleness and half melancholy mood of thought, when Mr. Scarsdale suddenly flung open the door, and appeared, as he had once appeared to his daughter before, swift and sudden as a wind, white with passion, and lost in a fiery, silent excitement, which terrified and shocked her. He came close up to her, with a long, noiseless stride, and grasped her arm furiously: but for that grasp the man might have been a ghost, with his shadowy, attenuated form, his long open dressing-gown streaming behind him, his noiseless step, and face of speechless passion. Not entirely speechless either, though he might as well have been so for any meaning which she could comprehend in the words which fell hissing and sharp on Susan's ears.

"Where is it?" he cried, shaking her whole frame with the fury of his grasp—"where is it?—what have you done with it? Restore it instantly, dishonourable fool! Do you think it is anything to you?"

"What, papa?" cried Susan, trembling, and drawing back unawares with a shrinking of terror. It was a strange interruption of her innocent girlish dreams.

"What!" he cried, holding her tighter—"what! Do you dare to ask me? Restore it at once, or I shall be tempted to something beyond reason. Child! idiot! do you think you can cheat me?"

Susan stood still in his hold, shaken by it, and trembling from head to foot—but she shrank no more. "I have never cheated you in all my life," she said, raising her honest blue eyes to his face—that face which scowled over hers with a devilish force of passion; was it possible that there could be kindred or connection between the two?

He looked at her with a baffled rage, incomprehensible to Susan. "There is neither man nor woman in the world, nor child either, who does not lie to me and deceive me!" said Mr. Scarsdale. "Do you suppose I do not know—do you think I have no eyes to see you smile over that old fool's fondling letters? Give it up this moment, or I swear to you I will cast you out of my house, and leave you to find your way to him as you can! Give it up at once, I say!"

"Do you mean Uncle Edward's letter, papa?" asked Susan. "I will get it this moment, if you will let me go; all of them, if you please."

But instead of letting her go, he grasped her pained arm more fiercely.

"You know what letter I mean," he said; "that letter which only a fool could have written, and which I was a fool to think of answering. What would you call the child who takes advantage of her father's absence to go into his room and rob him of it? Was it for love of the writer?—was it for your miserable brother's information?—or is it a common amusement, which I have only found out because this was done too soon? Thief! have you nothing to say?"

Susan drew herself out of her father's grasp with a boldness and force altogether unprecedented in her, and grew red over brow, neck, and face.

"I am no thief—I will not be called so!" she said, in sudden provocation; then falling as suddenly out of that unusual self-assertion, she continued, trembling, "Papa, I have never entered your room; I never went into it in my life except when you were there; I never robbed you; I know nothing even of what you mean."

Her father looked at her closely, with a smile of disbelief and a fixed offensive stare, which she could not tolerate. He did not attempt to lay hands upon her, but stood only looking at her with eyes which were incapable of perceiving truth or honesty, and saw only fraud and falseness. "Where is the letter?" he said. Those sincere young eyes, which everybody else in the world would have trusted, conveyed no security to him.

Susan turned away from him, with a sudden outbreak of tears—tears of mortified and passionate impatience. He was her father, in spite of the small tenderness he showed her, and had a certain hold upon her habit of domestic affection. She felt the injustice keenly enough, and she felt still more keenly that his eyes were intolerable, and that she could not bear them.

"I have no letter save those my uncle has sent me," she said, indignantly, when she had overcome her emotion; "they are all here in this box—I have no other. I can only repeat the same thing, papa, if you should ask me a hundred times—I have no letter but these."

And Susan opened the pretty inlaid box, with its key hanging to it by a bit of ribbon, which Uncle Edward had brought her, and which she had appropriated, with a fanciful girlish affection, to hold his letters—opened it hastily and threw out the little store upon the table with trembling hands. Some trifling circumstance, perhaps the mere odour of the sandal-wood which lined the box, recalling some subtle association to him, produced a start and flush of angry colour on Mr. Scarsdale's face. He thrust the little casket away with some muttered words which Susan could not hear, but, even in spite of that touch of nature, turned over with a cold suspicion the letters which it had contained. Nothing like what he sought was there, of course; but he was not convinced. No one else was in the house, or had been here—so far as his knowledge went—save Peggy; even Susan did not know of her brother's hurried visit, and Peggy was beyond suspicion, even to Mr. Scarsdale;—his daughter, and she only, could be to blame.

"I know," he said, coldly, when he had scattered the good Colonel's letters over the table, throwing them scornfully from him, "that my desk has been opened and my papers stolen. You are clever in hiding, like all women; but such an artifice cannot deceive me, when my loss is so evident. Take this detestable thing away! the smell is suffocating," he cried, with an interjection of rage, and once more pushing violently from him the pretty box with its pungent odour. "But stay, understand me first; it is late, and you are young; I will not turn you out upon the moor to-night, little as you deserve my consideration; but if this letter is not restored to me before to-morrow, nothing in the world will prevent me expelling you from this house—do you hear? I will have no thief under my roof. I perceive you are ready to cry, like all your kind. Crying is a very good weapon with some people, but I assure you it has no effect whatever on me."

Susan could not have answered for her life. She stood still, gazing at him with her eyes dilated, a convulsive effort of pride keeping in her tears, but a sob bursting in spite of her, from her suffocating breast. There she still stood after he had left the room, speechless, labouring to contain herself, even after the necessity for that effort was over. But when she dropped at length into a chair, and yielded to the hysterical passion of tears and sobbing which overpowered her, beneath all her shame, mortification, and terror, a guilty gleam of joy which frightened her shot through poor Susan's heart. She thought it guilty, poor child. She was dismayed to feel that sudden pang of hope and comfort breaking the sense of this calamity. To be expelled from her father's house, cast out upon the moor and upon the world, with the stigma upon her of having robbed and deceived him! She repeated over to herself that accumulation of horrors, to extinguish this furtive and unpermissible glow of secret hope, and cried bitterly over her own wickedness when she found it inextinguishable; but even with that secret and unsanctioned solace, the thought was miserable enough to her youth and ignorance. To be turned away like a bad servant; to be called a thief; to be driven from her father's house; Heaven preserve her! a young girl alone and penniless—what could she do?

CHAPTER XXV

In this stupefied condition of mind, stunned by the change which seemed about to happen, yet moved now and then by a strange intolerance and passionate inclination to resist and protest, Peggy found her young mistress when she came to spread the table for that hateful dinner, the thought of which made

Susan's heart ache. The poor girl still sat listlessly by the table on which her letters, the treasures of her affectionate disposition, were still carelessly scattered, and where the pretty box stood open and empty, as Mr. Scarsdale had thrust it away from him. Susan was by no means above a fit of crying, and had her disappointments and vexations like another, little as there seemed to wish or hope for within her limited firmament; but this listless attitude of despair was new to Peggy, who was somehow frightened to see it. What had happened? Had she expected a letter, and falling into a fit of passion not to receive any, had she thrown out recklessly on the table that cherished correspondence, the comfort of her life? But fits of passion were very unlike Susan. Peggy had come upstairs early, that she might have some private, confidential talk, and inform her of her brother's hurried visit; but she paused in anxiety and compassion before entering upon that subject. "Hinny, what ails you?" asked Peggy, with the kindly, local term of caressing, laying her hand softly on Susan's shoulder. The girl started, gazed in her face, and then suddenly recollecting this one, long, faithful friend, whom she must lose, hid her face upon Peggy's shoulder, and burst again into passionate tears.

"What is it then, hinny?—aye trouble, and nought but trouble. Bless us all, has the master been upon ye again? And what did ye know, poor innocent?" cried Peggy, caressing the young head that leaned upon her; "has he found it out, for all the watch I made? Hauld up your head, and let me hear—it was none of your blame."

"Found out what?" cried Susan, grasping her suddenly by the hand.

"No great comfort if a person mun speak the truth—just that Mr. Horry was here when you were out. Yes, Miss Susan," said Peggy, "I ought to have told ye sooner, but what good? He came for no end as I could see, and departed the same. Aye the owld man—a bitter thought in his heart, and an ill word in his mouth. Eh, the Lord forgive us! To think we should have the bringing up of childer!—that can make sure of nothing to give them but our own shortcomin's! He said he was leaving Kenlisle, but no another word, and was out of the house before I could come down to ask him wherefore he was goin', and where."

"Horace!" cried Susan, who had followed this speech breathlessly, with an interest almost too eager for intelligence, and whose face had reddened with a painful insight, as it came to an end. "Horace! Has Horace been here?"

She clasped her hands together with such an anxious entreaty not to be answered, that Peggy paused involuntarily. "Peggy," said Susan, under her breath, "don't tell papa—for pity's sake, don't tell papa! He will do nothing worse to me than he has threatened. I am only a girl—he would not strike me nor fight me. But Horace! Peggy, for mercy's sake, if you love me or any of us, let him believe that I did it. Let him never know that Horace has been here."

"There's something happened! Let me hear what it is," said Peggy, almost as anxiously, "and then I'll know what is behoving and needful. Eh, Miss Susan, you're ignorant and innocent yoursel', you moughtn't understand him. Let me hear what he said."

"He said nothing," said Susan, shaking her head mournfully, with a sadness very unlike Peggy's expectation, "but that I had stolen away a letter from his room while he was out. Oh, Peggy, I am so very, very thankful that I had not seen you, and did not know Horace had been here! And he said if I did not give it back to him to-morrow, he would turn me away. Turn me away, Peggy, out of doors upon the moor, to go anywhere, or do anything I pleased! I, who never was farther than Tillington except once with Uncle Edward! I, who know nobody, and have no money, and no friends! To send me away from Marchmain, and from—from you, who care for me. Oh, Peggy, what shall I do?"

Peggy stood irresolute for a moment, wringing her hands. "The Lord help us all! If the devil has a man bound hand and foot, what can I do?" cried the faithful servant. "God preserve us! That's what it's come to. Eh, mistress, mistress! Did I think what I would have to put up with when I gave you my word? Let me go, Miss Susan. I've know'd him thirty year, and he's know'd me. I'll speak to him mysel'."

But Susan hung round her with a clasp which would not be loosed, entreating, with a voice scarcely audible, which, notwithstanding, went to poor Peggy's heart. "He will think you know—you will tell him—he will find it out!" cried Susan; "and, Peggy, they will kill each other. Peggy, Peggy! think! father and son! Let him believe it was me; he will not kill me, and I am ready to go away."

"Poor lamb!" said Peggy, smoothing down the pretty fair braids of hair on Susan's young head, which had once more drooped forward on her own compassionate shoulder. "But it's no' her; I'm no thinking of her, bless her! It's him. God forgive him! He had but one chance, as any mortal could see. He had his childer, his daughter—an innocent that had no share in't, and was wronged as well as himsel'. And now the Lord help us! he'll bereave himsel', and send his one hope away. I'm no' thinking of you, hinny," said Peggy, tenderly, while a few slow tears began to fall, gleaming and large, on Susan's hair—"nor of me—one heart-break, more or less, is little matter to an owld woman; and if I wasna like to sink with fret and trouble, I would see it was best for you; but, oh, weary on the man himsel'! What's to become of him? There's no more houp, as I can see, no more!"

Susan, sobbing upon Peggy's breast, naturally felt, in the youthful petulance of that sudden calamity, that it was herself who ought to be sorrowed for, and not her father. She raised herself a little, wiping her eyes, with a flush of momentary independence and involuntary self-assertion. For once in her life the forlorn pride and excess of unappreciated suffering, so dear to very young people, came in a flood of desolate luxury to Susan's heart. She thought of herself, lonely and friendless upon the moor, cast out from her home, and ignorant where to turn, with nobody in the world so much as thinking of her, or sparing a tear for her sorrow. Peggy mourning for Mr. Scarsdale—for her father, he who dwelt secure and supreme at home, and cast out his woman-child upon the world. Horace, for whose sin she was to suffer, gone away without caring to see her, without even saying where he had gone; and Susan in her youth and desolation all alone and friendless! The picture was sad enough in reality; and Susan lifted her head with momentary pride from Peggy's breast, tears of self-lamentation flowing out of her eyes, and proud mortification and loneliness in her heart; not even Peggy felt for her.

"And I—what am I to do?" she said, half to herself, turning her wistful weeping eyes upon that moor which was the world to her at this moment, and no bad emblem of the world at any time to the friendless and solitary. It was true that Susan's heart had palpitated with one sudden flush of joy at the thought, beyond that moor and yon horizon, of reaching Uncle Edward, and the home of her dreams; but Uncle Edward was far off, and she had no means of reaching him. What was she to do?—wander on day and night, like a lady of romance, seeking her love, with nothing on her lips but "Uncle Edward" and "Milnehill"?—or lose herself and die upon those wistful far extending roads, out of reach of love or human charity? Anything sad enough would have pleased Susan's imagination at the present moment. She could see no brighter side to the picture. Nobody in the world cared for or sympathized with her strange dismal circumstances, and the only home she had ever known in the world was about to close its remorseless doors upon her. Darkness fell upon the moor, and the spring breezes blew chilly over it, but from that darkness and those breezes she might have no roof to shelter her after to-night.

From these fancies she was strangely enough interrupted. Peggy, absorbed in her own thoughts, and almost forgetting the young victim of this day's misfortunes, had not disturbed her hitherto. Peggy's own mind was wandering back through a painful blank of years and hopeless human perversity; but the sure touch of habit recalled her to herself more certainly than Susan's silent tears, or the melancholy thought of losing Susan, which, though she said little about it, lay heavy at her heart. The growing darkness startled her suddenly—"Gude preserve me!—and he must have his dinner, whether or no," said Peggy, darting forward to gather up the letters and restore them to their box. Not a moment too soon, for Mr. Scarsdale's study-door creaked immediately afterwards, and his step was audible going upstairs to dress. Susan took the box out of Peggy's hands with youthful petulance, and left the room, carrying it solemnly, and proudly restraining her tears. Nobody should be offended again with the sight of Uncle Edward's present. Nobody should find herself in the way after this melancholy night; and the dinner, that dismal ceremonial—the dinner which Peggy could not forget, though Susan's heart was breaking—she had that trial, too, to get through and overcome. To meet her father's eye and sit in his presence all the miserable evening; to eat or pretend to eat for the last time at his table; and to do this all alone and unsupported, the poor desolate child feeling a certain guilt in her heart which she had not known when he spoke to her first—the secret consciousness, not to be revealed for her life, that if she had not taken the letter she knew who had done so; and that secretly, like a robber, Horace had been here.

CHAPTER XXVI

The dinner passed as these formal lonely dinners had passed for years at Marchmain. There was no perceptible shade of difference in the manner of Mr. Scarsdale, who addressed to his daughter polite questions about the dishes she preferred, as he had been used to do to Horace, driving his son wild; and himself sat upright and stiff at the head of the table, dining, as usual, without any symptoms of the passion which he had exhibited to Susan. He was deeply angry, it is true, still, but he was entirely without alarm, believing, as a matter of course, that Susan must have taken his letter, and contemptuously receiving that instance of dishonourable conduct merely as a visible specimen of the womanish meanness and cunning which belonged to such creatures, and which, perhaps, was scarcely to be considered guilt. He believed she would return it to him that evening. He did not believe she had boldness enough to retain any copy for Horace, and he knew that to herself it would disclose nothing; therefore, he showed no more passion, was no more repulsive than he always was, and scarcely deigned to turn his eyes more than usual upon his unfortunate child.

She sat there at table, with the light shining on her, answering him in humble monosyllables when he spoke—for Susan's heroics had failed long ere now—receiving humbly what he sent to her, but unable to eat a morsel, her heart almost choking her as it beat against her breast. It was not now the desolate moor, nor the forlorn idea of being thrust out homeless upon it to wander where she would, that oppressed Susan. It was the terror of being put to further question, of her father once more addressing her, as he was sure to do, about the theft, of which she no longer felt herself quite innocent. She could scarcely restrain her start and thrill of terror when he turned his head towards her; her frame trembled throughout with desperate apprehensions; she feared herself, and her own ignorance of all the arts of concealment; she feared to say something or do something which would betray Horace; and she feared her father—that bitter tone of passion, that terrible incredulity of truth. The poor girl sat still, rigidly, upon her chair, with a feeling that this was her only safeguard, and that she must infallibly drop down upon the floor if she tried to move. When Peggy removed the cloth, and placed Mr. Scarsdale's little reading-desk, his glass and decanter, upon the table, Susan still sat there in spite of many a secret touch and pull from her humble and anxious friend. Peggy was alarmed, but durst not say anything to call the attention of her master; and at last brought Susan's work to her, and thrust it into the poor child's trembling fingers, with a look and movement of anxious appeal. Susan took the work mechanically, and applied herself to it without knowing what she did; and thus the evening went on with a thrilling, audible silence, of which, dreary and long though she had felt these nights many a time before, she had never been sensible till now. The long, gleaming, polished table, with the two candles reflecting themselves in its surface in two lines of light; the solemn figure of Mr. Scarsdale in his formal evening dress, seated upright at the head, turning with mechanical, automaton regularity the leaves of his book; the dead blank of the surrounding walls, no longer diversified even by a flicker of firelight; and Susan, almost as rigid and motionless as her father, afraid to breathe, lest it should call his attention to her; her ears tingling to the dreadful silence, and her heart fainting at thought of the words which some time this evening were sure to break it. Looking upon this evening scene, it was strange to believe that Susan Scarsdale could tremble at the idea of being thrust out of this cold and gloomy refuge, or find no comfort in the thought of trying rather the strange world and the solitary moor, which, unknown as they were, were still crossed by paths which led to human homes.

But she thought neither of the world nor the moor at the present moment. She would have been glad if she had been sufficiently courageous to fly out into the darkness and lose herself for ever rather than meet this impending interview; but it was not in her to escape or run away. Susan's mind was the womanly development of that steady British temper which cannot deliver itself by violence, but must wait orderly and dutiful for the natural accomplishment of its destinies. She sat trembling but still, afraid of what she had to bear, doubtless, but incapable of running away.

The long night passed in this pause and silence, without a word said on either side. The tea came in, and was made and swallowed without any interruption of the blank. And still Susan's fingers moved at the work which she could scarcely see, and her father turned over the pages of his book. He perceived beyond doubt, as he sat mechanically reading to the bottom of every page, with that dull, steady attention which had neither life nor interest in it, the state of extreme emotion, excitement, and desperate self-restraint in which his young daughter sat before him; but pity found no entrance into his heart. He permitted her to remain so, sitting late and beyond the usual hour of retiring, with a kind of diabolical patience on his own part, which checked the words a dozen times on his lips. He was satisfied to see the entire power he had over her, and at the present moment had no thought of his threat, or of carrying it out. Perhaps even to him the room would have been more desolate, the dismal evening longer, had there been no young figure there, humbly ministering to him when occasion was, keeping respectful silence, bearing, without a complaint or effort to enliven them, these tedious, miserable hours; but he had no objection to see her suffer. At length, when the chill of almost midnight began to creep into that room where they had ceased to have any fire, Mr. Scarsdale's own physical sensations moved him. He closed his book, and as he closed it, saw Susan shiver in the climax of her agonies of anticipation. She should not be balked this time, and at last he spoke.

"I presume, Susan," he said, with a little solemnity, "that you have made up your mind."

"Papa?" said Susan, with a gasp of inquiry. Made up her mind to what? He so seldom addressed her by her name that some forlorn hope of his heart relenting towards her entered her head. Perhaps some lingering touch of compunction had taken him at the thought of sending her away.

"Must I speak plainer?" he said. "I presume you have decided what you are going to do. Are you ready to restore my letter, or to leave my house? Which? You understand the alternative well enough, and you know that I am not to be trifled with—have you the letter here?"

"Oh, papa!" cried Susan, clasping her hands, "I have not the letter here nor anywhere! I never had it! I never saw it! Oh, papa, did I ever tell you a lie, that you will not believe me now? And how can I give it back when I never took it?—when I do not know what it is? Will you not believe me? I am speaking the truth."

"Where is my letter?" cried Mr. Scarsdale once more, growing white with passion.

Susan sat looking at him, trembling, unable to speak; her lips moved, but he could not hear what she said. She could hardly hear herself say under her breath, "I cannot tell! I do not know!" Her terror had taken breath and voice away from her. How could she answer such a question?—she did not know—and yet she did know. Oh, Horace! She could have been so much bolder, so much stronger, if she had never known of his coming there.

"You are obdurate, then, and determined!" cried the father. "You think, perhaps, your brother will take up your cause and protect you. Fool! do you suppose he cares for you more than for an instrument; or your meddling uncle, who has made perpetual mischief since his prying visit here. Think! I give you one opportunity more: will you restore me that letter—once for all, yes or no?"

Susan staggered up to her feet, hysterical and overwhelmed.

"You may turn me away out of the house!" she cried; "you may do it, for you have the power—you may kill me, if you please; but you cannot make me give back what I never saw and never touched in my life!"

Mr. Scarsdale looked at her intently, as if thinking that his eyes, fiery and burning, could overcome her if nothing else would. "In that case," he said, with cold passion, "this is our last meeting—the last occasion on which I shall have anything to say to you. I am now alone, and shall remain so while I live. Be good enough to give Peggy directions where your wardrobe is to be sent. In consideration of your youth, I give you the shelter of my roof to-night; but I trust I shall not need to encounter another such interview. Good-bye—I wish you better fortune in your future life than you have had here."

Susan held up her hands, overpowered, in spite of herself, by the position in which she stood.

"Father, where can I go?" she cried, with a wild appeal. He looked at her once more, fixedly and firmly.

"You know that much better than I can tell you. Good-bye," he said; and so left the room, with those long, silent, passionate steps, the light he carried gleaming upon his passionate face. Susan sank down where he had left her, alone and desolate. It was all over now!

CHAPTER XXVII

Susan could not tell how long the interval was till Peggy came softly stealing into the room, in her big night-cap, and with a shawl over her shoulders. Peggy had waited till she heard Mr. Scarsdale sweep upstairs; she could see him out of her kitchen, where she sat in the dark, silent and watchful as her own great cat, with her eyes turned towards the closed door of the dining-room; and as soon as she supposed it safe, she made haste to the succour of his poor daughter. Susan was sitting in despair, where she had sat all the evening, pale, stupefied, and silent—not sufficiently alive to outward circumstances to notice Peggy's entrance; overpowered by her own personal misfortune scarcely more than she was shocked in her sense of right, and ashamed to be obliged to expose her father's cruelty and injustice. A new horror on this point had seized her; she was not of that disposition which is pleased to appear in the character of victim or sacrifice; she would have suffered anything sooner than disclose the grim ghost of her own house to the public eye; notwithstanding this was what she must do, in spite of herself. When Horace left his home it was not an unnatural proceeding, nor was his father to be supposed greatly in the wrong; but she, a girl, what would any one think of a man who expelled her from his unfatherly doors? Her heart ached as this new thought fell with afflicting and sudden distinctness upon it, and she had now no more time to weep or bemoan herself. This night only was all the interval of thought or preparation to be permitted her. Already, indeed, in the chill of that deep darkness the day had begun which was to see her cast forth and banished; and already her mind sickened and grew feeble to think that she could not take a step upon the road without revealing to some one how hardly she had been treated; and that her own very solitude, helplessness, and necessity were all so many mute accusations against the father who had no pity on her womanhood or her youth.

Notwithstanding, Susan was recovering command of herself, and felt that she had no time for trifling; and when she felt Peggy's hand on her shoulder, and heard the whisper of kindness in her ear, she did not "give way," as Peggy expected. She looked up with her exhausted face, almost worn out, yet at the same time reviving, full of what it was necessary to do.

"I am to go away," she said, slowly, with a quiver of her lip—"to-morrow—early—that he may never see me again. I am to tell you where to send my things, and to go away, Peggy, to-morrow."

"Weel, hinny, and it's well for you!" cried Peggy, herself bursting out into a fit of tears and sobbing. "Oh, Miss Susan, what am I that I should complain and grumble?—but it's all that heartbreaking face, my darling lamb! What should I lament for? Nothing in this world but selfishness, and because I'm an old fool. The Lord forgive us!—it's a deal better for you!"

"Oh! hush, Peggy—don't speak!" said Susan—"and don't cry—I can't bear it! There is very, very little time now to think of anything; and you must tell me—there is nobody else in the world to tell me—what I am to do."

"Nobody else in the world? Oh, hinny-sweet!" cried poor Peggy. "There's a whole worldfull of love and kindness for you and the likes of you. There's your uncle—bless him!—that would keep the very wind off your cheek; and many a wan ye never saw nor heard tell o', will be striving which to be kindest. Say no such words to me—I know a deal better than that. I'm no' afraid for you," cried Peggy, with a fresh burst of sobbing—"no' a morsel, and I'll no pretend. I'm real even down heartbroken for the master and mysel'!"

Susan could not answer, and did not try; she was but little disposed to lament for her father at the present moment, or to think him capable of feeling her loss. She put her hand on Peggy's, and pressed it, half in fondness, half with an entreaty to be silent, which the faithful servant did not disregard. Peggy took Susan's round soft hand between her own hard ones, and held it close, and looked at her with sorrowful, fond eyes. She saw the young life and resolution, the sweet serious sense and judgment, coming back to Susan's face, and Peggy was heroic enough to forget herself, for the forlorn young creature's sake.

"Ay, it's just so," said Peggy—"I knowed it from her birth. She'll never make a work if she can help it, but she'll never break down and fail. Miss Susan, there's one thing first and foremost you mun do, and you munna say no to me, for I know best. You must go this moment to your bed—"

"To bed! Do you think I could sleep, Peggy?" cried Susan, with involuntary youthful contempt.

"Ay, hinny—ye'll sleep, and ye'll wake fresh, and start early. You wouldn't think it, maybe, but I know better," said Peggy. "You munna say no to me, the last night. Eyeh, my lamb! you're young, and your eyes are heavy with the sleep and the tears. I'll wake ye brave and early, but you mun take first your nat'ral rest."

"It is impossible. I do not know what to do—I have everything to ask you about. Oh, Peggy, don't bid me!" said Susan, crying; "and I have no money, and nobody to direct me, and I don't know how to get there!"

"Whisht! Youth can sleep at all seasons; but it's given to the aged to watch, and it doesna injure them," said Peggy, solemnly. "Go to your bed, my lamb, and say your prayers, and the Lord'll send sleep to his beloved; and as for me, I'll turn all things over in my mind, and do up your bundle: you mun carry your own bundle, hinny, a bit of the road—there's no help; and rouse you with the break of day, and hev your cup of tea ready. Eh! the Lord bless you, darling! you're a-going forth to love and kindness, and a life fit for the likes of you. Am I sorry? No, no, no, if ye ask me a hunderd times—save and excepting for mysel'."

"Oh, Peggy, you'll miss me!" cried Susan, throwing herself into the arms of her faithful friend.

"Ay; maybe I will," said Peggy, slowly; "I wouldn't say—it's moor nor likely. Miss Susan, go to your bed this moment; ye'll maybe never have the chance of doing Peggy's bidding again."

Moved by this adjuration, Susan obeyed, though very unwillingly; and smiling sadly at the very idea of sleep, laid herself down for the last time on her own bed, "to please Peggy." But Peggy knew better than her young mistress. Through those deep, chill hours of night, while Peggy, in the same room, looked over all the different articles of her wardrobe, selecting the dress in which she should travel, carefully packing the others, and putting up the light necessary articles which must be carried with her, Susan slept soft and deep, with the sleep of youth and profound exhaustion. She had been tried beyond her strength, and nature would not be defrauded. When Peggy's task was over she sat down by the bedside, a strange figure in her great muslin nightcap, and with her big shawl wrapping her close against the cold of the night. Peggy was too old to sleep in such circumstances; she sat wiping her eyes silently, though not weeping, as far as any sound went, thinking of more things than Susan wist of; of Susan's mother, who had succumbed so many years ago under the hard pressure of life; of the unhappy man in the next room, who was consuming himself, as he had consumed everything lovely and pleasant in his existence, by the vehemence and bitterness of his passions; and of yet another man who was dead, an elder Scarsdale, whose malevolent will worked mischief and misery, after he had ceased to have any individual action of his own. Susan would have thought it strange and hard if she had known that she herself, the darling of Peggy's heart, came in only at the end of this long musing upon others; and that even her brother, with his hard and ungenerous spirit, had a larger share in the sorrowful cogitations of the old family servant than she herself had. Susan was only a sufferer—she was young, she had friends who would love her. Peggy would "miss" her sorely and heavily, but it was well for Susan. She had nothing to do with that long line of perversity, and cruelty, and guilt which ran in the Scarsdale blood.

The dawn was breaking gray and faint when Peggy woke her young mistress. Susan sprang up instantly, unable to believe that the night was really over. Peggy had made everything ready for her, even to the unnecessary breakfast and comforting cup of tea down-stairs, set before a cosy fire, and the girl dressed herself with a silent rapidity of excitement, listening to the directions which Peggy, not very learned herself, gave to her inexperience. Peggy, out of the heart of some secret treasure of her own, which she kept ready in case of necessity, and had done for many a year, with a prevision of some such want as the present, had taken an old five-pound note, which, stuffed into an old fashioned purse, she put into Susan's hands, as soon as her rapid toilette was completed.

"They'll no ask more nor that, Miss Susan," said Peggy; "they tell me they're no as dear as postchays, them railroads. Now, hinny, I'll tell you what you'll do—you'll take across the moor to Tillington, to John Gilsland's, at the public; it's a long walk, but it cannot be helped, and it's early morning, and no a person will say an uncivil word to you. You'll tell him to get out his gig and take you immediate to the railroad, and you'll no pay him. Maybe he might impose upon you, though he's a decent man, if it wasna his wife; and maybe they might ask moor nor we think for at the railroad, and put ye about. Ye can tell him to come to us for his payment, and so I'll hear how ye got that far. Then, Miss Susan, ye'll make him take out a ticket for you—that's the manner of the thing—as near till the Cornel's as possible—you knaw the names of the places better nor me; and then, my darling lamb, you'll buy some biscuits and things, and take grit care of yoursel'; and you'll come to Edinburgh, so far as I can mind, first; and then you'll ask after the road to your uncle's. I canna believe, not me, that there's a man on the whole road as is fit to be oncivil to you. And you'll tell John Gilsland to take your ticket for the best place; and look about you, hinny, till you see some decent woman-person a-goin' the same road, and keep beside her. Miss Susan, my dear lamb, you'll have to think for yoursel', and no be frightened. Eh, if I could but go and take care of ye! but the Lord bless us, hinny, we munna leave him, poor forlorn gentleman, all by himself."

"I will think of everything you say. I shall not be frightened. I'll take care, Peggy," cried Susan, through her tears.

"Whisht, whisht!—you're no to go forth greeting. My lamb, it's best for you—I'm no sorry for you," cried Peggy, with a sob; "here's your tea—a good cup of tea's a great comfort; and here's some sandwiches—eat them when you can on the road, for I see you'll no put a morsel within your lips at Marchmain. And now, my darling hinny, it's good daylight, and here's your bundle, and you'll hev to go."

The parting was sore but brief, and Susan stood without in the early sunshine before she knew what had happened to her, holding unconsciously but tightly the bundle in one hand, and Peggy's old leather purse in the other, and hearing closed behind her, with an inexorable certainty and swiftness, which was poor Peggy's artifice to hide her own grief, and to shorten the pang of their farewell, that remorseless door of Marchmain. The desolate girl stood for a moment, blind with tears, on the step. Her fate was accomplished. There lay the moor, with the world beyond, strange, unfamiliar, bewildering—and her home, cold as it was, had closed upon her for ever. The first thrill of that reality was so dreadful to Susan, that she might have fallen and fainted upon the cold threshold where she still stood, holding by the doorpost to support herself, but for an incident that roused her. A window opened above—the window of her father's room. She looked up eagerly, thinking that perhaps he might have relented. Something, magnified and blurred in form by the tears which filled her eyes full, fell from above, and descended heavily at her feet; but no one appeared at the window, which was instantly closed. She stooped down to lift it, trembling. It was another purse, not so homely as Peggy's, containing no note or word of farewell as she had hoped for a moment, but merely another five-pound note. With a strange access of anger and disappointment, Susan threw it from her upon the step of the door. "Give it to Peggy—her money is better to me!" she cried aloud, with involuntary indignation; and then brushing the tears from her eyes, set out upon her journey without looking behind, her whole heart and frame tingling with wounded feeling and injured pride.

That cold and grudging provision for her wants, thrown to her at the last moment, transported Susan with a sudden touch of passion foreign to her nature; it sent her across the moor at a speed which she could not have equalled under any other circumstances. The dew was on the early heather-bells, and the solitary golden flower-pods which lighted the dark whin bushes opened under her eye to the morning sun; but though the scene had many charms at that hour and season, and though the whins and straggling seedlings caught her dress as if to detain her, the young wayfarer made no pause.

"The tears that gathered in her eye She left the mountain breeze to dry."

And pushing forward, with all the sudden force of a sensitive nature, urged beyond strength or patience, pressed along the rustling moorland path, without once turning her eyes to look upon that house from which the last gleam of hope disappeared with her disappearance. Henceforth all life of youth and light of affection were severed from Marchmain.

VOLUME III

CHAPTER I

It was still early, when Susan, somewhat flushed by her rapid walk, and somewhat tired to the boot— for, elastic and strong, and accustomed to exercise as she was, six miles of solitary road, with a bundle to carry, not to say the burden of her desolate circumstances, and the natural timidity which, after a while, replaced her flush of indignant vehemence, was rather an exhausting morning promenade for a girl of nineteen—arrived at Tillington. And, in spite of Peggy's injunctions and her own sense of necessity, it was only with lingering steps, and a painful reluctance, that she at last summoned courage sufficient to present herself at John Gilsland's open door. Once there, however, matters became easy enough, smoothed by Mrs. Gilsland's eager and ready welcome, and by an incident of which Susan had not thought.

"Eyeh, miss! but he's gone no moor nor half an hour since," cried Mrs. Gilsland. "Bless us awl! to have a young lady like you come as far, and o'er late, when awl's done! But he was in grit haste, was Mr. Horry. Come into the fire, and rest yoursel', for the like of them long walks at this hour in the morning, they're no for leddy-birds like you. You'll have heard from the Cornel, miss? And how is he?—the dear gentleman! But you're not agoing to stand there, with that white face. Dear heart, sit down, and I'll get a cup of tea in a twinkling. She's clean done with tiredness, and the disappointment. John! if ye had the spirit of a mouse, ye'd goo after Mr. Horry, and bring him back to satisfy miss—there, do ye hear?"

"No, Mrs. Gilsland," said Susan, eagerly; "but, please, if John will get the gig, and drive me to the railroad, and perhaps we might overtake my brother. I'm—I'm—I'm—going to see my uncle to Scotland; and Horace would—might, perhaps—see me away."

"But, dear miss, your boxes?" cried Mrs. Gilsland, gazing at the young pedestrian with astonishment, and throwing her wonder into the first tangible thing that occurred to her, as she took the bundle out of Susan's hand.

"They are to come after me," said Susan, with a blush of shame; "but we had better make haste, and overtake Horace. He does not know I am going; but I think—thought—he would, perhaps, go with me to the railroad," added Susan, availing herself of that unexpected assistance, to cover her strange departure alone from Marchmain, yet blushing at the falsehood of the inference. "Oh, will you please to tell John? I have had breakfast. I could not take any tea, thank you, Mrs. Gilsland, but I want so much to overtake my brother."

This was so reasonable and comprehensible, that the good woman left her guest immediately, to startle her husband into unusual speed, and urge him on to the harnessing of the horse, and preparation of the gig, with such wonderful expedition, that John, who, contrary to his usual habits, had no time whatever to think about it, was perfectly flushed with the exertion, and scarcely knew what he was doing. Susan, grateful to be left unquestioned, sat alone in the meantime in the little parlour, feeling half glad, and half guilty, in the strange relief afforded her by Horace's recent presence here, and the excuse it served to give for her own appearance. It saved her entirely from the halting and timid explanation of a sudden visit to her uncle, and there being nobody at Marchmain who could be spared to accompany her, with which she had been trying to fortify herself, as she approached Tillington; and the momentary rest and quietness was a relief to her tired and excited frame. Then the very room recalled to poor Susan recollections which warmed and strengthened her heart. Uncle Edward!—the only person in the world, save Peggy, who had ever looked with tender, indulgent eyes of affection upon her youth; and it was to him and his house she was going! She sat there motionless, in the dingy little inn parlour, too much fatigued and strained in mind even to unclasp her hands, but unconsciously recovering her courage, and feeling the light and flicker of a happiness to come about her heart.

This sensation of comfort increased when Susan was fairly seated in John Gilsland's gig, most carefully wrapped about with shawls and mantles, and began to feel the exhilaration of that rapid passage through the free air and over the open country. The youth in her veins rose like mercury in spite of herself, and she was not sure that she was so very glad in her heart as she ought to have been when John Gilsland assured her of her certainty of overtaking Horace. She was not a very attentive listener to honest John's talk, profuse and digressive as that was. She made gentle answers, for it was not in Susan's nature to show even unintentional rudeness to anybody; but with so much to think about, and possessed by the thrill of novel excitement which their first necessity of acting for themselves gives to very young people, she made but a very indifferent listener in reality. Then her heart kept beating over the thought of this approaching interview with her brother, and leaped to her mouth, as people say, when any distant figure became visible on the road. She did not know the road, nor whether her conductor was taking her direct the nearest way to the railway. They were making progress on this earliest stage of her long journey; and it was still morning, and all the long spring day was before her; that was almost enough for Susan in her present state of mind.

She was roused at length, and startled into an instant access of renewed excitement and anxiety by a shout from John Gilsland.

"Holla, Mr. Horry! Holla, lad! hey! hear ye! Maister Horry! here's me and your sister fleeing after you this six or seven miles. Mr. Horry, I'm saying—holla!"

Horace was before them, at some little distance. He stopped when the shouting reached his ear, and turned to look back. As they came up to him, Susan had full leisure to observe the changes which this year had wrought upon her brother's appearance, and a little sensation of affectionate pride gladdened her at the sight. But she was anxious, a thousand times more anxious, to make sure that he should speak to her with ordinary kindness, and without exposing rudely the nature of her sudden journey, which he was sure to guess, than she was to think how Uncle Edward would receive her when she went to throw herself penniless upon his charity; and felt herself approaching him close and fast with a degree of trepidation strange to see between two persons so nearly the same age, and so closely allied. He for his part stared at her with utter amazement as the gig approached closer. "Susan! what on earth has brought you here?" he exclaimed, with an astonishment which was by no means free of anger. Susan trembled and faltered in her answer, as if her father himself had asked the question.

"Oh, Horace! to ask you to go to the railway with me," she said, stooping closer towards him, and pressing the hand which he slowly extended towards her, significantly and closely, to make him understand that she had more to say: "I am going to Uncle Edward—will you come and see me away?"

He looked at her with a strange, half-envious, half-contemptuous smile. "So, he lets you go!" he exclaimed; "he has grown amiable all at once, it would appear."

"Oh, Horace, hush!" cried Susan, stooping closer, with a sudden rush of tears to her eyes. "I will tell you all whenever we stop. Oh, Horace," she added, in an inexpressible yearning for sympathy, and sinking her voice to a whisper, "don't look so unkind and cold; he has sent me away!"

"The mare's fresh and spankey," said John Gilsland; "she's enough to manage without any whispering in her lug. Jump up behind, Mr. Horry, and tawlk as we goo. It'll be straight to the railroad now?"

"Have you not been going straight to the railroad?" asked Susan, in surprise.

"Straight! I trust you thought me of sufficient importance to bring you five miles out of your way," said Horace, sharply, "and lose your train too, most likely. Why didn't you drive as she ordered you, Gilsland? What good can I do her? Look sharp now, then, can't you? Well, Susan, what's this sudden journey about?"

"Oh, Horace! can't you guess?" said Susan, looking at him wistfully. "But, hush!—never mind," she added, as she encountered his angry stare of inquiry. "Oh, hush! I'll tell you everything when we get there!"

And from that moment the most eager wish to get there moved poor Susan. His angry dissatisfaction at being stopped; his cold salutation; his apparent resentment at the idea that he could know anything about her journey or its cause; the tone in which he repelled her confidential whispers, and repeated aloud what she had said to him with all the little pantomimic exhortations to secrecy which were possible to her; brought a renewed chill upon her heart. They went along at a great pace, the mare, however, being the only individual of the party who showed the least exhilaration or pleasure on the road. Would that John Gilsland had been less considerate of the sister's desire to overtake her brother!

Would that he had gone the straight road, and made less demonstration of his kindly intentions! After all, the straight road is the best; but to hear Horace Scarsdale angrily insisting upon that plain fact, and upon the folly of making so long a detour to overtake him, was not calculated to raise anybody's spirits, or to make the drive more agreeable. John Gilsland's talk, which Susan had only half listened to, was much better than the sharp, dropping conversation which now went on at intervals; and Susan bought at a sufficiently hard price her momentary ease and relief.

"Where are you going, Horace?" she asked, with hesitation—"away from Kenlisle, Peggy said—"

"I am going to Harliflax," he said, shortly. "I have got a better appointment there. I have managed to make my own way so far, you can tell my uncle—without being obliged to any one," he added, with a sneer.

"And will you write sometimes, please, Horace?" said Susan. "There are only two of us in the world; and tell me, where shall I write to you?"

He laughed, as if this was an extremely unimportant matter. "I shall be with Mr. Stenhouse," he said— "Julius Stenhouse, Esq. I daresay your letters will find me, with his name."

"Stenhouse, said ye? Eyeh, Mr. Horry, will that be the Stenhouse that was i' Kenlisle, in ould Pouncet's office?" asked John Gilsland, suddenly looking round.

"And if it should be, what then?" asked Horace, insolently.

"Oh, little matter to me," said honest John. "He's a great scoondrel, that's awl—and married that bit silly widow, poor thing!—her as didn't know when she was well off, and had good friends; though the Squire would have done for her, as I have reason to know, like a sister of his own."

"What widow?" demanded Horace.

"It's no concern of mine," said John Gilsland, touching the mare with his whip for a grand final dash up to the railway station. "She wasn't my widow, I reckon, nor belonging to me. Her first man was a sodger captain, another chance kind o' person, like his son, one Mr. Roger that was. What the deevil has a woman to do with a new husband, that has house and hyame o'er her head, and a likely son? Serve her right, as I aye said, and will say. They're away out of this country—but he's a great scoondrel, as I tell ye, wherever he may be."

In spite of himself Horace started, and was shocked, as well as astonished, for the moment by this information. While Susan gazed at the railway, glad, and yet trembling to reach it, with thoughts of launching forth by herself, without even those familiar faces near which she knew well, though they smiled little upon her, Horace was busy with this strange bit of news. It was somewhat astounding even to him to think that the man who had betrayed the interests and appropriated the estate of the son, should be the husband of his mother. Running on with this contemplation, and biting his thumb, as was his custom when he addressed himself to the task of arranging something new among his stores, and finding out where it fitted best, his eye suddenly caught in the group before the railway-station the stooping and decrepid figure of his old pitman, carefully dressed in his "Sabbath clothes." Horace sprang from the gig, though it was still in rapid motion, with an impulse of alarm, and hurried up to his strange acquaintance. The mare drew up immediately after, with a great dash and commotion. John Gilsland helped Susan to descend, and finding some of his own friends immediately, while her brother's presence freed him from all responsibility concerning her, left the timid girl to herself. She stood alone for a moment, frightened and discouraged; then, seeing nothing better for it, followed Horace, who was in close conversation with the old man. She was not curious, nor even interested, in what they were saying; but she had never stood by herself before, exposed to the wondering gaze of strangers, and she felt secure when she could glide up beside her brother and stand close to him, even though he paid no attention to her, nor noticed she was there.

"Well, and what were you going to Armitage Park for, eh? What business have you there?" said Horace, imperatively, to the old man.

"My lad, that's no' the gate to speak to me," said the pitman, "that am owld enough to be your grandsire. I'm a-gooin' for awl wan and the same reason as ye cam' to me, my young gentleman. Sir John he's at the Park, and we've ta'en counsel, the neebors and me—them as seen me sign the paper, at your own bidding—and what we've settled is, Sir John's young Mr. Roger's friend; and if it was worth a gold sovereign to you, it's maybe worth a 'nuity or a bit pension to the man himsel'; so I'm a-gooin' to the Park to see Sir John, and try my loock—and that's awl."

"Sir John? Do you think Sir John will see you?" cried Horace, "you impatient old blockhead! Do you think I can't manage for you? Why don't you trust to me?"

"I'm an ould man; if it's to be ony gud to me, there's little time to lose," said the pitman, stoutly. "You're a clever lad, I'm no' misdoubting, but ye're nouther the man himsel' nor his near friend. I hevn't ony time to lose, and a bird in the hand's worth twa in the bush—no meaning ony distrust of you, young gentleman. If the young Squire should find his advantage in knowing what I know, he mought weel spare a bit something by the week, ten shilling or so, to an owld man as won't be a burden upon nobody for lang."

"Don't you understand this is the very thing that I intended?" cried Horace, making—as Susan, who had gradually become interested, could perceive—the greatest effort to keep his temper. "To be sure, I'm trying all I can. I meant to let you know as soon as I could tell myself, but you'll spoil all if you interfere. Go back to Tinwood, like a sensible man; I'll see you in a day or two. A bird in the bush is better than no bird at all, I can tell you; and do you think Sir John, with a score of servants about him, would see you? Trust to me, and you shall have what you want in two or three days. I give you my word—are you not content?"

The old man grumbled and hesitated, but Horace's arguments were strong, and at last overcame his opposition. Horace was not content, however, with the reluctant consent to give up his project which he at last extorted. He followed the tottering old figure out of the place, negotiated with a carter who was going that way to give him "a lift" on the road to Tinwood, and stood in the road watching till he was quite out of sight, with a total forgetfulness of Susan and the train by which she had to travel. Susan followed him at a little distance, and stood doubtfully behind waiting for him, not knowing what else to do. He had forgotten her totally in the stronger interest of this more important concern; and when he did turn round, with a vexed and thoughtful face, the start and frown with which he recognized her standing so near him were anything but flattering to his sister.

"What do you mean, following me about and listening to my private affairs?" he cried, roughly. "Eavesdropper!—but I suppose that's like all women," he added, with bitterness, and an adoption of his father's look and sentiment, which drove Susan to desperation for the moment.

"You are very wicked to say so," she exclaimed; "you!—do you not know why my father sent me away? Oh, Horace, is there no heart in you?—because of that letter; he said I took it—me!"

"And why not you?—you are so very virtuous, I suppose," said her brother, with a sneer; "you who can listen behind a man when he does not know you're there. However, this is not a place to cry and make a scene—come along, and get your train. If you are fortunate you can cry there, and make yourself interesting to somebody. Where is your money? I suppose you've got some money. I'll get your ticket for you; but remember, Susan," he said, turning back again, after he had proceeded a step or two before her on this errand—"remember! you may have heard something I'm concerned in without my knowing it—tell it to my uncle, if you dare!"

Susan made no reply—the menace and the insulting words roused her; she followed him, without the slightest appearance of that inclination to cry with which he taunted her, with a flushed cheek and steady step, and no intention or thought of yielding any obedience to him. Fortunately the train was expected instantly, and there was small leisure for further leave-taking. He shook hands with her slightly as he helped her into the carriage, turned his back at once, and went away. It was so that Susan parted with her two nearest relatives. Honest John Gilsland, waving his hat as the train plunged along on its further course, touched her into those tears which her brother had checked in their fountain, but she choked them up in her handkerchief, with the remembrance of his taunt strong upon her; and so went forth alone, upon her first voyage and enterprise into the world, which scarcely could be so cruel to her as those she had left behind.

But Susan, deeply wounded as she was, did not lose all the long, silent, exciting day in tears or melancholy; her mind ran astray a little after the old pitman, and the story he had to tell to Mr. Roger, which might gain him an annuity; and then escaped into anticipations which roused her out of herself. Shy and quiet in her corner, too much excited to eat Peggy's sandwiches, too shamefaced to venture forward to the book-stand, when the train stopped, to provide herself with amusement, keeping still in the same seat at the same window; shyly remembering Peggy's precaution, and ready to change only if the "woman person" who occupied another corner of the same carriage did so; Susan arrived at Edinburgh. She got there while it was still daylight, to her great comfort; and having argued the question with herself for an hour or two previously, and recollected that Uncle Edward had once spoken of taking a cab at the railway and driving to Milnehill, proceeded with trembling intrepidity to do the same thing. The cabman, whom the poor girl addressed with humble politeness, conveyed her in somewhere about two hours, along the darkening country road, during which time the beating of Susan's heart almost choked her. But she got there at last—saw the little door in the wall opened, and recognised, in the perfumed breath of the atmosphere around her, the fragrance of those great, white turrets of chestnut-blossom, which built their fairy pinnacles in the garden of Milnehill. How she got through that darkling garden-walk Susan could not have told for her life; and the bright light and rejoicing welcome at the end of it; the start of delight, the warm embrace of the new house and unaccustomed love, were too much for the traveller. She could not speak to her uncle, and neither saw nor felt anything but a vague sensation of unspeakable rest and comfort, as they half led and half carried her over the safe threshold of Milnehill.

While the rapid railway, of which she was half afraid among all her other fears and excitements, carried Susan across the border, her brother hastened by himself along the country road to Kenlisle. It still wanted an hour of noon, but Horace was angry to be so late, and his thoughts were not of the most agreeable description. It was, to be sure, no personal loss to himself which could be brought about by the mission of the old pitman to Sir John Armitage, which he had stopped for this time, but might not be able to stop again; but if the story was actually told to Roger Musgrave's real friends, who would use it for the interests of the heir, there was an end of "the power" of Horace over the two attorneys, whose breach of trust could no longer be concealed. Then he was furious to think that his sister had heard something, much or little, of his conversation with the old man, and might have it in her power to give a clue to the secret. While mingled with this immediate concern was a renewed impression of the importance which his father attached to Colonel Sutherland's letter, or at least to the information contained in it; and the most eager anxiety to get to London to resolve his fate, if that was possible, by investigations at Doctors' Commons into the will. Whose will was it? Was he justified in believing that even the name of Scarsdale was the real name of the family, or at least of the testator who had willed a "posthumous punishment and vengeance" upon his father? Horace could give no answer to these questions; he could not even resolve on hastening to town immediately, for his time was bound to the will of another, and his funds were exhausted. To wait was the only possibility which remained to him, and he did that with a sufficiently ill grace.

Mr. Stenhouse, however, was still at Kenlisle. As soon as he reached the office, and had ascertained that Mr. Pouncet was in his private room, in conference with his former partner, Horace lost no time in demanding an audience. He was received by the Kenlisle lawyer with the greatest evident reluctance and hesitation. Mr. Pouncet gave him the veriest little nod as he came in, and glanced from Horace to Mr. Stenhouse with an expression which seemed to say that he was the victim of a conspiracy, and that some new complot was hatching against his peace. He did not even ask the young man's business; the whole affair was growing unbearable to the man of character, who knew his reputation and credit to be in the hands of these two, yet who, frightened as he was, could scarcely veil his repugnance and impatience. Mr. Stenhouse, however, shook hands cordially with his new friend. "Well, Mr. Scarsdale?" he said, in his frankest tone, "any news?" He was not afraid; and to show that he had no occasion to be so, but that the whole burden of legal peril lay upon his unfortunate colleague, was a pleasure and refreshment indescribable to Mr. Pouncet's amiable "friend."

"Not very pleasant news," said Horace; "I have just seen old Adam Brodie, the pitman, and stopped him on his way to Armitage Park. He has taken it into his head that Sir John might like to hear his story, and that it might be worth Mr. Musgrave's while to give him an annuity. He will make the whole public if his mouth is not stopped. I came instantly to let you know. He thinks the young Squire might give him ten shillings a-week; he thinks me a friend of the young Squire, so I have persuaded him to let me try what I can do."

"Ah! Pouncet, my dear fellow, this is your concern," said Mr. Stenhouse, with his broadest smile.

Mr. Pouncet grew graver than before; he raised his head a little from the papers over which he was bending, and spoke with the greatest hesitation, clearing his throat and stammering at every word.

"I—I don't see how it can be my concern," he said; "who is Adam Brodie?—I—I never—heard the name."

"Unfortunately I know him, and so does our young friend here," said Mr. Stenhouse—"the old fellow who happened to be present when—ah, I see you recollect now! Awkward business, very—and Sir John Armitage himself is a client of yours; how very provoking! I'm afraid you'll have to do something about it, Pouncet; it would not answer you at all to have this affair known."

Mr. Pouncet did not look up; rage and provocation almost beyond bearing had risen within him, but he durst not show them. His very integrity and honour in other matters made the bondage of this one guilt more intolerable; he was enraged to be compelled to bow to it, but he dared not resist.

"The matter can be easily arranged, if Mr. Pouncet does not object to the cost," said Horace, trying the new rôle of peacemaker.

"If I do not object—what do you mean, sir?" cried Mr. Pouncet, with uncontrollable impatience; "what have I to do with it more than Stenhouse? This is a pleasant improvement, certainly. D— the whole concern!—I wish I had never had anything to do with it, with all my heart!"

"My dear fellow, compose yourself; it is too late for that; and, besides, it is you who are endangered," said the bland Mr. Stenhouse; "think of your own interest, my excellent friend."

Mr. Pouncet immediately betook himself to his papers as before, turning them over rapidly; he made no answer; habit had accustomed him to the civil taunts of Stenhouse—but he could not bear the same insulting inferences from a new voice.

"There is a very easy way of managing the matter," said Horace, once more; "the man is old, and has been long in your service. He lost his son in an accident at the pit two years ago; it is perfectly practicable to pension him on that account."

"And leave him free to seek another pension on the other," said Mr. Stenhouse; "won't do: no—they are rapacious, those people; that would only rouse his appetite, the old rogue. A man who gets one thing easily always hankers for another. He'd try Sir John immediately, and double his terms. No, no; if he gets anything, he must understand distinctly what he gets it for. If I were you, Pouncet, I'd lose no time, either. He can't live long, that's one good thing."

"I never have bribed any man!" cried Mr. Pouncet, vehemently—"I'll not begin now. I don't mind doing my share for any old servant; but I—I can't stand this, Stenhouse! What do you mean by turning it all on me?"

"Simply because he can do me no harm, my dear fellow," said the smiling Mr. Stenhouse. "Stop now! don't let us get impatient; here is our young friend has something to say."

Mr. Stenhouse was already benevolently aware that the remarks of "our young friend" were gall and bitterness to his old partner, and perhaps if anything could have made Horace's new patron more gracious, it was this fact.

"I was about to say," said Horace, with a little eagerness, "that the old man believes me a friend of the young Squire, as he calls him, and that I am quite willing to be made the channel of communication with him. If you trust it to me, he shall never know that the money does not come from Roger Musgrave; and my own opinion is that this will be the best arrangement. If he wants more money, at least he will come to you to seek it, and not to—"

The young man stopped short prudently, and went no further. Mr. Pouncet could not bear the emphasis upon that you, or the look of personal appeal which accompanied it, at least from any one but his old partner. He got up abruptly, and pushed his chair from the table.

"Stenhouse, will you settle this business? I'll agree to your decision," he said, pushing hastily away. "I've—I've got an appointment at twelve o'clock. I'm rather too late already; you can settle it without me."

Mr. Stenhouse smiled as he went, and so did Horace, almost without being aware of it. They had both a certain pleasure in the sufferings of their victim—a pure amateur enjoyment, entirely distinct from any consideration of advantage; however, they settled the matter between them easily and rapidly enough. To be liberal with another man's means is no difficult matter. Mr. Stenhouse arranged that a sum sufficient for a year's stipend to the old pitman, at his own terms of ten shillings a-week, should be paid into the hands of Horace, who undertook to dispense it; and Horace, on his part, lost no time in demanding from his new employer a few days' leave of absence before proceeding to his post. Mr. Stenhouse was very curious to know why this sudden permission was asked from him—so curious, that he granted it only on condition that Horace should first be settled in his office, and ascertain the nature of his new duties. After he had spent a week in Harliflax, perhaps he might be spared for another week; and as he was going to London, as he said, why, Harliflax was so much nearer London than Kenlisle, and indeed on the way. With which decision Horace chafing considerably, but compelled to assent, had no alternative but to declare himself satisfied. It was so arranged accordingly. Mr. Pouncet, when he returned, put his name to the required check, which certainly committed him to nothing, and might indeed appear nothing but a gratuity to the clerk who was about to leave him; and Horace put twenty pounds out of the six-and-twenty in his own pocket. Not that he meant to defraud the pitman, or anybody else, but he was completely indifferent whether the money he used for his own immediate purposes was his own, or Mr. Pouncet's, or the property of old Adam. He made full arrangement to have the weekly stipend paid to the old miner. He saw him indeed, paid him the first instalment himself, and persuaded the poor pensioner that his own bounty was the immediate source of this little income; his own bounty, subject to the approval of the young Squire. Then having done this Christian office, and procured for the ungrateful Mr. Pouncet the unwilling virtue of doing good by stealth, Horace, with Mr. Pouncet's twenty pounds in his pocket, started on his journey to Harliflax, full of hope, ambition, and expectation, with Doctors' Commons and the unknown will occupying most of his thoughts. But a week—no more—and he should know what was his "singular and unhappy fortune," and what the mysterious document which was supposed to have influenced him in his earliest childhood, and had broken all ties of nature between himself and his father, actually was.

CHAPTER III

Mr. Stenhouse, whatever his motive or purpose might be, received Horace, on his arrival at Harliflax, where the lawyer had preceded his new clerk by a few days, with great civility and kindness. Perhaps

Mr. Stenhouse was not much more beloved in his present residence than he had been in Kenlisle; but he was now a man of some wealth and importance, and his house had other attractions, which kept "society" in Harliflax on very good terms with him. The lawyer's household was a little out of the common order of such dwelling-places. It was divided by a singular separation, but not divided against itself. Two distinct and incompatible phases of life went on within its walls; but the one displayed no antagonism, and fought no battles with the other; and any Quixote who had chosen to take up arms for a wife neglected and a mother set aside, would have been as completely in the wrong as ever Quixote was. The family consisted of three daughters, aged from fifteen to nineteen, and of one boy, a child five years younger than his youngest sister, a hopeless little invalid, born to suffering. The girls were the daylight surface of the family, the pride of their father, and the supreme influence in the house. Two of them were pretty, the eldest as near beautiful as it could fall to the fate of an imperfectly educated provincial belle to be; and all three expensive and extravagant to the very verge of their means and opportunities. Over such a trio of young uncontrollable spirits—and the Misses Stenhouse were innocent of sentiment, and neither had nor pretended any devotion for their mother—the nervous and timid woman who was the nominal mistress of the lawyer's house could exercise no sway. Years ago, when Amelia, the beauty, was but just beginning to be conscious of her own perfections, and to assert herself accordingly, Mrs. Stenhouse had retired from the contest. The lovely young termagant had scarcely put off her last pinafore, when she found herself triumphant mistress of the drawing-room, while her mother fell back upon that never-failing interest and occupation which the poor woman wept over and believed one of the sorest afflictions of her life, but which was in fact its great preservative— the illness and weakness of her boy. Little Edmund and she lived together in a touching and perfect unity in the comfortable parlour downstairs, while the young ladies entertained their own friends and enjoyed their own pleasures above. Perhaps Mrs. Stenhouse did not do her duty by consenting to this tacit arrangement; but, like most weak people, she was so perfectly convinced that she could not help herself, that she was quite unable for the task from which she shrank, and would have done her daughters more harm than good by keeping up an unavailing contest, that her conscience did not disturb her in the loving performance of her other duty, her unwearied care of little Edmund, from which nothing ever diverted or withdrew the entire heart of his mother. This invisible fireside in the back parlour, where Edmund, despotic and imperious as only a child-invalid can be, tyrannized over his constant companion, and shared every thought she had, seemed no very important influence in the family to a cursory observer; but the household itself was perfectly aware that any distinct desire proceeding thence from little Edmund's sharp, high-pitched, childish voice, was law even to Edmund's father; and that the decrepid child, who did not even particularly appreciate or return his affection, was the very apple of that father's eye; his son, his heir, his representative; though nobody, save the two most deeply interested, the father and mother, believed or expected that the child could ever live to be a man.

This second domestic centre of Mr. Stenhouse's affections and interests was, however, invisible and unknown to Horace Scarsdale, when the unusual distinction of an invitation to dinner opened his employer's house to him a day or two after his arrival. He saw, it is true, the silent mother seated at the head of the table, nervously and quietly impatient of the time occupied there; and he observed that she disappeared from the drawing-room very early in the evening, and took little or no part in what was going on there. But Horace had neither eyes nor curiosity for Mrs. Stenhouse: he was more agreeably occupied. He who entered the lawyer's house with all his usual disdainful indifference—except in so far as they might serve him—to the people whom he was about to meet, had encountered a new influence, which proved too much for him at that undreaded table. All unprepared and unarmed as he was, a sudden and alarming accident, altogether beyond his calculations and out of his reckoning, happened to Horace; the young man fell in love!

This extraordinary and unexpected event took Horace much by surprise. It was the first time in his life that he had not scorned womankind and all its influences; but Amelia Stenhouse was an entirely new development of feminity. She was very—extremely handsome, in the first place, and she was authoritative and imperious, and had a kind of wit which her beauty made brilliant and successful. Used to homage and admiration, accustomed to believe that it became her, and was her privilege to do unusual things and make unusual speeches, and audaciously confident in her own powers, she shone upon Horace like a new species unknown and undiscovered before; and the contrast offered by her exuberant beauty, "dash," and presumption, was irresistibly piquant to the brother of Susan, on whom a tamer and sweeter beauty might have shone for years in vain. Horace neither knew the moment nor the means by which that amazing accident befell him; but it had happened long before the other people had eaten their dinner, transcending such common earthly occupations as much in speed as in importance. Neither did he know how the evening passed, in his sudden and strange intoxication. His new passion partook of the nature of all sublime and primitive emotions, so far, at least, as to blot out the little cross-bars of time from the young man's consciousness, and blur these hours into one exciting moment. He was transported even out of himself—a more remarkable result—and turned his back upon Mr. Stenhouse, and forgot his own interest, in devouring with his eyes, and pursuing with his attentions, this new star called Amelia, whom already—arrogant even in his love—he determined upon appropriating, however she or any one else might choose to object.

Uncareful of either etiquette or propriety, Horace stayed as long as he could stay, and only took his leave at length in obedience to hints which there was no mistaking. He went downstairs hurriedly, wrapt in his dream, all the air before him filled with two objects, intensely visible, and eclipsing all the world besides; which two objects were, Amelia Stenhouse, and that unknown document in Doctors' Commons which was to reveal to Horace his fate; when his course was suddenly and singularly interrupted. He had just reached the foot of the staircase, when a door was timidly opened, a glow of firelight came flushing into the hall, and the quiet little woman to whom he had been presented a few hours before, but whose voice he had not yet heard, stood doubtful and hesitating before him. Only for a moment, however, for, urged by an exclamation from within, Mrs. Stenhouse hastily addressed the stranger: "Mr. Scarsdale! Oh, come in here for a moment, please!" she cried nervously. Taken by surprise, and scarcely knowing what he did, Horace followed her. The room was very warm, carpeted and curtained into a sort of noiseless, airless luxury, which was half suffocating to the healthy and vigorous senses of the unwilling visitor; and near the fire, in an easy-chair, sat a small boy, pale-faced and sharp-featured, restlessly wide awake, as children are when kept up beyond their usual hour, and full of eagerness about something, with a whole volume of questions in his face. This was the little hermit of the luxurious seclusion into which Horace, who knew nothing about the boy, and had not even heard of his existence, was thus mysteriously introduced. The little fellow measured his visitor with those sharp inquisitive eyes, and addressed another adjuration to his mother. Edmund's "Now, mamma!" exclaimed somewhat impatiently, acted like a spur upon the timid woman. She started, and tremulously began a string of confused yet eager questions.

"Oh, Mr. Scarsdale! I beg your pardon! They told me you came from Kenlisle," cried Mrs. Stenhouse. "There is some one near there—Yes, Edmund, darling! wait an instant. Some one who—his name is Roger Musgrave. Did you ever hear of him? Do you know him? Could you give me any news of my—of—of—the young gentleman? Perhaps you may have heard of Tillington Grange, if you know the country. Do you think they have heard anything there of—of—. Oh, I beg your pardon! it is too much to expect that you should know."

"I used to know Roger Musgrave very well," said Horace. "I lived near Tillington when I was a boy."

"I say, sir, we've got a right to know," cried the sharp little voice out of the easy-chair. "He's my brother, he is; don't mind what mamma says. I am not afraid to ask for him. I've sat up on purpose. I want to hear all about Roger. How much is he bigger than you?"

"Oh, my darling child, the gentleman will be angry! He's a sad invalid, Mr. Scarsdale; everybody indulges him," cried poor Mrs. Stenhouse. "Pray, pray, don't be displeased!"

"He's a good deal bigger than me," said Horace, half amused, and half spiteful, answering the question with an involuntary grudge, and increased impulse of dislike to poor Roger, whose additional inches— poor advantage though that was—it galled him for the moment to remember.

The child clapped his hands. "How much?" he cried, with a little childish shout of triumph. The sight would have been touching enough to any one who had the heart to be moved by it. But Horace saw nothing that was not ludicrous in the poor little dwarfish invalid's eager and exultant curiosity about the size and strength of his unknown brother. He laughed in spite of himself.

"About two inches, perhaps," he said; "I have not heard anything of Musgrave lately," he continued, turning to the mother; "you know, perhaps, that he enlisted and went abroad; but I have an uncle— Colonel Sutherland, you may have heard of him—who took poor Roger up; he is very likely to know."

The scant civility and supercilious tone of this reply lost all its effect upon Mrs. Stenhouse from the name contained in it—"Colonel Sutherland! Oh, Edmund, darling! the dear old Colonel who was so kind to Roger!" she said, with tears in her eyes; "and to think a relation of his should come here! Oh, Mr. Scarsdale, if there is anything we can do for you, I or my poor boy (and Mr. Stenhouse will do anything to please Edmund), you have only to say it—oh, thank you, thank you, a hundred times! My dearest child, it is very late, we must not keep Mr. Scarsdale longer to-night; another time perhaps he will come in and see us and tell us more. Good night, good night! Say good night, darling, to the gentleman; and thank you a hundred times, Mr. Scarsdale. I am so very, very glad you have come here!"

Saying which, Mrs. Stenhouse preceded her visitor to the street-door, and opened it for him with her own trembling hands.

He went away with a smile on his lip; but it was only a smile of momentary ridicule, and bore no kindly meaning. That sad little secret romance of domestic life had neither charm nor sentiment for Horace. Without discovering what was in it, he plunged back into his own novel passion and excitement, in which, as was sufficiently natural, the young man passed that night and the remainder of his week in Harliflax as in a rapid and exciting dream. Falling in love was no softening enchantment for Horace; it did not involve affection, or respect, or tenderness, those sentiments and principles which act upon a man's whole nature. It made no difference on his opinion of other people, or his dealings with other people, that he had fallen in love with Amelia Stenhouse. No sweet imaginations of home or hearth clung round the object of his sudden passion; he neither endowed herself with imaginary perfections, nor thought better of his neighbours, for her sake; but still, according to his nature, he was "in love." His thoughts burned and glowed about the lawyer's beautiful daughter; he wanted her, without inquiring what, or what manner of spirit she was—a sturdy principle of love on the whole, and one which perhaps wears better than a more sentimental preference; but its immediate influence upon Horace was not particularly elevating. If it had been necessary, however, to fix and intensify his anxious curiosity concerning that unknown document in Doctors' Commons, this sudden attachment was the sharpest spur which could have been applied; for here alone lay the means by which the beauty might be appropriated and taken possession of. And every circumstance concurred to convince Horace of the importance of the discovery he had made at Marchmain. He saw the position of affairs there without any mistake or self-deception; perceived, with perfect clearness, that the letter which he had taken had been missed from his father's desk, and coolly contented himself with the knowledge that Susan had been banished from home for his fault. "So much the better for Susan," he said to himself, with entire composure; and it did not trouble him in the least that both Susan and Peggy must be quite aware who was the real criminal. He hoped, indeed, to be able very shortly to make the consequences of that theft apparent enough; for in all Horace's calculations the thought of some immediate issue followed without pause his investigation of the will. The impatience of youth and inexperience—mingling with all the calculations and designs of his unyouthful and ungenerous intelligence, the foresight and cold selfishness of age—made his very imaginations covetous and grasping; but the youth in his veins betrayed him into dreams of a conclusion as rapid as it was brilliant. He could form his schemes with all the coolness of an old man, but he could not wait for his fortune; like a young man, he was determined to have it now.

This point accordingly was one on which he concluded without doubt or hesitation. He did not know what fortune might have in store for him; he could not tell what mysterious inheritance lay waiting, till he should make his momentous discovery; but he felt convinced that to enter upon the immediate enjoyment of these unknown and concealed riches he had but to find this secret out. With all the cold blood of age, totally careless and indifferent to any results which did not affect himself, he leapt at the rapid conclusion of youth, and found wealth, love, and luxury in a sudden windfall of extraordinary fortune. So, happily unaware of his own inconsistency, Horace lived in a fever through the few tedious days which he was obliged to spend in Harliflax, in the monotonous occupations of Mr. Stenhouse's office, with only one other glimpse of Amelia before he could start on his important journey. Steady though his selfish intelligence was, the hours danced and buzzed over him in a dizzy whirl. He stood on the threshold of a dazzling and splendid fortune, the future of a fairy tale. He stood like a knight of romance, with his lady's name upon his lips, impatient to enter the charmed gateway, and read in the enchanted scroll the secret of his fate; but the talisman which should roll back these solemn gates of the future was no spell for the lips of a true knight; and romantic as his position might be, Horace Scarsdale occupied it in no romantic frame of mind. The romance of his attitude was all unwitting and unwilling, the work of circumstances. And it was not to conquer fortune, but to hunt for a cruel bit of paper, that, burning with suppressed eagerness, he set out for that London which to him meant only Doctors' Commons, bent upon two ideas which occupied his whole being—Amelia Stenhouse and the Will.

CHAPTER IV

While Horace made his beginning full of new emotions and interests at Harliflax, Susan entered into a kind of miraculous happiness and comfort, which her very brightest dreams had never ventured to imagine before. For none of the wonders of romance had happened to Susan; she had not "fallen in love," nor entered even to the precincts of that charmed condition in which everything is possible to the youthful fancy. No gallant knight had dropped out of the skies or come across the moor, to transport her into that perennial garden of enchantment, which will always remain a refuge for young imaginations while the world lasts. Yet Susan, seated in Colonel Sutherland's cosy dining-room, making tea at the round table, where the white tablecloth fell in fragrant shining folds over the crimson cover, and where all the agrémens of a Scotch breakfast showed themselves in dainty good order; with the windows open, the sun shining upon the garden, the birds singing, the sweetness of spring in the sweet morning air, which had found out all the hidden primroses and violets, and some precocious lilies of the valley beneath the trees, before it came in here to tell the secret of their bloom; and all those secondary delights, warmed and brightened by the face of love, beaming across that kindly board—the tender, fatherly face, indulgent and benign as the very skies—happy in all her pleasures, happy with a still dearer charm and unintended flattery in the very sight of her, and the consciousness of her presence; Susan did not know how to contain the joy of her heart. To think of Marchmain sitting here safe in Milnehill dining-parlour; to think of all her past life, with its melancholy solitude and friendlessness!—to think how little account anybody had ever made of her, whom all this bright house brightened to receive, and whom everybody here looked to as the crown of comfort and pledge of increased happiness! Susan had cried over it a dozen times during these first wonderful days—now she began to grow accustomed to her happiness. It touched her still with a sweet amazement of gratitude, in which there mingled a certain compunction. It seemed scarcely right to feel so happy when she could still return by a thought to that dreary moor and melancholy house, and remember how her father lived miserably by himself in his austere solitude, and that she was an outcast, banished from her natural home. But it was difficult to give importance to the passion of Mr. Scarsdale, and the contempt of Horace, in the sunshiny presence of Uncle Edward. The old man inclining his deaf ear towards her with that smile upon his face, put Susan's troubles to flight in spite of herself; she could not entertain either pain or grief in those bright rooms, where she was installed so joyfully as mistress; she could not have the heart to spoil Uncle Edward's pleasure by a sad look, even if she had been able to preserve sad looks through so much astonishing gladness of her own.

Everything was new to her in this new home. The friends who hastened to see her on the Colonel's invitation, and whom he took her to see; the young people like herself, who were pleased to make Susan's acquaintance, but of whose "education" and "accomplishments" Susan all unaccomplished and uninstructed stood in awe. The wonder of finding that her own ignorance, fresh and intelligent as it was, rather attracted than repelled many of her new friends; the very necessity of making an evening toilette, and having to interest herself in pretty fashions of evening dress; and to get Uncle Edward's Indian muslins, in their impossible delicacy, the things that she had once wondered over as ornaments of her drawers, but beyond all mortal use, actually made into ordinary gowns, and to wear them!—everything bewildered Susan into additional happiness. And that breakfast-table, with its post arrival, its letters and news—the epistles of her young cousins, the bits of pleasant gossip from the Colonel's old correspondents, all communicated to herself, with an evident pleasure in having her there to listen to them; the common family confidences and comforts which make up the daily life of most young people, made Susan's cup run over with unanticipated refinements of delight. At first every additional touch of domestic happiness was too much for her composure, and the spring skies were not more showery in their joy than those blue eyes, which could scarcely be convinced to believe themselves or acknowledge the reality of the sunshine and light around; but before the first week was over, Susan had begun to wonder how she could have managed to exist through the past, and to feel as though she had lived only in those happy days, the first days she had spent in a home.

About the same day as that on which Horace set out for London, Susan sat making tea at Milnehill breakfast-table, while Uncle Edward read his letters opposite. One of these letters, as it happened, was from Roger Musgrave. Something had been doing among the Caffres, in which Roger had distinguished himself, and an account of the affair appeared that very morning in the Times, where a brief but flattering mention of the young volunteer delighted beyond measure his fast friend. Susan, it is impossible to deny, listened with unusual interest both to the letter and the newspaper report. It was wonderful how clearly she remembered Roger Musgrave, how he looked, and all about him. She even liked to continue the conversation in that channel, and keep her uncle from digressing to Ned or Tom, or old Sinclair of the Forty-second; and with this shy purpose suddenly bethought herself of Horace's encounter with the old pitman, of which she had been a witness, but which happier events had driven until now out of her thoughts.

"Had Horace anything to do with Mr. Musgrave, uncle?" she asked, somewhat timidly.

"Eh? Horace? Not that I am aware of," said the Colonel; "but your brother, my love, is inscrutable, and might have to do with the Rajah of Sarawak, for anything I know."

"I never heard they were friends," said Susan, musingly. "I wonder what Horace could mean? You would have thought he was managing something for Mr. Musgrave, to hear how he spoke to that old man; and he told me—oh!" cried Susan, stopping abruptly, growing very red, and looking somewhat scared, in Uncle Edward's face.

"What, my dear child?" said the benign Colonel, with a smile.

"Oh, uncle! he told me not to tell you," said Susan, with a mixture of fright and boldness. "It must have been something wrong."

"Then perhaps you had better not tell me," said Uncle Edward, rather gravely. "I should be sorry to have a suspicion of either Roger or Horace. Never tell anything that seems to be wrong until you are sure of it, Susan. It may be safe enough to praise upon slight grounds, but never, my dear, to blame."

"That is how you treat me, Uncle Edward," said Susan, looking up brightly with recovered courage—"but this is different. What could anybody have to tell Mr. Musgrave, uncle, which would be worth paying a pension or an annuity for?—ten shillings a-week the old man said; and he was going to Armitage Park, but Horace would not let him. Horace seemed to be managing it all, as if it was for the young Squire: he said so even in words. Uncle, I wonder what it could be?"

"A pension of ten shillings a-week!" exclaimed Colonel Sutherland. The old man reddened with a painful colour. Unsuspicious of evil as he was, he had lived long in the world, and knew its darker side. The first idea which occurred to him was that of some youthful vice which this payment was to hide; and he was grieved to his heart.

"It sounded like—" said Susan, who was perfectly ignorant of her auditor's thoughts, and innocently went on pursuing her own—"it sounded like as if something had been found out about Mr. Musgrave's property or something, and that it would do him good, and that he would be so thankful to hear it that he would give the money directly; and Horace must have thought so, too, for he promised to get it for the old man. I wonder what could have been found out; for all the land was sold—was it not, uncle?—and Mr. Musgrave was poor."

"I doubt if he has ten shillings a-week for himself of his own," said the Colonel, hastily.

"Then, uncle, something must have been found out!" cried Susan—"I am sure of it, from the way the old man spoke; and Horace promised to get him the pension, and would not let him go to Armitage. That was a little strange, wasn't it?—because Sir John, you told me, uncle, was Mr. Musgrave's great friend, and I never believed that Horace even knew him until that day."

"Odd enough, to be sure. I did not know it either, Susan. They don't look much like a pair of friends," said the puzzled Colonel; "and your brother—hum—Horace is very clever, my dear," said Uncle Edward, with a grieved look, and a slight sigh. He did not want to think any harm of his nephew, but the old man could not make the young schemer out.

"I hope, uncle, it is not anything very wrong," said Susan, faltering a little.

"I hope not, my dear," said the Colonel; but they concluded their breakfast much more silently than usual, neither of them looking very comfortable; and, for the first time, Susan was rather glad when the meal was over, and herself at liberty. She went out into the garden among the flowers, as was her wont, but even that sweet exhilarating spring atmosphere, the rustle of leaves and ripple of sound that gladdened the morning, did not withdraw her thoughts from that perplexing subject. The more she hoped that it was nothing wrong, the more settled became her conviction that it was, and that deceit, or treachery of some kind, was involved in the transaction. And then a battle ensued in her private heart. Roger Musgrave was nothing to Susan, and Horace was her only brother; was it her part to search into the secrets of her nearest relatives, in order to befriend a stranger? With an uneasy consciousness of undue interest in one so little known to her, Susan blushed, and shrank from this idea; yet her honest thoughts, once roused, were not to be put to rest even by a scruple of girlish delicacy. To see harm done, and stand by passive, was as impossible to this girl as to the strongest champion in existence. It was against her nature. She could not do it, were the wrong-doer her nearest and dearest friend.

An hour or two later Colonel Sutherland came into the drawing-room, where Susan sat at work, with her thoughts busy about this matter. The old soldier loitered about, poking his gray moustache into the pretty bookshelves, as though he had suddenly grown short-sighted, and impending with the stoop habitual to his deafness over Susan's chair. He had something to say, but was reluctant to say it, lest he should wound, even by implication, the feelings of his young guest.

"Susan," said the Colonel, at last, abruptly—he thought he spoke as if the subject had suddenly occurred to him, while, in reality, it was most distinctly visible that he had been pondering nothing else since he entered the room; "thinking over what you told me this morning, I rather think it might be as well to write to Armitage—eh? Very likely it is nothing, you know; but still, if any one in that district does know anything that might be of service to young Musgrave—why, my love, it seems as well that we should know."

He looked at her doubtfully from under his gray eyebrows, laying a caressing hand upon her hair. He was afraid she would not like this proposal, and still more afraid that, alarmed in the quick and tender pride of family affection, she would guess and resent his suspicion of her brother. But Susan looked up quickly, without any shade of offence upon her face, which, however, had become very grave.

"I am afraid of Horace, uncle," she said, simply and sadly; "he is my own brother, and it is dreadful to say so; but I am not sure of him, as you are of my cousins. Since I think of it, I am afraid it is something wrong."

"Then you do not object, and I may write to Armitage?" said Uncle Edward. "Thank you, my dear child; perhaps we shall find it all a mistake, and Horace the most upright of us all. I trust so; he is very clever,

Susan, and clever boys are sometimes tempted into scheming—eh? And besides, poor fellow, he has had little justice in his own life. I will write, then, my love, and I hope everything will come perfectly clear."

So saying, the Colonel went away, to confide Susan's story to Sir John Armitage, and beg his attention to it. To seek out "an old man," who knew something to Roger's advantage, without either name or place to trace him by, was rather a hard task to impose upon the indolent baronet; and so Susan thought as her uncle left her. But still, it was a satisfaction to have the letter written. It is always satisfactory to transfer a portion of one's own personal uneasiness to somebody else. They hoped a little and wondered a great deal each in private, with very little communication on the subject, while they waited for Sir John's reply; and if Roger had wanted anything before of the requisites necessary for a hero in Susan's imagination, he had fully acquired it now. He was young, brave, handsome, generous, and perhaps he was injured—could any knight of romance require more?

CHAPTER V

Forgetting totally for the time all lesser projects, and suffering Mr. Pouncet and old Adam, Roger Musgrave and his lost property, to fall behind him into complete oblivion, though it was the Kenlisle lawyer's sovereigns which paid his fare to London, Horace set out to seek his fortune. He had never been so confident in his expectations; and if any one had informed him during that journey of the suspicions which his uncle and Susan discussed slightly and pondered deeply, the doubts of his own honour and uprightness which both entertained, and the inquiries which were likely to be set on foot to satisfy them, he would have laughed his laugh of supreme disdain, spurning that past transaction as too insignificant to help or harm him. Adam Brodie, and the "power" over Mr. Pouncet and Mr. Stenhouse which his story gave, had been sufficiently important to Horace a short time before; but the young man was in an elevated and dizzy state of mind. He was going to find out an unknown fairy fortune; the crock of gold was almost visible; he did not feel sure that he should return to Harliflax in less than a coach-and-six, with an old-fashioned braggadocio of triumph; and what were all the previous schemes and expedients of his humble fortune to the exultant heir who was coming to his kingdom? By dint of constant thought on the subject and intense desire, he had succeeded in convincing himself that this kingdom only awaited discovery, and was just about to fall into his full possession. A hundred Adam Brodies could not harm Horace, and what was Mr. Pouncet and his secret to him?

In this condition of mind, though growing somewhat anxious as the moment of certainty approached, Horace, in strong but restrained excitement, pale with the fire that burned in his veins and withdrew the blood from his cheek, hastened from the City tavern, where he had found a lodging, round the quiet side of St. Paul's, to that strange old den of fortune, where tragic family secrets by the thousand lie recorded, and where the domestic history of a whole nation accumulates in silence. He disappeared beneath the archway, anxious yet confident; the blaze of his triumph ready to burst forth, his thoughts rushing forward in spite of him to the splendours which lay almost within reach, to his marriage with Amelia, to all the pleasures and domination of sudden wealth. An hour or two afterwards he came out again a different man. He had found his fortune—but it was passion, and not triumph, that burned in his downcast eyes. His face was no longer pale, but red with a sullen flush of impotent resentment and hatred. He went through the crowd elbowing his way like a man who had a quarrel with all the world; he went straight across the crowded streets, and pushed his way among waggons and omnibuses with a certain fierce defiance of accident, and impulse of opposition. When he got to his tavern, the first thing he did was to call a cab, into which he flung his little carpet-bag, as if that homely conveniency had done him mortal injury, and in a voice of passion desired to be driven instantly to the railway. Alas! that was no coach-and-six, either morally or visibly, in which Horace returned to Harliflax, and to the clerk's life in Mr. Stenhouse's office, which this morning he regarded with lordly and lofty disdain. He sat back, an image of silent and self-consuming rage, in his corner of the second-class railway carriage; rage which dried up every comfortable sensation out of his mind; rage at himself, who had been thus deceived; at the dead man who had left him, in the first place, this bitter vexation and disappointment, and at the living man, who lived to thwart him, and keep him out of his rightful possessions. Not a remorseful thought of the lifelong wrong which had soured his father's spirit and destroyed his life occurred to the congenial temper of his father's son. A true Scarsdale, Horace proved his legitimacy by the unmixed self-regard which plunged him into that sudden passion. From his own point of view he took up the expressions of his father's letter. They were rivals to the death. That event, long ago accomplished, which Horace knew for the first time to-day, had abrogated the bonds of nature between them at the very beginning of the son's life; and already a horrible impatience of the father's existence stole unawares over the mind of the young man. That lonely, miserable, misanthrope's life which the recluse endured at Marchmain kept the heir out of his inheritance—kept the youth from his will—the bridegroom from his bride; and Horace set his teeth, thinking of it. In that chain of resentful and selfish cogitations one idea followed another too rapidly to be checked. Horace could not help it, and was scarcely aware at first how the thought, vexatious and galling, stole into his mind, that Mr. Scarsdale was still in the fulness of his days, and might live to thwart him for many a long year. The red colour flushed deeper to his face, and his hand clenched involuntarily as the idea occurred to him. Day after day, and year after year, till his own youth had died out of his veins; till Amelia Stenhouse was out of his reach, and life and wealth had lost half their charms; that unlovely existence might linger on at Marchmain, and keep him out of his inheritance. What sudden rush of breathless suggestion, not daring to breathe in shape of words or definite expressions, flooded his mind for one violent moment after that we will not venture to say; but the next instant Horace wiped his wet forehead, on which great drops of moisture hung, and threw open the window to draw breath, and hide himself from himself. When he looked in again, he had made a violent effort, and turned his mind into another channel. Crime or madness—heaven knows which—lay the way he had been going, and the first glance had sickened him with mortal terror. He turned away from the dread unwilling thought with the first conscious effort against evil which he had ever made. The evil was monstrous, and appalled him: he was not bad enough to cogitate that, even in his most secret thoughts.

But here stood the facts, certain and unchangeable. Fortune, as dazzling as he had ever hoped for, lay within Horace's sight, his lawful inheritance; but between him and that glorious vision stood the black figure of the disinherited—his father, through whose lineal hands the family wealth ought to have flowed. What did he live for—that unhappy, solitary man?—what was the good of an existence which dragged its melancholy days out after such a fashion? Horace understood now what was the meaning of "posthumous punishment and vengeance," and what bitter effect the disappointed man had given to his father's cruel will; but the heir was not sorry for the hermit of Marchmain. Pity found no entrance into the self-absorbed mind of Horace; he saw his own position merely and no other, and thought as little of Mr. Scarsdale's lifelong tragedy as if the recluse had been a wooden image; a scarecrow to keep him off his enchanted land. Yet something more; though he resisted it, the dark thought would return to increase the turmoil of his mind. His father was still young, a strong man in the vigour and flush of life. Again and again that dark red flush rose to the young man's cheek, and the dew hung heavy on his forehead. Ten years, twenty years—who could prophesy how long that dreary life might hang and linger out yonder on the dreary moor? The good, the just, the lives most loved and prized, fade out of human ways; but the man accursed and excommunicated lives on. This man, perhaps, whose death would scarcely call a tear to any eye, would die most likely a very patriarch of disappointment, hatred, and misery; while his son, the heir, lingered out the blossom of his life in daily drudgery, unconsidered and poor.

This idea pertinaciously clinging to his mind might have crazed a better heart than that of Horace; him it persecuted with a shuddering chill of inarticulate suggestions which paled his cheeks, yet stirred his mind with the wild excitement of temptation and crime. Crime! he was familiar enough with wickedness; but that ruffian whispering in his ear sickened him to the heart, yet moved his pulses with a tingle of passion. Wealth beyond his reckoning, power, riches, and Amelia, and only one desolate life standing between his strong arm and that threefold prize. The whisper which horrified him, but which he still listened to, stole into his heart as he went on; he had not closed his door against it. Already a fiercer excitement than he had ever known grew upon him and consumed him: he was innocent—he had never lifted his hand against life, nor shed blood; yet the passion and horror took hold upon him as if he were already guilty. How the hours and miles of his journey passed he was ignorant; when he had mechanically alighted at Harliflax he called himself fool not to have gone on; on, he did not know why, to that charmed spot, charmed by enmity and hostile passions, where his father, his hinderer, the bitter obstacle between him and fortune, dragged through his melancholy days. There was no influence upon the miserable young man to dispel the gloom of incipient murder from his heart; his very love, such as it was, urged him instead of staying him. He went on to the lodging which he had left yesterday with such different thoughts, in a brooding fit of hatred and disgust with himself and everybody else, afraid of the dreadful thought which made his pulses leap and his veins tingle, yet yielding to its fierce excitement, and permitting its fire of hideous temptation to light his path. A ghastly light; but it strung his nerves so high, and excited his mind so intensely, that by-and-bye the intoxicating influence was all that he was aware of, and the idea growing familiar ceased to horrify him. What was it?—but not even in the deepest silence could the coward crime shape itself into words. It was there, and he knew it. That was enough for the devil who had led, and the spirit which followed. He went through the darkness and the peaceful streets with this deadly inspiration within him; his thoughts hovering like so many spies, and closing in dark battalions round the house on the moor, where childhood and youth had passed for Horace. He had still almost a week's freedom—what was he to do?

CHAPTER VI

When Horace arrived at his lodgings he found two letters awaiting him, which gave a momentary diversion to the dark current of his thoughts. One of them was from Colonel Sutherland, being an innocent device of that innocent old soldier to draw a candid and frank reply out of his nephew's uncandid soul. Out of his dismal passion and murderous thoughts Horace came down to something like his old everyday contempt of other people, as he read his uncle's letter, which ran thus:—

"MY DEAR HORACE—I have lately learnt by accident that you know Roger Musgrave, which I was not aware of; and as the youth has interested me very much, I would gladly know what you, with your superior penetration, think and know of him. I will tell you frankly what makes me wish this. Susan had begun to tell me of some encounter of yours with an old man at the railway, in which mention was made of young Musgrave, when she suddenly remembered that you did not wish her to mention it. This, of course, as you will suppose, knowing the nature of garrulous old men and gossips like myself, made me ten times more curious, and I managed to get out of Susan some vague story about a pension and something that had been found out. Susan is ignorant as a girl should be of a young man's follies, but I unfortunately know better. I wish you would tell me, if you can without breaking confidence, the rights of this story, and whether it is to hide some youthful sin that Musgrave is expected to pay somebody a pension. If it should be so, believe me, my dear boy, who know life and the world, that it is far better to tell all. Pay the money if need be, but hide nothing; it is fatal policy, trust an old man's word.

"Susan is very well and happy with me, where I hope you will come and see this flown bird, and where we have always a bed and a welcome for my sister's son. Come when you can—the sooner the better; and while this unfortunate difference lasts between you and your father, it would give me great pleasure, my dear boy, if you would look upon Milnehill as your home.

"Affectionately your uncle, "E. SUTHERLAND."

This simple-minded letter brought Horace back to himself for the moment. He read it over a second time, with one of his familiar sneers, and, with scarcely the pause of a minute, hunted up writing materials in a cold corner of his half-lighted room, and rushed into a premature and imprudent reply.

"Your acuteness, my dear uncle," wrote Horace, "has not led you astray. Of course I could enter into no explanations with a girl like Susan, from whose ears one would naturally keep everything of the kind. But you are quite right in your supposition. Such insight as yours into our little concealments is a more effectual argument than any other to prevent us young fellows from trying to bide what cannot be hidden. I cannot enter into any particulars, and it seems needless to say anything more than that you are right.

"Thank you for your kind offer of a home at Milnehill; and with love to Susan, believe me in haste,

"Your dutiful nephew, "HORACE SCARSDALE."

This letter was closed and thrown aside before Horace perceived the other one which lay on the table before him. He turned it over half suspiciously. In a female handwriting, and sent evidently by some private messenger, the look of it puzzled him who had no correspondents. Then the signature threw him into a flush of eager anxiety. What could induce Amelia Stenhouse to write to him? But, after all, the contents were commonplace enough. It was a very brief note, dated from her father's house the morning of this same day:—

"DEAR SIR—Papa is suddenly taken ill. The doctors fear it looks like cholera, and he is rather alarmed himself. He wishes to see you immediately, if you can come. I hope this may reach you soon, and that you will be able to return directly, for he seems anxious to see you, as if he had something to say.

"Yours sincerely, "AMELIA STENHOUSE."

It was some little time before Horace understood distinctly the contents of this note; for he was a lover, unlovely though his love was, and the first communication moved him into a momentary tumult, in which the words lost their due meaning. When he turned over to the address, however, and the "to be forwarded immediately" caught his eye, he began to rouse himself to a consciousness of the urgent circumstances. Mr. Stenhouse was ill, and wanted to see him. Twenty-four hours ago Horace would have supposed that his employer knew something of his father's secret. Now he was somewhat indifferent as to any communication which Mr. Stenhouse might have to make. But he was Amelia's father, and she was likely to be there. He got up accordingly, in the haste which was congenial to his agitated condition, and made his toilette rapidly, but with unusual care. He was pale, and his passion of evil thoughts had left traces upon his face; but the very excitement of those murderous fancies lighted an unusual fire in his eye, and animated the countenance, which, in common times, was not a remarkable face. As he went out he took up the letter he had written to his uncle, and tossed it carelessly into the post as he passed, thinking, with a momentary contemptuous wonder as he did so, of the simple old man who had opened his arms and heart to Susan, and who held open for Horace himself that warm domestic shelter, the home of which the young man felt no need. The contrast was wonderful enough—Uncle Edward and his Susan in their bright, peaceful room at Milnehill, in the evening calm and sweet comfort of that home life; and this young solitary, hurrying by himself through the dark streets of Harliflax, the wind flaring the street-lamps overhead, and a crowd of hurrying phantoms rushing through the darkness of his mind, where the air was wild with the excitement of a storm, and lightning gleams of evil intention threw a fitful illumination. He went on, hurrying through the night, with a careless intuition that he was going to a death-bed. It was nothing to Horace. He was going to serve his own purposes, to see Amelia. His pulse beat high at last, with a rising exhilaration. In the changing tide of his thoughts he began to remember that fortune was secure to him, though not now, and he was going to see the first and only creature who had ever touched his selfish soul into passion. His spirit rose into a thrill of expectation and dark enjoyment. That inarticulate horror lay darkling still among his thoughts, but it did not disturb the rising flush of youthful elevation and hope.

The lawyer's house was lighted all over, but not with lights which could be mistaken for an illumination of pleasure. Even in so short a time the whole place had acquired a look of painful hurry and anxiety. The daughters and the servants were wandering restlessly up and down the stairs, making ceaseless inquiries, and keeping up a perpetual disturbance at the door of the sick-room, where Mrs. Stenhouse, restored to her due place, by the visitation of trouble, watched by her husband, and where even Amelia was not permitted to enter. Amelia was not very anxious for the privilege, it must be owned. She kept up a perpetual succession of messages, sending her sisters and her maid, and every half hour going herself to ask whether papa was any better?—whether there was any change?—with cheeks paled half by anxiety about her father, and half by fright and apprehension for herself; for the cholera had come to Harliflax, a dreaded visitor, some months before, and still made itself remembered in fatal droppings of poison, here and there a single "case" renewing in the public mind its original panic. The beauty was glad to escape from her fears and the troubled atmosphere of the house, into a burst of hurried conversation with Horace, who was not sentimental enough to require of her any great degree of devotion to her father, and did not find it at all unsuitable to the agitated condition of the household that Amelia turned to himself so readily for occupation in her restless idleness. She swept down upon a little sofa, which was lost and disappeared under the covert of her ample skirts, and shaded her face with her hand, and declared that she was so unhappy she did not know what to do. "For it really is the cholera, Mr. Scarsdale," said Amelia; "and we may all be gone in a week, for anything any one can tell. Poor papa is so bad, it is dreadful to think of it! And I am sure, ever since I knew what it was, I have been in such a state! If you were to listen now, you could hear my heart beat."

"I am listening; but my ear is too far off," said Horace, with bold admiration. "I should like to study that sound at a less distance, if I might—"

"Oh! Mr. Scarsdale—if I were not so anxious and so agitated, I should be very angry," said Amelia. "Pray, go away, sir. You are a great deal too bold, you gentlemen. But to think of poor papa: quite well yesterday morning, and to-night—oh dear! oh dear!"

"Perhaps he is not so bad as you suppose," said Horace.

"He is a great deal worse than anybody supposes," cried Amelia, with a little sob. "Here, you—Harriet—Emma! Run up this moment, and knock at the door, and ask how dear papa is; whether there is any change. I am so afraid to hear there is any change; the words sound so dreadful—don't they, Mr. Scarsdale?—and when it is one's father! Oh! what a long time that child loiters. I must run myself! Wait just a moment, please."

And Amelia swept away, upsetting a chair in her progress, and almost puffing out one of the candles on the table by the current of air which attended her movements. She came back again a few minutes after, breathless, but walking with great solemnity.

"He is no better—there is no difference, Mr. Scarsdale," she said, with a great sigh, seating herself with the deepest seriousness, casting down her eyes, and shaking her head. Horace watched her through all this pantomime with glowing eyes. Not that he remarked or commented on the character which thus showed itself: he cared no more for Amelia's character than he did for her grandmother's; but from the splendid black hair wreathed round her head, to the little foot which came out from under her wide drapery, and upon which her own downcast eyes were fixed, the young man devoured her with his gaze of bold and selfish passion. He should have her yet, whoever might object: she should belong to him, whether she would or not. That was the pivot of his fancy; and all Amelia's pretty trickery was nothing to her thorough-going admirer, nor did he even feel himself reminded of his special errand here, or of the suffering man upon whom "as yet"—ominous words—there was no change!

Perhaps neither of the young people knew very well how long Horace remained in that deserted drawing-room, which had so strange an air of agitation to-night upon all its familiar aspects, and which, though nothing was changed, bore somehow so clear an impression of being no longer the centre of interest, but rather a forsaken corner out of the current. After a while, however, the tête-à-tête was rudely interrupted by the staggering entrance of Mr. Stenhouse's man-of-all-work, carrying in his arms the invalid boy with whom Horace had made private acquaintance on his first visit here.

"Mr. Edmund's sent for up to master," said the man, confusedly, as he saw that his young mistress was there. "Beg your pardon, Miss Amelia; but I didn't know no one was here, and come in to rest—he's mortal heavy, for all he's so little," he continued, as he staggered out again, somewhat dismayed by his blunder. Miss Amelia was not the gentlest of rulers. Little Edmund, meanwhile, clung to his bearer's shoulder, with his suspicious eyes gleaming large and eager out of his little white child's face. Edmund was not the person to come and go without a word.

"I say, sir, you!" cried Edmund, "papa's ill. You're not to come a-courting, as Stevens says you all do, to-night. I won't have it—I won't! I'm papa's son, and when he's ill there shan't be strangers in the house!"

The end of this harangue was lost in the depths of the stairs, where Stevens had borne forth in alarm his dangerous charge. Amelia started, half rose, shook out her great skirts, and turned with graceful condescension to her lover.

"Don't mind that little savage, Mr. Scarsdale. But really I had quite forgotten that papa asked to see you; this has been such an agitating, anxious day. Pray call Stevens, and make him tell papa that you are here; and please," she continued, rising up suddenly, and laying her hand on Horace's arm, "please do let me know what he says to you. Oh, I'm sure it's about little Edmund—that little wretch is such a pet with papa, and it's so unfair to us. Will you?" she cried, with animation, making no resistance when Horace took and held her hand. "Will you really? Oh, do, there's a dear good—oh no, I did not mean that; I meant, there's a kind friend; now don't be foolish, Mr. Scarsdale; go up directly to papa."

"I will, because you tell me," said Horace; "for your sake—it would be hard to go on any other argument; and when I promise to tell you what he says, promise that you will see me again."

"Oh, yes, yes," said Amelia, hurrying him to the door, with a little fright, adding piquancy to her gratified vanity. She had seen various people "in love," and was a little indifferent to the manifestations of that youthful delusion; but the eyes of Horace glowed upon her with no commonplace fervour. She was flattered, but she was a little afraid, even though she was not aware what black companion she had in the young man's dangerous heart.

CHAPTER VII

Without any awe, or indeed much interest—with the indifference of a man absorbed in his own affairs, and the still more revolting carelessness of one who had begun to play in his dark thoughts with other human lives, and to find them obstacles in his way—Horace Scarsdale entered the sick room of his employer. Mr. Stenhouse lay, huddled among his pillows, in all the exhaustion of his terrible disease, shivering and blue beneath the load of coverings with which his attendants vainly endeavoured to restore vital warmth to his frame. He was not dying yet—he had still force enough to retain the dismal, anxious look into which that malady writhes and puckers the suffering face; but he had reached to that condition of entire occupation with his own pangs, which sometimes happily, sometimes miserably, beguiles the departing soul out of the shrinkings of nature on the verge of death. The appearance of Horace, recalling him from that absorbing consciousness of pain, he perceived with all a sick man's impatience. He had got free of his thoughts by means of those bodily tortures through which he had just passed—and to feel himself brought back to the more delicate agony of heart and conscience, seemed an infliction of wanton cruelty to the sufferer. He turned aside his chilled and colourless face, and closed his eyes on the unwelcome apparition of the man he had himself desired to see. He did not desire to see him now, nor to return to the anxieties of a living man in contemplation of death. He was no longer at a sufficient distance from that event to be able to contemplate it. Almost in the river, he would rather have forgotten what these dark waters were, and be left at the present moment to himself and his pain.

But as Horace drew close to the bed, a little cry of impatience from the sharp voice of little Edward, who was then being carried downstairs, startled the father. He was still open to the touch of human love and anxiety in that point. He opened his eyes instantly, and made a sign of recognition to the young man standing beside him. "Go away, let them all go—Mary, leave me," he said faintly; then louder, as Mrs. Stenhouse lingered timidly—"leave me, do you hear; I have something to say to him; go, I tell you, or it will be all the worse for your boy. Scarsdale," continued the sick man, watching with his anxious eyes his wife's figure disappearing, "come closer—no one is aware of it but you—sit down here."

Horace obeyed, bringing his ear near to the wavering voice. He was not sympathetic, and did not pretend it; he listened without a look or a word of pity, and the sufferer's spirit rallied into its wonted expression at the sight of his cold, business face.

"I've left everything to Edmund, if he lives," gasped the dying man; "here, Scarsdale, are you sure you hear me?—and about that young Musgrave's concern, you know. I don't want the boy to hear of it; eh, do you understand?—I had nothing to do preserving Musgrave's interests; do you hear me?—the boy is not to know."

"I shall not tell him," said Horace, briefly.

"Tell him!—that is not enough. He is not to know. Do you hear me? The child's a Quixote. How can I tell what he would do? He is not to hear of it! And, Scarsdale," continued the sufferer, almost piteously, in a tone of deprecating cunning, "there's Amelia; she has a little fortune, and if she'll have you, I shan't object."

"No," said Horace, looking with his eyes still fiery in their excitement, and all the superiority and contempt of youth and health upon the dying man, whose will, twenty-four hours hence, would be impotent as the grave could make it. "No!" There was almost a smile upon his lip; it was cruel life exulting over the vain intentions of the dying. A few hours, and what would his objection signify? Undisguised and manifest, that thought rung in the mocking tone of the young man's reply, and looked out of his uncompassionating face.

Perhaps the congenial spirit lying there felt it!—and knew his own impotence. He threw out his shivering hands in a gesture which might be appeal—which might be passion—which was actual physical agony, a paroxysm of returning pain. The wife and her assistants came back, and Horace stood aside from the bed, without the sufferer being aware of it. "Remember, Scarsdale, the boy is not to know!" he shouted out in the height of his sufferings. Horace remained in the room with a morbid curiosity strange to himself, though his eager thoughts were with Amelia below. He was not aware that few men depart in a paroxysm of pain, and he stood there with a strange excitement, almost thinking that, for the first time, he should see a fellow-creature die.

When those pangs subsided the sufferer was nearer the last act of life; a merciful haze and dimness of exhaustion had begun to creep over him. Through this mist he spoke faintly out of his wandering mind—words only half audible, only half intelligible. One of these murmuring sounds was over and over repeated, until the watchers recognized it:—"In its mother's milk—in its mother's milk; seethe a kid in its mother's milk; Scarsdale!" said the dying man, opening his dim eyes with a sudden renewal of energy—"isn't it in the Bible so?—ah! the Bible, boy—you know!"

"Yes, Julius dear—yes!" cried poor weeping Mrs. Stenhouse, eager, poor soul, to thrust into his mind, even then, more hopeful words—"and a great deal more, and better, about the forgiveness of sins. Oh, Julius! let me read—you can hear me yet!"

"Oh! you are there, are you?" said Stenhouse, raising his eyes with an effort. "I thought it was Scarsdale—ha!—he's off to Amelia, is he? to court the girl when her father's dying? But I tell you, Scarsdale," cried the sufferer, raising his sharp voice high and ghastly in the stillness, "the boy is not to know!"

These were the last words Horace heard from the man who had crossed so actively, yet so briefly, the current of his life. Warned by the unspoken appeal of Mrs. Stenhouse, and feeling that even decorum forbade him to remain, he left the room; nor had even he hardihood sufficient to linger long with Amelia, who awaited his return in the drawing-room. He told her a rapidly-invented fable as to what Mr. Stenhouse had said to him, and left the house almost immediately. His regard for ordinary proprieties was small enough, certainly; but he was not quite bold enough to come from the father's death-bed and make violent love to the daughter below. He postponed it for that night.

This episode turned the young man's thoughts back a little into a more familiar and less tragic current; and now that the lawyer's secret threatened to become known, Horace bethought himself of one way still remaining by which he might have, even although nothing happened at Marchmain, some benefit by his grandfather's will. That merciless document precluded the heir from availing himself of the aid of money-lenders, under penalty of losing the inheritance; and it was, accordingly, vain to think of availing himself of the common resource of impatient heirs. Mr. Stenhouse dead, and Roger Musgrave's friends aroused to the first inklings of a discovery, Mr. Pouncet's character and credit, and no inconsiderable portion of his wealth, lay absolutely in the power of Horace. If he could exercise that power so as to procure such support as he felt himself entitled to from the unwilling lawyer, it might save him yet from the deadly, secret, and unexpressed impulse in his hidden mind. Something might happen at Marchmain, without any agency of the unnatural son. Was it a good angel which put the lesser sin of deceit before those covetous eyes, to guard them from the bigger sin which loomed darkly within their vision? Heaven knows: but, at least, the phantoms crowding round his bed that night were less hideous than the latent horror which still cowered darkling in a corner of his heart.

CHAPTER VIII

"Armitage is the most indolent man I know, Susan," said Colonel Sutherland; "here is his letter, my love, saying he has written to his attorney to make inquiries. And yet, after all, they're sharp these country lawyers—perhaps it was the best thing he could do; and here's—eh?—why, a letter from Horace! Come now, that's satisfactory—let us see what the boy says."

"What does he say, uncle?" asked Susan, when, after a considerable pause, and two readings of the letter, Uncle Edward carefully refolded it, laid it down by his own plate, and went on with his breakfast without another word.

"Oh, hum—nothing particular, my dear child—nothing of any importance," said Colonel Sutherland, with a troubled face, opening the letter again and glancing over it; as if he might perhaps find out somewhere a key to the moral cipher in which it was written. He was slow to take offence; but its tone affronted the old soldier. There was a shade of mockery, visible even to Uncle Edward's earnest, unsuspicious eyes; and whether it was true, and Musgrave was to blame—or false, and a disgrace to Horace, there was equal pain in the alternative; in either case it was not for Susan's eyes.

"Uncle, has Horace been doing something very wrong?" asked Susan, after a little interval, with the moisture rising to her eyes. Colonel Sutherland made a little use of his infirmity at that moment. He bent his deaf ear towards her, asking, "What, my love?" as if he had neither heard nor could guess what her question was; and before she could speak again, made an exclamation of surprise over another letter, the postmark of which he was regarding curiously. "London! why, Susan, Musgrave has come home!"

And before the Colonel could assure himself of this unexpected event by a glance over his letter, a commotion was heard outside; Patchey intent upon showing into the drawing-room somebody who was equally intent upon finding his way direct to the Colonel's presence.

"Why, man, I have come all the way from the Cape to see him," burst at last upon their hearing, in a manly voice, somewhat loud, and full of exhilaration, from the hall. "I tell you, he'll give me some breakfast; the kindest friend I ever had in the world, do you think he'll refuse to see me?"

"The Colonel's a kind friend to many a person, but it's agin his principle to be disturbed at his meals," said Patchey, obstinately. "I'll tell him whenever the bell rings, but in the meanwhile you'll walk in here."

And Patchey's pertinacity would have gained the day but for the interference of Colonel Sutherland, who got up hastily from the breakfast-table, with an exclamation very rare on his gentle lips, and threw open as wide as it would go the door of the dining-room. There outside stood Roger Musgrave, brown and manful, in his dark Rifleman's uniform, and restored to such a degree of self-confidence and social courage as became a man who had been living among his equals for a couple of years, who had earned his place, and made himself a modest degree of fame. He grasped the Colonel's hands in his own with an exuberant satisfaction, which the poor Squire of Tillington's penniless heir would not have ventured upon. He came in boldly, overflowing with honest gratitude and pleasure, secure of finding his place, and delighted to be "at home" once more. But Roger was suddenly interrupted, and struck dumb in his jubilant and rapid account of having been sent home with dispatches, and arriving suddenly without due time to warn his old friend of his approach. Susan rose from her place by the breakfast-table, and the young man lost his head and his tongue in an instant, scared by that formidable apparition. After a minute's interval, turning very red, and stammering out, "Miss Scarsdale?" Roger shyly approached the unlooked-for mistress of the house; while Susan on her part, with an equal blush, and a faltering exclamation of "Mr. Musgrave!" made an imperceptible step of advance, and gave her hand to Uncle Edward's "young friend." Uncle Edward himself, much amazed and amused by this pantomime, looked on till it was over. Then he covered the embarrassment of the young people in his own fashion by innumerable questions, which Roger was only too glad to answer; but Susan, mortified and troubled, and finding herself sadly in the way, could not but perceive that her presence was an effectual damp upon the stranger's high spirits, and had subdued him in the strangest fashion. How could it be? Susan took the earliest opportunity of leaving the room, dismayed at the influence she had unconsciously exercised, and more than half disposed to run upstairs to her own room and have a good cry over it. She had imagined to herself, perhaps, more than once, what might happen at this very arrival—but her thoughts had never pictured any such scene as this.

When Susan had left the room, however, Roger's silence and diffidence, instead of lessening, rather increased; he followed her to the door with his eyes, and made a confused pause; and then he burst into the very middle of a little lecture upon strategy which the good Colonel was delivering to him, with the very inconsequent and illogical remark:—

"I was quite taken by surprise to see Miss Scarsdale here."

"Why," said Colonel Sutherland, swallowing the affront to his own eloquence, "you knew Susan was my niece, did you not?"

"I—I suppose I had forgotten," said Roger, with another blush over this inexcusable fib. And as the young man seemed disposed to make another pause after this false statement, and to fall into a state of reverie, the Colonel bethought himself of applying the sharp spur of Horace's letter to bring him to himself.

"I would have delayed for a little speaking to you so gravely," said Uncle Edward; "but as we are talking of Miss Scarsdale, it is just as well to enter upon the subject at once. Now, remember, I don't want to steal into your confidence, or urge you to tell anything you may wish to conceal; but let me know this much, Musgrave. When you left Tillington did you leave anything behind you; any foolish connexion, any boyish entanglement, anything you wished to conceal? My dear boy, I don't want to make myself your judge—such things have been, and have been repented of—only tell me, 'yes' or 'no'?"

"Foolish connexion!—boyish entanglement!" repeated Roger, in amazement; "I know you don't mean to insult me, Colonel Sutherland—what do you mean?"

The old man looked into the young man's face, bending towards him with that stoop of benign weakness—the touch of physical imperfection, which put a tender climax to his fatherly words and ways.

"I will tell you what I mean by-and-bye; but in the meantime say to me in so many words—'It is not true.'"

"It is not true!" said Roger, with emphasis.

The young man was certainly roused now—he sat quite upright, carrying high his soldierly head, not defiant as he might have been at Tillington, perfectly grave, conscious of nothing which slander could build upon. The old soldier's eyes glistened over him—he was proud of his volunteer.

"I knew it all along," said Colonel Sutherland, joyfully; "but to know you perfectly right, as I always believed, is not so much pleasure to me as it might be, since it proves somebody else entirely wrong. I'll tell you now how this came about. Susan on her way here overheard part of a conversation between her brother and an old man, in which your name was introduced, and mention made of a pension which the man thought you might be induced to give him, in consequence of some discovery. This Horace forbade his sister to repeat, but Susan told me, thinking there was something wrong at the bottom. You will forgive me, Musgrave, if the idea glanced into my mind for a moment that there might be something to conceal. With that idea, thinking to appeal to my nephew's generosity, I wrote to him, and this is the answer; see—I am assured now that there is something of importance to your interests beneath this veil."

Roger read the letter with a rising colour; he saw the trick of it, and had hard enough ado to restrain his impatience.

"He is brother—I mean he is your nephew, Colonel Sutherland," he said, returning the letter with a somewhat proud gesture. He thought of nothing else in his sublime, youthful contempt for this effort to dishonour him; he was innocent, and his veins tingled with momentary rage, proudly subdued; but he gave no second thought to the discovery, or to the something important and secret which this impotent slander had concealed.

However, the Colonel proceeded to question him upon the condition of his relation's estate, and the chances there might be of some discovery of consequence. Roger answered at random, being very ignorant, quite hopeless of any good, and otherwise occupied in his mind. The old soldier was at last compelled to break up the conference from manifest signs of impatience on the part of his guest, who was anxious to go to his room and refresh himself after his journey. When Roger had really got his release, however, and was on his way to the door, the young man came back again with another inconsequent question:—

"May I ask, Colonel Sutherland, if Miss Scarsdale was aware of this—of your suspicions?" he said, fumbling wrathfully with the handle of his travelling-bag.

"Certainly not—not a word," said Uncle Edward, gravely; and while the young man went away relieved, the old one mused in his chair, with a little humour in his smile. "I wonder, now, what it mattered if she had?" he said to himself; "they never exchanged three words in their lives." That was very true; but there are more things than words in the world when people are young.

CHAPTER IX

When Susan and Roger met again late in the day they had somewhat changed conditions. Lieutenant Musgrave—for that was now the rank of the young volunteer—had, to his own pleasurable consciousness, improved his personal appearance during his hour of seclusion. Though he was rather too tall for a rifleman, that excess of stature is a drawback easily sustained in general by those afflicted with it; and perhaps Roger had a little satisfaction in thinking that the dress became him tolerably well, in spite of his inches. It is to be feared that the thought did glance into his mind as he finished his toilette, that his own was such a figure as might catch a lady's eye, especially while the placid firmament of Milnehill was disturbed by no apparition of a rival knight; and that the likelihood of spending some days under the same roof with Susan was, when he realized it, rather exhilarating to the young man's spirits. Susan, however, was in a very different position. She had seen what she supposed to be a sudden chill of discomfort fall upon the stranger at sight of her. She had observed his silence, his fallen looks, his diminished brightness, and it was impossible to attribute this change to anything but her own presence. Susan was very much mortified by this supposed discovery. She had known herself to be unregarded and unloved for the most part of her life, but never before had she felt herself in the way; and the result was that a sentiment of injury, melancholy and heroical, arose in Susan's heart. She was sad and dignified, when Roger appeared full of animation, and anxious to please. She thought he had recovered the first shock of seeing her, and was training himself into friendly behaviour; and she repulsed him as much as she could by her monosyllables and downcast eyes. After a little, he began to grow puzzled: he could not rouse her to interest, though he exerted all his powers; she was dull, saddened, and pre-occupied. Perhaps, after all, there were rivals to disturb the peaceable atmosphere at Milnehill.

Uncle Edward, who observed the two with quiet interest, and a little mingling of amusement, beheld the shadow, and was puzzled in his turn; for Susan hitherto had shown no lack of interest in Musgrave's affairs. Colonel Sutherland's anxiety, however, relieved itself by the instant despatch of Patchey with a note to the Colonel's dear friend and ally, Mrs. Melrose, his sister-in-law, who was now his referee on all feminine topics. The tender-hearted old man concluded that Susan might possibly feel her position somewhat uncomfortable as hostess to the stranger, "especially if she likes him," thought Uncle Edward; and, obedient to his summons, an hour or more before dinner arrived a Portobello "noddy," containing Mrs. Melrose, her pretty maid, and her best cap. The old lady was almost as much disposed to make a pet of Susan as was Susan's uncle, and the reproof which she administered to his solicitude was of the lightest.

"Here I am, Edward, you perceive," said his old friend; "but why I should be sent for at this express rate is more than a quiet person like me can divine. Because Susan feels awkward at having a young man to entertain, and no other woman in the house? Nonsense! Susan is just the last girl in the world to be so foolish. What's a young man more than any other person? It's your punctilios, Edward, that put things into the bairns' heads; but I'm here, for all that. If the truth must be told, I am growing very fond of that young creature myself."

"I am very glad to hear it," said Colonel Sutherland, conducting that short, bright, pleasant figure most carefully and gallantly through the garden; for Mrs. Melrose was older than the Colonel, and owned to a good many infirmities, and had almost given up walking by this time. Then he began to recommend Roger very specially to her notice; and then he had to hear Mrs. Melrose's news; that the mail which came in yesterday had brought a joint letter from Charlie and his wife, and that the regiment was ordered to Outerabad, "where we were when my poor General got his first step," said the old lady. "I hope it will be as fortunate with his son," answered Uncle Edward; and so they entered the house, to receive Susan's glad, astonished welcome. The advent of Mrs. Melrose almost delivered Susan from that rare fit of romantic and heroical sullenness. There was no necessity now for Mr. Musgrave being specially civil to herself. Now she had some one to talk to, to release "the gentlemen" from the imperative claims of politeness. She seized upon the old lady with all the fervour of pique, resolved to show Roger that if she was in his way, he was an object of great indifference to her; and succeeded so well in this laudable attempt, that before the two ladies left the dining-room poor Roger was as distrait and silent as ever. Susan's cruel experiment, like the surprise of her first appearance, had puffed him out.

"But, my dear boy," said Colonel Sutherland, "you must do something in this matter. I wrote to Armitage about it, but, considering how he managed matters when you went, I can't say I have much confidence in him. And he is not married yet, the poor old sinner! My nephew, Musgrave, is—my nephew, as you said to-day, but I don't know the boy at all. I don't understand him, and therefore I don't know what to think of this concealed matter, which evidently concerns yourself, whatever it is."

Roger made no answer. He had not a vestige of belief in his heart that anything could be found out to his benefit, and he was consequently careless of it.

"What I should recommend you to do," continued the Colonel, "would be to go at once to Kenlisle, to see this lawyer whom Sir John has written to, Mr. Pouncet. Most likely he had the management of your godfather's affairs as well—and urge him to take all possible steps for hunting out the mystery."

"The mystery!" cried Roger, with a momentary impatience; "I beg your pardon, Colonel, but what possible mystery can there be about such a history as ours in these days? My dear, good, excellent old godfather, my tenderest of friends and benefactors," said the young man warmly, reddening with that deep consciousness of blame cast upon the dead, which made his language more fervent than was any way needful—"was an old-fashioned country gentleman, and lived to the full extent of his means. Why should not he?—he had no children to provide for. It is so usual a story, that any county in England could match it. He had a liberal hand while he lived, and when he died nothing was left. What possible mystery, what concealment or secret, could be here?"

"I cannot tell, indeed," said the Colonel; "but on the other hand, what possible reason could induce Horace Scarsdale, who is penniless himself, to promise a pension to a countryman of the district in your name, for the sake of some discovery connected with you?"

Roger mused over this an instant with a troubled face.

"Perhaps," he said at last slowly, not so much in pique as might have been supposed, but slightly inclining that way, with visions of unknown rivals crowding darkly before his eyes, "perhaps—I never wrote to ask if I should be welcome—perhaps while Miss Scarsdale is here—"

"Miss Scarsdale has nothing whatever to do with the subject. Why, Musgrave, man!" cried the Colonel, "what is the use of bringing Susan in? Susan is as my own child in my own house; think of your own interests, my dear young fellow, and leave Susan alone, though she is a very good girl."

"A very good girl!" repeated Roger; "then you don't mind us being together sometimes, Colonel, if she pleases," added, with a blushing burst of frankness, the self-convicted lover.

The Colonel shook his head. "Oh, young fools, young fools!" groaned, not from the depths, but only from the surface of his heart, that bewildered veteran; "what's to come of your being sometimes together? Not much increase to your purse, Musgrave, nor advantage to either of you. If you have begun to entertain such fantastic thoughts, your best plan is to think over what I am saying. There must be something, depend upon it, worth hearing, before my clever nephew, Horace, could make up his mind to offer an old countryman such a stipend as six-and-twenty pounds a-year."

"Ah!" cried Roger; the young man was struck with momentary conviction, partly by the fact and partly by the argument. He made a hasty memorandum in his own mind, that he would certainly look into it; but his thoughts at the present moment did not very well bear such an interruption. "It looks as if there must be something in it; but, Colonel, won't you postpone it till later?" he said, in a deprecatory tone; "I think, by this time, we ought to join the ladies. They'll blame me already for detaining you. I know you never sit long over your wine."

Once more the Colonel shook his head, but this time he smiled. He found the young man's behaviour altogether so natural, that he could not criticize it severely; and perhaps, having once been young himself, was all the better pleased with Roger, that the youth had heart enough to be shaken entirely off his balance by this deepest of disturbing influences. They went across the hall together into the drawing-room, where Susan sat by the side of Mrs. Melrose, hearing the old lady's stories. She had many a story in her mind that cheerful mother—a mother in everything, though she had but one child—many an exciting drama of life and sad domestic tragedy, brought out under yonder burning Eastern skies, lay within her memory; but it was not one of these to which Susan listened. It was to an account of Mrs. Melrose's Indian establishment, when she lived at Outerabad, "where my poor General got his first step," and where her son Charlie was now going. That practical and homely tale pleased Susan. She liked to hear of the economics of the young subaltern's wife; how she managed to do without superfluous servants, and strenuously laboured at the mending of that strange little hole in the purse through which their money seemed always running. Her contrivances about dress, when she and her lieutenant had an invitation to the Colonel's bungalow to dinner; the thrift with which this capable woman had managed that strange, half-savage, yet highly artificial and civilized household, with all its Anglo-Indian wants and luxuries. Susan was never tired of that long prolonged story, which always unfolded some new episode: "Did I ever tell you about so-and-so?" said the old lady, and forthwith ran into a variation which enlivened and animated the original strain. Susan was a capable woman, too, though she had not yet much tried her powers. She enjoyed hearing of these wonderful thrifts, and labours, and victories, as boys love stories of shipwrecks and hairbreadth escapes. "What I should have done myself!" ran through the whole like a golden thread. It roused Susan's spirits and her heart—it was to her like the reading of a possible future, instead of a certain past. She did not think of the things dolorous and heavy which cheerful Mrs. Melrose dwelt on little. She did not pause to remember that the heroine of all that active existence was now an infirm old lady, dwelling alone. Susan only thought of the life, and the love, and the labour; the capable hands, the cheerful heart, the years and hours so well filled and liberal. The fashion of that existence charmed her congenial thoughts.

"For you see," said Mrs. Melrose, after a long chapter of that history, which she meant to make an end of as soon as the gentlemen entered the room, "you see, Susan, we were poor then, the General and me."

"But you were happy all the same, happier than if you had waited till you were rich," cried Roger Musgrave, suddenly, in her ear.

"Happy!" cried the old lady, turning round upon him with an echo not to be described by words in her voice. Then she paused, with a humorous smile on her face; "I'm an old woman, and should be a good adviser; but I never was a good adviser, as your Uncle Edward will tell you. Now everybody knows that when two young fools marry upon nothing, it's not only one of the greatest follies the world is acquainted with, but exceedingly wrong."

Mrs. Melrose pronounced these words with great unction and emphasis. Could anybody doubt that she believed them thoroughly? But there was meanwhile a suspicious twinkle in her bright old eyes.

"And yet General Melrose was only a lieutenant," said Roger, "when—"

"When I married him, blessings on him!" cried the old lady, "he was but an ensign—that I should dare say so before young people!—but you can make an example and a beacon of me, Susan, my dear. Yes, it was years and years long before he was General Melrose, Mr. Musgrave; such years! years of trouble and toil and misery and happiness. Ah! Edward, they're gone and past, these years! Nothing but one thing will happen now to you and me, and that, please God, will give us back to them all."

To them all! There was a silence in the room after these words. Tears sprang to the eyes of the young people in that tender, pitiful youth of theirs, which could not understand how to be content without happiness; but there were no tears in the old eyes which met in such a pathetic cheerful glance, and understood each other beyond all interpretation of words. Dear life, which they could still live cheerfully, all shorn and diminished as it was, for His sake who gave it, and out of the most natural humanity of their Christian hearts!—but dearer was the end and termination, the day of that holy death which should restore them all.

But the evening was not sad after that, as a vulgar fancy might suppose. The old people were very cheerful, brighter than youth itself in the serenity of their old age; and Mrs. Melrose, who had been considered a very clever woman all her life by half the Indian service, and who had more actual humour and appreciation of the same than all her three auditors put together, kept Roger and Susan breathless with her recollections, her anecdotes, her sallies of quiet fun. She consented to stay all night, at her brother-in-law's request and Susan's anxious entreaty, and took Roger entirely under her protection, and treated him "like a boy of her own." "But I cannot understand," said the old lady reprovingly, as she bade her brother good night, "when you spoke of Susan and her delicacies, why you did not say there was anything particular in the business, or that this was not any person, but the special young man."

Was it the special young man?—the true knight? Susan asked herself no questions on the subject, but made great haste to get to bed and avoid speculation, which, seeing it was after twelve o'clock, a very late hour for Milnehill, was doubtless the most sensible thing she could have done.

While Roger Musgrave travelled full of hope and pleasant anticipation towards Milnehill, Roger's mother had been mourning over her dead husband. And now, while that happy evening party gathered in Colonel Sutherland's drawing-room, the widow and her little boy were spending the slow hours together in the warm parlour, where Edmund spent his invalid childhood. His father's death had given a shock more than it could bear to the nervous and weakly frame of the ailing child; his father was dead, and he was the heir. An unnatural excitement stimulated the precocious little mind, and rose to fever in the throbbing pulse and little pinched cheeks, now flushed with a hectic brightness. The little fellow had visions too magnificent to be safe, and projects as wild and impossible, as they were childish and simple-hearted. After the first pangs of his childish grief were over, Edmund, who knew nothing about guardians nor minority, began to speculate splendidly what he should do with his new wealth. He poured into his mother's ears a flood of intentions, vain, lavish, childish dreams of universal help. He was to send for Roger and give the greater half of all he had to his elder brother; he was to get everything she could desire for Mrs. Stenhouse; he was to send a present of the most beautiful horse in the world to Colonel Sutherland; and henceforward they were all to live together, and "my brother Roger" was to be supreme in the joint household. Mrs. Stenhouse, afraid to check him, and at the same time trembling for the effect of this excitement upon his weak frame, looked on with a troubled heart. She knew Edmund would not get his wild will now, as he supposed he should. She knew very well that nobody would permit him to do a tenth part of what he meant to do. But when he roused himself up out of his chair with that light of pleasure on his face, and that hectic flush which she persuaded herself into supposing "a healthy colour," and amused the languor of his lonely days with these imperative fancies, what could the poor woman do who had been his bondwoman and servant so long? And then she was full of sorrowful thoughts about "his dear father," as Mrs. Stenhouse now called the careless partner of her life, mourning him as many a man is mourned who does little to deserve that remorseful tribute of late affection. Now that he was gone, she thought it must have been her own fault that they did not get on better; and it grieved her to find how impossible it was to check Edmund into sadness, and to make him feel that the loss of his father was a matter far more important than his supposed mastery of his father's wealth. Edmund had cried all his tears out the first day, and had no more lamentations to make.

"What do you cry for?" he exclaimed at last, impatiently; "aren't you glad to send for Roger, and have him at home? I shouldn't wonder if he'd join the Edgehill Cricket-club, and get to be captain of the eleven—wouldn't it be famous. And I mean to get strong, I can tell you, mamma. I don't mean to live in this stifle and coddle, now I've come into my fortune; for papa said it was all for me."

"Oh, Edmund, dear child, your father was so fond of you!" cried the poor mother; "have you no thought to spare for him, now that he is gone? He loved you more than everything in the world. I wish—I wish you would think more of him than of what he leaves behind."

Little Edmund looked up keenly at the weak, weeping, timid woman.

"Were you fond of him yourself?" said the child, half suspiciously; "now you love him and cry about him; but it is different with me. He was very good to me, was papa," continued the little man, with a reluctant tear in the corner of his eye; "but all of you say he's a deal better off now, and that we'll see him again. If that's true, why do you cry?—and besides, mamma, I used always to think that you liked Roger's father best."

Mrs. Stenhouse covered her face with her hands, and only cried the more; she was vexed, humiliated, and ashamed, as well as full of grief. It seemed somehow sacrilege to speak of Roger's father to the son of her second husband; and Roger's father was little to herself now but a bright, brief dream of her girlhood, too short, too happy to influence her life. Now the second, longer, harder, more serious portion of her existence had concluded also; but while she sat crying these tears of mortification and wounded feeling, some one beckoned her to the door of the room and gave her some letters. One of these was from Roger himself, announcing his arrival, and that he had gone to Milnehill; for Roger as yet did not know what had happened in his mother's house. This surprising announcement raised her out of her distress in a moment and dried her tears. A thrill of new freedom ran warm through her heart, stirring the blood in her dull veins. Roger, her first-born, whom she had not seen since he was almost a baby—whom Mr. Stenhouse smilingly disliked, and would not permit to come there—Roger, her brave soldier, her handsome boy! Now she could have him under her own roof, without asking anybody's permission; now she could enjoy her son's society in fullest freedom. Poor soul! it gave her a compunction to feel how glad she was; but she could not deny even to herself how exquisite for the first moment was that unaccustomed delight.

"Oh, Edmund, darling, look here!" cried poor Mrs. Stenhouse, crying again, but this time with joy; "Roger has come home—your brother, my love;" and with an outcry of mingled terror, compunction, and delight, to feel herself daring enough in this house to pronounce these words aloud, Mrs. Stenhouse thrust the letter into Edmund's hands, and relapsed once more into tears.

Her other letters had fallen on the floor at her feet. When Edmund had finished Roger's, his inextinguishable childish curiosity discovered these. His mother was still crying, and he was her lord and master, the autocrat acknowledged and apparent of the house; he slid out of the easy chair as a cripple slides, and snatched up the nearest. Though it was addressed to Julius Stenhouse, Esq., the arrogant little imp did not hesitate to tear it open; but he did it with some haste, to make sure of the epistle before his mother uncovered her eyes. It was a communication somewhat puzzling to brains so young. Edmund, though his pride would not acknowledge it even to himself, did not understand half of Mr. Pouncet's letter, but he gleaned enough out of it to know that something that concerned Roger had been a subject of importance likewise to his father and his father's friend; and that the writer of the present epistle, which had, it appeared, been delayed in the transmission, was in a state of considerable alarm and trepidation about something. What it was that Mr. Pouncet feared Edmund could not make out, but he jumped at the conclusion that something was wrong as rapidly as Susan had done. Afraid!— why should a man be afraid?—Roger wasn't. Roger was the epitome of Edmund's faith. He had been badly educated, this poor child. He knew very little in heaven or earth save his prayers and Roger, and trusted in nothing as he did in that unknown, never-to-be-acknowledged, secret, invisible brother, whom his mother told him of in whispers, and whom he thought of by day and dreamt of by night. Now glorious times were coming. Papa and this other man, whose letter rather baffled Edmund, had doubtless entertained some project of keeping Roger down; but behold the tables were turned, the conspirators were cheated, and the details of the complot had fallen into the hands of Roger's little knight and defender. True, he did not understand them very well, but still they were here.

"Roger shall come home directly," said the little despot, waving aloft in his hand these two epistles. "I'll give him half of all my money, mamma. He shan't go for a soldier any more; and I'll find out if anybody wants to do him any harm, and punish them, I will! Look here; it's something about Roger, but I don't quite know every word what it means. You can't tell any more than me. I say, mamma, let's have Scarsdale here, and ask him."

"What is it, love?" asked Mrs. Scarsdale, wiping her eyes.

"I wish you'd mind what one says," cried the impatient little invalid. "I told you I didn't know quite all it means, neither could you if you was to try. Mamma, ring the bell and send for Scarsdale—he's got no master now but you and me; send and tell him I want him, and he's to come directly. Mamma, do you hear?"

And when Mrs. Stenhouse had glanced over the letter, which she did understand rather better than Edmund after all, she thought the boy's suggestion wise. She had not the smallest gleam of discrimination in respect to character, and to be Colonel Sutherland's nephew was enough to give her a blind confidence in Horace; and as to the possibility of acting for herself, that did not enter into the poor woman's head. She sent for Scarsdale accordingly, not in little Edmund's imperative mood, but with a pleading message that Mr. Scarsdale would be so very good as to come to her as soon as it was quite convenient for him, as she was so anxious to consult him about a letter she had received. Her heart beat higher in her breast that day with a deeper individual throb than it had known for many a previous year; a little flutter of tumultuous independence was in her mind; she would receive Roger into her own house unreproved; she seemed on the very eve of finding out something which might be of service to that cherished but unknown son; and her whole nature was stimulated by these unaccustomed hopes.

CHAPTER XI

In Mr. Stenhouse's office, where affairs were being wound up, Horace Scarsdale held his clerk's place in greater personal discomfiture than he had ever previously known. Mr. Stenhouse's executors knew of nothing extraordinary in the position of this young man. His mysterious prospects were totally unknown to them, and he had no secret to hold over their heads and enforce his claims withal. To them he was only the newest and least acquainted of the lawyer's clerks, and nobody cared for his black looks and assumptions of superiority. He remained reluctantly at his desk, because he could not afford, in present circumstances, to sacrifice the salary which would shortly be paid to him, nor could he make up his mind, in spite of all the dark excitements which distracted him—the fascination of enmity and evil purpose which bound him to Marchmain, and the covetous and tyrannous impulse which placed so plainly before his eyes his power over Mr. Pouncet—to leave the place which contained Amelia, and where alone he had any likelihood of seeing her. After their last interview the lover was daring enough to have stood upon small punctilio at the next meeting. But Mrs. Stenhouse's door was still decorously closed, and Stevens, at the present moment much more disposed to take Master Edmund for the tyrant of the house than Miss Amelia, was inexorable, and gave no admission. Mrs. Stenhouse's message accordingly found the young man in a propitious mood. He made haste to obey it, extremely indifferent as to the subject of the consultation, but deeply excited with the more personal emotion of once more finding himself under the same roof with the lady of his love.

Mrs. Stenhouse would willingly have seen him alone, feeling instinctively that little Edmund's interference was not quite expedient here; but she had submitted her inclinations too long to that small autocrat to have any chance of freedom now. It was accordingly into Edmund's parlour that Horace was shown. There was still a fire warming into a state of semi-suffocation that invalid chamber; and there sat the child, consciously regnant and despotic, with his eager eyes blazing out of his sharp little face, and the hectic flush upon his cheeks. The mother watching always, to whom Edmund's illness had become quite a domestic institution, a thing which should last for ever, saw no change save of improvement; but the cold stranger's eye saw differently. The little blade was wearing out its tiny sheath—all this excitement was too much for the feeble little body; and as distinctly as the doctor, highly skilled and richly feed, who should come down from town after awhile to pronounce the child's death-sentence, Horace perceived that before he could do one of the splendid things he purposed, little Edmund, like a shadow, should have faded away.

But Horace thought no more of Edmund when he cast his eyes upon the letter which Mrs. Stenhouse hurriedly and with agitation put into his hand:—

"DEAR STENHOUSE—I wish fervently I had broken my leg or taken a fever on that unlucky day when I was persuaded into that Tinwold business of the coal-pits. I have never had a moment's repose or comfort since, and from the day that young Scarsdale poked his inquisitive nose into the business everything vexatious in life has clustered about this unfortunate affair. I do not deny that it has paid very well as a speculation, but the profit twice over would not have paid for the annoyance which first and last it has caused to me. This morning I have a letter from Sir John Armitage. It has oozed out, somehow or other, through young Scarsdale doubtless, that there is an old man somewhere in the district who knows some secret worth telling about young Musgrave. It is true, they have not an idea what it is, but Sir John charges me with the duty of searching it out and 'doing the boy justice.' Armitage of Armitage Park, my father's clients before mine—one of the oldest families in the county! I know his affairs better than he does himself; and he dares not cut down a tree on his estate without consulting me; yet he breaks forth upon me as peremptory and absolute about this miserable business as if I could set it all square in a day. It is all very well for you, you are out of the way; you are never appealed to; the Musgraves never cross your path; but I am aggravated entirely out of patience. Would to heaven that I had never heard of your scientific friend and his discoveries! Such an accident is misery to a man of character, and if ever man was thrust and jostled into temptation that man was me.

"My temper has been so tried with this unhappy business, that I scarcely know what I am doing. Advise me how to answer Armitage, and send me Scarsdale if you can spare him. I want some assistance besides my own head and hands.

"O. POUNCET."

"Now, I say, mamma," cried Edmund, in a loud whisper, "don't give him time to make up a story—ask him what it means. Oh, Mr. Scarsdale, we're very surprised about that, we are. It's something about Roger—what is it?"

Horace was taken by surprise. Looking up, he caught the child's sharp glance, and the imploring look of the mother, both fixed upon him; and he was disconcerted. Not for the last injunction of Edmund's father—not because that worldly man, without repenting of the wrong, would have suffered another death rather than allow this secret to be known to his child. Horace had given no promise, and thought no more of that last adjuration; but what was to become of the secret if he shared it with a woman and a child?—the woman Roger's mother, the child his earnest champion. And they already knew so much of it, without any aid of his. He faced round upon them, ready to defend this fancied talisman of his power.

"What reason have you to suppose that I was in Mr. Stenhouse's secrets?" said Horace. "I had not been a fortnight in his employment. I had not known him above a month when he died. Was he likely to be confidential with me? Surely you know him better than to imagine anything so foolish."

"Ah, Mr. Scarsdale," cried Mrs. Stenhouse, trembling all over, and with tears which almost choked her— tears of anxiety for her son, and distress for her husband, mingled yet antagonistic; "he sent for you on his deathbed; there was something—something—God forgive me if I disregard this last wish of his! but it is for my Roger's sake—there was something that you were not to tell the boy."

"And is that the argument you use—you his widow!" cried Horace, with a sneer; "to induce me, a man of honour, just a week after, to tell the boy? That may be a woman's argument, Mrs. Stenhouse, but—"

"You hold your tongue, Scarsdale!" shouted little Edmund; "nobody shan't bully mamma. And I should like to know why I'm not to be told—me! I'm my father's heir, and I ought to know everything; and if you think me a child, it's because you don't know. Look here! I'm going to give half my money to Roger; but you shall marry Amelia, and have the half of my share, if you tell me honest what it is."

Horace rose up with a laugh of ridicule at the child's folly, but before he could reach the door Mrs. Stenhouse came before him. "There's some sad mystery here," she said, wringing her hands; "Edmund was not to know I heard him say; and then about seething the kid in his mother's milk. It's something that will harm my Roger! What is it, Mr. Scarsdale? I charge you, as you had a mother yourself, to tell me!"

"I never had a mother myself," said Horace, with his cold smile; "and if Mr. Stenhouse was a good step-father to Roger Musgrave, and took care of his property that the poor boy might not waste it, what was that to me? I can't tell you—how can you suppose that I know?"

While he was speaking he made his way steadily to the door. He was pleased to go out and close it after him, leaving that reflection with the mother and child; that to be sure the dead man, their nearest relative, had defrauded his wife's son; what was that to Horace Scarsdale? He went crushing Mr. Pouncet's letter in his hand; he had got possession of that, at all events, and he felt sure that poor trembling Mrs. Stenhouse could not make much of its hints, even though coupled with her husband's death-bed adjuration, and that strange maundering of his weakness, at which Horace smiled—seething the kid in its mother's milk. Unlikely words to enter the mind of that hard, unrepentant man of the world, who, even at his last moments, wished not to amend but to conceal.

But he had not seen Amelia; it was hard to reconcile the contrary accidents of his fate. He could not deceive them blandly, as Mr. Stenhouse could have done, and he had no resource but to go away with abruptness, losing all chance of future admittance to the feet of the beauty, who was now Mrs. Stenhouse's daughter, dependent upon her, and not the caressed and flattered mistress of the house. The cholera and the fright had unmanned Amelia. She had not been able to strike in at the proper moment and assert her sway; so that in the stillness of the house of mourning her mother and Edmund had unconsciously and tacitly won the supremacy. Fortune, however, gave him the advantage he had forfeited by legitimate means. He met the lady of his heart that very same afternoon, as she took languidly a solemn walk with her sisters, all crape and propriety. Amelia was sadly tired of decorum by this time—decorum which lasts so much longer than grief, and is so exacting and punctilious. Though she put down her veil, her heart fluttered at the approach of Horace; and she was quite well pleased that he should turn with her, and accompany her back almost to the door of the house. He told her of his magnificent prospects, as he had never yet told any one; that when his father died he could make a very fine lady of her, and give her a house in town, and all the unhoped for delights of fashion; but that might be years hence—and in the meantime would she marry him? Amelia was too wise to say yes without due consideration; but she blushed through her veil, and was quite sure Mr. Scarsdale would give her a little time to think—would not be too urgent in the sad, sad position of the family. How could she think of such things, and dear papa only a week in his grave? and some bright tears fell, easily shed. Horace was abundantly satisfied. He had excited her fancy with his hopes of fortune; and he thought she liked him, as it is so easy for people to believe; though in reality it was only the amusement, the admiration that Amelia cared for; and he wanted no more at the present moment. He said farewell, like an accepted lover, and went away jubilant; his dark purposes swelling in him, and a whole world of pleasure, wealth, and exaltation lying before him. A whole world, and only one dark, melancholy, unlovely shadow of life—a ghost alien to the sunshine, an unenjoying, unloving, dismal human thread of existence—hanging black between him and his enchanted kingdom. Accidents are rife and many in this troublous world—who could tell what might cut that thread?

CHAPTER XII

With Mr. Pouncet's letter in his pocket—that self-betraying document, which he had estimated at once at its due value—Horace set out the next day for Kenlisle. Yet not for Kenlisle direct: the young man, with the oddest, uncharacteristic trifling, stopped half-way, to visit a remarkable cathedral town which lay in his road. What did Horace Scarsdale care for cathedrals? Yet he paused, in that most anxious and exciting moment, to inspect this one, and marched doggedly round and about it, as if to persuade himself that he was interested. In his progress he paused before an apothecary's shop—but did not enter there, nor till hours after, when he rushed in on his way to the railway, and made certain purchases. In haste to get his train, he did not permit himself time to look at the things he had bought, but hurried them into his pocket, and rushed on again as though it had been only a sudden thought which moved him. Yet he had never looked so darkly pale and dangerous as when, seated in the railway-carriage, he felt in his pockets these little sealed packets. That day was a Mayday, warm and bright; but Horace shivered in his corner with a chill that went to his heart. For a moment the colour went out of his face, and the light out of his eye; he gave a stealthy glance round—a glance full of the intolerable terrors of guilt. Did any one guess what he had in his pocket? Could any one tell what he had in his heart?

The next morning he presented himself to the troubled eyes of Mr. Pouncet, an image of conscious power. That unfortunate man of character knew by this time of the death of Stenhouse, and had spent a day or two of agony wondering into whose hands his letter was likely to fall. The advent of Horace was a relief for the moment: here he had, at least, an assistant, who could do any further lying that might be necessary, without burdening Mr. Pouncet's personal conscience. That was a great point gained. But the answer to his first eager question was far from satisfactory.

"Your letter was put into my hands by Mrs. Stenhouse," said Horace; "and you know who she is—Roger Musgrave's mother."

Mr. Pouncet scratched his head in dismay. "She could not understand two words of it!" he exclaimed, at last, endeavouring to re-assure himself.

"Perhaps not—but one word, most likely, is enough. She is alarmed, and curious, and knows very well that something is wrong, though she cannot tell what; and that to expose you is for the interest of her son."

"To expose me!" cried Mr. Pouncet, with a gasp of rage and mortification.

"Yes," said Horace, coolly; "but," he added, producing that document out of his pocket, "I managed, fortunately, to bring away your letter."

Mr. Pouncet writhed silently under this persecution, which he dared not resent; for it was quite true that the story of that past transaction, once laid open to the world, would empty those solemn boxes labelled with his clients' names, which made his private office look so important, and would banish him at once from Armitage Park, and many another great house. The unfortunate lawyer was at his wit's end. That secret would have died with Stenhouse but for the discovery of this cold-blooded and unmanageable young man; and Mr. Pouncet cursed the day when, in defiance of all accustomed rules, he admitted Horace to his office. What was a romance of possible expectations to him?

"Have you ever learnt anything more of your own circumstances and the fortune," said Mr. Pouncet, with a slight sneer, "which you expected when I saw you last?"

But when Horace answered—as he did at once, having previously resolved upon it—with a very succinct account, quite unencumbered by any reflections or exhibitions of feeling, of what he had discovered, the lawyer opened his eyes. The heir of such a heap of money, penniless though he was at the present moment, was a very different individual from the poor Horace Scarsdale, with nothing but his cunning wits and unscrupulous mind to help him on in the world. The revelation reconciled Mr. Pouncet even to himself. It was no longer so sadly humiliating to acknowledge himself in the young man's power.

"And what will you do?" he asked, breathlessly, with already a difference in his tone. One does not speak to an attorney's clerk, even when he knows one's cherished secret, as one speaks to the heir of a good many thousands a-year.

"What can I do?" said Horace, rising in due proportion, and tasting the first sweetness of his wealth. "Forbidden to borrow—debarred from all ordinary means of reaping some present advantage; unless—I can be of use to you, if you make it worth my while—unless you can help me, Pouncet. You can if you please."

Mr. Pouncet winced a little at this familiar address. "Had you not better try," he suggested, "to make some arrangement with your father?"

"Arrangement with my father? What for? He has less power than you have: the will is expressly constructed so as to make arrangement impossible, and shut him out entirely," cried Horace, with a certain suppressed exultation of enmity. "Besides, he hates me, and I'd much rather arrange with you. Look here, Pouncet—I want to get married. Give me a thousand a-year, and I'll give you my best services, and my word of honour to pay you a reasonable sum, by way of acknowledgment, when I come into my property. Will you? There is no use lingering over it—say Yes or No."

"A thousand a-year!" cried Mr. Pouncet, in dismay.

"Less would be useless," said Horace, in his high-flying arrogance. "Besides, I could earn half as much anywhere, without asking any favour from you."

Poor Mr. Pouncet took his hand out of his pocket, and grinned at the young man with a helpless spite and disdain. Words were so incapable of expressing all the mingled mockery and mortification with which he heard that last speech, that the unfortunate lawyer would have made derisive faces at him had he dared. As it was, he turned away to his desk, and growled under his breath, "Catch me giving you fifty if you hadn't known," by way of relieving his feelings. Stifled as it was, the expression did him good. He turned round again with only some spasmodic remains of that grin agitating the corners of his mouth.

"And you're going to marry? Any money—eh?" he said.

"I don't think it," said Horace—"but I should like to know your decision at once, for I have some arrangements to make."

"A thousand a-year for the whole term of your father's life? Why, I suppose he is no older than I am?— he may live for twenty years," said the unhappy lawyer, rubbing up the scanty hair upon his head.

"He may," said Horace, briefly; but, as he spoke, a terrible throb convulsed, in spite of himself, the young man's heart, upon which those deadly packets seemed to press like an intolerable weight.

"He may! And you ask me, a man in my senses, to undertake paying you an income of a thousand a-year for, perhaps, twenty years!"

"I ask you only to consider the matter, and what I might be able to do for you at the end of my probation," said Horace, loftily—"not to say my services for the present time. Don't do anything against your will. A lawsuit promoted by young Musgrave—by that time most likely my brother-in-law—would, I have no doubt, be quite as profitable to me."

The lawyer gave a gasp of rage and derision beyond words. "You could conduct it, you suppose?" he cried aloud—"you!"—which was very imprudent, but a burst of nature. Then he cooled himself down, with a little shiver of passion: he dared not irritate this remorseless, immovable boy.

"I could, easily, with all these facts in my possession," said Horace, with a careless gesture; and Mr. Pouncet saw his whole substance, his business, and, worst of all, his reputation, falling like so many card-houses at the touch of that unpitying hand.

But the interview did not end so. Mr. Pouncet consented at last, with many a grudge and inward compunction, to pay Horace the large stipend he claimed, on the tacit understanding that one-half of it was to be repaid to him when the young man came to his fortune; and the lawyer, though he had guessed rightly when he judged Mr. Scarsdale to be about his own age, notwithstanding, with the reckless boldness of humanity, began to reckon in his mind all the chances against the recluse's life. The wonder seemed to be that such a man, in such circumstances, could last so long: there could not be much vigour of existence left in him. A very short time now should surely make an end of these deplorable, hopeless years. So reckoned the lawyer, who cared nothing about Mr. Scarsdale; while that unhappy hermit's son, with all the desperation of an unnatural enmity, cherished a darker kind of speculation in his hard heart.

The conclusion of all was, however, that Mr. Pouncet wrote a placid business letter to Sir John Armitage, informing him that he had just dispatched a confidential clerk, in whom he could place the most perfect reliance, to make the fullest investigation throughout the district. Mr. Pouncet very much regretted that Sir John could not furnish him with particulars, or indeed any clue whatever to the name and residence of the suspected old man; but had every confidence, if there was any such person, in the abilities of his clerk, who would leave no means untried for finding him out.

Sir John thought this epistle so completely satisfactory, that he forwarded it to Colonel Sutherland, with some uncomplimentary suggestions about a "cock-and-a-bull story," and feminine powers of imagination, which the Colonel did not read to Susan; and all the parties concerned were comfortably lulled out of their anxiety by the prospect of so complete an investigation. What might not be hoped from the researches of Mr. Pouncet's confidential clerk?

CHAPTER XIII

While the simple household at Milnehill felicitated itself on the reality of the search about to be made, Mr. Pouncet's confidential clerk left Kenlisle. Horace went slowly through the country, though he was not looking for any one. He did his journey on foot, and did it by very slow and gradual degrees— perhaps to favour slightly his worthy employer's fiction of a search, but in reality playing with, resisting by fits, yet always entertaining, the horrible attraction which drew him to Marchmain. He had nothing to do there which could give him a pretence of a lawful visit. The last time he had gone like a thief into his father's house, anxious to search into the secrets there; this time how was he going?—in pretended friendship, or in open war? He could not tell. He only knew that a fascination too strong for him drew him on and on, though he fluttered in many a circle, prolonging his way, like a charmed bird, towards that house which contained the father of his life and the obstacle to his happiness. As he walked sullenly through these well-remembered paths, hovering round the borders of that moor which in May, sunshine, and daylight, a man with such black thoughts might well have feared to enter, he seemed to see perpetually before him, as in a picture, that pale spare figure in the dressing-gown—that formal attenuated man who sat by the polished dining-table, with his glass of purple claret, his two tall candles, and his reading-desk. Was that dismal existence life? Was there any pleasure in it to the forlorn endurer of all these nights and days? Would there be any cruelty in hastening his withdrawal from this bitter and impoverished existence? The questions formed dimly, and died away without articulate answer in the mind of his son. He wanted to persuade himself, as he gradually neared the climax of his temptation and of his fate, that he came with no object, but simply because curiosity drew him to the old house, to see how things were going on there.

Horace came upon Marchmain from behind, on an afternoon of May. The moor was no wilderness at that season. The whins were burning under the sunshine, the heather blooming purple and fragrant, thrusting its flowery spires against the foot that disturbed their growth; and the young seedlings, sown here and there in little clumps, waved their delicate young leaves to the soft air, and glittered in the light with a genial spring triumph over the intractable soil. Even the dark moorburns and rivulets of water in the deep cuttings caught a grace from the sky, and brightened over their brown surface with a gleam of the blue heavens and white clouds above. Everything was sweet, and bright, and hopeful in that dull waste of unproductive soil, which at other times could look so dreary. The clump of firs on the hill-top looked down wistfully, no longer weird spies, but gentle gazers upon the changed scene. But no change had passed upon Marchmain. The house, if any thing, was a little more lonely than of old, betraying unconsciously that some of the little life it had, had ebbed out of it. Susan's flowerpots stood naked in the window, with withered stalks of plants, long since dead, standing up dead and dismal from the dry mould in which they had once grown; left here by Peggy as a grim reminder to her master of the daughter—the only chance of love and kindness which he had remaining in the world—whom he had thrust remorselessly away; and with that calm sky declining towards evening, the sun slanting westward, the home-going hour lengthening its shadows over the long stretches of moorland, where by-and-bye a few labouring men should cross the sunlight to cottages clustered somewhere on the road, hid in the lower nooks of the hills, few objects more desolate and solitary than the house of Marchmain could have been imagined. Human step or human shadow was not near. The undisturbed heather almost brushed against the step of the door. In most of the windows the blinds were down, as though the heart within was too sick to bear the light. This was how Horace found the house which had nursed his childhood and imprisoned his youth.

When the young man essayed to enter at the kitchen door, he found even that entrance, once hospitably ajar, now closed and bolted. He had scarcely courage to seek admittance boldly. He hovered about, making a faint noise among the rustling herbage and broken stones, enough in that solitude to bring Peggy peering to the kitchen window. Peggy had changed for the worse, like the house. She looked, at last, as if patience and strength were being exhausted out of her: her eyes were peevish and dilated, with dark rings round them; and she looked out with a keen, suspicious glance, as if even confidence in her own powers—that last stronghold—was failing her. When she saw Horace, a softening sentiment came over Peggy's face: she came softly to open the door to him, and brought him into the kitchen, without a word either of welcome or comment. Then she wheeled her own cushioned chair out of the immediate range of the fire, and half led, half forced him into it. "You'll be tired," said Peggy, under her breath, with a tear twinkling bright in the corner of her eye. The surprise overcame her for the moment, and made her forget the sad difference between Susan's brother and Susan herself.

And Horace, too, for that instant was not like the Horace of old times. He was subdued by his own thoughts. An involuntary tremor seized him, to think of the dark purpose in his mind, and of why he had obtruded himself into this melancholy-familiar house. He could have supposed that his dreadful secret impulse—the horrible secret instruments he carried about with him—were betrayed and visible to any eye that looked keenly at him. But Peggy did not look keenly; she faltered with a real emotion at the sight of him, and he trembled before her salutation with an intense anguish and remorse, of which he could not have supposed himself capable. Warnings sharp and terrible, of the remorse not to be removed, which should cling for ever to the traces of the deed done; but Horace shut his eyes to that consideration. In another moment he was fully himself—recovered from his rare and strange qualm of feebleness—pleased to find, in Peggy's softened mood, no suspicion of him or his intentions, and resolved to make the most of that unusual grace.

"I came to see how you were. How is he, Peggy?" said Horace, pointing to the door which opened into the hall.

"Speak low!—oh! speak low, for your life!" cried Peggy, in a whisper. "If he knowed I let you into this house he would murder me!"

"I should like to see him try," said Horace, grimly, with a smile over the fantastic idea; that, indeed, would be a better mode of removing this hindrance than any expedient he could devise. "He hates me so, does he?" he added, with a white smile of enmity. He was glad to hear of it—it spurred him to a passionate emulation in that unnatural art.

"'Tis himsel' he hates and mortifies—the Lord forgive him!" cried Peggy. "Eyeh, Master Horry, if you knowed the wreck and the ruin that the devil, and pride, and ill-will have made of that man!"

"I daresay he has not much pleasure in his life?" said Horace, half interrogatively.

"Pleasure! I'm the auldest friend he has in this world, though I'm but a servant," said Peggy, her eyes dilating still more with tears, which did not flow, but only reddened and expanded the limits which they filled; "but there's scarce an hour in the day, nor a day in the year, but I would see him die sooner than live as he's living now."

"You speak," said Horace, playing with his own self-terror, and turning a pale, ominous look upon her, before which she shrank instinctively, "as if you thought it would be a charity to rid him of his life."

"Eh, Mr. Horry?—the Lord forgive ye! Would you put such an accursed thought on me?" cried Peggy, with an ebullition of violence as tearful and faltering as her kindness. "God help us, master and servant, two lone people, without comfort in this world! But it would be a new sight, and a strange sight, to see comfort come from you."

"Why, Peggy, you said as much," said Horace, with momentary weakness.

"Then, I tell you, sir, murder's no charity," said Peggy, sharply. "I've little pleasure in my life by what I had in my young days, but I would have died more cheerful then nor now; and the master takes grit care, moor care nor I ever knew him take before, of his health and strength, as behoves a man at his time of life. He's aye at his medicine-chest off and on; and has the doors bolted and pistols in his room, for fear of robbers, though I'm aye saying there's no robbers like to come here. He's afflicted his flesh in the times that are past, but he's a careful liver now."

"That he may keep me a little longer out of my inheritance," said Horace, between his teeth.

Peggy stopped short in the middle of the kitchen, where she had been hastily laying out a rapidly prepared meal for her master's son.

"Keepin' ye out of what?" she said solemnly, and with a scared look in her eyes.

"Of my inheritance—it's no use humbugging me any longer," said Horace—"I know it all."

Peggy set down the dish she had in her hands, dropped upon the stool before the fire, and throwing her apron over her head, rocked herself for a few moments back and forward, in silence.

"Amen! it ought to have comed sooner; it must have comed some time," said Peggy at last to herself; "but the Lord forgive me, didn't I say and prophesy that when wance the bairns knowed it the end would come? Oh, Mr. Horry! for the love of God and your mother, if you have any love in you, go your ways, and tarry not a moment in this doomed house."

"You are not very charitable, Peggy," said Horace, who, by some diabolical impulse, began to recover his spirits at this stage of the interview; "especially as I presume your preparations were for me—and I'm rather hungry. You can't surely refuse me a dinner, if it is in the kitchen, in my father's house?"

Peggy rose without a word, and placed bread and ale on the table beside the little dish of meat which she had abstracted from her master's dinner for his son's benefit.

"Eat, if ye can eat in this house and with sitch thoughts," said Peggy; "but I crave of ye to give God thanks ere ye break the bread."

As Peggy stood over him, severe and disapproving, the remembrance of many such scenes in his childhood came to the memory of Horace; scenes in which Susan appeared, sweetly saying her child's grace, and he himself rebelling and refusing, with Peggy standing by exactly as she did now—her judicial eye fixed sternly on him. He was a man now, and had bigger rebellions in hand. With a little sneer and levity in that momentary diabolical exhilaration of spirits, he said the child's grace which Peggy herself had taught him nearly twenty years ago. When he had repeated the amen, his father's faithful servant turned away from him to go about her needful business, for it was drawing near to Mr. Scarsdale's dinner hour. But Horace put down his knife and fork upon his plate with a shudder of self-horror—the food choked him—he could not swallow the bread on which his lips, without any help from his heart, had dared at that terrible moment to ask God's blessing. The time of opportunity, which he tried to persuade himself he did not premeditate, but which was forcing itself upon him, approached moment by moment. He got up from the table with a nervous, imperceptible trembling, and went to stand by the fire where Peggy was busy, and then to wander through the apartment, always restlessly returning to that bright spot. An impulse of flight seized him at one moment—at another, a wild thought of thrusting himself into his father's very presence, by way of escaping the devil within him, and rather getting into hot words and a violent contest than this miserable guilt. But while he was at the height of his horrible excitement, Peggy, calmly doing her usual business, went out of the kitchen to spread the table in her master's lonely dining-room. Horace, wild as in a fever, drew with trembling hands out of his pocket one of his mysterious packets. He burst the paper open clumsily, awkwardly, with fingers which seemed made of lead. A great shower of white powder fell upon the floor at his feet, but none reached the dish to which he supposed he had directed it. Trying to remedy this failure, he was startled by a sound, as of Peggy's return. With a great start, which spilt still more of that fatal dust, he thrust it back into his breast, and in a horror of discovery snatched at something near him, he could not see what it was, and swept into the fire that evidence of his purpose. Having done, or thinking that he had done this, he threw the cloth out of his hands into the fire, and rushed out of the room and the house. As he escaped he saw somehow, by virtue of his passion and fever of overpowering excitement, Peggy coming quietly with a napkin over her arm, and her great white apron shining through the obscurity of the narrow passage, into the kitchen. That home figure, in its everyday occupation, struck him bitterly in his own tremor; he had failed, but he was guilty. No harm to his father had the parricide left behind him, but he was his father's murderer in his own heart; and all the world and all its riches could never make of him again the same Horace Scarsdale who scowled sullen but innocent upon that same Peggy, before the baleful knowledge for which he thirsted had scorched all nature out of his heart.

CHAPTER XIV

Horace never knew how he passed that night; during the twilight and the early darkness he hovered about the moor, lying down among the fragrant heather, when now and then for a moment he could keep still, and feeling the penetrating damp of the bog steal into his limbs, and the dark, noiseless prick of the whin bushes, startling him into energy as he rose out of that feverish, momentary rest. When the night had quite fallen—a dark summer night, soft, but gloomy, with a few faint stars, but no moon—he stole once more, circling and sweeping about the house, towards Marchmain; for no purpose, only to look in at the uncurtained window, and see sitting there in his utter solitude the formal figure, erect and motionless, which had shadowed, like a baleful tree, all his own young life. There he sat, a little turned aside from his familiar position at the head of the table, as though even he was glad to seek a little companionship in the morsel of evening fire which Peggy lighted in silent compassion every night; with his little reading-desk upon the table, and his glass of claret reflected in that shining surface, and the two tall candles lighting his white, worn visage, and the open page. There he sat, reading like an automaton, turning the leaves at regular intervals, doing the business to which he enforced himself, with his pale fingers and his rigid face. To think that one wicked, lawful expression of a dead man's will could have drained the humanity thus out of one who was a woman's husband and the father of children, when that devilish stroke smote him in full career! The woman was dead ages since, and the children banished; and dead down in its miserable solitude had stiffened that vexed heart. Did he ever have a heart, that dismal man, at his dreary occupation, forlorn by the evening fire?—or was this life which he lived, hugging to his bosom through all these years that big wrong which he had made the pivot of his impoverished existence? Who could tell? but there might, at least, have been pity in the kindred eyes which watched him through that melancholy night.

There was no pity, however, in the eyes of Horace: when his first guilty fear of being discovered was over, he stood and gazed, with a burning, steady gaze, upon his enemy. Years and days of his own existence rose before Horace as he looked; he heard himself once more addressed with that killing politeness which murdered nature in him; he saw himself once more lowering in a fierce, unnatural restraint at that same miserable table, cursing, and not blessing, the very bread he ate. He saw Susan's head drooping, in timid and terrified silence, opposite that lonely man. Had there been heart or hope in him, would he have banished the harmless girl, to whom Horace did contemptuous justice for once in his life? And as the young man gazed the fire burned. For a moment he seemed to see, by a better revelation, all the injury—a thousand times worse than disinheritance—which his father had done him; and became aware furiously, without regretting it, by some extraordinary magic of hatred, of his own unlovely character, the malicious creation of his father's cruelty. These were dreadful thoughts; but he did not seek to get rid of them—rather encouraged the baleful imagination, and wrapped himself in its hostile suggestions. Nature! that was abrogated long ago by Mr. Scarsdale's own words. They were rivals to the death—nothing but the bitterest dislike and mutual enmity could exist between that father and son; and Horace felt himself acquitted from any tie of nature by the thought.

While he stood thus, watching, Mr. Scarsdale, innocent of any enemy at the window, put up his hand to his head for a few minutes, as if in suffering, and then, rising, left the room. When he entered again he carried in his hand a mahogany box, bound with brass, not unlike a small desk. Horace, who watched all his proceedings keenly, with excited attention, saw him take out a vial, hold it up to the light, and then measure out for himself a minute dose of the medicine it contained. With eyes that burned through the darkness, Horace watched and noted. The box was left standing by his father's side on the table—where had he brought it from? The young man watched and waited, shivering for long hours, till Mr. Scarsdale's time for retiring came. Then he followed eagerly with his eyes the ghostly figure which glided out of the room, with the box under one arm. The light reappeared a few minutes after in the window of Mr. Scarsdale's bedroom, into the secrets of which he had no power of spying. Then he wandered away blindly over the invisible heather, feeling nothing of the pricks that caught him on every side, insensible to the fresh night breezes blowing about his cheeks, unthinking where he went. When the morning came he could have fancied that he had slept there, so profound was his miserable preoccupation. But he had not slept there. The other man within him had struck out resolutely across the night, and gained shelter in a roadside public-house, from whence it was, refreshed and resolute, that he now came.

That same afternoon Horace once more essayed an entrance at Marchmain. Peggy received him with a suspicious face, but thrust him into the kitchen with a haste and force which betrayed to Horace that, as once before, her master was out, and everything propitious for him. He asked the question hurriedly.

"What does the like of you want here, Mr. Horry, two days running?" said the startled woman; "and what's your business if he's out or in? I tauld ye last time, and ye know what came o't. It's no' your meaning that you came to see him, like a dutiful son?"

"No, Peggy; but only to look for something I want in my old room. I confess I got frightened yesterday," said Horace, with a grim, and somewhat tremulous smile. "I had no desire to meet him, fierce and furious as he used to be, or polite, which is worse. I ran away: but to-day you will surely let me go upstairs?"

"And what for," said Peggy, steadily fixing her eyes on his face, "did you throw yon napkin in the fire?"

Horace grew pale in spite of himself. "A napkin? Did I throw it in the fire? I was not aware of it," he said, with all the boldness he could muster. "However, let me go upstairs."

Peggy looked at him, and shook her head. "Ye'll be a-going and rummaging again," she said, with a voice of grieved uncomprehension. She had brought him up, and her heart warmed to him, unlovable as he was.

"I tell you I have found out everything. What should I rummage for?—and a great deal of good it is to me, now I know all," said Horace, in a tone more natural than Peggy had yet heard from his lips. "Go you and watch, Peggy, and let me know when my father appears."

Peggy followed him mournfully. Still, shaking her head, she went in after him with suspicion, and looked round the bare walls of his old room. "I'm bound to say I can see nowght to look for here," said Peggy, sharply; but, after another inspection, she went reluctantly up to her watch-tower—the store-room—to look for her master's approach. Whenever she was gone, Horace stole noiselessly as a ghost into his father's apartment. It was not a murderous light that shone from the May skies into that room, the most comfortable in the house—but the young felon had night and darkness in his face. The box stood on the dressing-table, beside that chair of Mr. Scarsdale's, in which some malicious ghost might have sat, it looked so occupied and observant. With a trembling yet rapid hand, Horace opened the box, and took out of it the little phial which he had seen his father use. It was carefully closed, with a piece of pink leather tied over the cork, and a very peculiar knot, which Horace, with his excited fingers, found great difficulty in opening. When he had succeeded, he poured out its contents, and replaced them from another of his own sealed packets. He did this mechanically and methodically, but with the cold dew bursting on his face, and his fingers, in their haste and tremble, fumbling over the knot, which he did not seem able to tie as it was before. When he had replaced it, and closed the box, he stood, trembling and miserable, looking at it. He could not tell whether he had placed the phial exactly as it was before: the box now would not close perfectly, and he could not remember, with his scared and desperate wits, whether it had been so when he opened it. At last, impatient, he put down the lid violently, with a jar which startled him into a fever of apprehension. Somebody must have heard it!—it went through his own head and heart with a thrill of terror. Then he skulked out, with that stealthy horror in his face which should henceforward be the prevailing sentiment of Horace Scarsdale's unhappy countenance. Twice a parricide!—without calling Peggy from her watch, or daring to look in her face, he stole out the back-way from his father's house, leaving Death and Murder there!

A week after, Mr. Pouncet's confidential clerk returned to Kenlisle. He was restless, and deadly pale, and went to his desk to look for letters with a horrible anxiety. There were no letters there; and he turned out again with a breathless flutter of excitement to see his principal, and speak as he best could about business. But neither Mr. Pouncet nor any other person had heard anything from Marchmain, and Horace went out again in a miserable fever, which all his efforts could not quite conceal. He had laid the train; but heaven knows how long it might smoulder before the spark was set to that thread of death!

CHAPTER XV

While these dark elements of tragedy were gathering about the lonely house of Marchmain, things went on very cheerfully in Milnehill, where everybody was vaguely encouraged by the idea of the investigation going on which might restore some wreck of fortune to the young Rifleman; and where a still more engrossing pursuit reconciled that hero himself to the necessity of waiting for news of this possible enrichment. Roger, who had no great hopes on the subject, bore the suspense with the greatest patience, and never, indeed, showed the least signs of anxiety, except when it seemed likely that a word or two of lamentation over his fate would call forth the compassion of the ladies—which compassion was very sincere on Susan's part, and good-humouredly satirical on that of Mrs. Melrose. "It's easy to see the poor young man's losing heart altogether with this waiting," the old lady would say with much gravity; "for you see, Susan, my dear, it's not to be expected that he can find anything here to amuse him, poor man, seeing nothing but two old people and a quiet little girl like you." Mrs. Melrose had quite taken up her abode at Milnehill since Roger's arrival. She said it was good for her health to smell the chestnut blossoms, and overlook Uncle Edward's gardening—and a very cheerful and lively addition she made to the happy house.

One morning, however, the quiet progress of affairs was interrupted by a letter, which Roger read not without a little agitation at the breakfast-table. When he had come to the end he handed it over suddenly, with a slight impetuous impulse, to the Colonel, who took it with his usual kind look of serious attention, put on his spectacles immediately, and addressed himself to the perusal of the letter with much gravity and earnestness. It was from Roger's mother, and written partly under the inspiration of little Edmund, messages from whom were mixed with everything the timid woman said—

"MY DEAREST BOY—Your dear letter and the news of your arrival brought the greatest pleasure I have known for many a long day, though it came in the midst of great trouble, my dear Mr. Stenhouse having been buried just a few days before; a very great affliction, which I trust, for all your sakes, my dear boy, yours and little Edmund's, and your dear sisters', I shall have strength to bear. Little Edmund interrupts me to say—and I must give you the very words of his message, or he will not be pleased—that, please, you're to come home directly, and that his papa has left him a great deal of money, and he means to give you half of it, and wants so very, very much to see his brother Roger. My own boy, I must ask you to be very good to dear little Edmund; he has been such an invalid, the dear child, that everybody has always yielded to him all his life, and he does love you so! Since ever he could speak he has kept on entreating me to tell him of his brother Roger, and he thinks there is not such another in the world; and he is very good, the dear little fellow, when he is not in pain, and one takes a little care and knows his way. However, I have something to tell you besides. The day before yesterday along with your letter there came a letter to my dear Mr. Stenhouse, which Edmund opened before I saw what he was doing. Edmund tells me to say that he does so hope you will come soon to see the cricketing in Leasough Park; and he thinks if you would join the Leasough eleven—Leasough is a village two miles off, where we always go for our drive, and where everybody knows Edmund—they would be sure to win. But about Mr. Pouncet's letter, my dear son. It seemed written in a great fright, saying that Sir John Armitage had written to him something about you, and what should he do?—and speaking in a very improper manner, actually cursing the day he did something, which it seems my dear Mr. Stenhouse must have known of, and asking that young Mr. Scarsdale, Colonel Sutherland's nephew, who seemed to know about it too, might be sent to Kenlisle at once. Edmund said, 'Mamma, send for Mr. Scarsdale directly' (he is so clever, the dear child), and so I did. But I must first go back to tell you that my dear Mr. Stenhouse himself had sent for young Mr. Scarsdale, and spoke with him in private, and charged him, as I heard with my own ears—dear Julius being taken very bad, and not knowing what he said—that 'the boy was not to know'—just the day before his death. When Mr. Scarsdale came, I am sorry to say he was not so polite as I should have expected from Colonel Sutherland's nephew, and would not tell either Edmund or me anything, but rather sneered at my poor child, and went off all in haste, keeping the letter in his hand. I should have sent it to you if he had not taken it away. Now, I do not know what this may mean—nor can it be expected that Edmund should, as he is only a child; but both he and I, my dear boy, beg of you to ask the Colonel what he thinks, and to try to find out yourself. And whatever you do, dear, don't trust to that Mr. Pouncet; for it was quite clear to me by his letter that he had somehow done you wrong, and wanted to conceal it. Edmund says, 'Tell Roger, mamma, he's not to trust Scarsdale either;' but indeed I scarcely have the heart to say so, remembering that he's the dear good Colonel's nephew—only he was not so kind as he might have been, you know, and I have some reason to think he is fond of Amelia—which should surely keep him from doing anything that would harm her brother.

"But, my dearest boy, come home. I have not seen you—my son—my baby—my first-born!—for so many years, and my heart yearns for a sight of you. Oh, come to me! Let me see you under my own roof! Roger—my son—my dear boy—come home to your mother! There is no other friend who can have so close a claim upon my darling child!

"Always your loving mother, "A. STENHOUSE."

"You will go at once?" said the Colonel, with some gravity, as he gave the letter back into Roger's hand.

Go at once! The words rung upon Susan's ear like a cannon-shot. She turned her blue eyes with a look of amazed alarm from her uncle to Roger; then she became suddenly very much busied with the duties of the breakfast table, swallowing down, as a very attentive observer might have noticed, something in her throat, and carefully keeping her eyes upon her tea-pot and coffee-pot. Roger had made no answer as yet. While the Colonel inclined his ear attentively across the table for the young man's reply, Roger was studying Susan's face; and it is not hard to explain that common paradox of youthful nature, which made Susan's silent signs of sudden disappointment and vexation the most exhilarating sight in the world to the young Rifleman. While Uncle Edward listened, and heard nothing, and fancied his own deaf ear in fault, Roger, quite otherwise occupied—thinking, it is to be feared, not much about his mother, and nothing at all about Mr. Pouncet—concentrated all his faculties on the honest face of Susan, with its womanly but unconcealable dismay.

"Eh, Musgrave?" said the Colonel, stooping towards his young guest, and putting up his kind hand over his deaf ear.

"I suppose so, sir," said Roger, in high spirits. Then, after a little pause, with sham sentiment, got up simply as a trap for Susan—"If one could only find out the secret of ubiquity, so that one might be able to content one's mother, and enjoy one's self, at the same time."

Yielding to this temptation, Susan glanced up at the young hero for a moment, with some tender tearfulness about her eyes; but, finding nothing but triumph and delight in his, returned, disgusted, and much more inclined to cry than before, to the contemplation of her coffee-pot.

"One may manage that, I hope, without any ubiquity," said the Colonel, still very gravely; for the old soldier was moved too seriously by this letter to notice the by-play of the youthful drama going on under his eyes. "But I am surprised you are not more excited by your mother's communication, Roger. My dear fellow, it is quite evident now that there must be something in it; and a pretty person to conduct an investigation this Pouncet must be, after what you have just heard. Why, to be sure, referring the search to a guilty party is the very way to keep ourselves in darkness. I'll tell you what, Musgrave; if you do not see after it at once, I shall take the liberty of constituting myself your guardian, and set out to-day."

Roger stretched out his hand to meet that of Colonel Sutherland, who had gradually warmed as he spoke. "Amen," said the young man. "Till I can persuade some still kinder and fairer hand to assume the reins, I could not have any guardian I should like so well."

"Pshaw!" said Uncle Edward, awakening to the fact that his young guest was speaking at Susan much more than to himself—"never mind fairer hands. What do you mean to do?"

Upon which, Roger perceiving that his last shot had taken due effect, grew serious all at once.

"It does look at last as if there was something in it," he said. "I have thought all along that if any mischief had been done Pouncet must have known of it; and he was a man of such character! I cannot think yet how it is possible that he could put himself or his reputation in danger to defraud me;—but certainly," continued Roger, growing rather red and wrathful, "the pretence of a sham investigation and a confidential clerk—"

"Ah!" cried Uncle Edward, with a sharp short exclamation like a sudden pang—"most likely it was—well, well, well!—we cannot help it; it is to his own Master that each of us standeth or falleth: let us not blame till we know."

"Uncle," said Susan in alarm, coming round to his side and sliding her hand into his, "it is something about Horace?—something more?"

"No, my love, nothing more—nothing at all that one could build upon," said the Colonel tenderly; "only I rather fear, Susan, as we both did when you came first to Milnehill, that Horace knows of some injury which has been done to Roger, and yet does not let him know."

Susan made a momentary pause of shame and distress as her uncle spoke, and then raised her eyes, full of tears and entreaty, to Roger's face. Poor Susan believed that these tears were all about her brother, and would not have acknowledged that a single drop of that gentle rain had relation to the "going away" with which this conversation arose.

Roger, however, could not bear these tears. He put his mother's letter hastily into her hand—would she read it? There was really nothing blaming Mr. Scarsdale, as she would see. And Susan stood shy and tearful, with the paper trembling in her hand—a maidenly, womanly, natural restraint forbidding her to read, while her heart yearned, notwithstanding, towards Roger's mother; while Roger kept looking at her with anxious eyes, as earnest to have her read it as though his fate depended on the issue. Did either of them think of Horace in connection with this letter? or what, between these two young dreamers, trembling on the edge of their romance, was Colonel Sutherland, with very serious thoughts in his mind and matters in his hand, to do? He got up after a few minutes waiting, with good-humoured impatience.

"Boys and girls," said Uncle Edward, "with all their life before them, like you young people, may waste a few hours of it without much harm done; but what I have to do must be done quickly. Make up your mind, Roger, my good friend; but as for me, I am going off to Armitage by the first train. Susan, my love, Mrs. Melrose will stay with you; for this young fellow's interests, you see, must be looked after, whether he wishes it or not—especially, my dear"—and Uncle Edward's kind face grew darker as he made that significant pause.

"Especially if Horace has had any share in it," cried Susan. "Oh, Mr. Musgrave!" and a few tears fell suddenly over Roger's mother's letter. The Colonel at the moment had stepped out of the room to give his instructions to Patchey, and Susan's one sole remaining intention, on which all her mind was fixed, was to rush after him; but that involuntary turn of her head and exclamation of her lips sealed Susan's fate. Roger was not the man to let slip so advantageous a moment—and had things to do of more importance than packing his portmanteau before he left Milnehill.

CHAPTER XVI

Colonel Sutherland and his young friend, who had by this time something to communicate which the discreet old soldier was perhaps not unprepared to hear, left Edinburgh that evening by the earliest train they could get which stopped anywhere near Armitage Park. The Colonel was most seriously in earnest, entirely occupied with the new position of affairs; while Roger, quickened by the change in his own personal circumstances, speculated a little on this new possibility of improving his fortune, and was exceedingly well content to dream of endowing Susan with something more than the old Grange, the empty and miserable condition of which came dolefully on his memory, now that he and his home were likely to have a lawful mistress. As they travelled, the Colonel exhausted himself in inquiries and suggestions as to what this hidden business could be, touching on every mode known to his innocence, by which an attorney could defraud a client, but of course never approaching within a thousand miles of the one method in which this attorney had succeeded in defrauding his; while Roger listened in a happy mist, half hearing—dwelling in his own mind on the plea he had already won, in the most arbitrary court in existence, and feeling the other plea important in consequence; but light, light and trivial, after all, a feather to his happiness. Thus they went on, very good companions, to Armitage, where Sir John received them with open arms; and in spite of all Colonel Sutherland's resistance, kept them four-and-twenty hours without doing anything. This delay postponed the execution of their business for a longer space than twenty-four hours, and produced other results not less important; for it left Horace time, in his restless wretchedness, to set out once more to Harliflax.

If Horace Scarsdale had encountered his uncle there, the chances are that he would have found very little difficulty in betraying his "friend" and principal. The young man had miscalculated the magnitude of those affairs in which he had embroiled himself. He knew well enough that there was nothing soft or sentimental, and not very much of human impressionable stuff in his own nature, but he did not know that a mind inaccessible to compassion or sympathy may still be desperately alive to all the selfish horrors of remorse and guilt, and that not even the promised income of a thousand a-year which he had forced from Mr. Pouncet's fears and hopes, or the expectation which he entertained of being able to persuade Amelia Stenhouse into an immediate marriage, could make him insensible to that dread horror of suspense in which he lived. There were no letters, no newspaper paragraphs, or country intimation of a sudden death—darkness and silence immovable had dropped like a veil over all that district which enclosed Marchmain. Every day and every night Horace could see that wild stretch of moorland brooding under its dismal sky; and there was scarcely a moment, sleeping or waking, in which his guilty imagination ceased to dwell in his father's lonely house. Had he met Colonel Sutherland in this miserable crisis of his affairs, the chances are that Horace would gladly have given a sop to his fevered conscience by telling all he knew of Mr. Pouncet's fraud. As it was, possessed with a restlessness which he could not subdue, he returned to Harliflax, the only other place in the world where he could find even a temporary interest—resisting, with all the strength he still could muster, the dread curiosity which drew him to Marchmain.

Mr. Pouncet accordingly was alone when Sir John Armitage, the Colonel, and Roger made an unexpected descent upon him. There was nothing to frighten a good dissembler in the entire three of them, honest sincere souls each in their way, who came here with suspicion, it is true, yet had a natural habit of believing what was said to them. Mr. Pouncet played his part very well. Knowing that his letter itself was out of their power, and could not be brought against him, he made his defence lightly. A lady's mistake, a thing most easily explained:—he had indeed written to his friend Stenhouse about some private matters of business, and his wife had made a woman's blunder about it, knowing nothing of business, and supposing, of course, that there could be no Musgrave in the world but her son. Of course Sir John might be perfectly assured that he should take every possible step to ascertain anything affecting Mr. Musgrave's interests—indeed, was not the late Mr. Musgrave his client? And now especially, when his own honour was involved, his exertions should be redoubled; he had already sent his confidential clerk—

Here Colonel Sutherland interrupted the fluent speaker: "Did the confidential clerk, whom you sent to make inquiries, happen to be my nephew, Horace Scarsdale?" asked the old soldier.

"Your nephew!" Mr. Pouncet stood dismayed. "The young man's name was certainly Scarsdale," he said, after a little puzzled pause.

"Then I have no doubt that accounts for the failure of the investigation," said the Colonel, who had been bending his deaf ear to the wily attorney with an earnest attention, strangely out of keeping with the insincere and untrustworthy voice to which he listened. "Much grief as it gives me to say so, Armitage, I am afraid Horace would hinder rather than help. I don't know how he has mixed himself up with such an affair," said Uncle Edward, musing; "but he certainly has to do with it somehow. He's—alas! very clever, this nephew of mine; unhappily brought up, poor fellow! fond of intrigue, I fear, one kind or another. Mr. Pouncet, I'd recommend you to employ another man."

"With the greatest of pleasure," said Mr. Pouncet, chuckling to himself; "of course, I yield any little knowledge I may have of young Scarsdale to the superior information of a relative—ha, ha! Your candid judgment does you credit, I am sure, Colonel. Mr. Scarsdale is not here to-day, I am sorry to say; very unsettled lately he has appeared to me. Ah, come in, Edwards! I've some instructions to give you before these gentlemen. We will lose no time, Sir John, and you shall hear my directions with your own ears."

"That'll do, Pouncet" said Sir John, with a slight air of disgust. "My own opinion is, you're a deal too easy in your talk to mean anything. Hope you don't know any more about it than you choose to tell us, which appears to me, begging your pardon, a long way more likely than not; for who's to cheat a man if it isn't his own attorney? Send your clerk if you like, I'll have nothing to do with it. If one wants a thing well done, one must do it oneself. Come along, Sutherland; no, I'm not satisfied, and I don't pretend to be."

Saying which, in spite of Mr. Pouncet's strenuous endeavours to explain, and to set himself right with his wealthy client, Sir John fought his way out, dragging along with him his young and his old friend. The Colonel looked very grave and rather sad, wondering what "motive" Horace could have for helping to injure Roger. Meanwhile, that young hero himself took, it is to be confessed, more amusement than anything else from the entire matter. His hopes were so slight that they did not at all excite him, whereas he could not but perceive that Sir John's little burst of ill-humour, and Mr. Pouncet's discomfiture thereat, was tolerably good fun. They went to the inn to have lunch, all three displaying their various humours—of which Sir John's was the most demonstrative and plain-spoken.

"I'll tell you what," said the baronet; "Pouncet's a deal too well up in his defence. I never like a man who knows just exactly what to say for himself when he's accused of a sudden—ten chances to one, look you, Roger, that he's guilty; for if he's guilty, of course he knew every word you were going to say—whereas if he's innocent, he's taken by surprise and shows it. That's my opinion; and, by Jove, if the rascal took in Musgrave, I'll bet you something he's taken in me as well. But you may rely upon it I'll have the whole affair looked into now."

"Eh?" said Colonel Sutherland, stooping over the chair into which Sir John had thrown himself, with his hand curved over his ear; "have the whole affair looked into now? Well, Armitage, if I have less concern in it one way than you, I have more another. There's still a week before my Ned comes home, I'll see what I can do with my own eyes and spectacles. I'm an old campaigner: twenty miles a day over a pleasant country is no extraordinary work for an old soldier like me."

"And I, Colonel—what am I to say to you for such painstaking kindness?" said Roger, forgetting his amusement in hearty gratitude and admiration.

"My dear boy, it's a great deal for your sake, but something for the sake of my sister's son," said the Colonel, with a smile and a sigh—"and only till my boy's holidays begin; but as for you, go on to whatever is the name of the place and see your mother, and the pretty sisters and the little boy, and if there's anything to be heard of Horace there, send me word; and don't forget if you do meet with him that he is, in spite of everything—"

"Susan's brother!—there is not a chance that I shall forget," said Roger, brightly.

Meanwhile Sir John, catching the sound of one word, which tickled the ear of his possessing demon, muttered to himself, "Pretty sisters!" Then added aloud, "Going to see your mother, Roger? Possibly she's got something further to tell us—I'll go too."

When Horace returned to Harliflax it was night—too late even for an accepted lover to gain admittance to the widowed house of Mrs. Stenhouse, and Horace was not even an openly accepted lover. These ten days had changed him greatly. This monstrous crime had indeed germinated in his mind from the very hour of his return from London; but that passion of temptation was very different from the horror of unbearable suspense and anxiety which consumed him now. While he was still only about to do it, his mind was buoyed up by a hideous fascination, which carried him over time and space as though upon a devil's wings. Now that he had done it, every hour was a staring, wide-eyed Medusa, watching and petrifying; and still, through the cold, creeping silence, there came no sound; no cry of the death-agony which he had contrived, nor shout of the avenger of blood behind; no sobbing forth of the dear life shed by his hands, and no cry of Murder! Murder!—only a convulsive whisper of the word among the grass and leaves, and secret spies of nature, which pricked him into madness, and turned the blood in his veins to fire. He was changed, imperceptibly to himself, but in the strangest way. Every day of this week in which he had been compassing his father's death had made him more like his father. His face had lost its colour and roundness—the soft outline of youth was gone; and in its place had come a sharpened distinction of feature, unusual at his years. His hair, which, to his great wonder, came out in handfuls when he dressed it, fell lank, like that of the recluse at Marchmain; and even his dress took the same resemblance, and flew back from his figure, as he went, with his restless haste of motion, from street to street. But the sneer and the disdain had almost gone out of Horace's face: he could no longer afford these light emotions. His whole soul was burnt up with passions more intense—self-horror—anxiety, more acute and devouring than ever was the anxiety of love, to know his father's fate; and, above all, that overpowering certainty of personal guilt, which all the world and all its powers could never again loosen from his self-convicted heart.

It was night, and nobody saw him. Few knew him, besides, in these streets of Harliflax. He rushed to his lodgings, and found there were no letters there; then out again, and did not draw breath till he stood in the dark, on the opposite side of the way, looking into the bright moonlight at the house where Amelia Stenhouse slept the untroubled sleep of youth. There he stood in the depth of the night-shadow, looking how the night-radiance and illumination of that weird moon brought out the long, lofty line of terrace, the line of great houses of which Harliflax was proud. The night was so bright, and the air so still, that one slow figure, gliding along there in front of the high, silent houses, was caught and wrapped in a silvery mantle, and drawn along noiselessly, like a pigmy, in the great flood of silent light. So white on that side of the road—so black here where he stood, among the shadows where the devils and lovers of darkness congregate. But, Amelia, which was she? He raised his eyes to the window which he knew was Amelia's, and tried to think of all the glories before him; fortune past counting, youth, love— nothing left out that was worth having, but—But!—that one miserable step out into the light across the blackness of darkness—the step which, God help his miserable brain, he was not about to take, but had taken, be the consequences what they might. When he thought of it there, opposite Amelia's window, standing in the darkness, his head swam and his tongue clove to his mouth. He had done it; he was not projecting, nor discussing, nor entertaining his subtle mind with the temptation; the temptation, with all its thrills of intoxicating excitement, its fascinations of fierce and hostile fancy—its wild impulses of passion—was over for ever, and for ever, and for ever!—and the victim, disenchanted, stood cold, looking always into the blanched face of the deed which he had done. And Horace could no longer think of Amelia; not of the delight of marrying, and carrying away, and making his own property of the beauty; not of the boundless wealth he should have to bestow on her one day; not of the thousand a-year which he believed would induce her to marry him immediately, and which for that sole reason, and no other, he had wrung out of Mr. Pouncet. He had pled his cause warmly with herself, and his love had blazed about her not so many days ago when he was at Harliflax; but he could not turn his thoughts to her now; he could not warm his torpid mind with remembering her beauty; he could not rouse his fierce animal passion. Something black and cold stood first in his mind between him and his fortune—between him and what he called happiness. Murder had overshadowed love, and killed it. He had no longer any thoughts to spare save for that horrible hag whom he had taken into his heart!

As he stood, however, thinking his own thoughts, it soon became vaguely visible to Horace that all was not entirely at rest in the house he was gazing at. Scarcely visible in the great flood of moonlight, there still was now and then the gleam of a light showing for a moment from one floor to another, as somebody went or came downstairs; and sounds began to be audible in the extreme stillness even where he stood. Shortly afterwards Stevens came to the door rubbing his eyes, and went down the street, with a sort of reluctant rapidity, to the doctor's house at the corner. Horace comprehended it as well as though he had been within and knew all. Edmund was ill. Death was not to be defrauded of that little victim: Edmund was going to die. When the servant came back with the doctor, Horace crossed the road and entered with them, nobody observing him in the excitement—entered he scarcely knew why, with a morbid craving after death and suffering. He was anxious to see how that child would meet the last adversary; curious to observe how the family would arrange itself around the deathbed of the little heir; the poor little heir! who had enjoyed for so short a time his childish importance, his eager liberality of intention. But Horace had no pity to spare for Edmund, or for any other person in the world.

Edmund Stenhouse was dying (as they thought) in the warm parlour where he had lived. He had been worse than usual for a day or two, and was laid there upon a sofa, so that he might not have the fatigue of removal; but though propped up with pillows, for the sake of his painful and hard breathing, he looked very little different from his usual condition. He was shouting out eagerly for pen and paper when Horace passed in at the door. He did not want the doctor; he would not be blistered any more, whatever the doctor said. He wanted somebody out of papa's office; he was going to make his will, and die.

"I tell you, mamma, I'm not going to take any more physic!" cried the poor child, thrusting aside with his hasty, feeble hand the glassful of some stimulating mixture which the anxious woman held to him. "I'm going to die! I tell you I've made up my mind!—what's the use of sending for doctors and stuff? Send for Scarsdale, or somebody. I'm going to make my will—I'm going to die!"

"I don't believe he is, though," said Horace, involuntarily coming forward, without very well knowing what he did. He was desperately interested, somehow, in this dread death which he had invoked. He was curious to see its workings, and how it approached; but he could not recognize that awful presence here.

Mrs. Stenhouse turned round with a little cry of recognition. There was a gleam of gratitude in her eyes: she could almost have taken into her arms the stranger who did not believe that Edmund was dying, and forgave Horace his former offences on the moment. "Oh, Mr. Scarsdale!—then you don't see a great difference in him?" cried the poor woman, with a flutter at her heart. She could take courage even from that feeble flicker of hope.

"Oh, here's Scarsdale," said Edmund, with a gasp of hard-drawn breath. "I want you to write out my will directly—directly, do you hear? because I'm going to die; you're to put it all down about me, Edmund Stenhouse, like papa's—I'd do it myself, only I can't write as well as a grown-up man; and I want to leave everything—except plenty of money for my mother and a little for the girls—to my brother Roger. Make haste, do you hear? because I'll die first if you don't be quick, and then what's the good of your coming here?"

"Humour him," said the doctor under his breath.

"Oh, doctor, is he so very, very bad?" cried poor foolish Mrs. Stenhouse, losing the morsel of heart she had picked up from Horace's words.

"He is very much excited—humour him," said the doctor authoritatively; "just now do exactly what he says. Thank heaven, there can't be much harm done in this way even by a spoiled child. The law don't recognize testators of ten years old."

"Doctor, go home to bed, and don't come if mamma should send for you again," said little Edmund; "I can die all the same without you looking at me; but first I'll make my will; I shall—and then I'll die; doctor, go home to bed."

"Thank you, I will," said the doctor, yawning; "but don't you be so very sure about dying, my young hero. I'll see him to-morrow, Mrs. Stenhouse. Mind what I say, humour him—he's very much excited, but he's no worse. Get him to sleep as soon as you can. Good night."

The doctor went away, and the unnecessary commotion subsided a little. The lingering housemaid went to bed, feeling somewhat defrauded of her tears, and tragically disappointed that the end was not coming to-night to poor little Edmund's tragi-comedy of life. So did Stevens, moralizing and very much disgusted at the interruption of his rest—"three nights all a-running!" said that injured man to himself, "and master, from he was took bad till he died, was only twenty-four hours;" while in the meanwhile a strange scene was taking place in the invalid's parlour. There, in the close stifling atmosphere and under the subdued sick-room light, sat Horace writing—Horace with murder in his heart and a personal burden too overpowering to allow him to remember the share he had taken in his employer's fraud, setting down mechanically, scarcely alive enough for a gleam of derision, the impotent will from the lips of that innocent, imperative, despotic child. Amelia herself had glanced into the room and withdrawn again contemptuously, without her lover perceiving her; but the youngest and gentlest of the three sisters was with Mrs. Stenhouse, to help her in her watching, and had already begun to slumber peacefully in a chair. The mother herself sat at the foot of the sofa watching her boy, with eyes enlarged and dilated by many a vigil, and by that constant fear and scrutiny of his face; while, propped up among his pillows, Edmund half sat, half lay, dictating, with many a digression, his arbitrary, generous intentions. The will was still incomplete, when sleep stole over the would-be testator. He drooped back among the cushions, and could no longer keep his fiery little eyes open. Was he dying with that last flutter of words, "my brother Roger," about his lips? No, only falling safe into the restless sleep of a sick child. When his sharp little voice had died away, and all was silent in the room, the two by his bedside looked strangely into each other's faces. What brought you here with your black thoughts, oh! dangerous, guilty man? He rose up alone in the still house inhabited of women, feeling for an instant a vague sensation of that power and freedom which the strong, unfettered by either law or virtue, may feel among the weak. What was to hinder him from ending by a touch that frail child's life?—he could have done it. What was to hinder him from going up in the darkness, and lifting out of her safe rest that beautiful Amelia? He stood looking for a moment at the timid woman before him, with a hundred suggestions and possibilities of additional guilt pricking him into life. What was it to him now what he did, he who had made the plunge and done the deepest crime of nature? But he only looked at her a moment, with a savage consciousness of his power to outrage and devastate; and then laughed a short wild laugh, and went out as suddenly as he had come. Poor Mrs. Stenhouse stole out to fasten the door after him, with a momentary sensation of relief, as though she had escaped from a wild beast; and, coming back again, relapsed into an anxious study once more of Edmund's little pale sharp face. Edmund's will, magnificent and powerless, his last toy and plaything, lay on the table beside him. Was Edmund to live or to die?

CHAPTER XVIII

A few days after this scene Roger Musgrave and Sir John Armitage arrived at Harliflax. Edmund was still living, and not less life-like than he had been for years, though his will was by this time signed and sealed. This will had been a ready means of renewing the flirtation, which was all the beautiful Amelia owned to maintaining with her father's clerk. Amelia was sadly tired of her mourning, and its inevitable decorums; she was glad to throw herself in Horace's way when he came to finish that child's will, which he did next morning, for Amelia's sake. Amelia wanted to ask him about this will; papa had been very unjust to the rest for Edmund's sake, and now somebody told her that the little wretch (though she was sure she had cried her eyes out about him, and hoped with all her heart he would get better) was making a will, leaving everything to mamma's son by her first marriage, whom none of them had ever seen. Was it true?—could a little spoiled monkey like that, only eleven years old, make a will?—had anybody any right to give papa's property away from his children? Mr. Scarsdale knew it was not of herself she was thinking, but poor Eliza and Fanny—what was to become of them if some one did not think of their interests?—for mamma cared for nothing in the world but little Edmund and her other son. All this flood of question and statement poured upon Horace, who incautiously set the beautiful doubter's mind at rest by telling her that Edmund's will was as useless as any other toy of Edmund's, if the child died. Horace proceeded immediately to enlarge upon his own prospects, and the income he had already secured, but Amelia's heart was shut against him. She was not more cruel or cold-blooded than a great many other people; she did not wish Edmund's death; but that being a thing which everybody calculated upon as "rather to be desired than otherwise for his own sake, poor child," Amelia's spirits rose a little with the idea of finding herself an heiress, and once more regaining command of the house. That sickly child made a vast difference in various matters to Amelia; without Edmund she could easily subdue her mother; with Edmund, she was only Mr. Stenhouse's eldest daughter, with two or three thousand pounds; but without him she was the mistress of a very pretty fortune. Perhaps it was not much wonder if the thoughts of the ambitious and uneducated young beauty availed themselves of this prospect without too much delicacy, and thrust Edmund out of the way. However, Horace found it very difficult to arrest her attention to the expression of his own wishes and arrangements. She was supremely indignant at the thought of anyone speaking to her of marriage at such a time. "Look at my mourning, Mr. Scarsdale, and think of Edmund, poor, dear fellow!" cried the virtuous Amelia. If Amelia came in for her proper share of papa's money, she saw no reason why she should make anything less than a very brilliant match. So after she had beguiled her tedium by means of Horace, as long as, in the circumstances of the house, that was permissible, she went away stately and affronted, though by no means casting him off even now. He was not afraid; he could not have been in less real alarm if she had been his wife, but he wanted sorely to get back to the old frenzy of his first love-passion; he wanted to linger about her and on her, and make sure that she belonged to him. For her and for fortune he had played these terrible stakes, which only he and God knew of; and it was tantalizing to have the prize of his wickedness drawn away from him, when, perhaps, if he but knew, the obstacle was removed already, and fortune incomprehensible and stupendous, big enough to have purchased twice an Amelia, was already in his hand.

But when Horace came next to the house he found a still greater barrier arisen between himself and Amelia. She no longer wanted to be amused—she was independent of him: he might come or he might go, and Amelia did not care. A new life had visited Mrs. Stenhouse's roof and family. Roger, the unknown brother, was there like a son at home, charming the little invalid, who had left all his wealth to him, out of the feverish excitement and unwholesome primary place, which were killing Edmund; warming his mother's heart into a late summer of peace and thankfulness; making himself acceptable even to the pretty sisters who admired him, and whom he admired. But it was not Roger who had displaced Horace with Amelia. A young man who was her brother, and, consequently, not to be fascinated, was of no account in the eyes of the beauty; but Sir John Armitage, if he was not very young, had many other qualities which made up for that want, and Sir John had already concluded to himself that he had seen no such fine woman since the days when he was young himself, and beauty was more abundant. Amelia did not lose an hour with the excellent baronet; she had not only baited the hook, but landed her fish long before anybody else suspected her; and as for Horace, though that pretty by-play roused another demon within him, he had still no suspicions of Amelia—or rather, so absolute was his own self-regard, that he did not believe it possible that he could be set aside for any man or woman in the world.

"Nephew of Colonel Sutherland—hum—Scarsdale—happy to make your acquaintance," said Sir John, doubtfully. "We didn't expect to meet you here of all places in the world; did we, Roger, boy? Got something to say to you by-and-bye, Mr. Scarsdale—if you'll do us the honour—about that confounded fellow Pouncet, and this—this young fellow here."

"When you please, Sir John," said Horace, with a giddiness about him scarcely bearable. Sir John was playing with a newspaper on the table—the Kenlisle paper, which always came there. Perhaps the notice, the intimation, the seal of all his breathless terrors and ghastly expectations lay there; but it was as unattainable as though strong walls had surrounded it, guarded by the trifling fingers of that stranger's hand. This newspaper, however—the common vulgar broadsheet—kept thus in his sight, yet beyond his reach, rapt the mind of Horace out of all excitement as to any other question. He knew well enough, with the dull certainty which other matters had in his mind, that Musgrave and his friend must have heard from Mrs. Stenhouse of his own connection with Mr. Pouncet, and call to the deathbed of her husband; but he felt no apprehension about their questions, cared nothing about the matter—in short, cared for nothing in the world at this moment but that paper rustling under the baronet's careless hand.

"Mr. Scarsdale is Edmund's man of business," cried Amelia. "Oh, poor dear little Edmund! I never shall forget that scene! Fancy, Sir John, Edmund taking it into his head that he was going to die, frightening poor mamma out of her wits, and sending for the doctor and Mr. Scarsdale long past midnight, when everybody was asleep. I peeped in at the door just after the doctor went, and there was poor Mr. Scarsdale at the table writing Edmund's will. I had such a laugh after I knew all was safe, and my little brother no worse than usual; for, only think of Mr. Scarsdale humouring Edmund, when he knew it was no good, and writing his will!"

"It was very kind of Mr. Scarsdale, Amelia," said Mrs. Stenhouse.

"Oh, it might be, mamma; but wasn't it an odd scene?" cried the beauty, appealing to Sir John, and laughing at her own penetration. That was Amelia's kind of wit—a wit which, being always played against one suitor for the amusement of another, was wonderfully successful. The baronet was extremely tickled with "the scene;" the fair artist went over it again for his behalf, with a ludicrous sketch of Horace, "though he knew it was no good" making little Edmund's will. While this went on, Horace gradually wakened up into a grim surprise at this ridicule, and began to perceive that the object of his love really meant to hold him up to derision, and had changed her tone. The discovery roused him into something of his former self. What had he not done to gain possession of this girl? But to her he was only a common one of her many admirers, to be laughed at and cast aside in his turn. Dead to all better emotions, Horace had yet a little of common life left in him through his intense arrogance and self regard, and this pin-prick found it out.

"When Edmund called upon me to help him, it was not the first time I had been honoured by the confidence of the head of the house," said Horace, with a sinister impulse of revenge—"the other scene might not have struck Miss Stenhouse as amusing, but, as it happened, it was more interesting to me."

As he spoke, everybody looked at Horace. And perhaps then everybody noticed, for the first time, the change which had fallen upon the young man—putting their various interpretations upon it, as was natural. Amelia saw nothing but a desperate struggle of passion, love, and jealousy, most flatteringly tragic, in the white fever which consumed him. Sir John regarded him with his head a little on one side, and made a moral remark upon the effects of dissipation, in his own mind; while Mrs. Stenhouse, leaping at the first troublesome idea which occurred to her, thought instantly, as he had meant them all to think, upon her husband's death-bed disclosure, and how it might affect her son.

"Oh, Mr. Scarsdale!" she cried, pleadingly, "you will tell Roger—you will tell Sir John, his kind friend, what it was that my dear Mr. Stenhouse had to say? It could be nothing against my son," she continued, nervously taking Roger's hand. Sir John roused himself up a little. It was much more agreeable flirting with Amelia; but, of course, as he had come to Harliflax about this matter, it was important to hear what the young man might have to say.

"If your late husband put his reputation into my hands, do you suppose I am going to betray him?" said Horace to Mrs. Stenhouse; but it was quite loud enough for everybody to hear.

"Mrs. Stenhouse will forgive you that—for her son's sake; we are all frail, and nobody can blame the defunct," said the baronet, with a hasty bow to the widow. "Come, my boy, out with it; or at least let's have a little private conversation, Scarsdale—there's a good fellow; a secret is the greatest humbug in the world—never does anybody any good to keep it. Should have been able to bring the late Mr. Stenhouse to reason, I have no doubt, if I could have seen him. My good fellow, with Mrs. Stenhouse's permission, step downstairs with me."

"Oh, do please, if it's a secret, tell it here. I love a secret of all things," cried Amelia.

But Amelia was cowed a little. She had caught Horace's wild eye, where so many fires lay latent and smouldering. How could she tell what the secret might be? She was vaguely afraid in the midst of her curiosity. If he had gone downstairs with Sir John, Amelia would have followed them, and listened at the door.

"May I have the paper to look at?" said Horace, seizing it suddenly, as Sir John rose. "No, I do not trade in my friend's secrets. Mrs. Stenhouse, good morning. I shall send back the paper, and I will see you again before I go."

So saying, Horace left the room almost before any one was aware—before any one, save Amelia, saw what he was going to do. She, foreseeing his intention, vanished while he was still speaking, and waylaid him on the staircase.

"Oh, Mr. Scarsdale, was it something very dreadful?" said the breathless Amelia, with a pretty affectation of alarm.

"Do you care about your father's reputation?" said Horace, with one of his old familiar sneers.

"I—don't know—that was papa's own business—if he did not mind, why should we?" said Amelia, with a toss of her pretty head.

"But suppose I had something to say which could make it quite sure that Edmund's will was of no good, Miss Stenhouse?" said the vindictive lover—"suppose I knew of a creditor who could empty this pretty house, and all your purses, and leave you nothing—what then would you have to say to me?"

The beautiful Amelia stood dumb for a moment, looking at him—trembling for her problematical co-heiresship—trembling lest she might have to forswear Sir John, and no longer dream of being called "my lady"—trembling most of all before the fiery eyes fixed upon her with so intent a gaze. "What should I say?" said the troubled flirt, with a little gasp—"why, that you were bound to make up for it somehow, you cruel creature—you who were to be so very rich, too;" and Amelia escaped, scared, when he chose to permit her—making up her mind to do anything in the world rather than marry this violent lover; while he went downstairs, roused by these last words into a renewed frenzy of excitement, carrying the Kenlisle paper in his hand.

The paper, which perhaps brought him news of his success, and that the vast unsunned hoards of his old progenitor were already his; the paper which he dared not read, for fear of attracting notice, in the dim cowardice of guilt, till he had shut himself up in his own room. But there was nothing in it; not a syllable in it about Marchmain or any sudden death. Had they both perished—both master and servant, in that lonely house on the moor? Or did the recluse of Marchmain live a charmed life?

CHAPTER XIX

Two days after, the same party met again in Mrs. Stenhouse's drawing-room. Horace had eluded all attempts on the part of Roger and Sir John to see or have any conversation with him; but he could not keep away from that only place where he had a chance of forgetting himself, or, at least, of counterbalancing one passion with another. He could not explain to himself why he stayed in Harliflax. It was against all his interests; it was trifling with Mr. Pouncet; it was exposing himself to a hundred risks, and leaving the citadel of the business to which he had bound himself undefended. But Horace cared no longer for Mr. Pouncet's credit, or for his own income. The young man was desperate: he was ready at any moment, in pure recklessness, to have flung that secret at anybody's head whom it had a chance of harming, or rendering unhappy, though, with a characteristic sullen obstinacy, he kept it out of reach of those whom it might have served. Nor could he any longer discern, out of the fiery mists which blurred his future, any prospects of his own; he could not make any definite stand upon that visionary thousand pounds a-year which he had extorted from Mr. Pouncet; he could not think, in that lurid haze out of which everything around him rose indistinct, like a phantom, of such a certain and settled act as marriage, with a household and steady beginning of life in its train. No such thing was practicable to the unhappy young man. He might have found some wild solace in breaking through the bounds of decorous life, and persuading Amelia Stenhouse to elope with him; but, except that, nothing tempted his fascinated mind. He could only sit and wait for the explosion—the terrible intelligence which, sooner or later, must come to him from Marchmain.

But he was once more in Mrs. Stenhouse's drawing-room, where there was no longer any newspaper to excite him out of his senses—calmly seated among people who were pursuing the common way of life, without any stronger stimulant than a flirtation or common project of marriage among them. Sir John, whose indolence was no match for the obstinacy of Horace, was carrying on, as well as he could, the talk with Amelia, which the entrance of "that cub" had interrupted; while Amelia herself did her best to subdue the tone of that exceedingly interesting consultation, in acknowledgment of the presence of her too ardent lover. Somehow, Horace's entrance, and all the restrained passion, unintelligible to them, which he carried about him, made the whole party uneasy. Amelia remembered with terror that, if provoked, he knew of somebody who could turn them out of doors, and leave them penniless. Mrs. Stenhouse regarded him with a vague awe, as holding in his hands at once her husband's good name and the well-being of her son; while Musgrave, with a good deal of natural exasperation, sat in the same room with the man who was in the secret of some conspiracy against himself, yet showed no compunction towards him, and who had tried to blacken his youthful character to his dearest friends. Nobody pretended that he was welcome in that house—not even timid Mrs. Stenhouse nor Amelia; yet he went—secure in his power;—went and set himself by Amelia's elbow, turning his passionate looks upon her, while, from one cause and another, nobody dared venture to say to him how little welcome he was.

That day, however, destroyed the strange incubus to which his presence had grown. The post came in while Horace sat in Mrs. Stenhouse's drawing-room. Roger had some letters, and opened them without waiting to be alone. When he had glanced over one he turned doubtfully, yet with some eagerness, towards the visitor. "Mr. Scarsdale," he said, quietly, "Colonel Sutherland is at Marchmain."

Horace did not fall down, or cry out, as he might have done; but, in the extremity of his startled horror, he rose bolt upright, and stood with his face blanched out of all natural colour. He could not speak, it was evident, for a minute; then he said, with a strange blank voice out of his throat, "My father is dead!"

"No, not dead—not so bad as that—but ill, I confess," said Roger, kindly, quite melted by what seemed to him an overflowing of natural feeling; "only ill; don't look so alarmed—not even seriously or alarmingly ill, so far as Colonel Sutherland says. Pray, read the letter yourself."

Horace took the letter mechanically, and sat down again, holding it up before his face. He could not see the writing, which swam and floated in variable lines before him. He had enough to do to control himself, that nobody might see the wild tremor, exultation, horror, which possessed him. And yet what did it mean?—not dead, but ill! His potion, surely must have done better work. Not dead, only ill? The words came to his very lips unaware. What did it mean?

"Take some wine, Mr. Scarsdale; you look quite ill. Nay, nay, perhaps it isn't anything to be anxious about," said Mrs. Stenhouse, stealing round the table with the charitable cordial to Horace's elbow. "How you did comfort me, to be sure, the other night about Edmund!—and that came true. Drink this to give you back your colour, and don't take on so; I hope your father will be spared to so good a son!"

"What do you mean?" cried Horace, hoarsely; "do you mean to taunt me?—as good a son as he was a father! Thank you, thank you! I was startled. I'm going off for Marchmain; good-bye."

He crushed up the letter in his hand, and went away hurriedly; but almost before they had begun to wonder and talk about him, came back and thrust his head in at the door.

"Musgrave," said Horace, in a broken voice, "when I come back, if—if I come back—I'll tell you something to your benefit. I say it freely, without any man asking me—I promise you I will."

With this mysterious intimation he disappeared once more, going out from among them upon his dismal way, leaving a strange suggestion of evil in everybody's mind. Great misery, it was clear enough, was in this sudden intimation. Was it the agonized apprehension of love fearing death?—what was it?—for of all the unlikely things in the world, that little company could have guessed at anything sooner than the truth.

"But I believe he expects to come into a great deal of money when his father dies," said Amelia; "not a common fortune—such a deal! I daresay that was why he looked so strange when he went away."

"And, oh, how do you know, Amelia?" asked her next sister.

"I wish you would not ask ridiculous questions," said Amelia, casting down her eyes with a pretty look of embarrassment, and a blush and simper, intended for the benefit of the baronet. "I know, of course, because—because Mr. Scarsdale told me; how else could I know?"

And Sir John Armitage saw, as clearly as if she had described it, a presumptuous proposal on the part of "that cub," backed up by promises of fortune, which the beautiful Amelia's delicate mind had remained totally unmoved to hear of; and entirely subdued by her fascinations, the bewitched baronet made up his own mind summarily. He flattered himself there was not much fear of rejection; and how famously that beautiful figure, which bent so often, and with such winning grace, towards him, would brighten the great rooms of Armitage Park.

Thus the waters closed in placid circles, widening out into smiles of well-pleased fortune, around the spot where Horace Scarsdale disappeared; and one of the great stakes he had played his deadly play for, slid out of his reach into the polished hands of a quiet spectator, who staked nothing. But he did not know that; he thought of nothing—not even of Amelia—as he rushed along to the railway, and flew by that iron road, at the swiftest pace, to the nearest neighbouring town he could reach in the vicinity of Lanwoth Moor; he was beyond thinking in the extremity of his haste and desperation. The black wings were spread over the lonely house. Death, whom he had invoked, was coming—his fortune would soon be all his own; but there was never spectator at a tragedy who held his breath for its consummation as Horace Scarsdale did, rushing out of his own black, unrepentant remorse and misery to Marchmain.

How that dark interval of time had passed at Marchmain no one could tell—for Peggy, the only individual who could have known, had long ceased to speculate on her master's sentiments and feelings, and learned to content herself with things as they came. But just as Colonel Sutherland, in single-minded devotion to the interests of his young friend Roger, and an honest and simple desire to set right the harm which he supposed to have been done by his nephew, had drawn close in his circles of laborious but unprofitable investigation to Lanwoth Moor, Peggy's attention had been called to her master's bodily condition. He had spent an agitated and restless night, as she could hear by his motions in his own room, and, for the first time in twenty years, did not get up in the morning. When Peggy went to him, alarmed by this extraordinary occurrence, she found him in bed, paralysed in one side, unable to speak, his face somewhat distorted, and everything helpless about him except his eyes. It was evidently and beyond any doubt "a stroke," and poor Peggy, alone in her solitude, and not knowing what to do—afraid to leave him to seek assistance, and unable to ascertain what were his own wishes—put the disordered room tidy by instinct in the first place, until she was driven out of it, scared and breathless, by those eyes which followed her movements everywhere. "Like as if an evil spirit had ta'en possession," she said to herself, as she went quicker than usual in her fright and perplexity down the stairs; and Peggy described many a day after how it was like an angel of mercy to hear "Mr. Edward, that is now the Cornel, the Lord bless him," knocking at the door all of a sudden, and asking if all was well at Marchmain. "I tould him all was as ill as ill could be; and he never so much as cam in to rest, but went forth with his staff in his hand five mile of road for the doctor and help," said Peggy; "and ye may all tell me about his own business and other things he had in hand, and owght ye please, but no man shall make me believe, if he preaches till Christmas, that it was aught but the very Lord himsel' in grace and mercy that sent the Cornel that morning, and no other, to the master's door."

That was a busy day for Colonel Sutherland. He sent not only the nearest country doctor, but an express to Kenlisle for a more noted physician there, and sent abundant help to Peggy, and everything which the surgeon could suggest as likely to be of use. The old soldier's heart of pity yearned over the unfortunate man who had shut himself out from all the tender charities of love. He despatched a letter instantly to Susan, bidding her come at once to nurse her father; and when he had done everything that his kind heart could suggest, went back slowly and thoughtfully across the moor, with very sad thoughts in that good heart. Not because he thought it sad to die; the Colonel had too many waiting for him on the other side of the river to compassionate those who were arriving at that conclusion of trouble; but it was sad to consider the ending of this melancholy and miserable life. Better for himself, for his children, for everybody within his influence, would it have been, if twenty years ago the grave had received him into its harmless quiet, instead of this miserable seclusion. And now, without even that privilege of a conscious pause upon the grave's brink, which sweetens so many memories, and endears so many of the dead, who, living, were less loveable, he was going away, this unhappy man. No wonder the tender heart of the old soldier was sad. It had been better not to be born than thus to die.

When Colonel Sutherland returned to Marchmain he was reluctant to enter the sick-room, fearing that even there the imprisoned mind, debarred of ordinary expression, would chafe at his presence, and put a cruel interpretation upon his kindness; but the importunities of Peggy, the silent surprise of the surgeon, and indeed the forlorn and pitiful loneliness of the patient himself, overpowered his objections. He went in and spoke to the stricken man lying there dumb upon his bed. He detailed all the circumstances of his own arrival, dwelling upon its accidental character—he spoke of Susan, he spoke of Horace—for the doctor had declared that to restore his speech and faculties it would be well to rouse him, even to passion; but all without effect. Mr. Scarsdale lay in his dressing-gown among the bedclothes, in that dead silence which looked almost malicious, and of purpose, contrasted with the wild watchfulness of his eyes. One hand lay powerless and numb beside him; the other held with a tight grasp some folds of the white coverlid. There he lay stretched out motionless, attempting no notice of the remedies they applied to him, suffering himself to be moved and shifted about like a log, but following every movement, every gleam of light, every passing shadow, with those eyes so desperately alive and awake. When he had once entered that melancholy sick-room, the Colonel for very pity could not leave it. He sat down by the side of the bed, his whole heart moved with a compassion unspeakable. He could not bear to think that no kindred blood or familiar voice was near the unhappy sufferer. Peggy, it was true, went and came; but Peggy was afraid of her master, whom she had served so long and faithfully. She was superstitious, with her long solitude and broken spirit; she thought her master had already gone to his account, and that it was some malignant spirit which looked out of these wild waking eyes.

After two days of this hopeless lethargy, during which Colonel Sutherland never left his post, but watched night and day, dozing sometimes for an hour in the arm-chair by the bedside, Susan arrived, under charge of Patchey, to whom the thoughtful Colonel had written. It was a strange home-coming for Susan, in the midst of all her sweet new hopes and beginning thrills of life. But when Susan, instead of being taken into Peggy's motherly arms, and kissed, and blessed, and cried over, as she expected, felt Peggy, after her first scream of welcome, bear heavily upon her shoulder, and drop off into a dead faint of exhaustion and over-excitement, she saw at once this was no time to think of herself. When Peggy was better, she took off her travelling dress, and went up without a moment's delay to her father's room, where Uncle Edward sat, pale with watching. Susan, too, was shocked and frightened more than she dared say by the sick man's attentive eyes; but she took the nurse's place with a natural and instinctive readiness, and begged her uncle to go away and get some rest. Why should they watch him with such careful, tender anxiety—the banished daughter and the insulted friend? Why, in this dismal need of his did these two come, whom he had sent away from him, and come as though that imprisoned spirit which they watched had been a heart of love? But nobody could tell in this world whether such thoughts touched the heart of the recluse, as he lay unmoving, unsleeping, speechless, upon that dreadful bed. The days which had now passed since he took any nourishment, the unnatural state in which he lay, made his condition, unhopeful enough at first, entirely hopeless now. He was dying slowly, no one knowing how it went with him in the depths of his hidden soul, and no one able to interpret if any late compunctions, any meltings of the shut-up heart, or touches of human charity, were shining at length, at last, when all utterance was over, out of these wakeful eyes.

When Susan took her uncle's place for the next long night—when through all the silent hours she could not move without attracting these sleepless looks, which were all that remained of this man's will and mind—Susan got frightened in spite of herself. So alive, so waking, so desperately conscious were these eyes, that the poor girl fell down on her knees by the bedside, and implored her father to speak to her.

"Only speak, say anything, if it was to curse me!" said poor Susan. It was impossible to believe that he could not if he would. And then one gleam of expression different from their usual strain of watchfulness appeared in Mr. Scarsdale's eyes; a strange gleam, as if tears were in them; a momentary melting of the hard heart, a wandering movement of the unparalyzed hand to lay it on her head. Susan hid her face, weeping aloud, the touch going to her heart as never tender father's blessing went, and her whole young soul heaving within her, at the thought how little she had loved him, he who relented over her and blessed her thus under the stony hand of death. Never in all his hard life had so sweet a gush of human gratitude followed any act of Mr. Scarsdale. It was well for him that it was his last.

At that moment when Susan, full of tenderness and compunction, knelt by her father's bedside, and Mr. Scarsdale's hand still trembled upon her hair—token, all too late, of the love which might have been—the door of the room opened stealthily for a moment, and Horace looked in. Whether it was that Mr. Scarsdale had preserved the sense of hearing as distinctly as he seemed to do that of sight, or that a strange magic of hostility drew his eyes to that quarter, it is impossible to say; but when Horace's gaze fell upon the bed and its ghastly inhabitant, his father's eyes met his, with a look which all the world and all its pleasures could never efface from the young man's mind. He staggered back, startled out of all self-control, and uttering, in spite of himself, a cry, half of defiance, half of horror; while the unhappy father of these two children, thrusting, with the force of extremity, Susan's fair head away from him, swayed round, by a desperate impulse, his half-lifeless body, and turned his face to the wall. Startled out of her filial delusion, and with her faculties confused by the sudden thrust away, which was given with feverish force, Susan stumbled to her feet in sudden terror. Horace was standing ghastly pale by the door, his bloodless lips apart, his eyes dilated, his manner so frightfully excited and unnatural, that Susan's first impulse was to interpose the frail protection of her own body between the helpless father and the frantic son. As she stood alarmed, protecting the bed, Horace gave a ghastly sneer at her, and said, "Too late!" hoarsely out of his throat. He saw well enough that she was afraid of him, and meant to defend her father; but nothing in the world could have initiated Susan into the horrible meaning of that "too late." When she thought of it, she supposed her brother to mean too late to be recognized, to ask his father's pardon—perhaps to gain his father's blessing, as she had done; and with that idea her feeling changed.

"Not too late, Horace," said poor Susan—"he is sensible—he knows me. But oh! before you speak to him, call Peggy first, and bid her tell the doctor. The doctor said he was to be called whenever papa moved."

"The doctor! What doctor?—what does he want with a doctor?" said Horace, in his hoarse, dreadful voice.

"The doctor is in the house—Uncle Edward would not let him go away. He has moved—he has all but spoken! Oh! call the doctor, Horace!" cried Susan, eagerly; "perhaps it may be a sign for the better! Call Peggy—she will tell you where he is!"

But Horace stood still on the threshold of the fatal room, looking round with wild, investigating eyes, as anxious, as desperate, as the sufferer's own. Where was it?—where was that little medicine-chest, which had dealt a slower death than he expected, but which, if it were found, might snatch the cup from his own lips, and abridge his lifelong punishment? Where was it? The dying man upon that bed, dreadful as was his son's curiosity about him, and terrible as the shock had been when their eyes met, was less important now than that chest and its tell-tale contents. He gazed around with his wild eyes—so like his father's—looking at everything but his father, who lay motionless, his dread eyes closed now, and his face turned towards the wall. Susan, in wild impatience, stamped her foot upon the floor, hoping by that means to attract somebody. There was a stir below, as of some one who heard her; and Horace, roused by the sound, approached the bedside cautiously. "He is dead!" her brother whispered in Susan's ears. It was the middle of the night, dark and still; and the poor girl, standing here between the dying man—who, perhaps, had died in that dreadful moment—and the living man, who looked like a maniac, lost all her self-command. She cried aloud in the extremity of her fear and anguish. Was Horace mad? And in that miserable moment, with his rebel son returned to vex his soul, had her father passed away?

The stamping of Susan's foot on the floor, the sound of some commotion in the sick-room, and at last her voice calling out in uncontrollable terror, brought all the other inmates of the house to the room—Peggy, the doctor half awake, the nurse, and Uncle Edward, all of whom, at Susan's earnest instance, had lain down to seek an hour's sleep. Among all these anxious people Horace looked still more like a spectre—but after another moment spent in inquisitive inspection of the room, he turned to the doctor and overpowered him with questions. As if in braggadocio and daring exhibition of his want of feeling, he urged the surgeon into descriptions of the complaint: what it was—and how it came on—and what were its particular features. While the astonished doctor replied as shortly as possible, and turned his back upon the heartless questioner, Horace hovered more and more closely about his father's bed. Another fit produced by the sudden appearance of his son had almost completed the mortal work which was going on in the emaciated frame of the recluse. It did not matter to anybody now that those eyes were faintly open, which a little while ago were full of unspeakable things; the force and the life had ebbed out of those windows of the soul, and the patient no longer knew anything of the agitated consultations going on over him, or of the hideous curiosity with which his son thrust into those, asking questions which horrified the hearers. When the doctor said that there were complications in this case, which made it difficult to treat, the young man laughed a short, hoarse, horrible laugh, and asked "how long do you think he will last?" in a tone which made them shudder. They were all afraid of his haggard figure as it swayed to and fro about the bed.

"You've been drinking, sir," said the doctor, in authoritative disgust. "You can't do any good here—be quiet and go to bed. He distresses the patient; some of you take him away."

"Mr. Horry, come with me," said Peggy, laying her hand upon his shoulder. He followed her out of the room without saying anything. He was mad, crazed, intoxicated; but with a deadlier poison than was ever distilled from corn or vine!

The old woman took him into his own room and left him there. She shook her head at him in sad displeasure, but understood nothing of the tragic misery which made him mad.

"I bid ye not to grieve," she said, reproachfully. "The Lord knows he's been little of a father to you, that you should break your heart for him; but be dacent, Mr. Horry, be dacent; if it's no for love's sake, as is no possible, yet have respect to death."

When Peggy left him Horace buried his haggard face in those hands which had grown thin and sharp like the claws of a bird of prey. "Have respect to death!"—to the death which he had invoked—to the destruction he had made. He sank down prostrate upon the floor, and lay there in a heap, helpless, overcome by the horror of what he had done. The strength of an army could not have kept him from Marchmain at that terrible crisis and climax of his fate; but now when he was here, he could but lie prostrate in the wildest hopeless misery, or, mad with his guilt, peer like a ghoul about his father's death-bed. It was easier to do that, noting horribly every slow step of the approaching presence, than it was to lie here in the dismal creeping silence, with that footstep creaking on the stair, and chilling the night, and a hundred deadly sprites of vengeance shouting Murder! murder! all night long, into his miserable ear.

CHAPTER XXII

Before that night was over the terrible visitor whom Horace believed his own act to have brought to Marchmain entered the lonely house; but the unhappy parricide did not hear or see the entrance of that last messenger. While his father sank gradually into the longer and surer quietude, sleep, feverish and painful, fell upon the son. He had not slept for many nights, and his great excitement, added to the fatigue of his journey, had completely exhausted his frame. The confused and painful commotion in the adjoining apartment as the mortal moment approached; the sobs of Susan, who saw Death for the first time, and found the sight of those last agonies intolerable and beyond her strength; the solemn bustle afterwards, when the last offices had to be performed—were all insufficient to awake Horace out of the deep but unquiet slumber, over which phantoms and fever brooded. He lay as Peggy had left him, in his travel-soiled and disordered dress, fatigued, haggard, bearing such weariness and exhaustion in his face, that it would have taken harder hearts than those of his sister and uncle to close themselves against him. But Horace was as unconscious of the visit of Susan and Uncle Edward as of any other incident of the night. They stood over him as he slept, talking in whispers; but those soothing voices did not enter into the fever of his dream. Susan was crying quietly, every word she spoke producing a fresh overflow of tears—natural tears, which she could not help shedding, but soon must wipe away. Nothing less was possible to her tender heart, and it would have been strange if the end of that unloving and unlovely life had produced anything more. "He looks so tired—poor Horace! Oh! Uncle Edward, he is not so hard-hearted as people thought!—he will feel this very much; think how troubled he looked last night," said Susan.

"Yes, Susan," said Uncle Edward, with a sigh, "more than troubled; but I do not blame him; it was not his fault—the evil was done before he was born."

"What evil, uncle?" asked Susan, looking up with wonder through her tears.

"My poor child, it would but horrify you," said Uncle Edward. "I cannot think but Horace, somehow or other, has found it out. Your brother lying there, Susan, is now one of the richest men in England; your grandfather's will passed over your poor father, and left everything to Horace. Ah, Susan! nothing but passion, and misery, and black revenge on one side and the other; and look at this young heir—poor Horace! they have heaped up money for him, but they have already robbed him of all the bloom and promise of his life."

"You don't think he has done anything very wrong, Uncle Edward?" said Susan, trembling and crying more and more.

For looking down upon that face, all darkly pale in its sleeping passion, with its deep-drawn lines of pain and stealthy curves about the closed eyes, it was hard to think of misery inflicted by other people. Misery self-made, and guilt actual and personal, lay even in the sleep of Horace Scarsdale's face. Susan's mind did not take in or comprehend that statement about her grandfather and his wealth, and "one of the richest men in England." The words had no meaning to her at that melancholy moment. She thought only of the brother of her childhood in that heavy sleep of exhaustion and misery, thrown down in a heap like one who had not even heart enough to stretch himself out in common comfort; and her heart yearned over him, whatever he might have done.

"I think, perhaps," said the Colonel, with hesitation, "that the journey and the excitement, and, perhaps, taking something he was not used to, overcame him last night. Sleep is the best thing for him; let us leave him quiet—he will be better when he wakes."

And so they left him; Colonel Sutherland really believing that to brave himself for a scene which must excite him painfully, but where real grief was not to be expected from him, Horace had come intoxicated to his father's death-bed, and Susan half-disgusted, half-comforted to believe that his maniac looks of last night might be attributed to such a cause. They went away, the Colonel to take an hour's sleep after his long visit, and Susan to weep out her heart, thinking over that one touch of natural sympathy, which, beyond death and the grave, gave her more hold of love upon her father, than she had ever before felt herself to possess. The morning was kindling over the moor, brightening the golden-blossomed gorse, and glowing over the purple beds of heather; but the blinds were drawn down and the shutters closed in Marchmain; the obscure and gloomy atmosphere of death reigned in the house. Peggy sat by the kitchen-fire, with her white apron thrown over her head—her mind lost in long trains of recollection, sometimes her wearied frame yielding to a half-hour's sleep, sometimes her troubled thoughts overflowing in a few natural tears. The woman who had come to be nurse and household assistant dozed on the other side of the fire. Colonel Sutherland, very grave, and full of the thoughts which death brings in his train, sat alone in the darkened dining-room, taking an hour's sleep as he said—though in reality the old soldier had only read his morning chapter in his old Bible, and was composing himself with the tender strength of these words of God; while Susan, withdrawn in her own room, gave the dead man his dues, and paid that duty of nature, a woman's lamentations, to the concluded life.

In this languor and stillness of the death-consecrated house, where no agony of living grief reigned, but only the natural pathos and the natural rest, Horace awoke at bright mid-day from his unnatural sleep. Accustomed to the noises of a town, and to the perpetual wasting of his own burning thoughts, the stillness struck him strangely, with a chill calm which he could not explain. He sat up mechanically, and put the lank disordered hair from his face, trying to recollect where he was and what had happened. Looking round at that room, strange yet familiar, the shelter of all his youthful years, he could almost have supposed that everything else was but a hideous dream, and that he himself was nothing worse or guiltier than the rebellious lad who once slept and dreamt within these homely walls. But then bit by bit the light brightened upon him; he traced out the whole black history line by line; the first suggestion of this guilt at which he had shuddered—the returning thoughts which grew familiar to him—the deed itself, black and breathless in its stealthy and secret crime; and now the consummation had come! At that thought he started from his bed, all his pulses beating with the strength of fear. What was he thinking of?—the great stakes he had played for and won? the big inaccessible fortune which made him this day, in this obscure house, as Uncle Edward said, one of the richest men in England? the wealthy inheritance, which was all his own? He thought of no such thing, poor madman, in his frightful success and triumph; far from that ruined soul and miserable house were now the delusions of love and fortune which had wiled him into crime; no exultant thought of fortune gained—no lover's fancy of Amelia won, warmed him in the first sharp access of misery. He thought of one thing, and one only, in the abject horror of that guilt, which he himself knew, though no one else did. The fatal box in which he had laid his train of destruction—the medicine chest where his father had gone to seek healing and had found death. Where was it? He saw it in his burning imagination a far more dread obstacle than had been that life which he had destroyed, standing between him and all the objects of his ambition; he could not look anywhere but that fatal vision glided before him, clear with its brass-bound corners, its tiny phials, and the lock which closed with such a horrible jar. It haunted his miserable eyes, a guilty spectrum—where was it?—had the doctor perhaps taken possession of if already to detect the secret felon, lurking murderous under its seeming innocence?—had the vindictive victim of that snare given it over into some one's hand, a witness not to be intimidated against the parricide? The heavy drops rained from his white face, his limbs trembled like palsy, his very youth and strength forsook him in that dread emergency. By a dark intuition he knew that his father was dead, that all was over; that, so far as superficial appearances went, the fortune and the triumph were his own; and so got up—God help him!—in a fever of hopeless misery, to look for that fatal token which might, his excited fancy supposed, turn all the tide against him, and take his very life. He went out trembling and feeble, out of the shelter of his room—afraid of the daylight, of the stillness, of everything about and around him—trembling, like a felon as he was, at his own dreary and hideous success. This was how Horace Scarsdale came into his fortune, in faithful fulfilment of his grandfather's wicked will!

CHAPTER XXIII

Armed by the extremity of his alarm, Horace ventured, no one being near to spy upon him, to enter, in his miserable search, the chamber of death itself. He dared not look towards the bed, on which lay that rigid outline of humanity, all covered and dressed with white. He could scarcely contain the horror of his trembling as he stood, dismayed and powerless, in the presence of his victim; but, after his first pause of involuntary homage, he turned—though still not daring to turn his back to the bed, overpowered with a terror which he could not explain—to pursue his search. Stealthily moving about, with his head bent, and his step shuffling as if with age, he examined every corner, peering into the wardrobe, where his heart thrilled desperately to see the well-remembered garments which it was so hard to believe could never be worn again; and turning over familiar articles of daily use with awed and trembling fingers, as though they could betray him; but he could not find any trace of the object of his search. Its very absence seemed to him significant and terrible. Had some enemy taken it to testify against him? Had the dead man himself taken measures to secure his own revenge? Heavy, cold, clammy beads of moisture hung upon the young man's face; a chill as of death entered into his heart; deep to the very centre of his being he himself knew and felt his own guilt—and now another mysterious, gnawing misery was added to his own self-consciousness. Some one else knew also; some one meaning him evil had withdrawn that dreadful instrument of death and vengeance. He had played his horrible game, but the great stakes were further off than ever. Already, in his miserable, excited imagination, he saw, instead of fortune and Amelia, a trial and a scaffold, and the dread name of parricide. A wild agony of impatience and intolerable suffering came over him. Rather than wait till this slow, deadly avenger of blood had found him out, he would rush forth somewhere, and denounce himself, and have it over. His punishment was more than he could bear!

But all was silent in the death-stricken house; not a sound, save the loud ticking of the clock downstairs, and the deep throbs of his own heart, could Horace hear as he stood, stealthy and desperate, at the door of his father's room. Susan's face, innocent and wondering; Uncle Edward's benign countenance, disapproving and sad; and, still more dangerous, Peggy's troubled eyes, watching where he went and what he did, haunted his imagination. He could fancy them all grouped together under covert somewhere, watching that guilty, stealthy pause of his—watching his secret, clandestine footsteps as he stole downstairs. But still he did go down, in the breathless cowardice of his conscious crime; fearing everything, yet with all his mind fixed, in an intensity which was half insane, upon that dumb witness against him. He did not expect to find it. He could have supposed it possessed by some malicious spirit, and with an actual animate will working against him; but he could not rest till he had, through every corner, sought it out—if, perhaps, it could be found.

When he had got downstairs he paused again to consider where he should go; a faint sound of Peggy's voice in the kitchen, and the slight stir made now and then for a moment by Colonel Sutherland in the dining parlour, confused and stopped him in his course. He stood for a moment irresolute and breathless, not seeing what to do, and then almost involuntarily opened the closed door of Mr. Scarsdale's study. The recluse was dead, and could harm no man now; but he was alive when his guilty son stepped into that room so deeply instinct with his presence, where now more than ever he lived and had his sure abode. Almost more awful than the actual presence of the dead was that presence unseen and terrible, the invisible life of life, which death could not touch, and which should remain here for ever. Horace dared scarcely breathe the air of this deserted room. An hour's imprisonment in it, in his present state of mind, would have driven him into mad superstition, if not to positive frenzy; but he saw something there, set out almost with ostentation on the table, which would have drawn him through fire and water. There it stood, solemnly by itself, the books and papers cleared away from its immediate vicinity, in malign and mischievous state, calling the attention of everyone who entered. Horace made his shuddering way forward, and seized upon it with the grasp of desperation. Yes, there it was, with all its evidence within his own reach, and safe, if he willed it so, to harm him no more!

The little medicine-chest was partially open, with the key in its lock; but this had been done of purpose, and was the result of no accident; and within lay something white—a sheet of paper—which assuredly was not there when he had opened it before. Almost too anxious to pay any attention to these elaborate marks of intention and design, Horace seized the box and the phial which he had filled. He could not pause even to look whether the leather which covered the cork had been removed, or any of the contents were gone, but hastened to the fireplace, where the ashes of a fire still lay in the grate, and with trembling hands broke the neck of the bottle against the grate, and emptied out its contents—for he dared not go outside, lest some one should see him. As he paused, kneeling on the hearth, breathless and with a beating heart, he tried to take comfort and re-assure himself. It was gone; no evidence existed now that the son had entered in, murderous and secret, to the father's chamber. He tried to persuade himself that he breathed more freely; then he grovelled down upon the hearth, and hid his face in his hands. God help him! what did it matter though no one else suspected?—deep in the bottom of his heart did not he know?—and was there anything in heaven or earth which could wash the horror of that certainty out of Horace Scarsdale's miserable mind? He had been selfish, malicious, unloving before; but never till now had he been a murderer—and, oh! the horrible difference, the change unspeakable, which that dread distinction made!

However, he got up at last, all shuddering and weak, with the remains of the phial grasped in his hand, and with a morbid curiosity returned again to examine the box. This time he set it open and took out the sheet of paper. He could scarcely distinguish the words at first, for the awe of looking at his father's writing, and receiving thus, as it were, a direct message from the dead; but when the sense slowly broke upon him the effect was like a stroke of magic. He stood staring at the paper, his eyes starting from his head, his face flushing and paling with wild vicissitudes of colour; then he dropped down heavily on the floor, thrusting aside unconsciously Mr. Scarsdale's chair, which stood in its usual place by the table. He could neither cry nor help himself; he fell heavily, like a man stunned by a sudden blow—voice, strength, consciousness went out of him; he lay prostrate, with his head upon the fleecy lambskin where his father's feet had been accustomed to rest, no longer a self-defending, self-torturing, conscious parricide, with a brand upon his soul worse than that of Cain; a figure blind and helpless, an insensible, inanimate mass of dull flesh and blood, conscious of nothing in the world, not even that he lived and was a man.

The paper fell fluttering after him and covered his face. It was of the kind and colour which Mr. Scarsdale always used—a blue flimsy leaf, and had been carefully cut to fit the box in which it was placed. What had tempted the recluse to record thus his suspicions and his precaution, no one in the world could now ever tell; save as the expression of a vindictive sentiment, and secret triumph to himself in his solitude for discovering and baffling a secret enemy, there was no meaning in it, and the chances are that nothing would have brought these words from the unhappy father's pen could he have known the overpowering transport of relief which at sight of them should overthrow all the strength and make useless the defences of the still more unhappy son. On the paper were written in large letters, in Mr. Scarsdale's distinctest handwriting, the following words—

"Tampered with by some person to me Unknown, and the contents of this chest left untouched by me since the 3rd May, on which day I have reason to believe this was done."

This was the date of Horace's fatal visit to Marchmain; and the solemn statement of the dead man relieving him from the actual guilt with which he believed himself accursed, had overpowered him with an emotion beyond words—beyond thought. Enough was left to sting him all his life long with black suggestions of ineffaceable remorse, but so far as act and deed went, he was not guilty. He could say nothing in his unspeakable relief. The desperate tension of his misery had kept him alive and conscious by very consequence of its sufferings—but when the bow was unstrung it yielded instantly. There he lay senseless where his father's feet had used to rest, smitten to the heart with an undeserved and unutterable consolation—guilty, yet not guilty, by some strange interposition of God. He could not even be thankful in this overpowering, unbelievable relief from his misery; he could only fall fainting, unconscious, rapt beyond all sense and feeling. He was deeply, miserably guilty; too deeply stained ever to be clear of that remembrance in this life; but he was not a parricide. In spite of himself he was saved from that horror, and human hope might be possible to him still.

CHAPTER XXIV

"And so the Cornel's at Marchmain; it's like you're acquaint with all the history of that family, Patchey, my lad—tak up your glass; ould comrades like you and me are no in the way of meeting every day, and you've a long road and a lone across the moor."

So said Sergeant Kennedy, possessed with a virtuous curiosity to learn all that could be learned from "the Cornel's own man," who, with the instinct peculiar to his class, had speedily found out that good ale and company were to be had at the "Tillington Arms," where Mrs. Gilsland showed great respect and honour to the important Patchey. Patchey had already taken glasses enough to increase his dignity and solemn demeanour. He had grown slow and big of speech, and eloquent on the great importance of his own services to the Colonel.

"He's a wise man for other folk," said Patchey deliberately, "but a child, and nothing but a child, where his own affairs is concerned. If it werena for me that ken the world, and keep a strict eye upon the house, he would be ruined, mum; ye may take my word for it—ten times in the year."

"Acquaint with all the family?—I'm no a braggart," said Patchey, in answer to this question; "but it stands to natur that in the coorse of our colloquies upon affairs in general the Cornel says many a thing to me."

"Not a doubt about it—especially," said the Sergeant, gravely, "as you're well known to be a discreet lad, and wan that's to be trusted—as was known of ye since ever ye entered the regiment, though I say it. Ye see, mistress, he was always a weel-respected man."

"The Cornel, as I was saying," continued Patchey, passing loftily over this compliment, "says many a thing to me that it would ill become me to say over again; but this ye a' ken as well as me. The gentleman at Marchmain was married upon the Cornel's sister, and died of a stroke, and the visitation of God, the day afore yesterday; and a' the great fortune that's been lying gathering this mony a year has come to his son."

"Eyeh, Mr. Patchey! but the fortin'—that's just the thing I cannot make owght of, head nor tail," cried Mrs. Gilsland; "there was never no signs, as ever I heard tell on, of fortin' at Marchmain, and for a screw and ould skinflint, that would give nowght but the lowest for whatever she wanted, I'll engage there's no the marrow of Peggy from Kenlisle to Cardale; and if you had asked me, I could have vowed with my last breath that the family had seen better days, and were as poor as ever a family pretending to be gentry could be."

At this statement, which he took to be derogatory to his dignity, Patchey squared his spare shoulders, and erected his head.

"Being near relations of my ain family," said Patchey, "where persons have oucht to say agin the family at Marchmain, I would rather, of the twa, that it was not said to me."

"Agin the family!" cried Mrs. Gilsland—"havers! wasn't Mr. Horry at my house five nights in the week, and the Cornel himsel' brought Miss here to dine? Do you mean to tell me its agin a family to say it's seen better days? Eyeh! wae is me! to think there's no a soul in the Grange but ould Sally, and the young Squire out upon the world to seek his fortin' like any other man! but where's the man would dare to say I thought the less o' Mr. Roger? That's no my disposition, Mr. Patchey. It may be the way o' the world, but it isn't mine."

"Leftenant Musgrave, if it's him you're meaning, he'll do weel, mum," said Patchey, with solemnity; "he's been visiting at our house, and the Cornel's tooken him up. I would not say but more folk nor the Cornel had a kindness for that lad; but these affairs are awfu' delicate. I wadna say a word for my life."

"Eyeh, man! I'll lay a shilling it's Miss!" cried Mrs. Gilsland, in great excitement and triumph.

"But all this has little to do with the family at Marchmain," said Sergeant Kennedy, as Patchey shook his head with mysterious importance—"what's the rights o' that story if wan might ask, Patchey, my friend?—for it's little likely the Cornel would keep a grand family secret like that from a confidential man like you."

"Ye're right there, Sergeant; he'll say more to me, will our Cornel, than to ony other living man, were it Mr. Ned or Mr. Tom, that are but callants," said Patchey. "I ken mair nor most folk of a' our ain concerns; but it's as good as a play to hear this. I've made it out, a sma' bit at a time, mysel'; and if it werena that the gentleman's dead, ye might hew me down into little bits, before ye would get anything that wasna wanted to be heard, out of me. But he's gane, poor gentleman, and a' the better for him, as I've little doubt; and Mr. Horry, as ye call him, has come into a great fortune. Ye see the rights of it was this:—the auld man of a', the grandfather, had been a captious auld sinner, though I say it that should not; and being displeased ae way or anither at his son, this ane that's now dead, he made a will, strick cutting him off, and leaving the haill inheritance at his death to his son, a baby in his nurse's arms. That's just the short and the long of it. I've read sichlike in print; but it's no often ye meet wi' a devil's invention like that in living life. And the Cornel's sister's husband, ye see, he took it savage, being but a young man then; and the poor lady died, and down came he here, with an ill heart at a' the world—and the rest ye ken as weel as me."

"Eyeh, man, is that the tale?" said Mrs. Gilsland. "I wouldn't say but it was dead hard upon Mr. Horry's papaw; but, dear life! was the man crazed that he would take it out on his childer?—for more neglected things than them two, begging your pardon, Mr. Patchey, were not in this countryside; and how they've comed up to be as they are is just one of the miracles of Providence. Neyther a play nor a lesson like other folks's childer, nor a soul, to see them frae year's end to year's end. It was common talk; that's the way I know; but, eyeh, Mr. Patchey! had the very Cornel himsel' no thought for them poor childer there?"

"The Colonel was at his duty, mum," said Patchey. "He was resident at Rum Chunder station, and me with him; and he served in the Burmah war, and wherever bullets were flying, as the Sergeant can tell you. There was little time to think of our own bairns, let alone ither people's, in these days. The Colonel was in Indeea, and in het wark, and me with him, for nigh upon forty year."

"Hot work, ye may well say, Patchey, my friend," said the Sergeant, authoritatively. "It's little they know, them easy foulks at home, what the like of huz souldiers goes through. Eat when you can and sleep when you can, but work and fight awlways: them's the orders of life as was upon you and me."

"Eyeh, Sergeant!" cried Mrs. Gilsland, suddenly facing round upon the self-betrayed veteran, "was them the words you said to my Sam, when the lad was 'ticed away and 'listed all out of your flatteries?—or to the young Squire, when he hearkened to you? Eyeh, ye deceitful ould man! Is't a parcel o' stories, and nowght else, ye tell to the poor young lads, that knaw no better? and make poor mouths, and take pity on the sodgherin', when ye're awl by yoursel'?"

"Whisht, mistress, whisht!" said the Sergeant, who had recovered during this speech from his momentary dismay. "Did I say owght but what's come true? Sam Gilsland's been home on furlough, Patchey—as pretty a lad as ever handled a gun—corporal, and well spoken on; and the young Squire's leftenant, and mentioned in the papers—and what could friend or relation, if it was an onreasonable woman, wish for more?"

"Ye may make your mind easy, mum, about Leftenant Musgrave; and your son, if he's steady, will come well on in the Rifles—'special when the Cornel's tooken him up," said Patchey. "Our Cornel, he's that kind of a man when he takes an interest in a lad he's not one that forgets. I should say he would do uncommon well if he's steady, being come of responsible folk, and the Cornel for a friend."

"The Lord be thankit, I have little reason to complain!" said Sam's mother, wiping her eyes with her apron; "and it's a rael handsome uniform, though it's no so gaudy as your redcoats. I took my Sam for an officer and a grand gentleman when he came in at the door, before I saw his honest face," cried the good woman, with a sob of pride; "and the Cornel's good word is as good as a fortin', and he's uncommon kind is the young Squire. I wish them all comfort and prosperity now and evermore," she concluded, with a little solemn curtsey, giving emphasis to her good wishes—"and Miss and Mr. Horry, as well; though he's no more like the Cornel than you or me."

"He takes after the faither's family—he's no like none of our folk," said Patchey; "but, though I wouldna say the Cornel altogether approves of him, he's much concerned about the young gentleman the noo. He's showed great feeling after a', that young man; he was like a lad out of his mind when the faither was ill; and the day of the death, what does the Cornel find but Maister Horace dead on his face, fainted off in the study, and in a high fever ever since. The like of that, ye ken, shows feeling in a young man."

"Feeling? They were none such good friends in life, if awl tales be true," said Mrs. Gilsland. "My man, John, was all but put to the door when he went for Mr. Kerry's things; and a lad like him, that was never greatly knawn for a loving heart, and was coming into a fortin' besides—feeling here or feeling there, I don't see no occasion for Mr. Horry fainting away."

"Nor me," said the Sergeant, emphatically; "but I ever said, and I'll ever say, that though he's the Cornel's nevvy, and doubtless well connected, and good blood on wan side of the house, I'll ever say yon's an inscrutable lad."

"That may be," said the solemn Patchey; "but scrutable or no, he's in a brain fever, and craves guid guiding, and here's me come for the medicine, if I hadna fallen in with ower guid company. Weel, weel—an hour mair or less will do the lad nae harm. I've little faith in physic for such like disorders. If ye've a good constitution and a clear conscience, and the help of Providence, ye'll fight through: if ye havena, ye must e'en drop out of the ranks, and anither man'll take your place. But I have Mr. Horace's bottle in my pocket a' this time; so, with your leave, I'll bid you good day."

Saying which, Patchey stalked out of the "Tillington Arms," and took his solemn way across the moor. His step was slow, and his cogitations momentous. If he did not think much about Horace and his medicine, he settled sundry knotty points in philosophy as he wended through the fragrant heather. Patchey's gravity and intense sense of decorum increased habitually with every glass he emptied; but, perhaps, when his moralities flourished most, he made least haste about his immediate business, and it is to be feared that the confidential communication which the Colonel made to him when he reached the house was not of a flattering character. Horace got his physic an hour or two later than the proper time; but Patchey's flowers of eloquence blossomed no more that day in the kitchen of Marchmain.

CHAPTER XXV

It was not till weeks after the mortal remains of his father had been laid to their final rest that Horace, out of his fever and frenzy, came to himself. Long before that time the popular opinion had changed concerning Marchmain and its inhabitants. The straggling country neighbourhood, with its little knots of villages, and solitary great houses, had eschewed for years that gaunt house on the moor; but, from the day on which the old soldier and the weeping girl stood alone together beside that grave—Susan, overpowered with a natural grief, which sprang more from her position as a daughter and a woman than from direct personal anguish, which could not exist in her case, weeping her tender natural tears, full of filial compunction and pity, on that quiet bed, where the unquiet man had at last found rest;

while Colonel Sutherland stood by gravely mournful, his noble old face clouded with compassion and sorrow, not for the death, but for the life that found its conclusion there—the mind of the countryside had changed. The group was one which those who saw it could not forget; and it began to be remembered, in the great houses near, that Mr. Scarsdale, on his arrival, had been thought worthy of a visit, and that the name of the gallant old Colonel was not unknown to fame. Then, when already the matrons near began to take pity upon Susan's lonely orphanage, and the dangerous illness of her brother, rumours, of which nobody could trace the origin, began to spread of the family history, and the great, unbelievable fortune which Mr. Scarsdale's death had put into the hands of his son. The story was tragical enough, and had shades sufficiently dark to bear dilution and variation. Then Roger Musgrave appeared in haste upon the scene, bringing his mother with him to his desolate old Grange—his mother, and little Edmund, and, of necessity, a train of servants. After a little they were followed—some hasty furnishing having in the meantime been done at Roger's ancient house—by the beautiful Amelia and her sisters. Amelia proclaimed herself most anxious to see and comfort Susan, her brother Roger's bride— but perhaps had a little curiosity besides to see with her own eyes what were the substantial attractions of Armitage Park. Edmund was not going to die, and Amelia had but little chance of being an heiress; so the beauty thought it might probably be as well, before Horace Scarsdale got better of his fever, to arrange matters with Sir John.

All these changes came about while Horace lay senseless in the wild turmoil of his fever, or, struggling with delirium and incipient madness, fought for his life. Susan had already received various matronly visits of condolence and sympathy; various young ladies unknown to her before had declared themselves ready to swear eternal friendship with the solitary girl; and many a flattering report of the wealth and importance of Horace, such as would have been balm to his soul a few months ago, had been spread through the county; while Horace lay all unconscious of the fortune which had after all come to his hands unstained by actual bloodshed. When he did come to himself at last it was a warm midsummer day, the blazing sun of which made vain efforts to penetrate into his darkened room; and that room was full of the luxuries of sickness—those luxuries which only the most close and affectionate care provides. In the wonder and weakness of his sudden awaking, he lay motionless for a time looking round him, unable to connect what he saw with any portion of his former life. Long experience and close observation of his nephew had convinced Colonel Sutherland that some great mental shock was the occasion of his sudden illness, and the tender-hearted old man, forgetting when he watched by Horace's bedside everything save that he was his sister's son, had caused every piece of furniture which could be changed in the room to be taken away, and replaced the familiar objects with safe unknown articles, which could recall no painful associations to his patient's mind. He was seated there himself grave and anxious, for this awakening was the crisis of the fever, and Uncle Edward had persuaded even Susan to leave him alone by his nephew's side. The Colonel's heart was heavy as he sat gravely pondering over the young man's face; it was no "feeling" which had driven Horace desperate when his father died; and the grieved watcher, himself so nobly innocent and unsuspicious, could not but fear some miserable connection between the young man's agony and that vindictive inscription in the medicine chest. He was afraid that Horace might say something to betray himself, or to convey some similar doubt to the mind of his sister, to vex Susan in her quietness; so he would have no one there with him to watch that awaking, but sat by the bedside grieved, anxious, and alone.

When Horace's wandering, feeble glance fell upon his uncle, a great cloud and shadow came over him even in the calm of his weakness. Everything came back to him in that first glimpse of Uncle Edward's face. He shut his eyes tightly again, with a longing to return to his insensibility, and gave a groan out of the depths of his miserable heart. He was cured—his fever was over: he had come back to life, with its agonies worse than fever. The very sound of that groan gave signal of recovery to the watcher by his side.

"You must keep quiet, Horace; you are better: you will soon be well, if you take care. And here is something you are to take," said the Colonel. "Hush! compose yourself, you live; and God is in heaven, and all will be well!"

But Horace did not answer; he kept his eyes shut for another bitter moment, gathering up the threads of his scattered recollections. Then the last incident of all returned to him—he was innocent!—so he said to himself, with a natural human casuistry; innocent! though it was in spite of himself. Innocent! at least, not guilty by the actual event. Then he opened his eyes and took the medicine, which his uncle had poured out for him. He was the same Horace as of old—subdued, but not changed; and in the sudden recollection that he was not a parricide, a rush of his old self-assertion returned to his awakening mind, and of his old sullen look to his face. But he did not say anything for the moment—he sunk back again upon his pillows, weak to extremity; almost the only sign of life in him being that uneasy guiltiness in his heart, which even the discovery, which had released him from the weight of murder, could only salve, and could not cure.

But he was uneasy, too, with the Colonel's grave, grieved, conscious face beside him—he could not help saying something. He remembered so distinctly now the study and all its familiar objects, the medicine-chest standing on the table; somebody must have brought him from that place where he lost consciousness, to this where he regained it. "Uncle, who found me?" he said, shutting his eyes once more, unable to bear that grieved look of knowledge which was in the Colonel's eyes.

"I found you, Horace," said Colonel Sutherland, quietly; "let your mind be quite at rest, no one else came near us. I put away the little medicine-chest," he continued, with hesitation, "and the paper which dropped out of it. They are locked up in one of your drawers; no one has either seen or touched them but myself."

Then there was a long, conscious pause; neither the sick man nor the watcher spoke—the one contending with his natural sullen pride, which would confess no sin, and the horror within him of knowing that so far as intention and purpose went he was as guilty as any actual murderer; the other grieved, silent, afraid, anxious not to hear that some diabolical purpose had been nursed in that young head, yet sadly fearing that, whether confessed or not, the wickedness had been there.

"Uncle," said Horace, at last, the words bursting from his lips in an eager paroxysm of defence against himself, and vindication to his own conscience—"Uncle, I did him no harm."

"I am very thankful to hear it, Horace," said the Colonel, very gravely; then he made another pause—"unless it will relieve your mind tell me no more," he said, quickly—"only, Horace, remember, you have been very near the grave; perhaps you know yourself that you have been near something more terrible than the grave; you should pause and think now while you can; for every evil intention, as well as for every act of sin, there is pardon with God, for Jesus' sake."

He said it simply, but with a solemn, almost judicial gravity. He could not help guessing what had been going on in the troubled spirit beside him, of which he knew so little; he could not help shuddering at the thought of the horrible guilt from which, by accident, as it appeared, and interposition of God, the young man had been unwittingly preserved. God help him!—so young, so wretched, to drag the hideous burden of that remembrance through all his days of life! The deepest pity, even amid his horror, struck the old soldier's noble, innocent heart. He could not comprehend the guilt—but he felt the remorse, with a compassion that was half divine.

Horace made no reply—he shrank, in spite of himself, as though he would have crept away morally out of his uncle's presence; for the instant the young man realized, with a desperate force of conviction, the "gulf fixed" between heaven and hell which none can pass over; he felt it in his guilt a thousand times more deeply than the pure heart beside him did, in its tender depths of pity. He lay still in his weakness, with a mortified consciousness of humiliation and inferiority, insufferable to his arrogant spirit. Then it occurred to him that there was still one thing, by which he might drag himself up fictitiously to that higher elevation, which he recognized vaguely in his downfall, and envied, though he knew it not. He turned once more towards the watcher by his bed with a sudden movement, which was so quick as to give him pain.

"You think very badly of me," he said, hastily; "but I have got something to tell you—something to tell Roger Musgrave, which will remedy one evil at least, and change, more than you can suppose, his position in the world."

The Colonel waved his hand, with the action of a man who knows what another is about to say. "My dear boy," he said, compassionately, "I am grieved that you cannot have the satisfaction of doing, at least, this piece of justice—but you are too late. The Kenlisle attorney, hearing of your connection with Musgrave, and of some promise you had made him when you heard of your father's illness, sent to beg an interview with Roger and Sir John, and confessed the whole transaction. That matter has been arranged while you have been ill."

"Do you mean Pouncet?—Pouncet has consented to his own ruin?" cried Horace, with a pang of disappointment. He had still been reckoning on this as a moral compensation which it would always be in his power to make, to balance more or less his personal guilt.

"Not to his ruin—they have made terms," said the Colonel. "He restores the property, and pays something to Roger besides, and there will be no prosecution or exposure. He loses Armitage's confidence, of course, and is no longer his man of business; but he preserves his character, and eases his conscience. All that is arranged. My dear Horace, you are extremely weak: try to compose yourself, and forget these troublesome affairs. If you can, for your health's sake, endeavour to sleep."

Horace turned his face sullenly towards the wall, and said no more. Perhaps this sharp pang of unexpected mortification and disappointment eased him of his heavier load. He set his teeth as he turned away and relieved himself from the sight of Uncle Edward's compassionate and kind face: everything humiliated him in that self-importance which was so strong a power within him. He once had it in his power to be at least Roger Musgrave's magnanimous deliverer, and to expose the fraud which had left the youth penniless; but he had lost his opportunity, and even that moral make-up for his other grievous guilt had slid away from him. He lay here powerless, known to one man, at least, in all the blackness of his evil intention, and to more than one man, stood revealed and visible, a willing accomplice in a fraud, left in the lurch by the principal sinner. His disappointment—his failure—the humiliation of his guilt—sickened him to the heart; he closed his eyes upon the light, disgusted and miserable. He had his reward!

"And so, hinny, you're to be married, and set up in a house of your own; and, 'stead o' solitude, and a wild moor, and ould Peggy, have all the county wishing ye joy. Eh, weel! I'm an ould fool, and nowght else: I think upon the mistress, and I canna forbear. The bride goes forth with joy and blessing, but the Lord alone He knows what will come to pass thereupon."

And Peggy, who was standing in the old dining-room—that room so strangely thrilled through, warmed, and brightened with the new life—examining one after another the pretty things which already began to be prepared for Susan's marriage, suddenly sunk down on a chair by the table, and covered her face, and sobbed aloud.

"But, Peggy, you should have a cheerful word for me," said Susan—"we have had so much trouble. Things will never happen with me as they did with mamma. For, Peggy," added the bride, with her honest eyes smiling frank and sure out of the warm blush that rose over her face, "we will trust and help each other through every trouble. Trouble never can be very heavy when there are two of us to bear the load."

"The Lord knows, and He alone," said the faithful servant of the house. "I'm ould, and my heart trembles; the like of me cannot see, Miss Susan. I look upon the bride-white, and there's shadows o' shrouds and widow's mourning a' covered ower and hidden in the bonnie folds. The Lord preserve ye from all ill and trouble that is beyond the strength of man!—and grant to me to depart and be at rest, before ever cloud or shadow comes upon the light o' my ould eyes!"

Susan was not discouraged in her own undiscourageable hope and happiness even by these melancholy words; but she was grieved for Peggy, who, broken and nervous with her long solitude, was no longer like herself. She came round to the old woman's side, and put her young arms, which had clung there so often, round Peggy's neck.

"Do you know Horace is going to give me a fortune, Peggy?" said Susan. "Horace is different, don't you think, since he has been ill? I thought it would have turned his head to be so rich—but he does not seem to care; he is so much quieter, older than he used to be. I did not suppose he would have felt so much for poor papa."

Peggy said nothing—but she gave an emphatic shake of her head, and, diverted into a less pathetic channel of thought, dried her eyes. Peggy's sentiments were changed. It was the younger generation who were now in the ascendant, and Peggy's magnanimous instincts, falling to the weaker side, turned all her sympathy towards the dead.

"But he is changed, though you shake your head," said Susan; "and I am to have a fortune—me! Everything is Uncle Edward's doing. How I wondered when he brought me these India muslins, Peggy—do you remember? I thought you were all crazy when you spoke of me wearing them—and now look here; and I suppose," said Susan, with womanful satisfaction and vanity, "we shall see the best people in the county at the Grange."

"And only your right, too," said Peggy, by way of interjection; for Susan, having fully launched herself, was quite qualified to keep up the discourse.

"Especially when Amelia Stenhouse marries Sir John. I wonder how she can marry that odd old man; and so pretty as she is too—don't you think she is very, very pretty, Peggy?"

"'Handsome is as handsome does,'" said Susan's oracle, with great solemnity.

"Oh, to be sure; but one likes to be handsome all the same," said Susan. "I don't say I like Amelia out-and-out. I suppose she's too grand and too accomplished, and too clever, and that sort of thing, for me; but she's very nice to look at, Peggy; and when she marries Sir John—"

"When who marries Sir John?" asked Horace, abruptly. He had just come rather feebly into the room—convalescent, but not strong, his mind working out all the vigour which should have gone to the strengthening of his body. That he was changed was certain, but it was doubtful whether the change was so entirely for the better as his sister charitably supposed. He did not look much more amiable at the present moment; he came in with the sullen shade of old upon his face. He had heard part of Susan's last words; but she did not know what a furious passion awoke in his heart when he asked, "Who marries Sir John?"

"Oh, it is Amelia, Horace—Amelia, Roger's half sister; did not you know about it?" said Susan, innocently—"you, too, who have known them longer than I; it was settled last week."

"Oh, was it?" said Horace, bitterly. He went out of the room the next moment, flinging down, half unawares, half consciously, a heap of his sister's wedding preparations. It was natural that the sight of such things at such a time should gall the young man; the next moment they heard him up in his own room, making a great commotion there. Susan was a little startled and frightened in spite of herself. Horace took strange fancies now and then. He was rich now, and could do as he pleased. Sometimes Susan, all unaware of the canker there, imagined that his mind was a little affected. She could not imagine what freak possessed him now.

A little while after Horace came downstairs, dressed more carefully than she had yet seen him. He told her he was going away "to town"—which Susan supposed to mean to Kenlisle—and should walk to the nearest roadside public-house, where they kept a gig. He would send for his things, but might not see her for some time again, and so he held out a hot, trembling hand, and bade her "Good-bye—good-bye!" Susan tried some remonstrances, but he hurried out in the midst of them, and strode away across the moor in the bright August sunshine. His sister stood at the window watching him, as she had stood many a day before, till his figure disappeared among the distant saplings and dark gorse bushes. It was the last time that Horace Scarsdale trod the familiar heather of Lanwoth Moor.

That evening Roger's mother came with him when he came on his daily visit to his affianced bride. They knew she was alone, and guessed she must be anxious. Horace had been at the Grange, where he saw only Amelia, and went away again in half-an-hour, leaving even that stout-hearted beauty, who was not too sensitive, fainting and overpowered by the violence of his farewell. That was the last any of the party saw of Horace for many a year. The marriages took place in due time, and all went well with the new households; but the unhappy heir of the Scarsdales went out and was lost in the world, and its great waves concealed him and his pleasures and wretchedness. He had put himself out of the reach of common blessings and sorrows, the dews and sunshine, of God's every-day world. He had his fortune, his failure, his dead burden of guilt, to begin his life withal; and so carried out among men, and the bustle and commotion of the world, a second bitter chapter of that hereditary curse, which had made a recluse and wretched misanthrope of his father, and a dismal prison and place of bondage of the solitary house upon the moor.

Margaret Oliphant Wilson was born on April 4th, 1828 to Francis W. Wilson, a clerk, and Margaret Oliphant, at Wallyford, near Musselburgh, East Lothian.

She spent her childhood at Lasswade, near Dalkeith, Glasgow before moving to Liverpool.

Her youth was spent in establishing a writing style so much so that, in 1849, she had her first novel published: Passages in the Life of Mrs. Margaret Maitland based on the Scottish Free Church movement. It met with some success and was a good start to her career.

Two years later, in 1851, her third book Caleb Field was published. It was also now that she met the publisher William Blackwood in Edinburgh and was asked to contribute to his well-received Blackwood's Magazine. It was to be a lifetimes endeavor. Over the course of the relationship she would have well over 100 articles published.

In May 1852, Margaret married her cousin, Frank Wilson Oliphant, at Birkenhead, and they settled at Harrington Square, Camden, London. He was an artist working primarily in stained glass. With the marriage she became Margaret Oliphant Wilson Oliphant.

Their marriage produced six children but three tragically died in infancy.

When her husband developed signs of the dreaded consumption (tuberculosis) they moved, on the advice of doctors, to warmer climes. In January 1859 it was to Florence, and then to Rome where, sadly, he died.

Margaret was naturally devastated but was also now left without support and only her income from her writing. She returned to England and took up the task of supporting her three remaining children by her literary activity.

By now she was being published both as an established novelist and regularly in Blackwood's Magazine, amongst others. Her incredible and prolific work rate increased both her commercial reputation and the size of her reading audience.

Against this her domestic life continued to be tragic, full of sorrow and disappointment.

In January 1864 her only remaining daughter Maggie died and was buried in her father's grave in Rome. Her brother, who had emigrated to Canada, was shortly afterwards involved in financial ruin. Margaret generously offered a home to him and his children, adding another demand to her already heavy responsibilities.

In 1866 she settled at Windsor to be closer to her sons, who were being educated at near-by Eton School. That year, her second cousin, Annie Louisa Walker, came to live with her as a companion-housekeeper. Windsor was now to be her home for the rest of her life.

Her literary career for three decades was one of constant delivery and success. Whether she wrote historical works or across several genres in fiction: domestic realism, historical, romance or supernatural she was successful.

For more than thirty years she pursued a varied literary career but family life continued to bring problems.

The literary ambitions she wished for her sons were unfulfilled. Cyril Francis, the eldest, died in 1890, leaving a Life of Alfred de Musset, incorporated in his mother's Foreign Classics for English Readers. The younger, Francis, who she nicknamed 'Cecco', collaborated with her in the Victorian Age of English Literature and won a position at the British Museum, but was rejected by Sir Andrew Clark, a famous physician. Cecco died in 1894.

With the last of her children now lost to her, she had but little further interest in life. Her health steadily and inexorably declined.

Margaret Oliphant Wilson Oliphant died at the age of 69 in Wimbledon on 20th June 1897. She is buried in Eton beside her sons.

At her death, Margaret was still working on Annals of a Publishing House, a record of Blackwood's Magazine with which she had enjoyed such a successful relationship.

Her Autobiography and Letters, which present a thoughtful picture of her domestic anxieties, was published in 1899. Only parts were written with a wider audience in mind: she had originally intended the Autobiography for her son, but he died before she could finish it.

Opinions on Oliphant's work are split, with some critics seeing her as a 'domestic novelist', while others recognize her work as influential and important to the Victorian literature canon. Critical reception from her contemporaries is also divided. John Skelton took the view that Oliphant wrote too much and too quickly. Writing a Blackwood's article called 'A Little Chat About Mrs. Oliphant', he asked, "Had Mrs. Oliphant concentrated her powers, what might she not have done? We might have had another Charlotte Brontë or another George Eliot." However not all of the contemporary reception was negative. The esteemed M. R. James admired Oliphant's supernatural fiction, concluding that "the religious ghost story, as it may be called, was never done better than by Mrs. Oliphant in 'The Open Door' and 'A Beleaguered City'. Mary Butts lavished praise on Oliphant's ghost story 'The Library Window', describing it as "one masterpiece of sober loveliness".

More modern critics of Oliphant's work include Virginia Woolf, who asked in Three Guineas whether Oliphant's autobiography does not lead the reader "to deplore the fact that Mrs. Oliphant sold her brain, her very admirable brain, prostituted her culture and enslaved her intellectual liberty in order that she might earn her living and educate her children."

Whatever the merits of their cases Margaret Oliphant has been shamefully neglected in modern years. She is now becoming more widely recognised as a leading writer of her day.

A canon of more than 120 works, including novels, travel books, histories, and volumes of literary criticism.

Novels

Margaret Maitland (1849)
Merkland (1850)
Caleb Field (1851)
John Drayton (1851)
Adam Graeme (1852)
The Melvilles (1852)
Katie Stewart (1852)
Harry Muir (1853)
Ailieford (1853)
The Quiet Heart (1854)
Magdalen Hepburn (1854)
Zaidee (1855)
Lilliesleaf (1855)
Christian Melville (1855)
The Athelings (1857)
The Days of My Life (1857)
Orphans (1858)
The Laird of Norlaw (1858)
Agnes Hopetoun's Schools and Holidays (1859)
Lucy Crofton (1860)
The House on the Moor (1861)
The Last of the Mortimers (1862)
Heart and Cross (1863)
Salem Chapel (1863)
The Rector (1863)
Doctor's Family (1863)
The Perpetual Curate (1864)
Miss Marjoribanks (1866)
Phoebe Junior (1876)
A Son of the Soil (1865)
Agnes (1866)
Madonna Mary (1867)
Brownlows (1868)
The Minister's Wife (1869)
The Three Brothers (1870)
John: A Love Story (1870)
Squire Arden (1871)
At his Gates (1872)

Ombra (1872
May (1873)
Innocent (1873)
The Story of Valentine and his Brother (1875)
A Rose in June (1874)
For Love and Life (1874)
Whiteladies (1875)
An Odd Couple (1875)
The Curate in Charge (1876)
Carità (1877)
Young Musgrave (1877)
Mrs. Arthur (1877)
The Primrose Path (1878)
Within the Precincts (1879)
The Fugitives (1879)
A Beleaguered City (1879)
The Greatest Heiress in England (1880)
He That Will Not When He May (1880)
In Trust (1881)
Harry Joscelyn (1881)
Lady Jane (1882)
A Little Pilgrim in the Unseen (1882)
The Lady Lindores (1883)
Sir Tom (1883)
Hester (1883)
It Was a Lover and his Lass (1883)
The Lady's Walk (1883)
The Wizard's Son (1884)
Madam (1884)
The Prodigals and their Inheritance (1885)
Oliver's Bride (1885)
A Country Gentleman and his Family (1886)
A House Divided Against Itself (1886)
Effie Ogilvie (1886)
A Poor Gentleman (1886)
The Son of his Father (1886)
Joyce (1888)
Cousin Mary (1888)
The Land of Darkness (1888)
Lady Car (1889)
Kirsteen (1890)
The Mystery of Mrs. Biencarrow (1890)
Sons and Daughters (1890)
The Railway Man and his Children (1891)
The Heir Presumptive and the Heir Apparent (1891)
The Marriage of Elinor (1891)
Janet (1891)
The Cuckoo in the Nest (1892)

Diana Trelawny (1892)
The Sorceress (1893)
A House in Bloomsbury (1894)
Sir Robert's Fortune (1894)
Who Was Lost and is Found (1894)
Lady William (1894)
Two Strangers (1895)
Old Mr. Tredgold (1895)
The Unjust Steward (1896)
The Ways of Life (1897)

Short stories

Neighbours on the Green (1889)
A Widow's Tale and Other Stories (1898)
That Little Cutty (1898)
The Open Door (1918)

Selected Articles

Mary Russel Mitford (Blackwood's Magazine, Vol. 75, 1854)
Evelin and Pepys (Blackwood's Magazine, Vol. 76, 1854)
The Holy Land (Blackwood's Magazine, Vol. 76, 1854)
Mr. Thackeray and his Novels (Blackwood's Magazine, Vol. 77, 1855)
Bulwer (Blackwood's Magazine, Vol. 77, 1855)
Charles Dickens (Blackwood's Magazine, Vol. 77, 1855)
Modern Novelists—Great and Small (Blackwood's Magazine, Vol. 77, 1855)
Modern Light Literature: Poetry (Blackwood's Magazine, Vol. 79, 1856)
Religion in Common Life (Blackwood's Magazine, Vol. 79, 1856)
Sydney Smith (Blackwood's Magazine, Vol. 79, 1856)
The Laws Concerning Women (Blackwood's Magazine, Vol. 79, 1856)
The Art of Caviling (Blackwood's Magazine, Vol. 80, 1856)
Béranger (Blackwood's Magazine, Vol. 83, 1858)
The Condition of Women (Blackwood's Magazine, Vol. 83, 1858)
The Missionary Explorer (Blackwood's Magazine, Vol. 83, 1858)
Religious Memoirs (Blackwood's Magazine, Vol. 83, 1858)
Social Science (Blackwood's Magazine, Vol. 88, 1860)
Scotland and her Accusers (Blackwood's Magazine, Vol. 90, 1861)
The Chronicles of Carlingford (Blackwood's Magazine 1862–1865)
Girolamo Savonarola (Blackwood's Magazine, Vol. 93, 1863)
The Life of Jesus (Blackwood's Magazine, Vol. 96, 1864)
Giacomo Leopardi (Blackwood's Magazine, Vol. 98, 1865)
The Great Unrepresented (Blackwood's Magazine, Vol. 100, 1866)
Mill on the Subjection of Women (The Edinburgh Review, Vol. 130, 1869)
The Opium-Eater (Blackwood's Magazine, Vol. 122, 1877)
Russian and Nihilism in the Novels of I. Tourgeniéf (Blackwood's Magazine, Vol. 127, 1880)
School and College (Blackwood's Magazine, Vol. 128, 1880)

The Grievances of Women (Fraser's Magazine, New Series, Vol. 21, 1880)
Mrs. Carlyle (The Contemporary Review, Vol. 43, May 1883)
The Ethics of Biography (The Contemporary Review, July 1883)
Victor Hugo (The Contemporary Review, Vol. 48, July/December 1885)
A Venetian Dynasty (The Contemporary Review, Vol. 50, August 1886)
Laurence Oliphant (Blackwood's Magazine, Vol. 145, 1889)
Tennyson (Blackwood's Magazine, Vol. 152, 1892)
Addison, the Humorist (Century Magazine, Vol. 48, 1894)
The Anti-Marriage League (Blackwood's Magazine, Vol. 159, 1896)

Biographies

Edward Irving (1862)
Francis of Assisi (1871)
Count de Montalembert (1872)
Dante (1877)
Cervantes (1880)
Life of Sheridan in the English Men of Letters series (1883)
John Tulloch (1888)
Laurence Oliphant (1892)

Historical & Critical Works

Historical Sketches of the Reign of George II (1869)
The Makers of Florence (1876)
A Literary History of England from 1760 to 1825 (1882)
The Makers of Venice (1887)
Royal Edinburgh (1890)
Jerusalem (1891)
The Makers of Modern Rome (1895)
William Blackwood and his Sons (1897)
The Sisters Brontë. In: Women Novelists of Queen Victoria's Reign (1897)